THE
SCRIBE
OF
SIENA

A NOVEL

MELODIE WINAWER

TOUCHSTONE
NEW YORK LONDON TORONTO SYDNEY NEW DELHI

Touchstone
An Imprint of Simon & Schuster, Inc.
1230 Avenue of the Americas
New York, NY 10020

First Touchstone trade paperback edition January 2018

TOUCHSTONE and colophon are registered trademarks of Simon & Schuster, Inc.

For information about special discounts for bulk purchases, please contact Simon & Schuster Special Sales at 1-866-506-1949 or business@simonandschuster.com.

The Simon & Schuster Speakers Bureau can bring authors to your live event.
For more information or to book an event, contact the Simon & Schuster Speakers Bureau at 1-866-248-3049 or visit our website at www.simonspeakers.com.

Interior design by Kyle Kabel

Manufactured in the United States of America

10   9   8   7   6   5   4   3   2   1

The Library of Congress has cataloged the hardcover edition as follows:

Winawer, Melodie, author.
The scribe of Siena : a novel / Melodie Winawer.
First Touchstone hardcover edition. | New York : Touchstone, 2017.
LCCN 2016025826 (print) | LCCN 2016034507 (ebook)
LCSH: Women physicians—Fiction. | Artists—Italy—Siena—Fiction.
  | Man-woman relationships—Fiction. | Black Death—Italy—Siena—Fiction.
  | Time travel—Fiction. | BISAC: FICTION / Sagas. | FICTION / Historical.
  | FICTION / Literary. | GSAFD: Fantasy fiction. | Historical fiction. | Medical novels.
LCC PS3623.I5894 S36 2017 (print) | LCC PS3623.I5894 (ebook) | DDC 813/.6—dc23
LC record available at https://lccn.loc.gov/2016025826

ISBN 978-1-5011-5225-2
ISBN 978-1-5011-5226-9 (pbk)
ISBN 978-1-5011-5227-6 (ebook)

THE CANONICAL (DIVINE) HOURS

HOUR	TIME	OTHER NAMES
Matins	Midnight	Vigils, Nocturns
Lauds	3:00 a.m.	Dawn prayer
Prime	6:00 a.m.	First hour
Terce	9:00 a.m.	Third hour
Sext	Noon	Sixth hour
Nones	3:00 p.m.	Ninth hour
Vespers	6:00 p.m.	Evening prayer
Compline	9:00 p.m.	Night prayer

PART I

EMPATHY

The problem with being a neurosurgeon is that when the telephone rings, you have to answer it. When the phone by my bed went off at 3:00 a.m. I went straight from sleep to standing. The emergency room attending sounded like he was having a bad night.

"Dr. Trovato? Dr. Green here, Area A. We've got an old lady with a cerebellar hemorrhage—she's unresponsive, and the CT scan looks nasty. How soon can you get in?"

"Eight minutes. Call the OR."

The pocket of skull housing the cerebellum is a dangerously small space with rigid walls; there is no room for an explosion of blood. The consequence is disaster—the brain gets pushed in the only direction possible: down through the foramen magnum, the big hole in the bottom of the skull, crushing the brain stem, the control center for all basic life functions. Unless a surgeon gets there in time. I drove to the hospital in the dark, planning my approach. Amsterdam Avenue was quiet, with a few yellow cabs roaming for nonexistent fares. I pushed my speed to hit all the green lights.

I scrubbed in at the vast stainless-steel sink and backed into the OR through the double doors. Linney, my favorite anesthesiologist, took her place at the patient's head opposite me while I pulled on surgical gloves. The anesthesiologist's job is to monitor every breath, heartbeat, and rush of blood pressure through the vessels. Linney, smooth and quiet, signaled to me—OK to cut. I looked at the back of the patient's neck: innocent, slightly wrinkled, hiding the catastrophe beneath. I made a quick incision on the back of the scalp, a few inches behind her ear, then running down the back of her neck. Down through skin, then muscle, then picking up the craniotome, I sawed through bone. I sliced through the dura, exposed the cerebellum . . . *there*. As I scooped out the fresh clot, I felt suddenly short of breath. For a moment I was drowning, flailing for the surface.

"Linney," I gasped, "is there a problem with the vent?" Linney looked up at me, startled, and then at the monitors. Three seconds later, a long three seconds, the alarms started ringing.

It was nearly noon before the patient opened her eyes, and by late afternoon she was awake and holding her daughter's hand. I headed to the locker room to change.

"Beatrice, lunchtime," Linney said as we stripped off our gowns and shoe covers. I followed her to the staff cafeteria. Linney did not have conversations like other people. If I called her up and said, "Hi, how are you?," she'd say, "Get to the point." We sat across from each other at a white melamine table. The cafeteria had aspirations of greatness it did not quite achieve. A letterpress sign read ARTISANAL BREAD SELECTION, suspended over a basket of plastic-wrapped rolls, and the chef's suggestion of the day was unintentionally thrice-baked ziti. I had an apple.

"Beatrice, how did you know that woman was hypoxic?"

"I felt like I couldn't breathe," I said, "but I knew it was the patient." I hadn't realized this until I said it out loud.

"So what you are saying, Dr. Trovato"—I knew I was in trouble now, since we were no longer on a first name basis—"is that you just *knew*?"

"I just knew," I said.

"You should have had more than an apple," Linney replied,

changing the subject with her usual abruptness. "We've got five more cases today." She got up from the table, leaving me holding the apple core.

I sat at the table for a few minutes after Linney had gone. Surgery seems so straightforward: open someone up, fix what's wrong, close. But even working inside the body doesn't necessarily get to the center of the problem. When I was training to be a neurosurgeon, I wanted to know whether a teenage girl's headache was a symptom of a bad home situation, or a herald of a leaky brain aneurysm. I wanted to be sure that the depressed patient I sent home with pain medication for a brain tumor wouldn't try to commit suicide by taking all of it at once. And I've always wished I could reach my patients silenced by loss of language or trapped in the blankness of coma, circling endlessly in their own internal darkness. I'd touched people's brains with my hand, but I couldn't know how it felt to actually *be* inside someone else's head. Today, though, it seemed I had.

I've been orphaned twice. The first time was at birth, since I never knew my father, and my mother and twin sister died just after I was born. I was twin A, though I'm not sure whether that counts, now that there is only one of us. My brother, Benjamin, had just turned seventeen when he gained a little sister and lost a mother; he was transformed suddenly from brother into parent. I can't imagine how he did it. All I know is his college education got postponed for a year; he didn't say more.

Ben told me Mom never bothered with finding fathers for her children. "A minute and a mother are all you need," she used to say. I quoted that when I was a kid without really understanding it, and I got some very odd looks. Once I hit adolescence, I realized why. I never met Mom, unless you count being inside her as meeting her.

All my nursery school classmates were jealous of my uni-parent. On Mother's Day when the moms visited and got their irregular heart-shaped cards, Benjamin came to class dressed up in a polka-dot housedress, a blond wig, and pumps. He had just started studying microbiology, so he brought in cookies in the shape of microorganisms. I liked the viruses best because they looked like jewels. On Father's Day he arrived wearing a double-breasted suit and a Groucho Marx mustache-nose-eyeglass combo. No one ever made fun of me for having neither a father nor a mother; they all wanted a Benjamin.

For kindergarten, Ben enrolled me at the Franciscan St. James Academy, the natural choice for reasons of tradition and nostalgia; Ben had learned his letters and responsorial psalms there thirteen years before. There was a black-and-white photo of him on the wall in his role as the camel in the annual nativity skit—I used to stop and look at it on my way to Tuesday Mass. I got to play the Virgin Mary, but part of me wished I could have been the camel instead.

While I was in elementary school, Benjamin put himself through graduate school twice: first microbiology, then medieval history. By the time I was dissecting my first fetal pig in ninth grade biology, he'd become an expert on the Plague, particularly as it applied to medieval Italy. Ben and I approached medicine from opposite directions. I went forward, straight to the patient, while he went back—to the past.

Having a sibling really takes the pressure off trying to do too much—you just divide everything up. I became the physician, Benjamin the academic, so my scholarly side didn't complain, and he never had to wonder whether he should have become a doctor. I suppose it might have gone another way—we could have vied for excellence in the same domain—but competition never occurred to me. Neither did collaboration, until it was too late.

When I was thirty, Ben followed a project to Siena, Italy, and fell in love—not with a person, but with the city.

"Little B, I'm head over heels," he wrote. *"It's like time travel but without losing all the amenities—medieval life plus hot showers and toilet paper. I'm set on buying a house big enough for family. Otherwise known as My Little Sister Beatrice."*

I liked seeing the word *family* on paper, but I wasn't used to letter writing. The last paper letter I'd turned out was at Girl Scout camp, on stationery decorated with mice curling their tails around an inkpot. But Ben was weird about email—I think the medieval scholar in him resisted the march of technology.

Ben eventually bought his house in Siena, but three years later I still hadn't made plans to go to Italy, and he hadn't come back to New York. It was the longest we'd gone without seeing each other. We kept in touch with rare precious phone calls across time zones, and resorted the rest of the time to Ben's favorite, if archaic, mode of communication. I had even gotten into the medieval spirit by digging up the old fountain pens I'd once used for calligraphy.

Dear Ben,

I know I need to visit you soon, and meet your new girlfriend, I mean, hometown. But I can't imagine getting out of here right now. I spend twelve hours a day looking at three square inches of someone's body, willing my hands to do exactly the right thing. One little mistake, and it's blindness, or left-sided weakness, or death, just like that. I've got one day off every seven, not really enough to get me to Siena and back. But soon, OK? The OR has been more intense than usual—I feel like my usual self-protective doctor's reserve is wearing a little thin and I need an antidote to all this surgeon stuff. What time of year is best to come?

Love, Beatrice

The OR had been more intense than usual, and not in a good way. The day before, Linney and I had scrubbed in on a far-gone basal cell carcinoma case. Skin cancer doesn't usually involve a neurosurgeon, but in this case the patient had kept pulling her wig down over the slowly growing lesion on her forehead. Fifteen years later, the wig was so low over her eyes she couldn't see. By the time she got to us, the cancer had eaten through her skin and skull, and she had a quarter-size hole between her eyebrows through which we could see the dural membrane covering the brain. The sight made me cringe when I saw her in the office. I have seen dura plenty of times—just never outside of surgery.

In the OR things took a downturn quickly. Just after I made the first incision, the heart monitors registered ventricular tachycardia—a dangerously fast rhythm that can deteriorate, preventing blood from going where it's supposed to. Not good. I took a quick look at the monitors—blood pressure was holding, but that might not last. Out of the corner of my eye I could see Linney moving quickly, asking for procainamide. Then, suddenly, I heard a hum in my ears, and after that, incongruously, the sound of my brother Ben's voice. My vision grayed, and then my heart and head filled with the fear of losing him.

Benjamin didn't tell me about his heart until I was in medical school. I'd reacted badly.

"Ventricular tachycardia? For God's sake, you're a walking time bomb!"

"My cardiologist says it's under control. In the meantime, please avoid doing anything shocking or sudden in my presence. . . ." He grinned lopsidedly while I fumed to cover the panic I felt.

"Why didn't you tell me before?"

"You were a kid—my kid, basically. I didn't think you needed to know. Now you're a big girl."

I hit him. He deserved it. Ben grunted, then started over.

"You're a big *doctor*, I mean. . . ."

"That's better."

"And I thought it was time you knew me from a grown-up perspective. It's been years; I'm fine."

I tried to incorporate this new frailty into my image of indestructible Ben. My own heart was pounding, though, in sympathy. *I don't want to lose him.*

"How about a hug, Little B," he said, "like the old days?"

I buried my head in his wool sweater and listened to his heart beating, slow and steady.

The next thing I knew Linney was whispering harshly in my ear. "Beatrice, blood pressure is stable, she's back in sinus rhythm. What's going on?" I wasn't sure what was going on, but it wasn't something that could happen again. There is no time for drifty emotional lapses when you've got a scalpel in your hand.

"I'm OK," I said. But I wasn't.

Siena, May 2

Hey Little B: What do you mean the OR is much more intense than usual? If you look up intense *in the dictionary I bet you'd find* NEUROSURGEON *right at the top of the page. I like thinking of you taking people apart and (ideally) putting them back together again. I try to get into people's heads too, but my subjects are already dead. You might say I'm a forensic pathologist of the distant past. I can imagine you saying "Come ON Benj, spare me the convoluted metaphors." I love it when you say stuff like that. Hey, happy almost birthday, Big Girl.*

I have some news, to the extent that any medieval historian could be said to have "news." There is something funny about the Plague and Siena. I've got my hands on some sources that explain why Siena did so badly during the Plague, and it will make a big splash when I'm ready to publish. In fact I think I might already have made a splash—I dropped hints at a conference of Tuscan medievalists, and a few "colleagues" got worked up about what I was suggesting.

They're probably upset because they wanted to get there first, but not only am I first, I've also got something they haven't—and it's something juicy. I wish you were around to puzzle over this stuff with me, the way you used to when you were a kid. I can still imagine the nine-year-old you, your straight black hair around your serious little face. Even then you had that laser focus; all you could see was the few fascinating inches right in front of you. I should have guessed you'd become a surgeon. For a while I thought you might turn out to be a historian like me, but you went for the knife instead. "Taking a history," you doctors always say, in that proprietary way doctors have. We historians prefer to call it "borrowing," since it's not ours to take.

You'd love Siena, and it's crazy that you've never seen the house. You should take a vacation and come help me with my little mystery. You don't want to be in the hospital in July anyway when the new residents come and you have to teach them not to kill people.

It's a great time to visit. The two Palios—the horse races that have taken over the city every summer for seven hundred years—are coming, and everyone is revving up for the event. We can read man-uscripts together—medieval Italian is close enough to modern that you'd be able to manage. Good thing I took your Italian upbringing so seriously, right? There is no way that Beatrice Alessandra Trovato was going to grow up without learning how to speak and write her mother tongue. Maybe Dante was a funny way to learn it, but you can't do better really.

Let me know. I'll change the sheets on the spare bed just for you. I love you, Little B.

Ben

_____

After I got Benjamin's letter I did something wildly uncharacteristic—I acted on impulse. It was after midnight when I finished reading, but I went online and searched for flights to Siena. The forty-eight-hour cancellation policy made me reckless, and I clicked on the "reserve now" button for an irresistibly affordable flight. Ben would be just waking up by now, so I picked up the phone and dialed.

"Ben, I bought a plane ticket. I'm coming to visit."

"For real?"

"I'll be there in three weeks." I imagined Ben's face with his habitual day's growth of beard, receiver pressed against his ear.

"I'll have to buy laundry detergent, but you're worth it. Send me your details, and I'll pick you up from the airport."

"Great. And hey—I love you."

"I love you too, Little B. Now go to bed. You have to get up soon."

As I fell asleep, I imagined poring over old manuscripts the way we used to when I was a kid. But it didn't work out that way.

I was orphaned for the second time a week later. The first time I had Benjamin; the second time I was on my own. The call from Ben's lawyer in Siena came the day after I'd renewed my passport, and the strange echo of the international call made me hear every word twice. Once was almost more than I could bear.

There was no way I could have imagined Ben's death—that moment when my one source of unconditional love collapsed into nothing and winked out like a dying star. Years before, when I'd first learned about Ben's heart, I'd thought: *I'll go crazy if I lose him; I won't survive it.* But now that he was gone, now that I had gone from having a brother to having none, I did not go crazy.

Or perhaps I did go crazy for those few seconds, as the world I knew tilted vertiginously sideways, and my legs slid out from under me. From the floor, I tipped my head back to look up at the haloed brightness of the hall light. *One bulb is out*, I thought, seeing the single bright circle where two should have been, *how strange that I hadn't noticed until now.* One minute Ben had been there, and now he was not. Had I gone crazy, it might have lessened the agony of understanding the truth. But my mind did not allow me that relief.

The used bookstore around the corner from my apartment has served as my second home for years. It's the kind of place that rarely exists anymore, with narrow aisles and big worn leather chairs where you can sit for hours getting lost in an out-of-print edition of some obscure writer's first novel. I have the dubious distinction of adoring authors whose books are mostly out of print, so I spend as much of my little free time there as I can. That's where I first met Nathaniel, who owns the bookstore and imbues it with unusual literary magic. Every time I go there I get lost in a book and look up hours later, having missed a meal, or the change from daylight to darkness. I'm cautious about who I get recommendations from, but Nathaniel knows how to pick a book, at least for me.

The first time I met him I was in one of those leather chairs, engrossed in a rare Jane Austen first edition, when a shadow fell over the pages. I looked up, blinking.

"Are you planning a purchase, or would you like to spend the night?" Nathaniel asked in his British accent. I felt the heat in my face as I leaped up out of the chair.

"How much?" He told me, and I sat down again, horrified.

"Why don't you come back tomorrow and finish it," he said. "Officially we open at ten, but you can knock at nine if you can't wait." That was the beginning of a beautiful friendship. I spent many hours in his store and, eventually, once we knew each other better, even more hours eating sumptuous meals cooked up by Nathaniel's husband, Charles, a forensic pathologist with a deft hand in the kitchen and a wry sense of humor about the origins of his knife skills.

Nathaniel was the first person I told about Benjamin. I showed up at the front door of his shop at closing time on the day I got the lawyer's call. Nathaniel had just bolted the front door when he saw me, but something about my face must have made it clear that he shouldn't start our conversation on the sidewalk. He waved me in.

"My brother died and left me his house in Siena." I said it all at once, before the words could retreat.

"Beatrice," he said, and guided me gently to an armchair.

"I'm going to Italy. Will you take care of my apartment while I'm gone?"

"It would be my pleasure and privilege," he said, his words formal but his eyes as warm as the hug I was not encouraging, though I clearly needed it.

"Thanks, Nathaniel, you're my savior. Now I need some guide-books."

"Would you rather plan a trip than talk?" I nodded. He looked at me carefully, as if checking whether I was safe to leave alone, and then disappeared behind a tall bookcase. He came back with a pile of reading material on Tuscany.

"Try these," he said. I leafed through them silently for a few minutes.

"There's a lot to see in Siena." I looked up from a color plate of Simone Martini's *Maestà*.

"Indeed there is, Beatrice." I was grateful he'd left the rest unsaid.

I kissed him on the cheek and left before I lost my composure entirely. I stayed up until 2:00 a.m. reading. Unfortunately, I had to wake up three hours later to operate on a tricky basilar aneurysm, but neurosurgeons are used to that.

An email from Ben's lawyers arrived a few days later. I translated from Italian to English in my head.

Gentilissima Dottoressa Trovato:

We are deeply grieved at the news of your brother's death and extend our most sincere regrets. We have known your brother for some time and mourn the loss of a well-loved scholar of our beautiful city and its history. As we discussed on the phone, you are his only known surviving relative and the beneficiary of his estate, which includes real property as well as material goods. We look forward to your visit to our Siena offices in the near future to aid in its disposition. We will send you the key to his residence in Siena to spare you the inconvenience of finding commercial lodging.

When Dottore Trovato first began working with our firm, he left instructions, in the event that any misfortune should occur to keep him from his research, that we send you the contents of his permanent carrel at the library of the Università degli Studi di Siena. You should expect to receive his notes and manuscript within the next few days. This is somewhat outside our usual procedure regarding timing of distribution of property before probate, but Dottore Trovato made it quite clear that you are his only surviving relative and that there is no one who would contest the intent of his will.

Although you are a Doctor of Medicine rather than Philosophy like your brother, we are certain you appreciate how regrettable it would be for the work of one of our city's great modern historians to fall into oblivion. We are the primary firm representing Tuscan academics and have taken the liberty of contacting several scholars who have graciously offered to study your brother's notes to determine what might be appropriate for publication. We will be happy to discuss the details further at your convenience.

With our sincerest hope for your solace in this terrible time of loss,
Avv. Cavaliere, Alberti e Alberti

Even though I didn't know exactly what Ben had been working on, the thought of other scholars getting their hands on it gave me a queasy feeling. I wrote a quick but polite reply asking the lawyers not to share anything with anyone. I wished I'd had a chance to hear Ben tell me about it himself. Now I never would hear him say anything again.

Three days later I came home late and overheated from my commute in a subway car with malfunctioning air-conditioning to find the package from Ben's lawyers waiting with the doorman. Inside the wrapping was a battered red accordion folder tied with a flat satin ribbon. *Ben held this folder, he tied the ribbon with his own hands.* I closed my eyes and took a deep breath. The folder smelled like a library, of course—old leather bindings and dust—not like Ben. I went to my desk and sat down to read. The papers were a jumble of typed paragraphs, interspersed with photocopies from original texts with notes scribbled in the margins. I could imagine Ben with his forehead creased in concentration, ink smearing along the heel of his hand as he wrote.

> *Agnolo di Tura, a 14th-century chronicler, recounted the impact of the Black Death on Siena:*
> "*The mortality in Siena began in May 1348 . . . in many places in Siena great pits were dug and piled deep with the multitude of dead. And they died by the hundreds, both day and night, and were*

thrown in those ditches and covered with earth . . . Father abandoned child, wife husband, one brother another . . . for this Plague seemed to strike through the breath and sight. I . . . buried my five children with my own hands . . . And so many died that all believed it was the end of the world."

Ben had scribbled a note in the right-hand margin around di Tura's words, and underlined for emphasis:

How many people died in Siena? Agnolo says 52K—Gottfried insists that can't be, since population was no more than 60K. BW claims that the population dropped 80 percent! Tuchman: more than half. <u>Was the mortality from the Plague worse in Siena than in the other Tuscan cities? Seems like it. Why?</u>

I went back to Ben's typed notes.

Siena at her heyday had a master plan to make the Duomo the largest in the world—the nave to become the transept of a vast cathedral. This cathedral would be the physical symbol of Siena's greatness among the Tuscan cities, what would become Europe, and the world. That plan died with the Black Death. The Plague heralded the collapse of a shining, self-governing city-state. After the Plague, Siena never recovered, unlike her longtime archrival Florence. Why?

For decades historians have tried to explain the particularly devastating effects of the Plague on Siena, her failure to recover, and the eventual fall of the great commune to her rival Florence. The pages that follow will introduce new evidence to explain Siena's suffering and eventual decline from power and political independence.

I'd been so engrossed by the medieval mystery Ben was writing about that for a few seconds I'd forgotten the present. Now, as I looked up from his notes, the reason I had them at all hit me again like a punch in the stomach. All those years I'd postponed going to Siena, and now I was going to deal with my brother's property and manuscript, rather than to see him. The consequence of my never having made time for a visit was nearly unbearable. I put Ben's papers back in their folder, carefully tying the cloth ribbon and trying to breathe. But —I could still see Ben's house, even without Ben in it. I could still visit the city that had drawn him in, even though he wouldn't be there to greet me. I needed to sort out the estate, and I needed to get away; I hadn't taken a vacation day in four years. The thought gathered momentum, and before the night was over I'd made up my mind. I fell asleep seeing Ben's hand curved around his favorite fountain pen as he wrote about the Siena Duomo that should have been.

"You're leaving New York for some Italian hill town?" Linney put her hands on her hips and glared at me. Linney reminds me of a small, fierce hawk. Her short red hair, so dark it's almost purple, lies close against her head, and from behind you can see the nape of her neck, oddly vulnerable, unlike the rest of her.

"Not just *some* hill town—*Siena*." I glared back.

The specifics didn't mollify Linney at all. "What's in *Siena*?"

"My brother left me a house there; I have to go settle his estate."

"Your brother died? You decided to tell me your brother died parenthetically while announcing that you're taking a trip to Tuscany? Beatrice, hello, are you in there?"

I looked down at the blue shoe covers on our four feet. Linney crouched down so she could meet my eyes from below.

"Come back," she said ominously. "The other neurosurgeons aren't as good as you are."

"Why wouldn't I come back? It's just a three-month sabbatical."

Linney didn't answer.

When the plane took off with me in it, I felt strangely light—as if the strings mooring me to the life I'd made had stretched too far, and had finally broken.

*　　*　　*

I stood at the door of Ben's house with the key in my hand—heavy and brass, nothing like my New York apartment key. I was about to put the key in the lock when I got the sensation that I had done this before—put this key in this lock, in this door, in this city. It must be déjà vu, I thought, because I had never been to Ben's house; I had never even been to Italy before. And yet I had a feeling of familiarity so strong, it had to be real. Déjà vu should be a dreamy sensation, not this sharp-edged clarity. I *knew* I had been here, and somehow that knowledge coexisted with the absolute certainty that I had not.

The heavy door stuck, but I managed to open it with a push from one hip. In the dark entryway, the smell enveloped me—the mustiness of a house left behind. I slid my hand along the wall, looking for a light switch, but found none. From the faint light filtering in through the open front door I could make out the entry hall with wood stairs rising to darkness above. I bumped into a hall table and almost knocked over a teetering lamp, caught it, then turned it on. I closed and locked the front door, and began to examine my new home.

Siena, June 4

Dear Nathaniel,

I'm writing a letter because Ben didn't seem to believe in home-based Internet service. Very medieval of him. No light switches either—I nearly killed myself the first night I arrived in the dark. The house has a typical medieval plan: a sala *(living room) in the front, and* the camere (bedrooms) in the back. Those back rooms open onto a central courtyard shared by all the houses around it, planted with a trio of blossoming orange trees—I wake up to the fragrance filling my bedroom through the windows. I wonder who owned this house before us, what merchant or artisan, wine dealer, painter . . . do you know how to find out? You always know everything. Were there surgeons in the fourteenth century? I'm not feeling very much like a neurosurgeon at the moment, and I'm enjoying playing hooky.

My first visit to the law offices of Cavaliere, Alberti and Alberti was like something out of a Fellini film. Cavaliere was rail thin, practically invisible from the side; the Albertis short and round with a total of six chins between them, and they all had sympathetic, meeting-a-bereaved-client looks on their faces. I realize you are probably worrying about me, but just remember that doctors make jokes when things get bad. It makes us feel better.

But these lawyers . . . the windows in their office are so dusty that barely any light comes through, and the antiquated lamps have at most ten-watt bulbs in them. I could hardly see where I was supposed to sign. But then I did, and now I own a house in Siena and everything in it.

The Albertis are pressuring me to relinquish the project to someone "more experienced." But I am not cooperating. There's this Tuscan scholar, Franco Signoretti, who claims descent from one of the oldest and most prominent medieval families of Siena. He gave an interview for the local television station that I watched on Ben's tiny black-and-white TV. (I know it's hard to imagine medieval history being newsworthy, but things are different here.) Based on the sharp comments this guy dropped during the interview he was clearly trying to discredit Ben's work. He described Ben as an "American-born young scholar in the making" who "had made a respectable effort, in his regrettably short career in Siena, to leave his mark on our long and illustrious history." It was unpleasant to hear about Ben in the third person this way, though I'm happy to say Italian has come back to me surprisingly *quickly. I'm glad now that Ben pushed me so hard to learn it when I was a kid, though at the time I fought him pretty hard. Listening to the guy rant on about how close he is to a discovery that the "young American" had been working on made me dig in my heels: not the reaction Alberti the Elder was hoping for. The more eager the lawyers get to pass Ben's research on to another scholar, the more stubborn I feel about hanging on to it. I might even be able to publish for him, with a little help from local experts. After all, Ben trained me. I wish he were here to help me now.*

How are you? Get any new books in recently? Thanks for taking care of my apartment. You can toss the plants if they're too difficult to keep alive.

Love, Beatrice

The morning after my visit with the lawyers, I woke up with the sun in my face in the second-floor guest bedroom—obviously for guests because it was so tidy, and had so little in it. I went downstairs to Ben's bedroom and stood for a few minutes at the door, looking in. The bed was made, but sloppily—he'd never been a hospital corners sort of guy. His spindly-legged bed table was stacked high with books, and more books stood in piles on the floor. The walls were covered with framed maps and pages of illuminated manuscripts, the dense black letters crowding together on the page. He loved his work, I thought—I loved mine too, but I wouldn't have wallpapered my bedroom back home with pages from neurosurgical textbooks. The sun wasn't as strong on the ground floor as it was in my room upstairs, and it came through the orange tree low and faintly green, speckling the walls of the room with leaf-shaped shadows.

I took a deep breath and stepped through the doorway, feeling like I might be invading his privacy—but what privacy do people have once they're gone? I felt the wave of loss rising then like a tide, here in this cluttered room that sang out Ben's memory like an elegy. I sat down on the wooden floor and watched the dust motes drift aimlessly in the light until my back ached and my body called out for coffee and breakfast. I closed the door on my way out.

I decided to visit the University of Siena, which was right near the Piazza del Campo—Sienese call it Il Campo for short—to see whether I could find more of what Ben had been working on. Nathaniel had recommended that I speak with a local archivist, Emilio Fabbri. It was too early when I got there, the doors locked and windows dark, but I could pass time in the Campo, along with half the population of the city.

The day was heating up by the time I reached the big piazza, so I stopped at a small shop to buy a bottle of fizzy lemonade. I drank it while sitting on a bench, watching the lines between the paving stones converge and bend in the heat. I counted the piazza's nine sections—for the Council of Nine, i Noveschi—who ruled Siena during its medieval heyday. As I sat, my mind went still. The sounds around me intensified; high individual voices rang out against a background of lower rumbles. I felt the ground vibrating as children ran past me chasing pigeons, and I inhaled the pungent smell of garlic wafting from a trattoria that faced the piazza. And into that moment of pure receptive blankness came a sudden wave of profound, absolute panic. It passed quickly and left my heart pounding. Seconds later, the terror hit me again. I stood up, and the lemonade bottle slipped through my hand and shattered on the pavement. That's when I saw the young girl a few feet away from me, alone in the crowd and white with fear. She looked up into my face, her dark eyes huge and brimming with tears.

"*Dov'è Mamma,*" she wailed, throwing her head back. "*Mamma, Mamma . . .*"

In that moment I knew that it was not my own fear I felt, but hers. I grabbed the girl's hand and looked desperately around the expanse of the Campo. At the other side of the piazza, under the awning of a souvenir shop where I'd bought postcards on my first day in Siena, stood a woman I'd never seen before. She had dark hair pulled back from a pale face, and her red dress was bright against the stone of the buildings behind her. The moment I saw this woman who should have been a stranger, all I wanted to do was run as hard as I could into her arms. And so we ran together hand in hand, the girl and I, both fueled by the same desire and knowledge, stumbling up the slope of the shell-shaped piazza, until we were looking into Mamma's stricken face—me from above and her daughter from below. Mamma thanked me in a wild outpouring of Italian and tears and enveloped her daughter in a tight embrace. I stood frozen, watching them. She was back with her family, but no one could help me find mine. I didn't have the energy left for the visit I'd planned to the university. I left the girl and her mother by the postcard rack and walked slowly home.

Back at the house, I sat at the kitchen table. I tried to re-create that blank feeling I'd had right before I'd found the lost girl, before her fear had taken root in my head. I'd had it before—in surgery. As soon as I'm scrubbed and gloved, my mind goes quiet and something else takes over. Looking back on all those surgical hours, I realized that when I operate, I am listening, and reacting to what I hear. And what I hear is the patient's body telling me how things are going, because it knows I'm paying attention. I can feel the blood moving, hear the air entering and leaving the lungs, see the winding thick gray gyri of the brain being pushed aside by an invading tumor. I know where it is safe to cut, and I know when things go wrong.

When I'd written to Ben about the OR being intense, he'd made a joke about it. But I hadn't been joking. At first, my extra sense had been a background hum, such a natural and useful extension of my work that I'd barely noticed it. That moment in the OR with Linney three years before, when I'd noticed a problem before the monitors did, was the first time my abilities had crossed the line. The ventricular tachycardia episode had been worse—my emotional response to a patient's condition had overwhelmed me enough to interrupt my ability to work. And things kept happening, things I no longer told Linney. I was afraid to tell Ben, who might worry too much from too far away. While I was operating, I'd know a hidden blood vessel was leaking because I could feel it in my own head. I'd wake up sweating at 3:00 a.m. to realize a postop patient had a brewing infection before the nurses called with reports of fever. And now, after that moment in the piazza, that tendency had broken into the rest of my life, outside the confines of the operating room. How far could this empathy go? And would it take me with it?

I can't help thinking that having been a twin, even so briefly, might have something to do with it. Maybe I feel what others are feeling because I've got an open edge where *she* used to be, and instead of having her at my side, buffering and shoring me up against the outside world, I absorb everything. Or maybe she is my window into *other*, because I knew, once, deeply, before I knew what it meant to know, how it is to be identical to someone else.

Ben witnessed the first time it happened, though neither of us realized what *it* was at the time. QUIET ZONE the sign read at the edge of the steep path leading up to the Cloisters, marking the entrance. Every Sunday Ben and I walked to the transplanted medieval abbey in Fort Tryon Park from our apartment in Washington Heights, on paths that opened to a view of the Hudson River through the trees. We entered through a doorway in the stone walls and up a steep dark winding staircase, then emerged into the sudden sun of the magical twelfth-century cloister garden, centered around a quiet fountain etched with lichen.

While we walked through the museum, Ben told me stories of knights, feudal lords, and the Annunciation—but the unicorn tapestries were always my favorite. This is probably true of all kids who visit the Cloisters—the hunt for a mythical creature beats paintings of a bunch of old dead saints any day. I'd sit in the gallery, staring at the intricate patterns of flowers woven into the background of the tapestries, imagining myself as the maiden who invited the unicorn to dip its horn in a woodland stream. When I was twelve, my brother decided I was old enough to hear the real story behind the tapestries, and I sat on a wooden bench at the side of the gallery listening in the high-ceilinged room.

Ben told me the story while I looked at the series of tapestries that told the story of the hunt for the unicorn: the hunters brandishing their weapons, the dogs sniffing out their quarry, the maiden who'd lured the unicorn to lay his head in her virginal lap. And near the end of the cycle, when I saw the unicorn's limp body draped over the hunter's horse, his white coat stained with new blood, I felt suddenly dizzy, and the sounds around me muffled. I smelled the sharp scent of horses, felt the bristling of a wiry mane under my hand, and heard the barking of hunting dogs. I saw dense forest undergrowth coming up to meet my face, then suddenly I was lying on the cold stone floor of the gallery, blinking up at Benjamin.

Ben helped me up and sat next to me. "Little B, what happened?"

"I fell off the bench," I said. "Did the maiden know what was going to happen to the unicorn when she agreed to act as bait?" Ben didn't answer. "She would *never* have agreed if they had told her!" Adolescents are very intense as a rule, and I was hardly the exception; I was almost at the point of tears. "*I* wouldn't have done it if *I* had known they were going to *kill* him, KILL him! Never, never, *never*. . . ." My voice cracked, and I looked down at my shoes. One lace had come untied and I busied myself with it, not meeting Benjamin's eyes.

"B, the unicorn comes to life again"—he lifted my chin with one hand and with the other pointed at the final tapestry—"and the red on its coat is not blood. It's pomegranate juice, dripping from the tree above the corral."

"That doesn't make it OK! It's, it's . . . BETRAYAL!!!" He nodded mutely while I ranted. I stayed away from the tapestry room after that.

After my incident in the Cloisters, Benjamin took me to a lot of doctors. At the time, I thought I had done something wrong, something dangerous. I saw our family doctor, then a general cardiologist, then a specialist in cardiac arrhythmia. They all proclaimed me to be a perfectly ordinary twelve-year-old, at least from a cardiac perspective. Seeing Benjamin's worry, I vowed to stay in the present, far away from the fanciful imagination that had triggered my outburst. It wasn't until many years later that I understood the source of his anxiety—his own, unpredictable, vulnerable heart.

Instead of attempting another trip to the library, I spent the next day at home making Ben's house feel more like mine. I started in the kitchen with its dark wood-beamed roof meeting thick white plaster walls. I spent a peaceful hour cleaning the old cast-iron stove while the breeze blew through the open shutters. I organized the small collection of chipped yellow and black enamel pots. As I picked up the smallest one, I remembered the first time Ben had taught me to make polenta in it. Finally, standing by myself over that piece of twenty-year-old kitchenware, I managed to cry.

When I could navigate the stairs safely again, I headed to the guest room—the room Ben had intended for me. I loved the metal-framed twin bed and its faded linen sheets, the creaky oak armoire where I hung my clothes, and the tiny sitting room that looked out onto the street. I found an old package of nails and a battered hammer and put up a few pictures I'd found at an antique store near the house, reproductions of old maps that showed how little the city plan had changed since the fourteenth century. As I hammered in the last nail, it crossed my mind that redecorating was the sort of thing you do when planning to stay somewhere for a while, somewhere you might consider calling home.

It was nearly two by the time I made it to the ground floor. I dusted off the chairs and tables in the *sala* and then went to the back. This had been Ben's study, his private sanctuary. The desk was his only extravagance, an antique Biedermeier drop-front made of satinwood and ebony. I turned the small brass key in its lock and dropped the leaf to reveal six drawers adorned with ebony pulls. The first held a collection of fountain pens, nibs dry. Another was filled with scribbled notes on bits of scrap paper and old envelopes, and the next held obsolete Italian coins grouped by size in small glass jars. The fourth was devoted to scissors: small gold ones engraved to look like a stork's beak, larger steel-bladed shears more useful than decorative. In the fifth drawer I found inks in every color of the rainbow—my fingers itched to dip one of the pens and write. The sixth drawer stuck, and I edged it slowly open to avoid cracking the veneer. Inside was a linen-wrapped package, and within that, a heavy cardboard folder with a card tied to the front that read: UNIVERSITÀ DEGLI STUDI DI SIENA. "Hello," I said out loud. I'd been alone long enough to start talking to inanimate objects. A single page of parchment was pressed between the covers.

Florence, Italy, September 1347

To Messer Salvestro de' Medici
My dear Cousin,

I am writing to you as I know not where else to turn. Since the death of his father my little Iacopo has been full of strange and troubled thoughts. I err in calling him "little" as he has attained the age of twenty-eight, but it is always difficult for me to remember that he is fully grown. Perhaps that is a mother's lot. A mother of a son, that is—I have heard that daughters seem to mature well before their youth should be spent! In truth, Iacopo has always had a strangeness about him, even when he was a boy. Such serious ideas, and held so fiercely. I could never distract him from a grudge. I recall when he was three years of age, he deliberately upset his cup of milk, something that every child has done at least once. But I, heated from too many tasks clamoring for my attention, took his cup from him and would not give it back, despite his screams. When I relented he refused to drink. It was months before he agreed to have milk again, and I worried for his health.

Ever since the misery that has befallen his father, my husband, the execution that has become the tragedy of our noble family, Iacopo has withdrawn into himself. He broods alone and writes endless pages in a small cramped hand. I do not know what he writes. It does not appear to be a letter. He avoids the company of his peers, and of the women of good families I suggest to him, hoping that betrothal might brighten his future. If you think perhaps you might advise him, from the perspective of a gentleman, I would be grateful if you would write to Iacopo. Perhaps he will listen to another man, now that his father is gone. I pray to see the joy return to my son's face, and lighten the shadow that weighs upon all our hearts.

With best wishes for the success of your business ventures in Venezia,
                              Immacolata Regate de' Medici

Why did Ben have a more than six-hundred-year-old letter from a Medici woman with an executed husband and a troubled son? Did it have anything to do with Siena's downfall? The letter made me apprehensive, but I didn't know why.

Siena, June 8

Dear Nathaniel,

Today I went to the University of Siena, and met the archivist you recommended—Fabbri. He was helpful but looks like he's spent enough time in the dark to develop vitamin D deficiency. I told him I was looking for information about the Plague in Siena. He was expecting a visit from me—thanks to your introduction. He actually bowed (so medieval!) and said he was delighted to provide me with material that would help me "imagine with great clarity the horror of the time." I guess you're bound to get some creepy reactions when you specialize in the Black Death. But Ben wasn't creepy. Maybe someday you'll come visit me here? I'm missing my old life. Or at least I'm missing you.

Love,

Beatrice

As soon as I started reading about places and dates, it became obvious that I needed a diagram. Referring to multiple sources, I pulled out a blank sheet of paper and started to sketch a graphical representation of the Plague's path through what would eventually become Europe, with Italy's boot at the center. I hunched over my sketched map, adding different-colored, multidirectional arrows labeled with dates. Fabbri periodically looked in on me courteously. I wondered whether he might have thought I was going to deface original manuscripts with Magic Markers. My chart looked like a kindergartener's drawing, but it was just what I needed. I have a good memory for many things; dates aren't one of them.

Over the next few days, I pored over modern epidemiologic treatises on the origins and spread of *Yersinia pestis*, the bacteria blamed for the epidemic, and learned about the digestive system of the infected flea, the main vector for transmission of the Plague from infected rats to humans. I read medieval chronicles describing the buboes—armpit or groin swellings—that burst, spewing purulence. People spouted blood from every orifice and worsened so rapidly that they might go to sleep well and never wake. I went home with a headache and thrashed around most of the night, imagining lumps in my armpits and wishing the sun would rise. But it made me feel a satisfying connection to Ben, who must have followed these paths many times before me.

On my third day in the archives, I began to feel like an underground animal. I attached myself to a hard wooden chair and took notes furiously. After three hours I got up and looked for Fabbri, but couldn't find him. I wandered through the aisles of books with faded titles and soon I was deep into unknown territory.

The books got darker and shabbier, and I began to feel an odd sense of unease. I ducked under a low doorframe into a small windowless room. There the feeling got stronger, as if someone were speaking just under the threshold of my hearing. The books were so crowded here that there was hardly space to walk, and nowhere to sit. I could feel my heart accelerating. *It's a library, Beatrice, not a haunted house.* Most of the books had no words stamped on their bindings. I picked up a small leather-bound journal, smooth from handling. I closed my eyes, dizzy, and put the book back on the table where it belonged.

I kept one hand on the table until I felt steady, but the book waited to be picked up again, inanimate but irresistible. As I reached for it, I heard a hollow sound in my head, like the echo in a tunnel, and smelled the scent of damp plaster and paint. When I opened the book the faded handwriting seemed unaccountably familiar. I glanced down at the first page and read:

Anno Domini 1343
Gabriele Beltrano Accorsi

Gabri-EH-leh. He would have said it the Italian way.

My good mother, I am told, lived more in the spirit than on the earth. With her final breath she carried me to the threshold of this world, then left me for the angels. I still bear the marks of that loss upon my heart.

I recognized the quiet hum, then the heightening of perception, and then I was flooded by this fourteenth-century writer's loss. It's one thing to read the words and sympathize—*how tragic, he lost his mother as he was being born, just like me.* But I didn't just think. I *felt* his grief, despite the fact that he had been dead for centuries. I closed the book but could not put it down. I made my way back to the table I'd huddled over for three days. As I was packing up my things, a voice behind my right shoulder made me gasp. I turned to see Fabbri standing at attention. His head came barely to my chin.

"Dottoressa Trovato, does this book have bearing on your research?"

"It's very informative, Signore," I croaked, unaccustomed to speech. "It comes from just the right time period." I think he expected me to hand him the book for safekeeping, but I didn't.

"Do you think I could take it home rather than try to get through it here?" Fabbri puffed his cheeks out once, started to speak, stopped himself, then started again. I hoped the internal battle he was having would end in my favor.

"I would hate to see any damage come to it in your hands."

It was time to name-drop. "I don't know whether I told you—I'm Beniamino Trovato's sister. I'm working on a project he left behind when he died." Fabbri's jaw dropped.

"You are *that* Trovato? Of course you know how to care for a manuscript! Under the circumstances I think the archive's policy can be waived. But might you be so kind as to leave some form of identification?"

I beamed at him and handed him a credit card I wouldn't miss. "Thank you so much." He helped me wrap the book carefully, and I headed back out to daylight. I walked home, holding the little book against my chest.

June 11

Dear Nathaniel,

Every night I dream stripes, stripes, stripes. The green and white cathedral has invaded my sleeping life. All this reading is really getting under my skin. Ben's project has become mine, and everything else fades to insignificance next to it. I'm so absorbed in Siena's past I feel like I'm actually there . . . or, maybe more accurately, THEN. Maybe I should have been a historian after all—Ben would be so smug if he could see me now.

This Franco Signoretti guy has become more insistent—somehow he got my address and sent me a letter that on the surface looks pleasant but between the lines reads as a threat. Probably an academic competitor who doesn't want me publishing what Ben dug up. So of course I will do just that, once I figure it out. The other option my lawyers are pushing doesn't look good either—passing Ben's research to a local Sienese scholar who looks like he just finished high school. I'm not rolling over for any of these guys.

The guidebooks say Siena's glory is frozen in time, suspended in the Middle Ages unchanged—all because of the Plague. Can you imagine what it would be like if more than half the inhabitants of New York City died within two years? It might be a lot easier to get a dinner reservation. Sorry, morbid humor. Actually, it's true—people ate a lot better after the Plague than before, with at least half the population gone. Poor consolation for losing half your neighbors and family, I know, but at least there was an upside.

I found an interesting book—I think it's actually a diary—from the 1300s. It's really bringing the past to life. Don't you just love primary sources?

Love,

B

I was hanging my long-neglected laundry in the courtyard behind the house when I noticed someone watching me. A little girl sat in the fork of the orange tree, staring silently as I struggled. I couldn't find any clothespins and the wind kept blowing things off the line, so I'd resorted to tying knots in my bras.

"What are you doing to your underwear?" she asked, and then, "Do you live here?"

It took me a minute to understand her little kid's version of Italian. "Now I do. This is my brother's house."

"Beniamino is your brother?" The girl snagged an orange blossom from a branch above her head and tucked it into her shirt, then scrambled out of the tree. I decided not to discuss death with a child I'd never met.

"Yes."

"I like him," the girl said. "He gives me really nice pens." She paused. "Do you have any pens?"

"I think so," I said, which apparently satisfied her. She came over and introduced herself. "I'm Felice Guerrini, and I'm five and two-thirds," she announced. "Want to come have some gelato? We've got *nocciola*."

I met the Guerrini family over hazelnut ice cream. Felice proudly announced her discovery of Beniamino's sister, and the Guerrinis welcomed me warmly. Donata, the mother of the family and an art historian at the University of Siena, looked like a figure from a Botticelli painting with her long golden hair tied up in a careless knot, but she acted like an ordinary human being. She pulled me aside to confirm what had happened to Ben, but we postponed further discussion.

Our house was in the Civetta—little owl—*contrada*, one of seventeen remaining medieval districts in Siena. Donata and her husband, Ilario, rapidly determined to make me an honorary Sienese, or, specifically, a Civettina, loyal to our particular neighborhood. Besides Felice, they had two other children, Gianni (eight), and Sebastiano (six months), each noisy in a distinctively age-specific way. It was a nice antidote to my last few days of self-imposed solitude.

My indoctrination into the intimate life of the *contrada* came a few days later, when the Guerrinis invited me to Sebastiano's baptism in the Civetta fountain.

The feast day of Saint Anthony of Padua, La Civetta's patron saint, marks the time for all the *contrada* babies born within the previous year to be baptized in the ward's own font. At noon on Sunday, Sebastiano, along with other infants and their families, waited his turn. Sebastiano was a perfect cherub of a baby, with golden curls and plump, dimpled arms and legs. At this moment he was angelically asleep for the *priore*'s words.

"I, in the name of Saint Anthony of Padua, sprinkle you with the waters of this noble fountain, so that from your heart the love for your *contrada* will flow eternally, blessing you with the great heritage of your ancestors." The *priore* dipped his fingers into the fountain and sprinkled Sebastiano's smooth forehead with water, at which point he promptly woke up and began screaming. Donata expertly folded down a flap of her shirt and shoved her breast in his open mouth. Draped with the black, white, and red silk scarf of La Civetta that would be his forever, Sebastiano realized that he was not being abandoned to starve to death on a mountaintop in the pouring rain, and soon dozed off to sleep again, to the obvious relief of his parents and the rest of the Civettini.

The next morning I woke up at dawn. Too restless to read or write, I dressed and left the house. In the faint gray of early morning, I wound through the narrow streets toward the Piazza del Campo. As I came around the corner of Via Banchi di Sopra, I saw a train of workers carting wheelbarrows piled high with yellowish dirt. A reverent silence hung over the men— as if for a religious occasion, rather than a menial task. Then I saw that the line wound its way down to the outer rim of the Campo, where the workers began to lay down the yellow earth, La Terra in Piazza, which would soon be a racetrack for ten Palio horses. I watched the workers, their manual labor imbued with their spiritual purpose, until I was too hungry to stand there anymore, and went to get a bottle of water and a wheel of *panforte* di Siena. The dried fruit and nut cake dusted with powdered sugar was delicious enough to transcend any demeaning fruitcake jokes, and it was dense enough to get me through the afternoon.

In the evening, the Sienese began to come to the Piazza to touch the earth and pay their respects. The Guerrinis found me there and invited me for dinner, which, after a day of *panforte*, was a welcome change. Felice and Gianni led the way back to Vicolo del Coltellinaio singing and chanting pro-Civetta songs boisterously all the way home.

Sitting on Donata's living room couch, I held the dozing Sebastiano while Donata and Ilario worked companionably in the kitchen preparing dinner. I'd never had the luxury of holding a sleeping six-month-old before. A sweet, powdery smell rose from his skin, and he radiated warmth against my bare arms. His chest rose and fell with his peaceful breathing, and every now and then a fleeting smile crossed his face. I looked up from the world of infant bliss to find Donata looking at me.

"No *bambini*, Beatrice?" She said my name the Italian way, with four syllables. Bey-ah-TREE-chay. It sounded impossibly romantic. "But I see you feel his magic."

I smiled, reluctant to break the wordless pleasure I had in Sebastiano's sleeping company. "I had no idea they could be so . . . magnificent."

Donata laughed indulgently. "Enjoy him while he's peaceful, I'll finish the risotto," she said, and went back to the stove.

I watched Donata as she stirred the risotto patiently, and vowed to slow down. Certainly with Sebastiano in my arms exerting his hypnotic dreamy power, I wasn't doing anything fast. Just as we were sitting down at the table, Sebastiano opened his mouth and turned his head toward my chest, searching for sustenance. Since I had nothing to offer him, I handed him over to Donata. He latched onto her breast with ecstatic concentration and ate with eyes closed, bliss personified.

That's when it happened again. First, sudden silence. Then I could hear Ilario, Felice, and Gianni talking, as if from far away. The scent of Parmesan from the risotto sharpened, and I felt the warmth of my left arm where Sebastiano's head had rested. Then I had a sensation I've never had before, first a gentle but persistent tugging on my nipples, then a rush of little electric shocks in my breasts, sparking downward, then a wave of heat and fullness, and an overwhelming feeling of peace, and I realized—*I'm breast-feeding.* Or more accurately, *Donata is, and I'm in there with her.* Donata was lost in a little world with Sebastiano and she didn't notice my intrusion, or my retreat.

The rest of dinner passed without incident, unless you count the moment when Gianni upended his glass of ice water into his sister's lap. After dinner, Donata and Ilario kissed me soundly on both cheeks and I walked the few steps through the courtyard to Ben's house, let myself in the massive door, and made my way to bed, with the sensation of Sebastian's evening meal still tingling in my body. It took me a while to fall asleep.

The next morning I dove into Gabriele's journal again.

> *I came into the world in the year that Duccio di Buoninsegna's Maestà was carried through the streets to the Duomo by a great and reverent crowd.*

I paused to look up Duccio—the *Maestà* was finished in 1311.

> *My father, spent from mourning the loss of my mother, died when I was still a babe, and my uncle took me into his household. On my fourth birthday, I begged him to make me a paintbrush. We cut a tuft of hair from our unwilling cat, and bound it to a slender twig. Thus began my career as a painter.*
>
> *Until my apprenticeship, I was a difficult child. I used the yolk of an egg to decorate the wall behind my chair, and the sauce from our midday stew created the outlines of a Madonna on the table. When it became obvious that I wished to paint more than eat, my uncle sent me to study with Simone Martini. Under his tutelage, my mischief was bent into study. When Simone finally let me work at his side, he directed not only my hands, but my soul.*
>
> *"Paint from the holy text, but let your soul give life to your brush," he whispered, as I lifted my arm to copy the Annunciation he had set before me. In my fingers the feel of the brush faded, and I was filled with the fear of the Virgin at her uninvited angelic guest's arrival. I took the Maestro's words to heart.*

Siena, June 28

Dear Nathaniel,

Sorry I haven't written back to you for so long. I'm trying to finish what Ben started before that smarmy Signoretti gets there first, wherever "there" is. I still don't know what Ben was looking for, but I don't want to give it up—I want to do Ben justice now that he's not here to finish the work himself. So I'm trying to map out what happened to Siena during the Plague, hoping to figure out what Ben was onto, instead of thinking about getting back to New York to repair aneurysms. I haven't found anything yet. But if Ben did, it must be somewhere.

In the meantime, while you're taking care of my apartment (thanks again) I'm enjoying hanging out in the fourteenth century with my very appealing fresco painter. It's a safe obsession, since he's been dead for over six hundred years.

The surgeon part of me seems to have gone dormant. Don't tell the department head, since I'd like to have a job when I get back . . . though I'm not sure when that will be. A long-quiet part of me is waking up, the historian born in my brother's study twenty years ago.

Would you like anything from Siena? Maybe something for the bookstore?

Love,

B

I didn't write what I was thinking. I did not confess that I had begun to live as much in the pages of that journal as in the real world around me. I did not express the nagging worry that my empathy, so useful to me as a doctor, was now sparked by words written by someone dead for centuries. I'd been happily lost in a book many times before, but this was different. This, I had no control over. Even then, I think I sensed the possibility inherent in that profound immersion in the written word—the possibility, and the danger. But it did not make me stop reading.

Two days later, I found a note from Donata under my door inviting me for coffee. I felt a rush of warmth reading this personal invitation from my first Sienese friend. We planned to meet at the Fonte Gaia the following day before heading to her favorite café. I stuffed her letter in my bag as I headed out to the piazza.

Donata arrived in a flax-colored linen dress, looking effortlessly perfect. I suspected that she looked this elegant even in her sleep.

"We take it for granted, the presence of water here," Donata said, sitting down beside me on the edge of the reflecting pool. "Water was scarce in medieval Siena, and its availability to the people of the *commune* changed lives. It took eight years to build the conduit to bring the water here, then the following year, 1343, the fountain was completed."

Donata had pronounced the word *commune* with three syllables: co-*mu*-neh. I'd never heard it out loud before. In my head, I'd been imagining the word *commune*, the hippie 1960s version.

"Nobody knows exactly what the original looked like," Donata said. "It's one of those puzzles that keeps art historians like me up all night." As we walked to the café, I looked back at the Fonte's pool glittering in the sun and wondered what it had looked like back when my artist was alive.

We ordered two espressos, and I watched Donata sip hers slowly.

She spoke first. "How are you managing?"

"I'm comforted by picking up the work Ben left, as if he's there inside me, telling me how I'm doing. The way he used to." I looked away and was glad when Donata changed the subject gracefully.

"I've always loved the name Beatrice. Do you know how your parents chose it for you?"

36

"I never knew who my father was, and my mother died giving birth to me. Ben chose my name. He was reading Dante in the hospital waiting room."

"He chose well for you," Donata said.

I was silent for a long time, thinking.

"Have you seen the *ospedale*, Beatrice?"

"No, should I?" I must have sounded unenthusiastic. "I don't really want to spend my free time thinking about medicine." My response sounded more irritable than I'd intended.

"Beatrice, I meant the Ospedale Santa Maria della Scala—across from the Duomo. It hasn't been a hospital for centuries." Her gentle reprimand made me blush.

"I'm sorry. The thought of visiting a working hospital in Siena is about as appealing as amputating my own leg." Donata snorted in a graceful, somehow Italian way. "I repent my brutish American manners—will you be my friend anyway?"

"Of course," Donata said. "I like your brutish American ways—politeness can get tiresome."

We walked companionably together back to the Piazza del Duomo, where the cathedral and the Ospedale faced each other. Donata stopped in front of the Ospedale entrance. "The facade of the Ospedale is another great mystery for art historians."

"I don't see any paintings."

"Exactly. It is believed there were once five frescos here, depicting the life of the Virgin Mary. But it's not clear who painted them. It was probably a collaboration among three of Siena's greatest painters: Pietro and Ambrogio Lorenzetti—the painters of the Sala della Pace in the Palazzo Pubblico—and Simone Martini."

Martini—Gabriele's teacher. Donata must have heard my intake of breath but misinterpreted the reaction.

"Yes, an extraordinary combination of painters, unprecedented and never repeated. Simone left Siena for Avignon around 1336, and did not return. The Lorenzettis died in the first year of the Plague. Four of the frescos—the birth of the Virgin, the presentation of the Virgin in the temple, the betrothal of the Virgin, and the return of the Virgin to the house of her parents—were probably painted by the Lorenzettis and Martini. But the paintings did not survive."

"I thought you said there were five?"

"The fifth is even more of a mystery. It might have been painted later than the others, and the attribution is uncertain. Four were painted over the arched doorways. The fifth may have been in the center, with two on each side flanking it."

"And the subject?"

"The Assumption of the Virgin—when she ascended to heaven at the end of her life."

At that moment, despite years of Catholic school, I suddenly saw the story from Mary's perspective for the first time. "Can you imagine being accosted by an angel who tells you that you are going to give birth to the son of God, then doing it, only to lose your son to a crazy bunch of rabble-rousers? I couldn't handle it, even with heaven at the end."

Donata fingered the beads at her neck. I wondered whether I'd offended her with my abridged version of the life of the Virgin. "I see Siena is starting to get under your skin," she said. "We Sienese feel a special connection to Santa Maria, who has protected us for hundreds of years, and medieval Siena was even closer to her embrace than we are now. When the gates closed at night and the mantle of the Virgin settled over the *commune*'s inhabitants, priests chanted the divine office through the dark hours of the night, keeping material and spiritual dangers at bay."

"Since I've been here, I've started to wonder what it might be like to be a historian instead of a doctor."

Donata turned to face me. "What is it like to be a neurosurgeon?"

"Maybe it's like having children. You are expected to be available at high intensity one hundred percent of the time, and the decisions you make have life-or-death consequences. But at least I can take a leave of absence."

Donata laughed and we walked through the gates into the *pellegrinaio*, the frescoed hall that used to house ailing pilgrims cared for at the Ospedale. Now it was a museum.

"Do you miss it now, the surgeon's life?"

I didn't answer Donata for a long time. I was thinking about the surprising, heady pleasure of watching the past come to life. The OR seemed very far away. "No, I don't miss it. Not yet."

"I'm sure your passion for surgery will return." Donata smiled. "After you've had enough time off."

I nodded, but I wasn't sure at all.

I went back to the library the next day, to grill Fabbri about Medicis beheaded in the 1300s, but I didn't get a chance. Fabbri was frowning as he greeted me. "There is a Signor Signoretti here, asking after you. He insisted, and not as graciously as I would expect from a gentleman of his stature, that he would wait."

"Where is he?" I looked around anxiously, having built an ominous picture of the man from what I'd heard.

The infamous Signoretti walked into the reading room. His black hair was slicked back from his high forehead, and his pale summer suit hung on him too perfectly. "Signora Trovato."

"Dottoressa," I said, correcting his address.

"Ah, of course, but the medical sort of doctor. Not like your late brother, whose expertise was history. My condolences. All who knew him mourn his loss."

"Thank you for your concern," I said, trying to suppress my irritation.

"You have not responded to any of my messages, Dottoressa."

"I appreciate your gracious offer of assistance, but I don't need it. I hope you will excuse me. As you know, we *doctors* are very busy."

It did not require paranormal abilities to feel the anger pouring off Signoretti as the clerk officiously showed him out on my behalf.

I spent the rest of the morning with the Medici collection, which was small, not surprising, since we were in Siena, not Florence. Most of what I found was from the 1500s, too late for what I was interested in. As I was leaving the library, the strap on my bag broke, sending the contents onto the floor.

I cursed inventively, then bent down to pick up my possessions. Fabbri appeared as I stood up with an armful of books.

"Would you like to leave the contents here, and pick them up tomorrow? Perhaps when you return the Accorsi journal?"

"Thank you, I'll take you up on that offer." I pocketed my wallet and keys and left everything else in Ben's carrel, careful to avoid Fabbri's second question. I tucked my broken bag under one arm, then headed home.

On the way, I had the sensation that someone was following me. Lately I'd had a constant feeling that there was some world hovering just beyond what I could see, the past edging into the present. But this was different.

I stopped at a neighborhood bar whose warm amber light spilled out onto the pavement, and after I had a glass of wine I felt ready to go back out again. As I walked home the unpleasant sensation returned. When I turned onto the deserted Via Cecco Angiolieri, I heard steps behind me speed up, and someone shoved hard against my hip, throwing me to the sidewalk. My broken bag was gone, along with the rapidly moving figure in the dark. I leaped up with my heart pounding, and stood shaking on the corner.

Whoever had mugged me would end up with a bag that was not only broken, but empty too. Part of me hoped it was Signoretti just for the pleasure of having thwarted him, but the idea that he'd resort to violent methods to get information made me nervous. What information could I have, or could Ben have had, that would be worth the risk? And why? Once I was home with the heavy door barred and double locked, I went to Ben's desk and searched the drawers to be sure all was as I'd left it. I found the small folio and Gabriele's journal where I'd stored them. I put the journal and folio into a battered leather backpack I found in the back of Ben's closet, and tucked it under the bottom of my laundry basket full of dirty clothes, just in case. I knew I should return the journal to the archives, but couldn't bring myself to let go of it yet.

The next morning I spent a futile six hours filing a police report that I was fairly sure would never go anywhere other than a sergeant's file cabinet. As I walked out of the station, I decided it was time to distract myself from my brush with Tuscan criminal justice by engaging in some tourist activity—I'd been in Siena for a month and hadn't done anything recommended by the guidebooks Nathaniel had given me.

I started with the biggest thing around: the Torre del Mangia, the bell tower of the Palazzo Pubblico. *Why am I paying good money to climb three hundred steps?* I wondered as I bought the ticket. Maybe I'd regret it later, but I'd heard the views were fantastic. The small entrance doorway to the tower was in the corner of the Palazzo Pubblico's inner courtyard. It was marked by wordy signs and a small light that turned from red to green at apparently random intervals. If it's red, you can't start the climb; if it's green, you can. Or at least you can try.

My ticket read 9:30 a.m., sounding very official, and the stony-faced guardian of the entrance was equally official and quite strict about counting the number of eager tourists (twenty-five, and that's *it*) going through for each time slot and green light, and a mandatory bag check too. Once I'd started up the staircase I realized why the rules were so unbending. One staircase ascends the 102 meters—335 feet—getting narrower and narrower toward the top, with hardly any room to turn or pass. The square spiral went on and on, winding past narrow window slits that offered no view and little air. Then the stone steps turned into rickety steep wooden ladders that led to successively more terrifying platforms; each one seemed like a very good opportunity to change my mind, or plunge to my death. Then my legs started to ache, then burn, and I had to press myself hard against the wall as the descending tourists squeezed past. Finally I was at the top, with a view of the red-brick *campo* spread out—crazily far below, surrounded by a sea of terra-cotta rooftops, then the city walls, then the green glittering *contado* beyond them. Climbing down was even harder: not as much effort, but more fear of falling. I wasn't eager to try it again soon.

Siena, June 30

Dear Linney,

Thanks for your letter; it was nice to see your handwriting somewhere other than a medical chart. It's looking like I'll be using the full three months of my sabbatical here. It's just as well I'm not spending too much time in the OR anyway—you know it's time for a break when you start losing it over an episode of VTach. I'll tell you a secret—I'm writing a book—the book Ben left notes for. I may not be the most erudite scholar out there, but this job is mine. Don't tell anybody; neurosurgeons aren't supposed to spend time daydreaming about illuminated manuscripts and poring over medieval frescoes. At least not publicly.

Love, B

On the evening of July 1, the day of the Palio-eve banquet, I ran downstairs to join the Guerrini family. They gathered solemnly around me on the sidewalk.

"We have a gift for you," Donata said, and nudged Felice forward. She held out a clumsily wrapped package in her hand, the wrapping clearly her own handiwork. But the contents trumped even the lovingly constructed wrapper—my own Civetta scarf. I bent my head and Felice draped it over my neck; I could feel her warm breath on my cheek as the silk slid over my shoulders. I hugged her tightly.

"It's perfect."

"Welcome to the family, Civettina," Donata said, kissing me on both cheeks. We continued our walk to the banquet through the darkening streets.

Felice wanted to hold my hand as we walked. I shortened my steps to match hers and we dropped behind the rest of the family. Glowing torches and lanterns bathed the buildings in gold, and white-clothed tables filled the piazzas. Felice, usually ebullient and silly, hardly spoke at all, and I could feel tension in her arm through our joined hands.

"Last year my papà cried after the Palio," she said, unprompted. "They call Civetta 'La Nonna' because we haven't won in so long." She frowned, clearly not liking the "Grandma" title applied to her *contrada*. "Mamma said Papà cried because his heart hurt." She paused again, looking at her sandaled feet silhouetted against the brick pavers. "I was sad too, but I didn't cry because I didn't want to make him sadder," she said matter-of-factly, and then her shoulders relaxed and she let go of my hand. She bolted ahead, yelling, "*Chiocciole—andiamo!*"

I watched her braids bounce against her back as she ran to join her family, happy to have been included as one of the snails. We stayed late at the *cena*, eating sweet and sour wild boar at long tables set in the candlelit streets. Ilario and Donata managed to sneak in a brief embrace when their children were otherwise occupied. Seeing them together made me acutely aware of how uninterruptedly single my life had been.

The week before I'd left New York, Nathaniel and I had gone out to a tapas bar for some very nice Serrano ham and even nicer sherry. We'd discussed my perpetually single state.

"Why do you think I've never been in love?" Nathaniel had smiled at my question indulgently. I always welcomed his incisive perspective, even though it wasn't always exactly comfortable.

"Do you want to hear my answer?" he asked. "Or do you want to enjoy your sherry?"

I swallowed the last sip of the Manzanilla that had gotten me to the point of being able to discuss this.

"I'm ready."

He took a breath and began.

"First: you insist that you want to work less, but there is no evidence to support this assertion. Second: you stubbornly resist being known. Third: I suspect this is because in fact you do not wish to be. Fourth: you sometimes intimidate people."

I opened my mouth to protest—I don't think of myself that way—but Nathaniel held up his hand to silence me. I closed my mouth again.

"Fifth: ideally, you would find someone at least as strong as you are, and that is quite difficult."

"Oh," I said, feeling a little sick. "Now what do I do?"

"Your best option at the moment is probably to go home and go to bed, since, as you told me at the beginning of our lovely dinner, you have a spinal decompression to do tomorrow." I nodded, since it was true. And with that, he took my hand and ushered me out of the restaurant. Maybe I shouldn't have asked.

The next entry in Gabriele's journal was short, but disturbing.

Midwinter 1344

My little Paola is ripe with our first child, and the midwife tells us her time will be soon. I see her illuminated from within, as if she bears a brilliant sun that will shed its warmth and light on our new life. There are times though when the light seems almost cold, like a low moon through clouds, a supernatural and uneasy brightness. I have not spoken of this to the priest who takes confession in the contrada church, preferring my private prayer. I look forward to the day when I can hold the baby in my arms and put these visions to rest.

I paged ahead in the journal to look for an entry announcing the child's birth but found none. In fact, there was no more mention of Paola either.

There are not a lot of places where a horse defecating in a church is considered a good thing. Siena, it turns out, is one of them. I squeezed into the crowded Civetta church to watch the blessing of Civetta's horse before the race. The air was thick with incense from swaying censers when the Civetta jockey walked in, holding his horse's reins in his hand, closely followed by the *comparsa*—the official delegation of the *contrada*. The horse flicked his ears restlessly, dark gray above his lighter gray head, and shied from the crowd as he was squeezed into the tiny church. The *contradaioli* kept the onlookers back, clearing a space around the horse and jockey, and I maneuvered to see from the side pews.

"Our help is in the name of the Lord," intoned the *contrada* priest, holding a cross over the horse's elegant head.

"Who made heaven and earth," the congregation answered.

The horse shifted and defecated onto the marble floor, and the crowd let out a cheer of delight.

"Guard, protect, and defend your servant from the dangers of the race to come . . . let your blessing fall upon him and upon this horse . . . and may they be safe from the approaching dangers . . . through the intercession of blessed Saint Anthony . . . amen."

And then a cry went up from the priest and the hundreds of *Civettini* packed shoulder to shoulder:

"Vai e torna vincitore!" Go and return a winner! I joined the yelling crowd and tried to stay on my feet as we pushed out of the church and emerged into the hot sun, thoroughly blessed and heading fast for the piazza. Someone must have stayed to clean up the floor afterward.

Donata guarded our places in the packed Piazza del Campo with all the ferocity of a Palio-charged Sienese art history professor. People crowded on rooftops, leaned out windows decorated with *contrade* banners—owl, unicorn, goose, caterpillar, all seventeen proudly flying their colors—and thousands, like us, pressed close together down on the ground. The huge bell of the Torre del Mangia began to ring, bells that had rung their warning for centuries. Then, to screams from the crowd, the horses entered the piazza with their jockeys. I tore my Civetta scarf off my neck and waved it frantically in the air like everyone around me. When the cannon fired the horses exploded forward, tearing around the piazza, hooves thundering on the yellow earth.

Ninety seconds—that's all it took for the ten horses to run three times around the piazza—the most breathtaking ninety seconds I had ever witnessed. Within the first turn one horse had slammed into the wall, and his rider was thrown to the ground, then rolled to escape the horses pounding past him. The horse kept running, riderless. At the San Martino corner, two horses went down, along with their riders.

"OCA OCA OCA!!" the goose *contrada* fans screamed. Their horse was in the lead, head free and low, with the jockey flat

against his horse's neck, green, white, and red silks flapping. Civetta was in the middle of the pack, edging forward around the second turn, but Oca crossed the finish line first. Screams of joy broke out from Oca's *contradaioli*, and despair from Civetta, La Nonna again. The Ocaioli poured onto the *terra*, crying, laughing, praising God, and hugging the winning horse and jockey.

"*Daccelo, daccelo, daccelo. . . .*" The chant of the Oca *contradaioli* rang through the Campo: "Give it to us!" and the Palio banner descended into their eager hands, rippling with the image of the Virgin Mary.

"Next year, Papà," Felice said, wrapping her plump arms around her father's bent neck.

That night, just before I went to sleep, I snuck in a quick read from Gabriele's diary. For the first time, I imagined his voice, reading the passage aloud. Through him, the saint's story came alive for me in a way it never had in my years of Catholic school.

Feast of San Pietro Martire, 1346

I have been fortunate to be granted a commission to decorate a section of the new city gates. I will paint Saint Christopher, protector of travelers, patron of ferrymen, and guardian of good death. A good death—not too sudden to pray for redemption. Since the commission was confirmed I have spent many nights awake, as I often do at the beginning of a project, staring at the beamed ceiling above me as my head fills with images starting to take shape. I have always been deeply moved by his story—in seeking to serve his holy Master he took on the task of ferrying travelers across a dangerous river. One day he found himself carrying a young child, a child who became heavier and heavier as the waters became more turbulent, so that Christopher bowed with the struggle, unsure he could continue, saying, "I feel that I carry the world on my shoulders." In fact, he did, as the child confided in him,

"I am not only that world, but its Creator, whom you serve through your efforts," and vanished. It is a tale worthy of depicting. All who enter or leave our gates will set their prayers by his image, and though I am certainly no saint, I take this weight seriously.

The next afternoon, I threw on my favorite sleeveless white linen dress, shouldered Ben's leather backpack with the journal in it, and took an afternoon to walk out the Porta Camollia through Siena's medieval walls and down the Via Francigena, the ancient trade route between France and Rome. I stopped to look at the inscription over the Porta as I left. *Cor Magis Tibi Saena Pandit*: "Wider than this gate, Siena opens its heart to you" the Latin read. So far, I'd found that to be true, and secretly was imagining a second, if only sentimental, citizenship. I wondered whether Gabriele's painting might once have decorated these walls. After a few hours' walk I made my way back to the Porta, then I went to the Museo dell'Opera del Duomo, on the site of what should have become the new cathedral.

Later, I would try to remember every detail of what happened next, but at the time I did not know how important that would be. A set of paintings depicting the life of Saint Christopher caught my eye, and when I saw them, I stopped short. The saint's face was filled with intense determination to ferry the small child safely across the frighteningly rough river, and the final scene, where Christopher and the child gaze into each other's eyes, was so intimate and beautiful I almost understood, for a brief moment, the power that pulls ordinary human beings into sainthood.

I glanced at the placard on the gallery wall: "*Studies for frescoes thought to have decorated a portion of the city gates, tempera on panel. Attributed to Gabriele Beltrano Accorsi, Martini School, 14th century.*" *My Gabriele*, I thought, and I felt the hair on my arms rise. And then I caught a detail at the edge of one of the scenes, almost small enough to miss. On the distant riverbank, a small crowd of anxious travelers stood, and among them was a woman in a green dress, with black hair braided in the shape of a crown. The painting was more than 650 years old. But the woman's face was mine.

I must have walked out of the Museo, because I was standing in front of the Duomo, surrounded by tourists. I ducked through the huge bronze doors into the cool of the cathedral, where the striped columns rose spectacularly to the high arches of the vault. The dome soared above me, decorated with golden stars gleaming against a dark blue background, and sunlight poured through the glass-paned oculus at the top, blindingly bright. Crossing myself reflexively, I counted the busts of popes along the cornice at the top of the nave, trying to calm down. *It's just a coincidence. I have a common Italian face: it just happens to have been shared by someone in fourteenth-century Siena.*

In the transept a circle of marble lions held up the columns of the octagonal pulpit. When I reached out to touch one, the marble of the lion's back was cool and worn smooth by many hands before mine. I took out Gabriele's journal, opened it at random, and bent my head to read the words of this artist whose writing had started to encroach on my modern existence, and whose art, for some inexplicable reason, depicted me.

July 1347

I find my paintings haunted by a persistent image that I cannot dispel, and whose origin I cannot fathom. One day as I knelt in the Duomo, my senses were overtaken by a strange quiet, and my surroundings—the Te Deum ringing around me, the church bells calling our citizens to prayer and chasing the night's demons away, the creaking of benches on which my neighbors knelt and shifted—went silent. At that moment I saw a figure of a woman, dark hair loose over her simple white shift. She appeared beside the lions of Pisano's pulpit, but when I leapt up to see the apparition it had vanished. I find the mysterious figure hovering at the edge of my paintings, watching the events unfold in the scenes I depict. It is as if she were seeking a path through my paintings and into this world.

This time as I read, my vision went abruptly dark, and I heard the last words I'd read reverberating in my head, as if someone had said them aloud.

. . . *a path through my paintings and into this world.*

And then I stopped hearing at all.

PART II

WIDER THAN THIS GATE

This episode did not fade like the others—I couldn't see or hear. Seconds passed, and I started to panic. What if I stayed like this forever? Finally sounds started to filter back, and I began to see shapes again, then details. My fear receded. *It's just nighttime and the lights are off*, I told myself. But the comfort of that explanation faded fast. *It wasn't nighttime a minute ago.*

Faint moonlight came through the cathedral windows. I'd been reading in the bright light of the afternoon. How had I lost hours without realizing it? I ran through possible diagnoses. Complex partial seizure? Bad. Transient global amnesia? Not as bad, since that was, by definition, transient.

I was still standing next to the marble lion and I put my hand out to touch its back, steadying myself. It felt different now, rougher under my fingers. Other than the lion, my hands were empty—Gabriele's journal was gone. I was still wearing Ben's backpack though, the straps cutting into my shoulders. I bent my arms and legs, making sure I still could. Now I had a strange headache at both temples. Could it all be a complicated migraine? I'd never had a migraine before. *Occipital aneurysm? God, I hope not.* I staggered over to a wooden choir stall and sat. From somewhere in the dark, a single disembodied voice began to chant the night office in Latin.

Then I noticed something very odd. Along the high cornice that ran the length of the nave, the busts of the popes I had just counted were missing; the space below the clerestory was empty. My heart pounding, I made my way to the great front doors of the cathedral, my footsteps echoing in the empty nave. The rose window in the facade had disappeared, leaving a gaping hole in its place, with the night sky beyond.

I stumbled out through the doors of the Duomo, which had inexplicably changed from bronze to wood. There were no lights anywhere. No lampposts, no warm yellow café windows beckoning travelers. And there was no one on the street. I had never seen a city, any city, so eerily empty. I made my way across the Campo, the slanting lines mysterious in the silvery light from above. A dream? It seemed too realistic to be a dream. Fugue state? Psychotic break? I was running out of diagnoses.

The streets had no signs but I managed to find Ben's street from memory. Once I turned the corner it was so dark I could hardly see at all. The buildings leaned in toward one another, blocking out the moon, and awnings further darkened the narrow alleyways. Was it a blackout? I touched the walls for guidance as I walked.

A votive candle in a niche that housed an image of the Virgin Mary faintly lit my street. When I found the doorway of Ben's house—my house—relief washed over me. Now I could climb the stairs to my bedroom, slide between the linen sheets, and fall asleep. Everything would be fine again.

But it wasn't. The lock looked strange, and my key didn't fit. I tried it upside down, then right-side up again, but it was clearly the wrong kind of key. *How could it be the wrong kind of key?* I felt along the plaster wall in the direction of Ilario and Donata's bell. But there was no bell. Instead of the flat front of the building, the wall extended into a shuttered storefront that I didn't remember seeing before. Shivering, I wrapped myself in the shawl I'd packed in my bag that morning, curled up on the doorstep of the house that I couldn't go home to, and waited for sunrise.

The clamor of bells woke me from a cramped sleep before dawn. Out of Donata's doorway came a mother and daughter arm in arm, both dressed for a Palio parade, in ankle-length gowns with long, tight sleeves. The younger woman stared at me while Mom clucked disapprovingly, and hastened down the street, pulling her daughter away. More doors opened and people poured out, heading toward the Piazza del Duomo. I joined the group and followed the pealing bells to morning Mass at the striped cathedral.

I sat in the far back, surrounded by strangers who should have been my neighbors but looked like actors in a historical reenactment. Were they celebrating some big feast day, maybe the favorite local saint? The priest's face emerged, lit by candles and serious under a miter. It must be a special holiday for the bishop to be giving Mass. But once the bishop started speaking, his Latin ringing through the nave, my last stubborn attempts to rationalize failed.

Feria Sexta Iulii Anno domini mille tres centum quadraginta et septem . . .

The rest of the service was wasted on me as my rusty high school Latin kicked in and I realized that the date was July 6, 1347. My head spun with the impossibility of the dislocation. I had often imagined that at some point in my life I would lose someone I loved, and I had. But I had never considered the possibility that I would lose my place in time.

After the service I stayed seated while the other congregants filed out of the cathedral. One word kept going through my head, over and over again: *impossible, impossible, impossible.* If you say a word enough times, it stops making sense. *This is impossible.* But that didn't mean it wasn't happening.

Panic rooted me to my seat. A young boy in white robes walked over to the altar and began to arrange the candles, removing the spent wicks and replacing them with new tapers. The idea was incomprehensible, but the evidence was all around me; I'd been transported to fourteenth-century Siena dressed in a sleeveless linen sundress. I knew no one. I had no home, no food, and no money. I had no idea how I'd gotten here, and, more importantly, no idea how to get back. I could hear my own breathing, shallow and rapid, and felt my heart hammering in my chest. I was about to have either a nervous breakdown or a heart attack.

Most people do not find it relaxing to recite the names of the arteries at the base of the skull in order of their appearance, but most people are not neurosurgeons. Fighting to keep control, I closed my eyes and resorted to my favorite strategy, honed by years of training. I imagined the weblike shape of the arterial Circle of Willis, and the vessels branching off from it. *Anterior cerebral artery, anterior communicating, internal carotid, middle carotid, posterior cerebral, basilar, vertebral . . . anterior cerebral, anterior communicating, internal carotid . . .* After the third repetition my heart had slowed and I could breathe normally again. The altar boy finished with the candles and started walking down the length of the nave toward me. I wrapped my shawl around my bare arms and shoulders and headed out of the cathedral.

I focused on my immediate needs first: finding a bathroom and suitable clothes. I discovered a foul cesspit in an alleyway behind the cathedral that was probably used to empty chamber pots and accomplished my first goal. I held my breath until I was back in the piazza again.

In the Campo, merchants were starting to set up market stalls, but I didn't see any clothing for sale, and in any case I had no medieval money. The Campo had filled with people. A few glanced curiously at me. Maybe I could find some drying laundry to dress myself in—people must do laundry around here. The key was not to get caught stealing, since I didn't want to end up being hanged as a thief. My thoughts were spinning, recycling all my historical knowledge in the hopes of finding something useful. I chose a street at random, turned right, then left. Farther from the cathedral, the streets got narrower and darker until I could touch the buildings on both sides with my hands. I wasn't finding the laundry lines I'd hoped for. There were probably courtyards behind the buildings, but I couldn't get to them. I kept walking, hoping I wouldn't have to spend much more time in the fourteenth century wearing the medieval equivalent of underwear.

I felt a wet drop on my head and looked up, trained by my New York City upbringing to see a pigeon. Instead, protruding from the facade of a four-story town house was a wooden pole a few feet long. It looked like it might have been used to hang a banner, but this pole had a wet cape hanging from it.

I'd been hoping for a dress, but I was willing to take what I could get. Unfortunately, the pole was far above my head. I stared at it, gauging the distance. If I could just get to the loggia on the first floor, I'd have easy access. I pushed against the wood front door, but not surprisingly, it didn't move. Just above my head was a hook, probably for a lantern. I reached and gave it a good yank to test whether it might hold my weight. It pulled right out of the wall and hit the pavement with a loud clang.

The wood shutters on a third-story window flew open. I flattened myself in the doorway. "*Chi è?*" a woman's voice called down sharply—who's there? I waited unmoving until I heard the shutters slam shut and, after a few minutes, chanced a peek out of the doorway. No one in sight. I jammed the hook back into the hole in the wall, willing it to stay.

I had decided to give up on the cape when a young woman with a large basket appeared from an alleyway in front of me. I followed her at a safe distance until she stopped at a house, put her basket down, and unlocked the door. She turned back to retrieve her burden when an elderly voice called from inside.

"*Vengo, Nonna*," she replied and disappeared through the door, leaving the basket. A wooden birdcage hung from a hook outside the window, with two larks singing inside and jumping from perch to perch; otherwise, the street was quiet. I approached casually, trying to look like I belonged, in case any neighbors should appear. The basket was full of wet clothing, probably washed in a public fountain. I grabbed a dark green garment at random, then walked quickly around the corner. My heart was pounding as I looked at what I'd taken. Fortunately it was a dress, made of light wool with long sleeves and skirt. Struggling with the wet fabric, I put the dress on over my own and kept walking, weighted down and dripping. I hoped the granddaughter wouldn't get in trouble.

After the adrenaline of my first criminal act subsided, I realized how tired I was. I headed back toward the Duomo. A low wooden building adjoined the cathedral; I found the door and ducked inside, hoping I could find somewhere to rest. I'd walked into a livestock pen; high openings in the walls let through enough light to reveal cows, horses, and donkeys staring placidly as I walked past. When I saw the ladder leading up to a hayloft, I almost cried with relief. Up above, surrounded by fragrant hay, I took off the wet gown and spread it on the straw, covered myself with my shawl, and went to sleep.

The angle of the sun had changed when I woke up to bells again, thirsty and with a growling stomach. I made a quick inventory of the contents of my bag. Fortunately, Ben's old leather backpack looked medieval enough not to attract undue attention. A wedge of *panforte* and a small steel water bottle, half filled. I wolfed down the slice of stale fruitcake, then emptied the rest of the items onto my skirt. The useless keys to Ben's house, and a wallet, also useless, since modern bills would do me no good here. I sorted through the rest: a slightly grubby cotton handkerchief, two safety pins, and a square mother-of-pearl pillbox containing the last five tablets of an antibiotic I was supposed to have taken for bronchitis two months before. At the bottom of my bag was the note from Donata inviting me for coffee. *Donata.* I stuffed the note, my shawl, and all my other worldly possessions back in my bag, wondering whether I might ever see her again.

Snorts, whinneys, and grunts drifted up from below. I peered down from the hayloft as a young boy filled feed bags with oats, forked hay into the troughs lining the stalls, and poured fresh water into stone basins. As he worked, he murmured softly to each of the animals with familiarity and warmth. *"Ciao, bella, hai fame?"* He rubbed the donkey's nose as her soft lips closed around the carrots in his palm. The carrots really got my attention.

The boy made his way through the line of animals and then disappeared through the door. After waiting a few minutes to make sure he wasn't coming back, I put on my damp dress, scrambled down the ladder, and walked down the row of munching animals, taking a scrap of something from each one to be fair. Fortified by my scavenged breakfast, I brushed the straw out of my hair, said good-bye to my new housemates, and headed out the door into the city.

Now that I was clothed, rested, and fed, the fear came back. My old life was hundreds of years away, and everyone I knew didn't exist yet. Figuring out how to get home depended on understanding how I'd gotten here. I mentally retraced my steps—the shock of seeing myself in Gabriele's painting, then reading his journal. What had the words said? Now I couldn't remember. One minute I was reading, then the next I'd gone straight into a night 650 years earlier than the day I'd started in. I have always preferred reason to blind faith, but what had happened to me was beyond my capacity to rationalize. Still, I tried to work systematically through the possibilities. If the journal held some key, it was lost to me now, since I'd arrived without it. The Duomo itself might be a gateway from the present into the past, but I had no inkling what the mechanism for reopening the gate might be. Or maybe Siena itself was the key; perhaps this city, which seemed magically suspended between times, had allowed me to step out of my own world and into this one. However I'd gotten here, could the process be reversed?

My loitering had started to attract unwelcome attention, so I chose a direction and started walking. My feet led me into the Campo by habit, and I emerged into the middle of the marketplace—a riot of color and sound. The midday sun was high now, the market I'd seen setting up hours ago now in full swing. I had landed in the seafood section. Eels wriggled in the stone trough outside one stall—succulent, according to the fish seller. Next to him, trout flashed silver scales in another basin, and in a third, bug-eyed cuttlefish bumped against each other, displaying their tentacles. While I watched, the merchant grabbed one for a customer and it shot out a jet of black ink—impressive, but futile.

I passed a large public fountain that looked familiar—the Fonte Gaia. The high, sculpted walls on three sides were missing, but the wolves spouting water were still there. With a pang I remembered Donata's impromptu lecture—this fountain was now just four years old. Women chatted with one another while they waited to fill their buckets at the spouts. A rectangular pool where the fish sellers were replenishing their basins was set beneath a graceful marble carving of the Virgin Mary nursing her infant son, her face suffused with gentleness. Like Siena with her citizens, I thought, feeling comforted, as if I were one of them. Beneath the sculpture was a stone banner inscribed in Latin; I translated slowly to myself:

On this day in 1343 the thirst of Siena is quenched
The Fonte is the heart of the Campo
The Campo the heart of Siena
The long sought source of life and joy from this day forth

Any lingering doubts I might have had about the possibility of time travel vanished as I read. I longed to tell Donata all about it—but maybe I'd never tell her anything again. I had to sit down and put my head between my knees to stop the spinning. *Get a grip*, I told myself. When that didn't work, I chanted the arterial Circle of Willis again. Once, twice, three times.

When the dizziness passed, I took a deep breath and stood up. I made my way into the produce section of the market, pausing at a fruit seller's stall to stare at a pile of purple grapes. The grapes were dotted with droplets of water that sparkled like gems. I began to have a near-hallucinatory experience of popping a grape into my mouth, feeling it burst with a rush of winey sweetness. A sibilant voice at my right shoulder startled me out of my reverie. "Signora, *mi scusi*, may I have a word?"

I looked into the pockmarked face of what appeared to be a law enforcement official because he said, with a gloating smile, "Need I remind you of the regulations concerning your neckline?" He looked down pointedly at my cleavage as I stared at the lace of my sundress peeking out from the low-cut gown I'd recently acquired.

I searched my memory of all I'd read frantically for the right medieval form of address. *"Ser?"*

He smirked again. "Certainly you recall the ordinance?" While he waited for my response, I tried to decide whether confession, denial, or silence would be the safest route. I'd gotten the "Ser" right, but the dress probably should have been worn over a higher-necked undergarment I didn't own. "In keeping with the statute, I will take your silence as a confession, and your acquiescence to document the infraction." He pulled out a tiny metal rod to measure the exposed area of my chest. "You have ten days to produce the required fine in the amount of a hundred soldi," he continued, "at which time you will present the appropriately tailored garment to the office of the Donnaio in the Palazzo for inspection. With"—he placed his hands on his belly beneath its black and white tunic and caressed it almost sensuously—"certain consequences should it not meet the required standards. May I have your place of residence, so we may find you should you need assistance complying?"

I was about to be fined for indecency, had no money to pay the fine, and had no address in this century to give to this representative of the government office responsible for enforcing sumptuary laws, one of which appeared to apply to my inappropriate neckline. What if the consequences of indecency in fourteenth-century Siena were imprisonment? Or worse? I felt myself starting to sweat. I had to say something, ideally something that sounded as authentically medieval as the letters I'd been reading in my own time. Left with no other options, I began lying as quickly as possible.

"I am a recent widow." Here I inhaled with a convincing almost-sob, though it came more from real fear than loss of my imaginary husband. "From the city of . . . Lucca. After the death of my beloved husband, I set out with my handmaid and guards on a pilgrimage to assuage my grief and purify my soul." I made sure to be clear that I would have backup in case things got unpleasant, but the official's eyes narrowed.

"Your dress does not become a penitent pilgrim nor a recent widow." He took me firmly by the wrist. "You will accompany me to the Palazzo Pubblico immediately, where i Noveschi are hearing claims. Unless, of course, you have the amount of thirty soldi on your person? I might be able to waive the presentation of your case to the council." I did not, of course, have any soldi, having just learned what soldi were.

The Donnaio's representative propelled me into the Sala della Pace. Lorenzetti's figure of Justice sat enthroned on the wall above me, larger than life and brilliant with color. I looked up at her face and I hoped, feeling a little desperate, that she would weigh in favor of my case today.

On the next wall, the *Effects of Good Government* sprawled out from city to *contado*, bustling urban center to verdant countryside. Looking at the painting, I felt everywhere at once—peering into second-floor windows, buying shoes at a storefront, exiting the city gates, and hovering over woodland and pastures. Eight figures danced in the street, celebrating to the music of a tambourine player whose instrument I could almost hear jingling. A birdcage in a window barely contained its exuberant feathered inhabitant, and men bent intently around a game of dice on a low wall. The bound figure of Justice on the wall depicting the *Effects of Bad Government* stared mournfully at me, her scales broken.

The hall was filled with milling petitioners lining up to make requests or present cases. A ripple of excitement passed through the crowd as nine robed figures entered, making their way onto a raised platform at the front of the room. These were i Noveschi, the nine celebrated leaders of the republic, who enacted laws, declared edicts, and exacted punishments—including possibly mine. I looked at other petitioners while we waited. A diminutive nun stood in line a few people behind me. She raised her head from a document she was holding and caught my eye. The bells rang again, as they did every three hours to mark the divine office—it must be noon.

The complexity of the Sienese legal apparatus was interesting enough to distract me from my own problems. The first petitioner wore a midnight blue damask tunic edged with gold embroidery, and his dark brown curls clustered around his face under a soft velvet hat trimmed in fur.

"I, Tancredi Lisini, representing my *consorteria*, wish to bring attention to the document here presented. My brothers and I were taken into custody for the injury to the father of the Regnoni family, but the heirs have hereby produced this *instrumentum pacis*, eliminating the possibility of legal recrimination, and allowing us to participate in the Feast of the Assumption. We request that the state drop all criminal action in the resolution of this dispute."

One of the Nine, centrally placed and apparently the chairman, squinted at Tancredi. "Even those producing instruments of peace must pay a penalty. The representative of the Lisini family must produce ten percent of the fine in lire for the crime with which the family has been charged, deliverable within seven days from this council."

Tancredi retreated, bowing. I made a silent note to add lire to my list of fourteenth-century Sienese currency.

After fifteen more petitions, I started to feel faint. My last meal had been much smaller and longer ago than I would have liked. I started fantasizing about the water bottle in my bag but thought it might draw unhealthy attention, since there was no stainless steel in fourteenth-century Siena. Plus I didn't want to have to find another restroom equivalent. Then, suddenly, it was my turn.

"Messer Stozzi, representative of the Donnaio of Siena, please step forward with your claim."

I tried to stay calm. I couldn't imagine my décolletage warranted hanging, but my lack of funds, inconsistent pilgrim story, and being a lone woman made a risky combination.

Stozzi began his formal address. "I Noveschi Onorevole, I present to you a self-proclaimed grieving widow and pilgrim from Lucca, incongruously dressed for her declared purpose. I discovered her parading in the piazza with no regard for modesty, and with no source from which to draw the required fine regarding her neckline. I present her case to you today rather than during the session established for pursuance of sumptuary infractions because of the singular nature of the situation in which I found her, and await your respected judgment."

A sharp, high voice broke the silence after Stozzi's account of my wardrobe offense. "The *mantellate* of the Ospedale della Scala—in particular I, Suor Umiltà, their humble representative—under the guidance of our esteemed rector, petition i Noveschi to fulfill their civic duty to the bereft widow and penitent pilgrim." The speaker was the nun whom I'd seen earlier. Her voice was surprisingly loud, coming from such a small body. She took a huge breath and continued with her appeal. "This is the duty to which the Ospedale has devoted itself for centuries, with the Grace of God and the support of our magnificent *commune*, in the hands of its greatest rulers, whose purpose is to make the light of this gleaming republic shine all the brighter." She had to take another breath. "I combine this plea for beneficence toward traveling pilgrims, whose good fortune it is to arrive at our gates, with a request for the funds to enable the completion of the fifth fresco on the facade of the Ospedale Santa Maria della Scala, the very site into which we welcome these souls in their journeys toward redemption."

By now most of those present were staring at the speaker. She was dressed in black robes over a white scapular but clearly not cloistered. I wondered what *mantellate* meant in this context—"cloaked" was as far as I could get from the Italian. Her black and white robes were decorated with a curious insignia of a golden ladder.

"We welcome the generosity and beneficence of the *commune* in supporting the Ospedale, an august institution whose walls await the further attentions of Siena's painters whose aim is to honor the Blessed Virgin who protects us." That sounded good to me; I hoped it did to the experts. "I humbly suggest that the portion of the fine required for the unfortunate error of this young woman's dress be subtracted from what I am sure will be a much greater sum intended for the beautification of the Ospedale with the aforementioned commission, which accounts can be settled at the next meeting of the Biccherna, until which time we request that this widow and pilgrim return with us to the Ospedale." With that, Suor Umiltà clamped her lips shut and smiled winningly up at the platform on which the Nine were seated. She was clearly an expert at this.

One of the Nine responded. "Granted, on both counts, Suor Umiltà. The lady can return with you to the Ospedale, hereby spared a sentence for her violation of sumptuary laws. And the rector may invite submissions for the new fresco, with communal support." I stopped registering anything after that, as my rescuer grabbed my elbow to hurry me out of the Sala.

"Whom do I have the pleasure of having snatched from Messer Stozzi's grasp?" The diminutive sister spoke to me in her surprisingly large voice. "Your plight became evident to me, aligned as it was with my request for a supplement to our communal funds. I usually achieve my aims, with God's help of course. Please allow me to introduce myself. You may call me Suor Umiltà."

The tiny woman's fingers were firmly around my wrist. She could have been anywhere from forty to eighty years old, and the pointed stare from her dark eyes made me feel like I was being X-rayed.

"I am Beatrice Alessandra Trovato, from Lucca, recently widowed and on a pilgrimage. I am very grateful for the Ospedale's welcome." I was getting good at that story. The word *ospedale* encompassed the institution's multiple roles as hospital, pilgrims' hospice, and protector of widows and orphans. I congratulated myself on having created a fictional identity that put me in more than one category that the Ospedale ministered to.

"Trovato: found, as in a foundling, or orphan. An auspicious name for a recipient of the beneficence of the Ospedale." Umiltà beamed, deeply satisfied with the linguistic tidiness of it all. "Do tell me of your travails, Beatrice Alessandra Trovato, and be assured that we will provide you the assistance for which the Ospedale is renowned." Faced with the first directly sympathetic ear since my arrival in 1347, I was overwhelmed with the desire to tell her everything. Instead I said:

"Thank you for rescuing me. I can't imagine what would have happened if you hadn't."

Umiltà smiled in a self-satisfied way. "Did you encounter difficulties in your trip through the Maremma? I have heard tales of vicious bandits along the route. I hope your traveling companions were not lost to violence?" I was stumped for a moment by the questions—Maremma, bandits, companions? What was the Maremma? It must refer to the land between Siena and Lucca. To buy time, I put my face in my hands. Umiltà put her arm on my shoulder and leaned in solicitously.

"The tribulations of pilgrimage weigh heavily upon those who take up the path, but rest assured it brings us closer to God in the process." I kept my hands over my face, still thinking furiously. "Can you speak of your losses?"

I opened my eyes inside the darkness created by my hands. The invitation to consider my grief brought back a memory of the day I'd said good-bye to Ben for the last time. "My brother," I said, my voice breaking.

"My child, you have lost so much in such a short time," Umiltà responded, her hand still firm on my shoulder. "Rest assured the *mantellate* will care for your spiritual wounds. Many come to us with losses such as yours, and we are well equipped to find balm for suffering souls."

"Mantellate?" I blinked back tears.

"We are religious women, doing the work of God by charitable acts in the world of men, rather than the cloister. Have you no equivalent in Lucca?"

"Yes, yes, of course, we just call them something else." It sounded lame to me, but she let it go. When Umiltà spoke again it was with a new undercurrent of interest.

"What can you do?" Umiltà looked at me appraisingly. "Sew, embroider, spin, recognize and prepare medicinal herbs?"

The question was clearly intended to discover whether I'd be of any use, or just a burdensome charity case. I considered my options. Most of my sewing had been related to wound closure. Billing myself as a physician might get me into trouble, and I knew nothing about herbal medicine. My first and only experience with a spinning wheel had been during an elementary school trip to a model early American village.

As we walked across the courtyard to the entrance of the Ospedale, Umiltà put her hand firmly on the small of my back to guide me through the doorway. I was still trying to think of something that would support my stay when I remembered my hours copying Ben's manuscripts.

"I can read and write. Is that helpful?"

She looked at me with new interest. "Assuredly. Of course, the charity of the Ospedale would extend to you in any case, but the additional assistance you might provide to our great institution as a scribe, supporting its noble mission through your skill, would be most welcome."

"It would be an honor to contribute to the Ospedale and its inhabitants, and by extension the *commune* of Siena, whose beneficence and protection serve as a beacon to travelers and citizens alike." I wondered whether Umiltà's verbiage might be contagious. But the more I sounded like the people around me, the less alien I'd seem, and that might keep me out of trouble. All those medieval documents I'd read back in modern Siena gave me language I could draw upon to sound more like a fourteenth-century native.

That thought made me wish that I still had Gabriele Accorsi's journal to keep me company.

✱   ✱   ✱

The fresco season had the brevity and intensity of an adolescent love affair. On this hot July day, well into the season of paint and plaster, Gabriele was deep in the passion of a work in progress. He awoke before dawn to the *mattino* bells sounding from the Torre del Mangia—marking the end of curfew and the opening of the city gates—and made his way to Mass in the little *contrada* church. Instead of focusing on the sermon, Gabriele imagined the face of Santa Anna, the Virgin's blessed mother, gazing with wonder at her newborn daughter being bathed in a basin. Gabriele felt the weight of an imagined brush in his right hand, and his left hand's fingers moved as if he were checking the plaster to be certain of its dampness. Gabriele could feel Anna's ache to hold her daughter, a child who would someday bear, to her joy and despair, the son of God.

"Dreaming about your painting again?" Gabriele's cousin Ysabella peered up at him as the congregation filed out.

"The arm of the Virgin's mother today, Ysabella, but, by the feast of the Birth of the Virgin, Anna in her entirety." Gabriele's face lit briefly with a smile, and Ysabella smiled back, looking at Gabriele for clues to his mood. Since his wife had died a few years before, Gabriele had become impenetrable. He looked like a Lorenzetti painting himself, with his still features. He was unlike anyone else in the family, tall where they were small, and with an unhurried long-limbed grace. Gabriele's uncle, Ysabella's father Martellino, was a baker with a round, cheerful face, and the spherical motif persisted throughout. His protuberant belly strained against his tunic, his short legs bowed out in an arch. Ysabella had inherited her share of roundness; she reminded

Gabriele of a nesting wren, bright-eyed and quick. But Gabriele had the look of a falcon. Gray had come to his hair early, and it gave him an otherworldly quality, striking against his olive skin. His arched brows remained dark, in contrast to his prematurely silver hair. Gabriele and his cousin walked next to each other through the lightening streets.

"Your paintings see more of you than we do," Ysabella jested, taking his arm. "If you can make your way home for supper, we would welcome your paint-spattered self. I'm making mutton tonight—perhaps that will entice you?" Gabriele nodded absently, in his mind already climbing his scaffolding. He saw his cousin to the door.

"Gabriele." Ysabella hesitated. Gabriele could see her reluctance to let him leave. Her cheerful presence was a pleasant distraction from his preoccupations. She was eminently practical, talkative where he was quiet, and she made him smile, even when he did not intend to. "I wish I could go with you."

"Ysabella," Gabriele said, smiling at her broad, open face, "my painter's life is not as thrilling as it might appear."

"It is thrilling compared to mine, assisting father in the bakery all day and trying to put off his suggestions of marriageable young men. He worries that no one will want a wife past her twenty-fifth year. As if I had any interest in marriage at all." Ysabella laughed. "All the girls ask me whether you might marry again."

"Your companions should turn their attention to more worthy targets of affection," Gabriele said. "The life of a painter's wife is not an easy one." He wondered, looking at Ysabella's bright, intelligent face, whether she would ever marry. Her father had only half tried to find her a match, no doubt welcoming his daughter's presence too much to imagine losing her, now that her mother was gone.

"But will *you* ever marry again, Gabriele?"

"Truly, I cannot arrive late to work for one of my few dedicated patrons. My reputation is at stake, and my imagined future brides can wait." Gabriele patted Ysabella's hand gently and started down the narrow street that led to the private chapel in the Signoretti palazzo. His performance on this commission might determine a future of more important work. Martellino's generosity was welcome, but Gabriele wished he could take less and offer more to the upkeep of the household. As he walked, practical concerns faded and he turned his thoughts to the patterns of light and shadow and the wings of angels beating at the edges of his vision.

Gabriele passed the Ospedale, which loomed above him, bright with the four painted scenes from the life of the Virgin. One empty space remained over the entrance, its blank stone beckoning. For a moment Gabriele lost his hold on the present, and he was high again on the scaffold next to his former teacher, working to finish the last of the four Ospedale frescoes before nightfall. The depiction of four-year-old Maria taking leave of her family always evoked powerful emotion in him. Maria's mother and father, blessed with the conception of a child long after it should have been possible, dedicated the unborn baby to God's service, and this promise was fulfilled when the time came. Maestro Simone Martini had sat down with him the night before Gabriele began to paint the Virgin's face.

"Her innocence is held in tenuous balance against the powerful future foretold for her. If you cannot feel the gravity of this moment, do not climb the scaffolding tomorrow."

Gabriele had stayed up long into the night imagining the state of the child Maria's heart. In that fresco, under Martini's tutelage, he had reached the pinnacle of his career to date, but since the Maestro's departure for Avignon and his death there, Gabriele's reputation had been slow to build. He was well regarded—"the silver-haired pupil of Martini"—but not yet renowned.

At the far edge of the piazza, he looked back toward the Ospedale. "I will find myself on scaffolding before you again, I swear to it," he said, under his breath. He smiled, imagining how Ysabella would poke fun at him for talking to a building. *Maria Santissima Annunziata should fill that space*, Gabriele thought, *and I should like to be the author of that prayer in paint.*

* * *

When Umiltà and I reached the entrance of the Ospedale, I stared up at the wall. In my memory I could see the blank brick of the facade, but in front of me the entry was painted with the scenes depicting the life of the Virgin that Donata had told me about. The fifth space over the doorway was still empty; Umiltà had only just petitioned the Nine for money to commission it. Umiltà peered up at me, squinting.

"I will show you to a room where you can rest and seek solace in contemplation. Have you need of food?" I started salivating when she said *food*. She eyed me speculatively. "Fasting may bring us closer to God, but at a price. I will have a meal brought to you this evening, rather than have you brave company in the refectory." Umiltà turned and led me through the doorway, under the stretch of blank wall.

As we stepped into the *pellegrinaio*—the pilgrim's hall of the Ospedale—I saw why Messer Stozzi had found my story hard to believe. Most of the pilgrims in the hall wore rough sackcloth, looking far more penitent than I did. Exhausted families huddled together while robed friars examined lone travelers. Part of the room was organized into curtained beds from which a few faces and hands appeared to accept bowls of food.

Umiltà narrated for me as we walked. "The physically infirm pilgrims stay here in the *pellegrinaio*. That young man is on a barefoot pilgrimage from Roma to Venezia to visit the *brachium* of San Magnus in the reliquary—his feet have required a great deal of our attention over the past few days." She pointed discreetly.

"He's walking barefoot across Italy to see the arm of a saint?"

"Ee-tah-lee?" Umiltà looked at me strangely. "I have not heard that word before. Is it Luccan dialect?" Neither the word *Italy* nor the unified country existed yet. I covered up as quickly as possible.

"Yes, we use it to mean . . . a great distance."

Umiltà accepted my explanation and went on. "His wife is ailing in childbed, swollen and full of ill humors. His parish priest advised he embark upon this journey for the sake of his wife and unborn child." This was probably pre-eclampsia—she needed medical attention to keep her blood pressure under control, not prayers.

"And that man is a knight from Orvieto on his way to Roma, seeking absolution for the blood he has shed on the battlefield." I stared at my first real knight, but he just looked like an ordinary, if muscular, individual. I suppose if you are on a pilgrimage to repent violent acts of warfare, you leave your armor at home.

"There don't seem to be many women in here." I hesitated, not sure whether I might be making another mistake.

"Our last rector, the esteemed Giovanni di Tese dei Tolomei, supported the creation of our new Ospedale delle Donne, dedicated to the care of women pilgrims and invalids. You will find your quarters there."

Umiltà stopped in front of a young man lying on a cot against the wall. He was drenched with sweat and covered with a rash—small, raised, pale, tense-looking bumps dotted his face, trunk, arms, and legs. He moaned in agony as Ospedale staff tended to him.

"We must find a place for him to bear out the remainder of his illness apart from the other pilgrims, however long it may last. Or however short," Umiltà said, ominously. She bent her head to consult with one of his caretakers. I stared at the suffering pilgrim's rash and fevered face, and suddenly it hit me. *This is the Plague, the great scourge of Europe. We'll all be dead by tomorrow.* I'd appeared right at the most dangerous time in Siena's long history, the time my brother had spent years studying. I was in the city that would be hit by the most devastating infection the world had ever seen, and it would be worse here than anywhere else, for some reason I still didn't know. My vision blurred, and I felt myself swaying. *Please don't let me die here, stranded in the past with only five antibiotic tablets.* Then my training took over. I'd seen that kind of rash before in med school textbooks—it was smallpox, not Plague. Smallpox had been eradicated in 1975, but we were a long way from 1975. I silently reviewed my immunization record and breathed a quiet sigh of relief. For everyone else's sake, I was glad Umiltà knew enough to insist on quarantine. But, in ten months, in the spring of 1348, the Plague would come to Siena. It would come to me, if I were still here, and to all my unsuspecting companions in this time and place.

Umiltà led me swiftly through the hall. On our way out, she pointed in the direction of the Church of the Santissima Annunziata. "If you find yourself able, you may join us for Vespers this evening, in the Ospedale's own chapel," she said, making me feel like a schoolchild contemplating playing hooky.

I followed Umiltà to the Pellegrinaio delle Donne. We passed through a small courtyard with a round stone well, then up two flights of stairs to a tiny cell just large enough for a narrow bed with a wooden chest at its foot. A small arched window faced the cathedral and the gleaming green Sienese countryside beyond.

"I hope you will find peace on this stage of your journey, and that your respite here will assuage your suffering," Umiltà said, standing behind me as I gazed out the window at the magnificent facade of the Duomo. I hoped so too.

A timid-looking young woman wearing a brown homespun gown knocked on the door as Umiltà was leaving. She placed a tray laden with a bowl of fragrant soup, a pitcher and goblet, a spoon, and a slab of crusty bread on the wooden chest and backed out of the room, leaving me to eat.

The thick, white soup was completely unfamiliar but delicious. It reminded me of warm vichyssoise without potatoes. The top was sprinkled with spices—cinnamon and nutmeg, what else? Cloves, definitely cloves. And cardamom, like the rice pudding in Indian restaurants. And in the soup itself, the heat of ginger. But I still couldn't figure out the main ingredient. I wiped the bowl clean with bread, then finished that off too. I looked into the pitcher: wine. I poured and drank, but cautiously. It was ruby-colored, sweet, and watered down—just as well.

The meal took me no more than a few minutes to eat. I sat on the chest, which appeared to serve as both table and chair. Besides that and the heavy canopied bed, the only other furniture in the room looked like a cross between a podium and a desk—one small wooden step and above it a tilted top. An *inginocchiatoio*—the Italian version of a prie-dieu. The supplicant was supposed to kneel on the step and put his or her arms and maybe an inspirational text on the desk above. The shelf was empty.

Although prayer hadn't been in my daily repertoire since grade school, my situation made me feel that I should at least try. I knelt awkwardly on the bench and put my hands together. No inspiration came, so I decided to start with the invitation that begins the divine hours, hoping things might flow from there.

"Lord, open my lips, and my mouth will proclaim your praise." I paused. More personal might work better. "Thanks for that really nice soup. This is a lovely room too, private, great view, quiet." I was praying, not reviewing a hotel. "And thanks for sending Umiltà. I wasn't sure what was going to happen with Stozzi out there." I hoped no one could hear me. The door, heavy and barred, was closed, and the walls looked like solid plaster. "So the thing I'm getting at is, this has been a really extraordinary experience, whatever is going on, but I'd very much like to know how to get home. I'm hoping to leave before May of 1348 ideally. Please." I realized my eyes were wet.

I wiped my eyes and face with the back of my sleeve and put my forehead down on the cool wood of the *inginocchiatoio*'s shelf. I knelt there until the light through the tiny window changed to the darker gold of late afternoon. As I unfolded myself I heard footsteps, and then the sound of the door swinging open. I looked up into the face of the same young woman who had dropped off the soup. She was a girl really, maybe thirteen years old, and light wisps of hair escaped from under the edges of her linen coif, floating about her face.

"What was in that remarkable soup?"

She stared at me as if I were from another planet, which I suppose I was, in a way. "The *poratta*, Signora?" she said.

I'd made another blunder by not knowing what I was eating. "I'm from Lucca." She kept staring. "I had always heard there was no match for the food here in Siena."

Her expression softened slightly. "I helped the cook make it myself, Signora."

I saw I'd hit on a matter of personal conceit. "You are certainly on your way to becoming an exceptional cook."

Her pale face flushed an appealing pink. "*Grazie*, Signora. The leeks come from the *mercato*, but we make the almond milk ourselves, with nuts from the Ospedale's own *grance*."

Almond milk: that was the elusive flavor I'd been trying to identify. The last time I'd had any was out of a cardboard carton at a vegan friend's house, but it had tasted nothing like this. "Can you tell me what that symbol means?" I said, pointing to a golden ladder embroidered on her dress.

"That is the insignia of our Ospedale—Santa Maria della Scala. The Ospedale gets its name from the steps of the Duomo, across the piazza."

I risked a personal question. "Do you live here at the Ospedale?"

"The Ospedale has been my home since the night my parents left me in the stone basin in the piazza, where orphans are found by the Ospedale *mantellate* at sunrise." She reached into her bodice and drew out half a metal disc on a narrow cord she wore about her neck.

"I was found with this wrapped in my swaddling clothes. Suor Umiltà says my mother left it with me so she could find me someday." She tucked the pendant back into her dress. "She also tells me I will be an excellent cook."

"I'm sure of it," I said. We smiled at each other.

"Were you praying? I'm sorry if I interrupted you."

I wasn't entirely sure what I had been doing. She picked up the tray and the bells rang again. "Vespers," she said, turning quickly through the door.

I headed out after her, tugging the bodice of my white underdress to make it cover more of my chest and draping my shawl over my shoulders; I'd have to come up with a more permanent solution later.

The small Ospedale chapel of the Santissima Annunziata was full. Some of the congregants looked like nuns, some like friars; others had the battered look of pilgrims. Many were dressed like the young cook-in-training I'd followed here. I realized I hadn't asked her name. The vault filled with singing, and I let myself drift along with it, for a blessed moment not thinking at all. After the service ended, I stayed in the back of the church as it emptied.

Umiltà found me staring up at the stained glass windows of the clerestory. "Our church is plain, but filled with the essence of Our Lord, is it not? It is our duty, and our pleasure, to provide a haven for those in need." Her tone changed abruptly. "Tell me again, of your origins, parentage, and purpose? Have you a letter from your local priest, or family, to support and sponsor your pilgrimage, a written certificate confirming your good character?" I made the disturbingly easy decision to lie again.

"I lost it in the *mercato*." Umiltà's eyes narrowed. Benjamin always used to say "When you have to lie, use the available facts." I did. "I never knew my father, and my mother died shortly after I was born. I was raised by my older brother Beniamino, who also died, recently and unexpectedly. He was a . . . chronicler. My husband, a notary in Lucca, is dead as well. I embarked upon this pilgrimage along the Via Francigena with my head bowed in sorrow and loss." I had a sudden image of my walk out the Porta Camollia, in my old time. Most of the story was true, including the sorrow and loss part, and being the widow of a notary would elevate my social status. "I hoped the journey would allow me to start a new life with a fresh heart."

"How long do you plan to spend on this stop of your pilgrimage, Monna Trovato?" I hadn't planned anything, of course, but didn't say that.

"I am finding such consolation in the welcome of the Ospedale that I would like to prolong my stay, if possible. I hope that my skills may offset the burden that the Ospedale's charity could engender." Now I was speaking her language.

"I am glad you have found succor here, Monna Trovato. Tonight you will rest, and tomorrow we will undertake to find work to busy your hands while your soul heals. You have met Clara, who brought you food this evening? She will find you in the morning and direct you to the *scriptorium* after Mass." With that informative pronouncement she sealed my immediate future, and I found my way back to my room.

I'd taken care of the basics now, escaped arrest, and made a few friendly acquaintances. That would have been fine if I'd moved to a new country. But this was time travel, not tourism. And if I couldn't get out of here soon, I'd have to deal with the Plague. No brilliant plan to address this problem came to mind, and finally, overwhelmed by fatigue, I fell asleep.

I woke to the sound of bells the next morning at dawn. For a moment I thought everything that had happened might have all been a dream, until I opened my eyes and saw the ceiling of my room in the Pellegrinaio delle Donne. *It's July 7, 1347*, I told myself, as if stating the date could force it to make more sense. I used the chamber pot in the corner, then tried my best to clean myself using a pitcher of water and a basin. I hadn't seen anything resembling a bathroom yet. I had slept in my white linen dress from the twenty-first century—it made a reasonable medieval nightgown and undergarment, and I'd left the green dress draped over the back of the *inginocchiatoio* overnight.

The door opened and Clara appeared holding a flickering lantern as I was getting dressed. She hung the light on a metal hook in the wall and watched me as I tucked my handkerchief into my offending neckline. The handkerchief wasn't entirely clean but neither was I, and I didn't want to end up breaking any more indecency laws. While Clara wasn't looking, I secured the handkerchief with the two twenty-first-century safety pins from my bag.

I stumbled down the dark corridor back to the Santissima Annunziata. The church glowed with candles; flickering light haloed the worshippers' faces.

Oh Lord, make haste to help me . . . I recognized the Latin of Psalm Fifty-nine from Catholic school. It was nice to hear the familiar words; that sense of belonging across centuries was one benefit of religion. I'd never needed it so much before.

Let the heavens and all life on earth praise him who created them.

I watched the light grow brighter through the tall windows, making the panes glow.

And in the shadow of your wings I sing for joy.

The last lines of the morning psalms echoed in my head as the congregants rose. The sun was streaming into the chapel as we walked out. Clara asked me whether I had committed to daily fasting during my pilgrimage; I opted for food.

This time it was broth flavored with smoked pork ladled over a piece of bread. I ate in the company of hundreds of pilgrims seated at long trestle tables set up in the huge refectory of the Ospedale, the clamor of voices startling after the church's quiet. After I finished eating, Clara led me to the *scriptorium* to meet the head scribe.

"Fra Bosi will be here shortly," she announced, leaving me to look around.

A wall of colonnaded windows glazed with small panes of thick glass let in the sunlight. The windows were wide enough to walk through, but didn't appear to open. There were two angled wood writing desks in the room, like drafting tables with a ledge at the bottom to prevent things from sliding off. Above each of the desks was a small shelf. I saw a book propped open on one; fresh empty pages rested on the desk below.

Along the walls, niches and wooden shelves overflowed with manuscripts and books. Some had elaborately tooled leather bindings closed with single or double clasps. Others were simply folded pages held between rectangles of wood. *Ben would have had a field day doing research in here. Maybe I could too, even in this century?* Before I could look more closely at anything, a robed man entered. He had a large, fleshy face, a round head topped by a bristling circle of short gray hair, and deep-set eyes shadowed by heavy brows. He wore an ingenious pair of red folding eyeglasses without earpieces that hinged at the bridge of the nose. It was hard to tell how old he was; aging seemed to have a different rhythm here than I was used to.

"I am told that you can write," he said doubtfully. This must be Fra Bosi. I nodded. "My former assistant, Guido Baldi, the younger of the two Baldi brothers, disgraced himself in the tavern several days ago, and I suggested he find other employment." It seemed I'd arrived conveniently at the moment of a job vacancy. Bosi continued, scowling. "I do not intend to waste my time training incompetent widows to hold a pen for charity's sake, but Suor Umiltà seems to think you might be useful."

"I hope to be," I said. Against the wall, a young boy pounded rags with a mallet while an iron pot boiled over a fire in a corner stone fireplace. Fra Bosi saw the direction of my gaze.

"We have taken on the modern techniques of making paper, in addition to parchment," he said, gruffly. "Egidio is competent at preparing the sheets, but he has not proven himself with the pen and stylus." I saw Egidio's shoulders hunch and the pounding got louder.

"I'm here to write," I said, bluntly. Fra Bosi's face reddened and his eyes bulged; I was afraid that he might be about to blow a blood vessel somewhere.

"We shall see." Bosi motioned for me to sit down and placed pages from an account ledger in front of me. Each row was headed by a phrase describing the nature of the expense or payment, and the columns were divided into credits and debits, like a modern double-entry bookkeeping record. The tiny cramped letters and numbers were all carefully ruled by hand.

"The Ospedale needs to provide to the Biccherna a copy of its accounts since the beginning of Lent." He deposited a stack of stiff, faintly translucent sheets of parchment on the desk in front of me. I'd read about the Biccherna, Siena's financial governing body, so I didn't have to risk asking Fra Bosi what he meant. "I will return at the Nones bells to check on your progress. The materials are costly, I am sure you know. I suggest you minimize error." He turned and left me with my assignment. I checked the quill points, arranged the inks, put the ledger on the stand, set out the ruler and square, and started copying. Nones was seven hours from now; I had some serious work to do.

Oddly enough, I felt more at home in the *scriptorium* of the Ospedale della Scala than I had almost anywhere in the past month, even in my own time. Maybe because it reminded me of working in Ben's office, doing my homework while he read and wrote, and then, as a treat when I finished, trying to copy rubrics, the initial red letters that decorated the more elaborate manuscripts. I'd done a class project on a history of books and gotten an A-minus. It would have been an A, but it was a day late because I'd made the inks myself. Ben had called me "my little scribe" after that.

The next time I looked up from the ledgers, Egidio was stirring a large tub of rag pulp and hot water; his face glistened pink from the steam. While I took a break to flex my fingers and shake out my legs, I watched him pour the pulp and water slurry into screened trays and let the liquid drip through the screens into a large stone basin. Along another worktable, trays held sheets of newly made rag paper beginning to curl away from the frames. Egidio turned to the completed trays, carefully removing the sheets from the mesh. He laid the pages out on the table in front of him and painted one side of each sheet with a thick liquid that looked like Elmer's glue. We hadn't spoken a word to each other in our hours working side by side.

"What is that?"

Egidio turned, startled; I imagined Fra Bosi didn't encourage a lot of idle conversation. "Sizing," he said, blushing furiously. "Fra Bosi says it keeps the ink from spreading on the paper. I cannot write like you so I do not know."

"Have you tried to learn to write?"

"Fra Bosi says I do not have the skill, Signora."

"You can learn," I said, unable to suppress my fundamental educational philosophy. "I don't know how to make paper and you don't know how to write. Both of our failings can be fixed." Egidio's small smile transformed his serious little face.

My hand was cramping agonizingly by the next peal of the bells—Prime, 9:00 a.m. I stretched for a few minutes, then went back to writing. When the bells rang hours later, the pain extended up to my shoulder. Sext—noon. Three more hours to go. No one had mentioned a lunch break. I sneaked a sip from my water bottle. I came to a long list of products from the Ospedale's agricultural landholdings, with the income associated with their sale:

80 soldi / 35 staia / grano / Grancia di Cuna
150 soldi / 15 staia / mandorle / La Grancia Spedaletto
60 soldi / 5 barili / olio d'oliva / Grancia di Grossetto

I didn't know how big *staia* and *barili* were, but writing about wheat, almonds, and olive oil made me uncomfortably aware of my lack of lunch. I tried to pay attention to the amounts. If I ever ended up with any money of my own, I would need to know what it was worth. I copied out several lines on payment of artists' commissions and contracts with architects. There was nothing about the fifth fresco on the facade, but of course Umiltà had only just requested funds for that; it wouldn't be recorded yet.

On the next page I found a familiar name: Vitalis Signoretti. The same Signoretti I knew? The family did date its prominence in Siena back to the fourteenth century. He seemed to be a patron of the arts—many of the sums by his name were for paintings on Ospedale property. Based on the numbers, he had a ton of money and was spending at least some of it on art.

By the time the bells rang for Nones, I had a headache, and my hand and sleeve were stained with ink. But I was done. Bosi appeared in the doorway as I was putting down my pen and came to peer over my shoulder. He picked up the pages, scrutinizing each one and comparing it with the ledger template. I waited, hearing my heartbeat in my ears.

"You will do, Monna Trovato," he said. "Return tomorrow after Prime." And with that, he left, Egidio trailing behind him.

I stood in the middle of the *scriptorium*, stunned by my success.

I'd just succeeded in landing my first medieval job, a symbol of permanence and stability in a place I wasn't sure I wanted to remain. I rinsed what ink I could off my hands and sleeve, ruminating. I'd been dismissed, but I wasn't ready to go back to my room yet.

I was surrounded by primary sources—thousands of books—sitting on the shelves waiting for me to pull them down and read. What if the answers to Ben's questions were in one of those books? I'd found that letter among Ben's papers from Immacolata de' Medici, mourning her husband's death, but found no way to connect it to Siena's downfall. Maybe there was something useful about the Medicis here.

I started looking at the spines of the books lined up along the long walls, but most had no words. I pulled out, inspected, and returned at least thirty books, climbing ladders to reach the highest. I'd settle for anything Florentine I could find, though it was even more of a long shot in a medieval Sienese library than it had been in the modern one. Then I got lucky.

It was a thin, bound transcript of the procedings of the city council, with the date, 1342, on the frontispiece. I looked through the pages. Walter of Brienne, Duke of Athens, who had briefly been the head of the Signoria of Florence, had visited Siena that year. He'd been received with a lavish banquet, which included a flaky pie of live songbirds that flew out during the party. The guests were listed too, and interestingly, Signoretti's name came up again, and later in the list, a Ser de' Medici, also visiting from Florence.

I stopped reading to think. Was this the same Medici—the executed Medici—mentioned in Immacolata's letter? This visit had happened five years earlier—if it was the same Medici, had he been going to Siena for all those years? Doing what? And if it was the same Medici, he'd been in the same room with Signoretti, the wealthy Sienese nobleman, at least once. I felt a strange chill looking at those names together: Signoretti and Medici, one from Siena, the other from her rival *commune*, both at this party with the head of the Florentine government. Had they met then? When I put it back on the shelf, my fingers were tingling, but I didn't know how to interpret what I'd seen. I wished I could have asked Ben what he thought.

After that, there was nothing else directly relevant to my questions. I spent some time poring over a gorgeous illustrated copy of Dante's *Divine Comedy*, and what looked like a mathematical treatise in Arabic before I gave up. Exhausted and starving, I made my way back to my room. There I found a savory pie waiting for me, still warm and smelling of saffron. When I bit into it, cheese, cinnamon, and raisins filled my mouth. I silently blessed Clara as I chewed, and washed the pie down with wine. I climbed onto the bed without getting undressed, and when I closed my eyes, I could see little black letters wavering under my eyelids.

*   *   *

July 7, 1347

Just after dawn, Gabriele started to climb the scaffolding in the Signoretti Chapel, his breath quickening from effort and anticipation. On the high platform he mixed fresh plaster for the *intonaco*, and with a trowel began laying down a thin layer at the seam he'd left the night before. The line of Anna's bed, where the plaid coverlet met with the border of the wooden chest alongside it, had made a natural stopping place, and the division between the dried plaster and fresh *intonaco* would vanish easily in the final painting. Once the plaster was firm enough, Gabriele polished the surface to an even smoothness.

The first hours of the *giornata*, a day's work for the fresco painter, set the whole day's work in motion. A calm beginning let the work roll forward with a sweet, measured cadence. Gabriele laid out the bags of *spolvero*—he would use this soot to mark the drawing's outline—and the jars of pigment he'd prepared. The bedside chest took shape under his brush as he worked. Some painters from Simone's workshop complained about painting inanimate objects in their eagerness to depict the human form, but for Gabriele it all pulsed with the same life and beauty—a line of inlay, a metal lock, the intricate geometric pattern of the carpet—all as worthy of attention as the Virgin's curving fingers, or the lines on Gioacchino's anxious face.

At the beginning of the day when the plaster was still damp the pigment absorbed slowly, as if the wall and the paint were shy lovers, but at the end of each day, as the angle of the sun sharpened, the wall avidly embraced the colors. Gabriele worked rapidly, aware of the urgency of drying plaster. He leaned back to examine the red of the nursemaid's robe against the rose of the infant Virgin, her right hand raised in a baby's first salute. The juxtaposition was just as he'd imagined it. He put his brush down reluctantly; soon it would be too dark to paint. He headed out into the busy streets as the light was just beginning to fade.

On the way home, Gabriele stopped to listen to a *trovatore* singing Dante's *Paradiso*. A small crowd had gathered in appreciation—an elderly cleric next to a restless young son of a nobleman, and a few scruffy-looking children. The singer's sweet voice held them all entranced.

> *Quando Beatrice in sul sinistro fianco*
> *Vidi rivolta, e riguardar nel sole*
> *Aquila sì non gli s'affisse unquanco.*
>
> *E sì come secondo raggio suole*
> *Uscir del primo, e risalire in suso,*
> *Pur come peregrin che tornar vuole;*

Così dell' atto suo, per gli occhi infuso
Nell' imagine mia, il mio sì fece,
E fissi gli occhi al sole oltre a nostr' uso.

When I beheld Beatrice turned to her left and gazing
    on the sun
Never did eagle so fix himself thereon.
And even as a second ray is wont to issue from the first
    and re-ascend
(like a pilgrim whose will is to return);
So from her gesture, through her eyes infused in my
    imagination, did mine own take shape;
and I fixed mine eyes upon the sun, transcending our
    wont.

Like an artist's muse, Gabriele thought. The singer had chosen one of Gabriele's favorite passages. He had a brief vision of his late wife Paola's face, but to his dismay, her features would not come into focus. She had been a timid almost-child when they wed; but a good match for Gabriele, fatherless and motherless, with only the painter's trade to support a new family. Gabriele had been inspired to protectiveness and in time, affection, though not passion.

Within a few months Paola had grown ripe with child, but their babe would never cry or find solace at his mother's breast. When Paola and their son died, Gabriele had returned to his art with greater intensity. He never spoke of Paola, despite his family's attempts to draw him out, or to find him a new source of feminine distraction.

But Gabriele's muse, to his consternation, did not have Paola's face. The woman he had painted on the riverbank watching Saint Christopher carry the Christ child came from some shadowy place of visions, not memory. He felt irrationally guilty, as if an imagined woman emerging from the spirit world could signify an infidelity to a wife nearly three years gone.

The sound of bells reminded him of his cousin Ysabella's promise of supper. He turned away from the performance and hurried back to his uncle's house.

"Gabriele has deigned to grace us with his artist's presence!" Ysabella's words were softened by her wide smile. She stopped short to look at Gabriele.

"Change your sleeves, else you'll cover us all with paint." He looked down at himself, seeing the spattering and smears of color along his arms and hands.

"Of course, Queen Ysabella," he said, bowing, and made his way through the shuttered bakery storefront of the house. Gabriele unbuttoned his dirty sleeves at the shoulder as he mounted the stairs to his third-floor bedchamber under the roof, where he attached clean sleeves. His tunic would have to do for now.

"Don't forget to wash your hands." Ysabella's voice carried up the narrow staircase. As he came down the stairs, Ysabella was smearing the shoulder of mutton with a paste of chopped parsley as the fat dripped and sputtered into the fire.

"You would make a Franciscan into a glutton with your cooking," Gabriele said appreciatively. His uncle Martellino entered the kitchen, hands on his belly.

"She's already managed that with her father! But I was no Franciscan to begin with." His broad smile creased his face.

"Where is our Bianca?" Gabriele asked.

"Upstairs praying to Saint Nicholas again to protect her unborn child," said Ysabella, pulling a pan of roasted onions from the fire, edges curled and darkened by the heat.

"You will see how it feels when your time comes," Martellino said. Ysabella shook her head but held her tongue. She clearly had no intention of acting like her brother's wife now or ever; Gabriele had never seen two women less alike.

The heavy wooden door slammed open against the wall, and Bianca's husband, Rinaldo, entered the house with his usual excess of noise.

"When do we eat?" Rinaldo bellowed. "The price of wheat has risen again, and a day at the bank always makes me ravenous."

"Food never comes fast enough for you, Rinaldo," Ysabella retorted, stirring vinegar into the roasted onions and shaking salt over the bowl.

"No one will want a bride with that tongue." Rinaldo stared pointedly at his father.

"I am certain that your sister will find a husband happy to hear what she has to say," Martellino said tolerantly. "What man would not put up with any amount of haggling for such meals as this?" He put his hand on Ysabella's shoulder to calm her obvious irritation. "And until such time as she does find a husband, we will certainly benefit from her ample skill in the kitchen. Your mother would be proud of you, my angel."

Bianca chose that moment to lower herself painfully down the steep staircase.

"Sit, Bianca, lest our child appear before his time." Rinaldo strode to Bianca's side, leading her to a bench at the table.

Gabriele sighed inwardly as Rinaldo sat beside him; they would be sharing a *tagliere* tonight. Most diners gracefully shared the wooden platter, but grace was not in Rinaldo's nature. Gabriele imagined he might not be eating much this evening, for Rinaldo's speed at the table was difficult to match.

The meal began with a brief prayer, then bunches of taut purple grapes to open the palate, followed by the fragrant salad of roasted onions. Martellino kept Rinaldo distracted with questions about new regulations from the city council for pricing loaves, allowing Gabriele to cut off a sizeable chunk of mutton before Rinaldo could attack it. Ysabella spoke into the contented silence before sweetmeats appeared.

"The crowds at the *mercato* were buzzing with news," Ysabella said. "I Noveschi granted the Ospedale communal funds to commission another painting to honor Santa Maria."

Bianca fingered a gold chain she wore around her neck. "There is talk about Simone's pupils, but others say the Lorenzetti brothers . . ."

"Gabriele is the obvious choice," Ysabella insisted. She slammed a wedge of creamy white cheese emphatically down on a board on the table, spearing it with a knife.

Martellino cut a slice from the cheese and chewed as he spoke. "We know our Gabriele's merit, but the rector of the Ospedale will have to decide for himself. And you, silent one, have you nothing to say about all this?"

Gabriele could feel his pulse beating at the angle of his jaw. He and the other members of Martini's *studium* had struggled to keep the work flowing after their master's death. He needed to pay the *calzoleria* to resole his shoes, and it had been some time since he had contributed his share to Martellino's household expenses.

"I will submit my name to be considered for the commission," Gabriele said levelly as he rose from the table. "And an example of my work stands before the rector, each time he enters the doors of the Ospedale. I hope that will guide him."

"No sweetmeats for you, Gabriele?" Ysabella looked incredulous. Her figure was a testament to her love of sweets.

"I have eaten enough to fill my stomach, despite obstacles." Gabriele's face remained impassive, making his words seem innocuous. Rinaldo, oblivious, wiped the bottom of the almond bowl with his fingers for the last grains of sugar. Gabriele pushed his chair into the table. "I hope you will excuse me. A day on the scaffolding has made me long for bed."

Upstairs in the top-floor chamber where his sketches and studies beckoned from the plaster walls, Gabriele pulled his tunic over his head, then his white cotton shirt. He hung the clothes on the pole protruding from the wall, extinguished the burning candle in its holder, and climbed up onto the large bed, where he said a prayer before he lay down to sleep.

"God in heaven, let the fifth fresco be mine, that I might serve you and Santa Maria in its painting," he whispered, closing his eyes. In the dark behind his lids, the image came alive: the Virgin ascending to heaven, borne by four angels with golden wings. As Gabriele's breathing slowed into the rhythm that precedes dreams, he saw the face of the woman he had painted on the riverbank, her gray-blue eyes the color of the sea.

> *So from her gesture, through her eyes infused in my imagination,*
> *did mine own take shape;*
> *and I fixed mine eyes upon the sun, transcending our wont . . .*

I shall make her an angel at the Virgin's side, Gabriele thought, half dreaming. He smelled damp plaster as he drifted off to sleep.

*   *   *

At last, Iacopo de' Medici thought as he entered his father's *studium*, *at last he has deemed me worthy of his trust*. For years Iacopo had passed by the closed office door, glancing at the rectangle of wood that barred him from the responsibility he longed to assume. This time, however, the door stood open, and Iacopo entered and bowed his head in deference to his father, who sat behind his desk, writing.

"You summoned me, Father," Iacopo said, knowing he should not let his sentence end in the questioning inflection that so infuriated Giovanni de' Medici. "If you speak in questions, you will be questioned, rather than obeyed," Giovanni had said, more times than Iacopo could remember.

Giovanni put down his pen. "Close the door behind you." It

took all of Iacopo's weight to swing the door shut. "I have business in Siena, Iacopo, and I wish you to accompany me."

"I am honored by your trust, Father." Iacopo ran a hand across the back of his neck where his headaches always began, for one had lodged there as he waited for his father's summons. But he would not complain now. On the last occasion before his father had left for Siena, one of his maladies had struck, and he had begged off seeing his father to the city gates.

"I have no patience for this weakness within you that invents ailments. You are a man, now, and a Medici son. You would do better to spend time learning the accounts, rather than lying on your back like a whore waiting for her next visitor. When I am away, your ignorance will be as clear to my associates and clients as it is to me. First master the ledgers. Then we will see if you can manage a business voyage of your own."

"I hope one day to earn your trust," Iacopo had said, pressing the nails of one hand into his palm. And now, it seemed, the day for trust had finally come.

Although Giovanni had begun to involve Iacopo in the family's merchant banking firm, he had been notably closemouthed about his trips to Siena. Iacopo had imagined a secret lover who might satisfy his father's needs, but the details Giovanni recounted came as a surprise.

"I must tell you of the business that has brought me to Siena for five years now, in the service of our *commune*. You are not too young to recall the year Florence submitted herself to the reign of Walter of Brienne, Duke of Athens? I seem to recall you had sprouted a few hairs on your chin by 1342."

Iacopo remembered it well. The Medici family's role in overthrowing Brienne a year after his installation as the head of the Signoria was well known throughout the city and had been a source of political clout for the already prominent Medici family.

His father continued. "Before it became obvious that Brienne was a disaster for our republic, several powerful families of Florence supported the duke's regime, in the hope that he would bring economic stability in the wake of their terrible banking failures and the costly war against Lucca. Are you listening?"

Iacopo shook himself back to the present. He had been thinking about his dinner, the capon that sat heavy in his stomach. Giovanni had always been alert to his drifts of attention.

"In the year of our Lord 1342, I joined with a group of *casati*—noble families in Siena—who were barred by law from serving among i Noveschi. Chafing at this insult, they provided a source of unrest worth harnessing. Under the protection and direction of the Duke of Athens, we attempted to incite a revolt against i Noveschi in Siena. We offered the *casati*, our temporary allies, their rightful place in the seat of government in Siena. We imagined that with these Sienese families on our side, most notably the Signoretti, we might undermine i Noveschi and reestablish a different sort of rule, one that would eventually allow Florence to take control from within. And of course those families would be promised the benefit of a role in the new government as an incentive to joining our cause."

Iacopo nodded. "Since we failed at the battle of Montaperti, conspiracy would seem a reasonable alternative." He heard the slap of his father's hand before he felt the sting on his cheek.

"Listen to me, idiot. You will have to eschew such talk if you are to work at my side." The pain in Iacopo's cheek radiated up to his temple, which began to throb. "This plan for Siena failed, and Brienne proved useless." Giovanni laughed harshly. "I was pleased to have a hand in his sudden departure from Florence. You know he barely escaped with his life."

Iacopo remembered Brienne's ousting from the city. He had been driven out in a violent uprising by the families who had initially supported him, once his despotic rule and harsh economic policies had alienated those who had called him to power. Giovanni continued: "Some of us still believe that through agitation of *casati* families we might find a manner in which Florentine influence could dominate. My visits to Siena have been to further that aim, through allies there that serve our purpose. Do you see now?"

"I do, Father."

"Prepare yourself, for we ride to Siena tomorrow morning. There, we will meet with Ser Signoretti, one of Siena's nobles, who may prove ripe for the picking. He has all that we need to forward our plan—power, wealth, and discontent. And I shall use those to my advantage."

"Yes, Father." Iacopo's head raced with what he had just learned. *My father leads a plan to overthrow Siena's government, and I, the heir to the Medici legacy, shall follow him.* Iacopo began to imagine the meeting with Ser Signoretti, himself and his father side by side, commanding respect, even awe. They would be served fine wine, their voices would be serious, hushed, dampened by tapestries on the walls, the servants dismissed while their important business took its course. The visions in his head eclipsed the present until Iacopo's father barked at him.

"I said prepare yourself, did you hear me?" Iacopo bowed once and fled, tripping on the marble lintel but managing not to fall.

✳   ✳   ✳

On the day after Ysabella announced the Ospedale commission, Gabriele failed to finish his work on the Signoretti Chapel by nightfall. He had timed the day's section poorly, and as the light dimmed, he stared grimly at the infant Maria's unfinished face. Hoping he would not regret the decision to stay late, Gabriele lit a candle and pressed onward until the baby's features materialized on the quickly drying plaster, her rounded cheeks flushed with rose.

Exultant, he extinguished his candle and descended the scaffolding in the near-dark. As he left the chapel, Gabriele saw a figure emerge from the Signoretti palazzo, cloaked and hooded despite the warm night. A second figure followed the first as he watched. It was late to be entertaining visitors, and most would have stayed the night rather than depart at this hour. Once he was certain that the men had gone, Gabriele crossed the courtyard and came out onto the street, staying in the buildings' shadows to avoid the night patrol. A fine for being out past curfew would be costly, and other dangers posed by walking the city streets at night might have even graver consequences.

Gabriele had walked only a few moments before he heard the watchman's voice; Cristoforo's rasping breath would mark him anywhere. Gabriele had seen Cristoforo the week before in the *mercato*, one arm proudly draped about his new wife's shoulders. Despite their acquaintance, tonight Cristoforo might have to charge Gabriele for violating curfew. Gabriele stayed hidden and listened.

"Halt, strangers, what keeps you out so late?"

"Our business is none of yours." This second voice was unfamiliar: low and ominous.

"Declare your purpose, and your identity, or you will find yourself in prison."

"A gentleman of Florence does not bow to Sienese enforcers," the stranger said. "I suggest you let me pass."

"You will give me your name, and recount your doings in detail, if not here, then before the Podestà himself. I am sure our chief magistrate would have great interest in your story."

The next voice was higher-pitched, wavering. "This is Messer Giovanni de' Medici of Florence, a city whose beauty makes Siena a cesspit by comparison. The purpose of our visit is no concern of yours, son of a whore."

Gabriele bit his lip, trying to remain silent.

"Florentine filth pollute our city. I will see that you are brought up before the Podestà for violation of curfew and insult of a city official. You can both spend tonight in a cell, and explain your late-night business to the Podestà in the morning."

"I regret you will not have the opportunity to see me safely to the Podestà's office." The first stranger's voice, which Gabriele now knew must belong to Giovanni de' Medici, was filled with malice but the sounds that followed were worse: the scrape of a blade unsheathed, Cristoforo's scream, then the pounding of running feet. Gabriele stood frozen for a few seconds, then he reached for a plaster trowel from his bag and leaped from his hiding place. The street was faintly lit by a votive candle in a wall niche before an image of Saint Ansanus staring sadly downward, and the light flickered on a tangle of black-and-white cloth on the ground. Cristoforo lay on the pavement, gazing up at Gabriele with wide eyes. His attackers had fled.

Blood seeped rapidly through two rents in Cristoforo's tunic and he patted them softly with his hands, as if he were simply looking for his spectacles, rather than trying to hold on to his life as it left him. "Gabriele Accorsi?"

Gabriele nodded, wrapping his arms around Cristoforo's body and lifting him to stand.

"Cristoforo, a surgeon lives nearby who once tended my uncle. Can you take a step?"

"Your efforts are wasted on me, but I'll spare you the curfew fine for your good intentions." He coughed raggedly. Gabriele hefted the watchman over his shoulder and stumbled toward the surgeon's house. Cristoforo's blood flowed down Gabriele's neck and shoulders and his weight made Gabriele's knees buckle as he walked.

"You'd best put me down," Cristoforo rasped, before they'd reached the surgeon's house. Gabriele let his burden slide slowly to the ground. "Denounce the Florentines," Cristoforo whispered, "and tell my wife that I love her with all my heart." He closed his eyes.

"My good man," Gabriele began, but Cristoforo had drawn his last breath.

Gabreiele covered his friend's body with the man's own cloak, and closed the staring eyes with one hand. Gabriele made his way home quickly, but once in bed could not rest, remembering what he had heard and seen—the harsh threats, and the look in Cristoforo's eyes as his life bled away. *I have been a witness to a murder*, Gabriele thought, *and I must act*. But what would it mean to act? To denounce a powerful nobleman from the rival *commune* whose force was a threat to Siena? *Would that I had not stayed late, this one night . . .* but he had stayed. Perhaps God willed that he be a witness, and bring the murderer to justice. Gabriele knew of the informers' boxes outside the office of the Podestà. Rinaldo never tired of recounting how he had once informed on a sodomite, penning his secret accusation on a sheet of parchment. The information had led to the man's trial, and death. Gabriele wondered whether Rinaldo would have been so proud to do his part to protect his *commune* without the shield of anonymity. Enough witnesses had stepped forward to allow Rinaldo to remain a silent informer setting the machine of the Iudex Maleficiorum in motion. Gabriele had tried to imagine how he might rise to the service of his *commune*, but knew that he would not find such pleasure as Rinaldo in the retelling.

The night after he had witnessed Cristoforo's murder, Gabriele again found himself unable to sleep. With the weight of what he knew bearing down on him, he penned a letter on parchment and quietly left the house, making his way toward the office of the Podestà. The words he had written hummed in his head:

I have witnessed the brutal murder of Cristoforo da Silvano in his course of duty to protect Siena, by the violent hand of Giovanni de'

Medici of Florence. Written this day by my hand, I do bear witness to the crime, and would swear before the Podestà and judges should this murderer be brought to trial. —Gabriele Beltrano Accorsi

The note dropped through the slot in the large wooden box outside the palazzo. Gabriele disappeared into the shadow of the shuttered buildings, quickly making his way home.

✷   ✷   ✷

One of the disadvantages of having such an angry husband, Immacolata de' Medici considered as she lowered herself slowly into her bath, was raising an equally angry son. Immacolata's maidservant stood behind her, pouring warm water into the wooden tub until the water lapped around Immacolata's shoulders. Rose petals floated on the surface of the bath, filling the room with their scent. The maid turned her eyes away, appearing not to notice the spray of bruises across Immacolata's back before they disappeared under the surface. Giovanni had been in an evil temper when he left for this most recent business journey.

Immacolata had held her husband's cloak as he prepared his horse and bags. "When will I have the pleasure of welcoming you home again, my husband?"

"Do not presume to delve into matters of my business," Giovanni had barked, pulling on his boots. "Whenever I return you will be prepared to receive me, or face the consequences."

Admittedly, Giovanni's absences provided a certain relief. A bath such as this was a pleasure she reserved for her evenings alone—Giovanni would have found it frivolous and wasteful. This current trip was lasting longer than usual. He had already been gone five days, and only to Siena; the distance certainly did not justify the time elapsed.

Immacolata watched her breasts floating on the surface of the warm water. The stab of distress she still felt looking at her body surprised her; after so many years her failures should have ceased to rankle. After all, she had a child. Though Iacopo was hardly a child now, twenty-eight years old and working at his father's side—and on this occasion traveling with his father to Siena. She was pleased to see Iacopo taking an interest in the merchant-banking firm, though his absence came, of course, with its attendant worry.

Sighing, Immacolata pulled herself out of the cooling bath. As she lay alone in bed, she allowed herself a moment of pleasure in the solitude afforded by Giovanni's absence.

✷   ✷   ✷

After I'd spent a week with the ledgers, Fra Bosi finally decided to trust me with a weightier task. Bosi set a wax tablet in front of me.

"Today you shall draw up a contract from this draft provided by our notary," he said gruffly. "See that you make no mistakes." He turned away with his usual lack of social niceties, and I sat down to read the words engraved in the wax, marveling at the medieval reusable notepad. I read, translating silently from the Latin.

On this 14th day of July, 1347, in the name of God, amen. I, the rector of the Ospedale della Scala di Siena, with the support of the Nine Governors and Defenders of the commune, hereby contract, with the goal of the beautification of our city through patronage, the commission for a fifth fresco on the facade of the Ospedale to honor and exalt the Blessed Virgin, heavenly protector of Siena. We grant this commission, for the amount of forty lire in gold, to Messer Gabriele Beltrano Accorsi, pupil of the late Maestro Simone Martini of Siena.

I dropped the tablet onto the desk, startling Egidio.

"Are you well, Signora?" His face creased in concern.

That's my *Gabriele, and he's going to paint the facade of this very building. And I've been asked to work on his contract.*

"I need some air," I said, and rushed out of the *scriptorium*, down the steep stone steps, and into the courtyard. I sat on a stone bench and took a few deep breaths. Gabriele was *here*, no longer a long-dead writer of a medieval diary. It was shocking, the sudden collapse of centuries that had separated us when I'd first read his words.

I shook my head until my thoughts cleared and my breath returned to normal. The courtyard was empty except for myself and a flock of sparrows gathered about the central fountain, and for a moment I watched the birds in the sun. I got up slowly and made my way back into the *scriptorium* and Gabriele's waiting contract.

PART III

THE LITTLE OWL

Bartolomeo stood behind the pulpit in the cathedral rehearsing his sermon silently. He'd waited longer than most for his opportunity—one year as an acolyte, another assisting the cathedral elders with preparations for their services, then months chanting the night office before he was allowed his own sermon. *Empty your mind. Be a vessel for the Holy Spirit.* Distractions were everywhere—the ache in his legs, the rasp in his throat that he feared might silence him when he began to speak today.

The other young priests strove to rise rapidly in the church, but Bartolomeo had dragged his training out as long as he could. Like many of his compatriots, he was the third son in a family of good worth. His eldest brother had inherited the family property while the second had the skill and temperament to train as a knight and was squiring with one of the Sienese *contado*'s largest landowners.

The clerical path suited Bartolomeo. He had always liked disappearing with a book; even as a child his attempts to play swords and lances had fallen hopelessly flat. As a result, he spent an inordinate amount of his childhood hovering around his mother in the kitchen of the great stone house. His brothers called him "little sister" when their mother was out of hearing, but she did not question his quiet nature. Education in the church was a perfect retreat from all that Bartolomeo found most challenging, with one small exception: public speaking. He had hoped repetition might soften the edges of his fear, but here he was, five minutes before the ringing of the bells, biting his nails to the quick.

"Today on this auspicious day——" *No, no, I cannot say* day *twice in one sentence.* "On this auspicious day, before the feast of Santa Maria Magdalena——" *TWO days before the feast. Can I not produce a single utterance without error? Oh, help me, Virgin, to survive this sermon.* Bartolomeo wiped his palms on his robe, cleared his throat, and started again: "On this auspicious day . . ." The bells began to peal. Bartolomeo said a brief prayer to whatever saint might be near enough to help and mounted the wooden steps to the pulpit.

Back at my desk, I spread out a sheet of parchment and prepared a fresh batch of red ink for the initial rubrics. I had always been a rule-abiding sort of person, taking written contracts seriously. But now that I was writing one myself, for someone I felt I knew, the words took on even greater weight. When Fra Bosi returned at midday to examine my finished work, he actually gave a complimentary grunt. After some practice, I had learned to distinguish those from the disparaging grunts.

"You are a scribe, you need a signature," he said. "The mark that identifies the work as originating from your hand, and declares your authenticity, and thereby that of the document you create." Bosi pulled a chair beside me, lowering his substantial bulk into it. "You must craft one that is uniquely recognizable and true to the path God has ordained for you. Think of the signs that have guided you to this point and marked you for who you are."

I picked up a pen and a blank piece of Egidio's newly made paper. My head filled with images—Felice draping the Civetta scarf around my neck, my scalpel slicing through dura to find a fresh collection of blood. I drew an outline of an owl, then beneath it a scalpel, the mark of the profession I had so recently left behind, like a branch beneath the owl's feet. I added a blend of my initials like leaves from the branch the knife had become. Fra Bosi picked up a cloth to blot the design I'd drawn. I felt as if I'd just clipped my first aneurysm, with a senior surgeon telegraphing silent approval.

"You may sign your work thus, Scribe Beatrice Alessandra Trovato, and take the remainder of the day to restore your strength for tomorrow's efforts." He rose slowly and left.

I headed out the front door of the Ospedale and for a moment I forgot my peculiar situation in the pleasure of the afternoon. But when I stepped into the Duomo's shadow I remembered. I looked up at the striped facade, at the place where I'd left my own time and entered this one. Could the path between the two times still be open? If Gabriele's missing journal had pulled me toward this century, I was out of luck, since I didn't have the journal anymore. But what if it were the Duomo itself? I followed the bells, up the stairs and through the great doors. I sat in a pew at the front this time and stared at the lions, remembering how the marble had once felt worn and warm under my hand. I followed the dizzyingly striped columns of the nave to the huge dome above. In this century, the gold stars on their background of twilight blue had not been painted yet; the vaulted arches were bare, austere stone. Still the dome felt, with the oculus at its apex bright now in the midday sun, like it might be a portal to another world or time. I stared up until my neck ached and my eyes burned, but nothing happened. I tried again, this time closing my eyes and envisioning the little guest bedroom in Ben's house, with its white curtains blowing over the linen-sheeted bed. All I got from that was a surge of homesickness—emotion, but no transportation.

Before I could make another attempt, a young priest appeared in the pulpit, cleared his throat, and began speaking in a tremulous voice. Then his voice squeaked to silence. The congregants around me shifted restlessly while the priest stood at the pulpit openmouthed, but making no sound at all.

I slid suddenly from looking at the panicked priest to being inside his head. He really had it bad. I felt his wave of nausea and heard the rapid beat of his heart in my ears. From the young priest's perspective the congregants looked scornfully at the pulpit, ready to pull him down from his perch. *I am unfit to give a sermon, unfit, unfit. . . .* His words echoed in my head. But this time I managed to keep a part of me separate. I approached the priest's anxiety the same way I used to stanch the flow of blood from a blood vessel—methodical, unhurried. *Slow down, breathe, it's OK*—I was talking to him and myself at the same time. *This is a great sermon; you're doing fine, keep talking. You're surrounded by fellow citizens patiently waiting to hear your words. Quiet heart, quiet mind, strong voice.* I sensed his fear ebbing as my own heart slowed with his. I backed out as quietly as I could.

"Well spoken, Bartolomeo," the usually taciturn deacon said as the congregation filed out. "I thought you might need to be rescued from your perch midsermon, but you found inspiration to go on."

"Indeed I did," said Bartolomeo, still a bit mystified by his sudden deliverance, and added: "With God's help, of course." Breathing a sigh of relief, he watched the congregants leaving the cathedral. Among them he caught the sight of a woman with dark braids wound around her head, her green gown swirling around her as she turned to depart. He had seen her before—on the night he had first chanted the hours, weaving with his voice the fragile thread of prayer that would guard Siena's citizens: *"Keep them safe, Lord, and guard them as they sleep."* Distracted by some sound in the pews he had seen the woman moving quickly through the nave, her black hair streaming behind her. He had feared then that a spirit might have found its way from the supernatural world, let in by his faltering prayer. It seemed that the spirit had stayed.

*　　*　　*

"Is it a love letter?" Ysabella stood on her toes, trying to see the folded parchment delivered to the house that afternoon, but Gabriele held it just out of her reach.

"Of a sort," Gabriele said, with a half-smile, "but not the kind you imagine. I have been granted the commission to paint a scene from the Virgin's life over the Ospedale entry."

Rinaldo smiled, but his words were barbed. "Now you may earn your keep, and repay my father's generosity."

"It is easy to be generous to such a generous spirit as our Gabriele," Martellino countered. "And as for the commission, it is no great surprise. Whom else would they choose?"

Ysabella's eyes lit up with interest. "Gabriele, how marvelous! When do you start, and what will you paint?"

"The rector has asked that I come to his office tomorrow, to begin planning the project. And the subject—I have long hoped to paint the Assumption of the Virgin, to crown the cycle of her life with her ascent into heaven."

Ysabella shaped her face into a dramatic rendition of a lovesick young adolescent. "Santa Maria, Gabriele's one true love. Who can compete with the Virgin? Perhaps you should have been a monk instead of a painter!" She dodged the swipe of Gabriele's arm and went to bank the fire with ashes.

Before bed there were beans to be shelled, almonds to blanch and skin, repairs to be made—the big cauldron had lost its wooden handle—and it was several hours before the family retired upstairs. Martellino's house was well appointed, with two good-size *camere*. Rinaldo and Bianca shared one of the bedrooms, and Ysabella and her father the other, with a large bed and smaller cot beside it. On the top floor under the wood-beamed roof, Gabriele had a modest space to himself where he might not only sleep but also spend time sketching studies for his future paintings on the plaster walls.

Alone in his room at last, Gabriele stared at the contract in his hands, touching the words. The handwriting was delicate, with a strange look to it—it reminded him of hearing his own language spoken with a faint accent, the cadence of a visitor whose home was far away. The signature too was unfamiliar: an owl, perched on a branch, with the scribe's initials entwined in its curve. A new scribe perhaps, or a visiting one.

Gabriele lay in bed, imagining his upcoming meeting with the rector. For hours he lay staring at shadows as they stretched slowly across the beamed ceiling. He despaired when he heard the sound of the Matins bells hours later with only a third of the night behind him. When he finally drifted off to sleep, he dreamed he was awake, watching the window for a sign of dawn. He woke groggy with fatigue to the smell of baking bread, afraid he'd overslept for his meeting. Martellino managed to press a small loaf into Gabriele's hand as he hurried out the front door.

*　　*　　*

To Monna Immacolata de' Medici
Palazzo Medici, Florence
Written by the hand of your Husband, Giovanni de' Medici
From the Communal Prison, Palazzo Pubblico, Siena
25th Day of July, three weeks before the Feast of the Assumption, 1347

It is said that a spendthrift wife is a husband's burden. I trust you are not wasting, in my absence, the funds that I require for my Deliverance. Business did not proceed as I might have hoped, and I have been detained

*here in this cesspit of a city. Iacopo ought now to be on his way back to
Florence, but in the interim, send a messenger with as much haste as you
can muster. Bid him carry fifty fiorini d'oro to speed my departure from
this pitiful edifice of communal Sienese justice. I expect to be released,
despite the efforts of these incompetents to detain me.*

Giovanni folded this first letter and affixed his seal in wax. There
had been a witness to their nocturnal encounter with the night
watchman, a witness who had denounced Giovanni for homicide.
When a knock had come on the inn's door, Giovanni sent Iacopo to
hide behind a curtain to minimize any trouble he might cause. But
trouble came notwithstanding, for the pair of thick-necked police
arrested Giovanni, marched him through the city like a common
thief, and imprisoned him in this grim cell to await trial. Iacopo
had had enough sense to stay hidden and had followed his father's
order to return home to Florence and await further news.

Giovanni spat into the viscous ink left by the guard that morning, and began his second missive. The guard had also allowed
him pen and parchment, though at an exorbitant price.

To My Son Iacopo de' Medici
With the grace of God

    *Spending these nights in a Sienese jail cell has done nothing to
improve my poor opinion of the commune's citizens. They pride themselves on their new facilities, as if their fledgling efforts to build a
modern prison should place them in the firmament of communal justice,
with the little shack they have appended to their so-called Palazzo
Pubblico. I am being held in a cell awaiting trial for the dispatch of
that night watchman who presumed foolishly to block our way. If he
had known that it is wiser to let a businessman go about his business
undisturbed, he might still be alive today.*

    *It appears some other citizen in disregard of curfew witnessed my
lesson to the night watch and took it upon himself to denounce me to*

the Podestà. On my arrival in the prison, I provided the warden with an incentive to better my accommodations. I managed in this way to avoid the common cells, but have not been granted the relative liberty that my station should warrant. I do not expect to remain long, but while I am here, I should spend my days in a fashion appropriate to our family's position. There is a Magnati ward here, but it appears that the treatment of "foreigners" and "serious crimes" prevents my placement there.

Your mother will send a messenger with funds to smooth my passage here, but I expect to see you before this Holy Sunday, so that I may communicate to you a matter of great importance regarding the instigator of my arrest.

Giovanni paused, rubbing his right hand with his left to soften the cramp that had lodged itself at the base of his thumb. As he picked up his pen to dip it again into the remaining ink, he forgot for a moment what he had intended to write. His usual certainty was replaced by an odd sensation, like hunger but higher in his chest. When he took up his pen again, his next words surprised him.

I find that the unexpected confinement and restriction of my liberty has made me long for the company of my family, those in whom love and loyalty for Firenze runs as deep as the blood that links us. I look forward to a face sympathetic to my plight, instead of these mocking visages that hint at a dark future for me and those who share my name. When I close my eyes to rest, I begin to believe I can feel the weight of the thick stone that surrounds me and bars my communion with the sun and air. I bid you to return to me with the greatest haste, not only to assist me in obtaining the justice and liberty that are my due, but also to stand at my side so that I may have some reminder of a life outside these walls.

From the hand of your father
Giovanni de' Medici
Detained awaiting trial and in God's hands
This 25th Day of July, 1347

Three aspects of imprisonment vied to be the most infuriating. First was the knowledge that he would be using his own gold to pay for his unwilling sojourn in prison—it made his dinner rancid in his stomach. The physical confinement provided greater misery. In this cell, only slightly larger than a horse's stall, he ached to stretch his limbs again. But the most maddening consequence of imprisonment was boredom. His two letters written and dispatched with a guard, along with the soldi required to assure their delivery, Giovanni was left with no other task to complete, no meeting to attend, no subordinates to command. The guards had taken his knife, or he might have enjoyed sharpening it on the whetstone he carried in his belt pouch, or even, for a moment of titillation, testing it on the edge of his thumb. The sight and smell of blood, even his own, would have provided some welcome stimulation in this bland stretch of hours.

Some relief came at the hands of the guard returning with an evening meal, but the bean stew left him sharply unsatisfied. As the guard retreated, Giovanni raised his hand to signal a question. The guard stopped, staring suspiciously—he'd been warned about these Florentines, their open disregard for Sienese law and order.

"Have you knowledge of any . . . shall we say, amusements, that might be afforded visitors with the means to support them?" Giovanni's hand went to the pouch at his belt, and he fingered the coins inside so their clinking could be heard easily.

The guard licked his lips. "I am sure you know, Ser, nocturnal visitors are strictly forbidden." But as he spoke the guard rubbed his fingers together, as if noting the absence of something.

"Of course. But we both know that the straightest rule can be bent."

The guard stepped closer. "Are those golden lilies you carry with you? They might call forth an equally lovely nocturnal visitor."

Giovanni laughed quietly. "The florins will take root nicely in your palm," he said, dropping two into the guard's upturned hand.

"Expect a visitor at the Matins bells," the guard said, and left. The sound of the bolts troubled Giovanni less now that he knew the distraction the night hours would bring.

The room was dark when the door opened again, awakening Giovanni from a light sleep. His visitor wore a robe and hood that hid her face. She placed a small candlelit lantern on the table by his bed.

"I would see what my lilies have bought," Giovanni said quietly, and he watched as two white hands emerged from the long sleeves to push back the hood. A surprisingly young and delicate face for a whore—perhaps she was new to her business. So much the better; fresh maidens were not yet hardened to the shock of their patrons' desires. Immacolata had long since ceased to arouse him, but Giovanni found ample opportunity for gratification elsewhere.

"I have never had the opportunity to plough Siena's fields," Giovanni said, and he was pleased to see the girl's hands tremble at her sides.

"My Lord, at your service." Her voice trembled too, appealingly young and frightened. Giovanni leaned against the wall, enjoying the tension in his visitor's face as he paused.

"Are you new to this . . . employment?"

The girl nodded. "Shall I lie down?"

"This is not a meeting of newlyweds. Turn your back to me."

"Ser?"

"I said, turn your back. I have paid for your body, not your conversation." She complied, and he saw with satisfaction the anxious hunch of her shoulders under the homespun gown. "Now listen closely—I do not like to waste my breath on repetition. Kneel on the floor and raise your dress over your head—but do not remove it." Giovanni felt himself grow aroused as the girl complied, and he saw her pale buttocks before him, invitingly parted by her position.

"Do I have the good fortune of having bought a virgin?"

"My Lord, I have been with a man only once."

"Well, then I shall use you where you haven't yet been. I like to be the first to break new ground."

"Ser?"

"And of course, I would prefer to avoid the chance that I might leave you with child."

"I cannot hear you, My Lord." Her voice was muffled under the fabric.

"I suppose you are a virgin to sodomy?"

"I am a woman, My Lord."

"That will not protect you. The anatomy you share with a man allows the same invasion." Giovanni's voice fell almost to a whisper. He heard her gasp and the fear in it brought him such delight he could not restrain himself a moment longer. His hands were soft, the girl thought—like a nobleman's—as they gripped her hips, but his intent clearly was not.

*   *   *

"Iacopo, are you in your chamber? The table is laid for supper."

Iacopo emerged into the light of the dining room, his habitual scowl deeper than usual. Immacolata smoothed her son's hair with one hand.

"Mother, I am no longer your little boy," Iacopo said, but he leaned into the caress. It seemed such a short time ago that his head had been at her waist, Immacolata thought, lowering her hand reluctantly.

"Can you not rest another night before you return to Siena?"

"My father has bid me return with haste, as you well know." Iacopo covered his eyes to block the last of the evening light filtering through the leaded glass windows of the *sala*.

"I have prepared a packet of dried fruits and almonds, those your father prefers, as well as all you might need for your journey. Your father's words to me were brief—did he explain why they have detained him?" Iacopo remained silent. In the darkness behind his lids Iacopo saw strange geometric patterns of light and shadow pulsating. When he opened his eyes the flickering lines remained, obliterating half of his mother's face. He squinted to bring the image into focus.

"My son, you are so thin, and since you first left for Siena you have grown even thinner. Please have a few bites of trout with me tonight."

"I cannot eat." Iacopo picked up a pitcher of spiced wine, then put it down again. "Father has killed a man of Siena's night watch. The guard deserved to meet his end, but that has not prevented the agents of the Podestà from detaining him." Iacopo de' Medici had not slept more than a few ragged hours each night since his father's imprisonment, and his head buzzed with unspoken words. *It is my fault that they have him now, my fault that my father is locked in a Sienese jail cell, awaiting trial. He gave me a chance to prove myself, and I failed him. I spoke my father's name, when I should have remained silent. I hid behind a curtain when I might have helped. I left Siena when I might have remained at my father's side. Is this how I should repay his trust?*

"They will try him for murder?" Immacolata put her hand flat on the trestle table for support. "God help us." She watched her only son open the door. She could still imagine his small boy self, plump feet peeking out beneath the hem of a child's red gown.

"We will need God's help," he answered, then disappeared into the courtyard as she wiped the wetness from her cheeks.

Outside the light was fading as Iacopo ducked into the stable adjoining the Palazzo Medici. The incessant company in the house tired him and he preferred the relief of the stables, the sounds of the horses' hooves shifting in the straw at their feet, the soft blowing of the mares against their foals' necks. He headed toward the stallions' pens to choose his mount for tomorrow's journey. In the dark the jagged lines of light had grown to fill most of his field of view, and he had to squint to see where he walked. A thread of headache began, the left side of his scalp burned as if he had slept too near the hearth, and a wave of nausea nearly made his knees fold. He steadied himself, swallowing bile, and waited for the spasm to fade. In a few more moments the lights had passed, leaving him with a dull throb beneath his skull.

As Iacopo approached, Pellegrino moved restlessly in his stall. The stallion was aptly named Pilgrim, loving always to be in motion. Iacopo spoke before moving; Pellegrino had a tendency to startle if approached too quickly.

"*Buona sera*, Pellegrino. Will you ride with me tomorrow?" Iacopo touched the white blaze on the horse's long nose. The animal's hair was smooth under his hand. The horse asked nothing of him but food, water, and the opportunity to run. Iacopo felt at home in the saddle; he could not have said that of the other tasks placed before him. Iacopo moved in closer to Pellegrino until he could rest his cheek on the long muscled neck, and closed his eyes for a moment. He could feel the twitch of Pellegrino's skin, flicking off a wayward fly.

Iacopo wished he might stay here forever in the stable, rather than return to the palazzo, his tapestried room with its imposing carved dark wood bed, the anxious words of his mother, and tomorrow's journey. He would have preferred to sleep here, surrounded by the smooth warm flanks of the horses and the sweet and musky smells of hay and manure.

When Iacopo left the stable, a sharp wind was blowing off the Arno. A bad portent for tomorrow's journey; rain could quickly turn the road between Florence and Siena to churning mud, difficult if not dangerous. Iacopo could feel the parchment of his father's letter folded against his skin beneath the fabric of his shirt, close to his own heart. The words appeared before his eyes as if he were reading them—

I bid you to return to me with the greatest haste . . . to stand at my side so that I may have some reminder of a life outside these walls.

He wishes my return, despite my missteps, Iacopo thought, and as the wind rose he felt it lift the hair from his forehead like a gentle hand.

The demon rain came on a *caroccio* of unholy wind, unnatural for the month of July. The drops began to fall just after Matins, at first tapping quietly on the awning outside Iacopo's window, then becoming more insistent, like the pattering of a hundred feet on the courtyard paving stones. A flash of blinding light, then a crack from the heavens heralded a deluge that cascaded off the tiled roof of the palazzo.

The streets had turned into streams by the time Iacopo left the following morning, and refuse overflowing from the alley cesspits made the air rank. Iacopo's fear for the condition of the road was well founded; as nightfall approached he had only reached a hamlet outside Arezzo, where he was forced to spend the night at an inn, along with other travelers who had failed to reach their destinations. Iacopo shared a bed with a corpulent and gassy wine merchant who talked endlessly until the Matins bells, then fell promptly asleep in the center of the bed, leaving Iacopo clinging to the edge of the mattress for the rest of the night.

The following morning, Iacopo struggled into his damp clothing and mounted Pellegrino with reluctance. The rain had slowed but the clouds stayed low and dense, dripping monotonously for the entire journey. Iacopo arrived at the prison mud-spattered, hungry, and short of sleep. The headache still lurked behind his eyes, waiting for the slightest provocation to worsen.

Iacopo secured his mount and entered the guardroom, greeted by suspicious looks when he announced his purpose.

"You're the Medici boy? You don't look a bit like him. Perhaps your mother looked elsewhere for a moment, during one of her husband's *business* trips." The guards guffawed loudly, patting their crotches. "You're a scrawny fellow. Is the bull proud of the little calf he's made?" Iacopo's vision swam with fury and he grabbed the pouch from his waist, slamming it on the table.

"I will see that my father and I receive the good treatment our station deserves. This should pay for your respect." The guards looked approvingly at the pouch from which two lily-stamped gold coins had spilled out.

"You may not be much to look at, but your money's handsome. Gerardo, show the *gentleman* to his father's cell."

Iacopo looked down at himself as he trailed the second guard through the prison corridors. The hose sagged on his slender legs and were streaked with mud. The wool of his cloak was damp and smelled like dirty sheep. He had no glass to see his face, but he knew his own flaws well enough. His long chin and narrow-set eyes attracted little admiration, though he suspected some feigned it because of his family's power and wealth. He had come of age without managing to elicit respect for his accumulating years— remaining always his father's underwhelming only son.

The guard stopped in front of a wooden door. His keys jangled as he opened the padlock and pushed the bolt back with a grunt.

"I shall be outside, lest you think to try any tricks, little calf."

Iacopo prayed that Giovanni did not hear the insult, nor the quiet "moo" and laughter that followed him into his father's cell. The guard shut the heavy door behind him.

The light from a slit of window illuminated Giovanni from behind, haloing his mane of hair but leaving his features in darkness.

"Late, as I might have expected, and looking more like a ditch digger than the son of a nobleman."

"The rain detained me, Father."

"I have no interest in your musings on the weather. I have a task for you that will require all the resources you can muster." Giovanni turned so that his features were lit from the high window, and Iacopo saw unfamiliar signs of strain lining his father's face. Iacopo searched for a sign of the spirit that had given rise to his father's last letter, but was not sure what to look for.

"Will they release you?"

"I thought promise of additional payment might afford me greater liberty, but I have not been allowed to leave this cell, even to take my meals." Iacopo produced the almonds and fruit his mother had packed the night before, holding them out to his father. Giovanni took a handful of dried figs, eating them rapidly. Iacopo tried not to stare as he watched his father devour the fruit, putting more into his mouth before he had finished the first handful. Iacopo had never seen his father in a position to want or need anything. "They have told me nothing. I intend to vouch I acted in defense of my life."

Giovanni had finished the figs and reached for the almonds, eating them quickly one after the next. "You look as if you've been rolling in a pen, and smell worse."

Iacopo did not contradict him. After a few seconds, his father sighed, as if resigned to make the best of the material he had been provided, however unsatisfactory.

"Now—the matter I alluded to in my letter. My arrest has resulted from the work of an informant who denounced me in writing. The guard told me the man's name—such information can be bought, for a good price: Accorsi. Now you must find him."

Iacopo swallowed with difficulty, his throat dry. "And if I find him?"

"You will do what must be done. Call upon the members

of our confraternity; there are men in the Brotherhood of San Giovanni who will follow your lead if I am indisposed." Giovanni did not speak for some time. From deep within the prison a man began screaming shrilly. The silence after the screams lasted a long time, and when Giovanni spoke his voice was quieter than before. "I may never leave this prison, Iacopo."

"Certainly the judges will accept the argument of self-defense?"

"In Firenze, where all respect the Medici name, my arguments would not have met with any question. But our power is worthless here. This place has robbed me of my certainty." Giovanni looked into his son's eyes, and Iacopo could not tear his gaze away. "In the event that I am not allowed to return to the life I once enjoyed, if the worst should transpire and I am hanged for my acts, you must avenge my death. I speak of the coward Accorsi who spoke against me, but also the city that dares to punish a nobleman of Florence for defending himself. A city whose pretentions to greatness we men of Florence have long had occasion to despise."

We men of Florence. Iacopo leaned in closer to hear Giovanni's words, close enough to feel the warmth of his father's breath, smelling of figs and the fear of death.

*   *   *

July 28, 1347

Dear Nathaniel,

I feel like writing to you even though I have nowhere to send this letter. Did you suspect before I did that my preoccupation with the past had gone too far? "You're getting in over your head, Dr. Trovato," I can hear you saying, as if you're standing here next to me, but of course you're not. You don't even exist yet but I like to think that somewhere you and Charles are rolling out of bed, emerging from your hem-stitched linen sheets, and padding into the kitchen to make espresso. God, I miss coffee. And toilet paper, and . . . Ben. I'm sure he'd be amused to be in the same category as toilet paper. But even if I came home I couldn't have Ben. Not anymore.

What I miss most is not the conveniences of modern life; I miss being known. Everything I say about myself is fabrication, but there's no alternative, because the truth is impossible. There are moments when I forget my old life, when I'm happily writing and the dust motes are swirling in the air above me, catching the light through the rippled glass windows. But underneath the day-to-day rhythm here, I'm homesick, or maybe timesick is a better word. With no way of getting home.

This is better than a postcard, right? I don't think they had postcards, I mean HAVE postcards, in the 14th century.

Love,

B

I'd made no progress on how to get home again, but at least I had a job, which at this moment entailed drafting an agreement with the Grance di Grossetto accounting for the proceeds of twenty bushels of barley. Egidio had been sent on an errand and I was alone in the *scriptorium*. I could hear street sounds as I worked—laughter from a group of children playing, a peddler calling his wares. That morning, an intermittent loud banging had started, as if someone were building something just outside, but I couldn't see anything through the leaded glass windows. As I finished the agreement, I began to feel sleepy. I'd slept badly the night before, awakened by nightmares of the Plague, reenacted by flat medieval figures from the chronicles I'd read in my old century. I slipped the letter to Nathaniel under the ledger and put my head on the desk. The agreement could wait a few minutes, unlike neurosurgery. Soon I was dreaming: I was lying on my belly in the sun on a sandy beach, letting the warmth soak into my back. Then I was feverish in my childhood bed, getting an alcohol rub from Benjamin to bring my temperature down. The images fragmented, a bonfire at the camp I'd gone to when I was nine, faces distorted through the wavering heat above it. When I woke up, I was lying in the street.

Gabriele had not asked for help from any of the laborers at the workshop, preferring to limit expense by doing the preparatory work himself. The single fresco over the doorway would not require a team of carpenters to build the scaffolding or painters' assistants to prepare plaster, bag *spolvero*, and mix the pigments daily. Tommaso, his closest friend from Simone's workshop, questioned his sanity, but Gabriele enjoyed the physical effort.

He extended the boards to allow access to the wall over the Ospedale entrance. Soon he was too warm for his tunic and worked in his linen long-sleeved undershirt, humming under his breath in harmony with the sparrows that gathered in the piazza. As he hammered, he began to smell the cooking from the Ospedale kitchens, smoky and pungent. But after a few more minutes, the smell became unpleasant, and his eyes stung. Gabriele rapidly made his way down the scaffolding to the front entrance. The two guards at the entrance moved to block his entry until they recognized his face.

"Fire," Gabriele barked, then raced past them into the Ospedale's entrance and up a flight of marble steps, following the smell of smoke. When he reached the landing he dropped to the ground and crawled until he reached a closed door. The door was warm to the touch but he rose and threw it open.

Gabriele's heart sank at the sight of billowing smoke and tongues of orange flame curling around stacks of books in the

Ospedale's great *scriptorium*. He could see a large cistern in the corner of the room with a bucket and dipper hanging next to it, and scrambled on his hands and feet toward the water source. As he passed the scribes' desks he stumbled over something soft and yielding. Looking down he saw, with shock, a woman's foot, wearing a sandal with fine leather straps. The billowing smoke isolated the foot strangely, as if it were disembodied. As the smoke drifted, Gabriele made out a calf above the ankle, and the edge of a skirt—all attached to a woman, slumped over the copyist's desk.

Gabriele pulled himself to stand. His mind allowed him a peculiar slow clarity, enough to capture detail despite the situation's urgency. The scribe's cheek rested on the ink-stained wood and her slender fingers still curled around a pen. A few fine strands of black hair escaped from her plaits to touch the curve of her neck. In that fraction of a second Gabriele caught the subtle lift as a shallow breath moved her shoulders. Alive.

He grabbed the scribe under her arms and dragged her toward the doorway. As he did, he heard a terrible splintering sound—a full bookcase detached from the wall near the door, swayed and pivoted, showering sparks as it fell. It crashed to the floor in front of him in flames, effectively blocking his exit. He pulled himself and his limp burden back down to the floor, scanning the room for possibilities. High windows paned with thick glass lined the left wall, and he could see a path through the flame and smoke to reach them. He grabbed a heavy inkwell from the desk and crawled, dragging the scribe behind him. At the windows he rose, hefting the inkwell with one hand, and swung hard to smash the diamond-shaped leaded panes. The windows broke around him, the thin seams of lead bending and fragments of glass showering him and the motionless scribe.

Gabriele had chosen his escape route well; outside the broken window were the poles of his scaffolding. He knelt down to lift the woman and threw her over his shoulder. As he struggled to climb through the jagged opening he found himself thinking, with the same odd crystalline detachment, how bizarre it was to be carrying another person, the second in a few weeks, to either death or recovery. He hoped for the latter as he flung the woman out the window onto the small platform he had built just that morning, and burst gasping into the fresh air after her.

With a final surge of effort, Gabriele managed to climb down, carrying the woman draped over his shoulder; later he could not imagine how. His knees buckled and he folded slowly onto the ground where he rested for a moment to catch his breath. He lay there, seeing the Duomo sideways, stripes flipped to vertical and changing color from green to black to green again as he watched.

A small army of young wards raced out of the Ospedale door carrying buckets, heading for the nearest fountain. Gabriele felt he might lie there forever, as if he were merely enjoying a languorous moment in bed, rather than lying on the ground outside a burning building. The sound of a ragged cough followed by a sharp intake of breath brought him back to the present, and he pushed himself up to a sitting position and looked into the scribe's face.

Gabriele held his breath and stared. He did not think to question why the vision that had haunted his dreams and populated his paintings should be a flesh-and-blood scribe in the Ospedale, now lying before him on the pavement. The woman's cheeks were flushed from the heat of the fire, but not a single hair was singed, nor the fabric of her green dress—somehow she had escaped the flames. And, he thought somewhat irrelevantly, he had guessed right by choosing a green gown for the bystander in his painting of Saint Christopher. Dante's verses rang in his head, and he spoke the name of the poet's muse aloud.

"Beatrice."

_____

Through layers of sleep I heard a voice say my name in that marvelous Italian way, the way Dante might have said it. The sound made me open my eyes, and I found myself lying on the pavement outside the Ospedale, looking into the face of a stranger.

"What am I doing out here?" My throat was raw and painful, and my lungs burned. The man moved back and I was able to focus on his face. His hair curled silver-gray almost to his shoulders, and his eyes were gray too, fringed with long dark lashes, and angled slightly upward at the corners, irises flecked blue-black.

His mystified look made me realize I'd spoken in English.

"*Mea scusi?* May I help you sit up, Signora?"

Switching quickly back to Italian, I responded. "I think I can do it myself." He watched me patiently as I struggled in my twisted gown, managing to get myself upright. I could hear a commotion going on inside the Ospedale. "How did I get here?"

"I found you in the *scriptorium*, my lady, and as it was engulfed in flames, I removed you from the building."

I stared at him. "I'm sorry if I was impolite."

"Not at all, Signora." He inclined his head gently in a graceful gesture. I still wasn't sure how he had known my name. Our interchange was interrupted by a horde of running Ospedale wards carrying buckets of water that splashed onto the paving stones. The yells of "*Fuoco, fuoco!*" drifted out from a shattered upstairs window along with tendrils of smoke.

"I suppose I can't go back to work now," I said blankly. Throngs of people were now rushing out of the open doors of the Ospedale. "But I should go help." My words trailed off into a fit of coughing. I was clearly in no condition to help with anything.

"I would be happy to escort you to your home and family, or to a physician."

"I live *there*. Or at least I used to." I pointed toward the Pellegrinaio delle Donne. I was relieved to see Umiltà on the other side of a crowd of people, giving orders to everyone in sight.

Clara stood beside her, staring upward. I hoped Egidio was still away on his errand.

"I hope you will accept an invitation to the home of my uncle where you can recover in greater safety and comfort. His home is not far, and if you find yourself unable to walk, I can carry you again."

"No thank you, I think I can walk," I said, but when I tried to stand my legs shook. "I need to tell Suor Umiltà where I'm going." Billows of gray smoke wafted toward us, starting me on another spasm of coughing.

The thought of pushing through the crowd back toward the burning building was overwhelming. My rescuer stopped one of the wards heading back out to the fountain with an empty bucket.

"Young man, please tell Suor Umiltà and the master of the *scriptorium* that the scribe is safe, and gone to the baker Martellino Accorsi's home in the Civetta *contrada*. I will return her when she is well and the danger passed." The ward nodded and took off with his bucket.

Accorsi, I thought, *that's interesting*. How common was the name in fourteenth-century Siena? I supposed I should have thought twice before leaving the Ospedale with a stranger, but I didn't. The last thing I saw as I looked back over my shoulder was Fra Bosi standing to one side of the Ospedale entryway with tears coursing down his ample cheeks.

Since my rescue from Stozzi's clutches I had rarely ventured beyond the Piazza del Duomo. I wasn't in the best condition to enjoy my first real excursion, but I couldn't help noticing the hum of Siena's life around us as we walked. Two young boys in parti-colored tunics and hose—half red and half yellow—juggled before a crowd of cheering spectators. They competed with a young peddler calling out her wares—a tray of buttons of different sizes and colors, some glinting metal, some whitish ivory or bone, others the brown of wood or leather. We passed a bookseller's shop crowded with gowned and hatted gentlemen who looked as if they might be university professors. I stopped, thinking of the last visit I'd made to the university—in my old time. Then I realized I knew the route we were walking very well, and I felt my skin prickle. When we passed under a curved archway and stopped in front of a three-story house made from stuccoed stone with an inviting bakery storefront, I knew exactly where I was—standing in front of Ben's house, my house. And, uncannily, it seemed to be my rescuer's home too. I stared at the open door, the door I had once opened with my own key. The front hall was dominated by a huge brick oven. Despite its dislocation in time, this house was a place I knew, and a place I had begun to love. It was the first thing I had found in this century that felt familiar, and it made my knees weak with relief.

A flour-dusted man met us at the door, a broad smile creasing his face. "Gabriele, how unlike you, to pay a visit before nightfall—how did you manage to tear yourself away from your work? Rinaldo has gone to purchase our grain, and Bianca is upstairs sleeping." He caught sight of me and his smile widened. "And who, may I ask, is this delightful guest? Will she be joining us for dinner?" *Gabriele*. I registered his name with a start. The baker, whom I assumed was Gabriele's uncle Martellino, bowed at the waist, producing a small puff of flour from his apron. Before Gabriele could answer, a young woman came out from the back of the shop. She was shorter than Uncle, and trying to see around his width without success.

"Father, *move*, I can't see through you!" The baker moved to the side and she squeezed through the doorway. "Gabriele, aren't you supposed to be painting the Ospedale?" The girl caught sight of me. "Were you planning to introduce your companion? Dinner is not ready yet." When she saw Gabriele her face changed abruptly. "Gabriele—your clothes are stained with ash—what happened?"

As my brain put the pieces together: Gabriele, painter, Ospedale, Accorsi, I felt the hair on my arms rise.

"This good lady is a scribe at the Ospedale, and she was trapped in a fire from which I managed to extract her. May I present my cousin Ysabella, and," he said, nodding toward the baker, "my uncle, Martellino."

Ysabella touched my hand solicitously. "What are you doing keeping this poor woman standing outside in the street? Gabriele, have you no sense?" She turned to me with a much kinder expression. "Come inside and sit; I'll bring you a cup of spiced wine to revive you."

I turned to my rescuer. "Your name is Gabriele?"

"Yes, Gabriele Beltrano Accorsi. It is my great pleasure to serve you. And you, Signora?"

"Beatrice." I said it the Italian way. "Beatrice Alessandra Trovato." Seeing Gabriele in front of me now, as real as my own solid self, unnerved me. I'd created a person in my head, based on the words I'd read. My imaginary Gabriele was pale, effete, and emotionally close to the surface, with no sense of humor. That virtual person had no relationship to the man standing in front of me at all.

The real Gabriele was much taller than I had expected—taller than me and taller than most of the other people I'd encountered in the fourteenth century—and although he was slim, no one would have described him as effete. He moved gracefully, despite his height. Oddly, I couldn't read him at all. His voice was quiet, but the sort of quiet that makes you aware of the power underneath, like an ocean without wind—peaceful, but you know you are no match for it.

Ysabella and Martellino led me to a low bench, inquiring after my health. Ysabella disappeared and returned with a tray of enticing items: a cup of hypocras—wine with spices and honey—a wedge of pale yellow cheese, and slices of fresh bread, still warm from the oven. I devoured it all shamelessly, thanking them between bites. While I ate, I took in the details of the room around me. Where there would someday be a hall table and a lamp that I'd almost knocked over on my first day in modern Siena, now a wooden flour chest—I'd heard Clara call it a *madia*—stood against the wall. A set of neatly organized weights and a scale were displayed in the front of the shop. The wood-burning oven with its arched opening proclaimed the baker's trade, along with the flat long-handled wooden paddles that reminded me of pizza parlors back home. What I'd known as a decorative fireplace had once been the hearth of this medieval kitchen.

A trestle table with benches on either side was set up in the room, ready for a family meal—dinner was the midday meal in this century; supper came at night. Two huge iron pots hung on a chain above a lit fire: one with water heating, the other releasing a meaty scent. A narrow shelf held several jars, a mortar and pestle, a salt box, a set of nested brass cooking bowls, a copper frying pan, and a set of earthenware dishes. A few impressively large utensils hung on pegs from the wall near the fire.

Once I had finished eating, Ysabella stood up and announced I must come upstairs to rest. She had clearly marked me as her project. Gabriele stood up to assist us, but Ysabella waved him away. "I can provide the lady all she needs," she said authoritatively. Gabriele looked at her with warmth, then turned to me. "You are in the best possible hands with our Ysabella. Just be certain to do everything she says."

I followed Ysabella up the steep stairs, reluctant to be separated from the author of the journal I'd pored over in modern Siena. At the top of the stairs, I could still hear Gabriele and his uncle talking in hushed voices below. Ysabella led me into what had been Ben's bedroom, but there were no books and papers piled on the floor, just fresh-smelling rushes over the wooden boards. Being there, but with no sign of Ben's presence, made me miss him acutely. But now, neither he nor anyone else I had known and loved in my old time even existed yet.

Ysabella's next question effectively distracted me. "Would you like to bathe? It will help dispel the smell of smoke from your skin and hair."

"You have a bathtub?" I hadn't had a real bath since my last access to twenty-first-century plumbing.

"We may not be *casati*," she began—I recognized the word that designated the noble classes—"but my father built our own tub. The public baths are better equipped, but I hope you will find our modest version pleasing."

What an idiot I'd been. For weeks I'd been splashing awkwardly with a pitcher and basin of water in my little room, and meanwhile all over the city, and maybe in the very building I lived in, people were luxuriating in big bathtubs. "I'm very grateful for your hospitality."

Ysabella smiled broadly, then yelled down the stairs at the top of her lungs.

"Fazio! Bring hot water, and be quick about it! There is a pot already on the fire." She disappeared out the door and soon returned, dragging a small round tub made of wooden slats, lined with heavy white oiled cloth. I got up to help.

"You must recover your strength." Ysabella pushed me firmly down onto the large curtained bed and took off down the stairs. I sat on the edge of the bed and looked around the room. The one window had no glass in it now; I could see the translucent oiled paper rolled up above the window opening and beyond it a rectangle of sky. After a few minutes Ysabella and a boy with floppy black hair came back carrying the first of several steaming buckets. When the boy had left, I stood to peel off my smoky dress. I unhooked my bra and stepped out of my underwear carefully, feeling wobbly. Ysabella was staring at my bra as if she were a naturalist discovering a new species.

"What manner of garment is *that?*" The most mundane things from my old life could get me into trouble.

"Oh, I made it myself," I said airily but held on to it so she couldn't get a close look. Hooks and eyes were probably medieval enough to avoid suspicion, but not elastic or nylon. Ysabella was gracious enough to leave me to my bath without further questions, and I lowered myself into the hot water, sighing with pleasure. I had to bring my knees against my chest to fit, but that couldn't diminish the exquisite sensation of immersion. I thought of the next letter I'd write to Nathaniel, telling him how offering a bath to guests was a normal thing here.

Ysabella returned as the bath was beginning to cool off. She carried a clean white linen chemise—a more appropriate medieval undergarment than my anachronistic underwear.

"I'll wash your gown with our other laundry," she said, briskly, and I didn't argue. I kept the bra and panties.

Ysabella handed me a gown made of blue-dyed light wool. It was long-sleeved like all the dresses I'd seen here, and laced in back, allowing for a snug fit through the body. I was comforted to see that the new dress had a higher neckline than my old green one. As I dropped the dress over my head I wondered whose it was. It would have been at least a foot too long for Ysabella. The thought that it might have been Paola's—Gabriele's late wife's—chilled me. I thanked Ysabella and she nodded quietly. As I dressed I felt dizzy again, and had to sit down on the wooden chest.

Ysabella motioned to the bed and I gave in to her command. She brought me a cup of milk mixed with honey and ginger, placed a moist cloth smelling of lavender on my forehead, and left the room, making the wooden steps creak.

I had a few sips of the warm milk and lay down. After a while the smell of lavender was replaced by a stronger scent wafting up the stairs. Something with anise maybe, or fennel, onions, chicken. It wasn't long before the soporific effects of the bath and warm drink began to wear off and my thoughts sharpened. *I just met Gabriele Accorsi.* The fourteenth-century journal writer, fresco painter, and rescuer all had to be the same man—and he would soon be eating chicken stew downstairs, in my brother's future house. The whole thing was implausibly coincidental, but not impossible—no more impossible than traveling back in time. I listened for Gabriele's voice from the kitchen but I mostly heard Ysabella. She was a force to be reckoned with, despite her youth, and I could see that the men of the household respected her imperious will.

That last meandering thought put an end to my easy idleness. Here I was, lying in bed with a scented cloth on my head while my colleagues back at the Ospedale were dealing with the after-effects of a devastating fire. I sat up abruptly and headed down the stairs to find Gabriele, Ysabella, and Martellino sitting at the table in the kitchen, eating.

"I must return to the Ospedale." Three heads swiveled toward me.

"You are not well enough," Ysabella exclaimed with outrage. I saw Martellino and Gabriele exchange glances.

"Monna Trovato, I hope you will accept our hospitality and the healing ministrations of my daughter Ysabella; she learned a bit of the womanly art from her mother, who lives now with the angels." Martellino stopped speaking for a moment before he resumed. "Her dress becomes you, Signora."

I put my hand to the smooth fabric of the skirt. It had belonged to his late wife, Ysabella's mother. I wondered how she had died. "Thank you for letting me wear it," I said, "I'm honored."

"Please keep it," Martellino added. "And do stay with us until you regain your strength, at which time we would be happy to accompany you back to your home, or the Ospedale."

I did not correct his assumption that my home and the Ospedale were two different places. I chose my next words carefully. "Ser Martellino, I could not have wished for better care than your family has provided. Your nephew saved my life, and your daughter has returned me to health. I feel hardly deserving of such generosity." I saw Ysabella and her father both smile. *So far so good.* "But I can't justify resting here, while my colleagues and friends deal with the fire and its consequences."

"I will escort you back immediately, if you feel well enough," Gabriele said. Ysabella opened her mouth to protest, but Gabriele put his hand on her arm. "You have done your part in returning our lovely guest to health, good cousin. But regrettably we both must leave your competent hands to return to our work—even more work than before, now that this terrible event has occurred. Thank God it was not worse."

As we headed back out into the street I registered that he'd said *lovely guest*. Of course it might have just been a polite turn of speech. I glanced up at him surreptitiously, but he kept his gaze forward. "Thank you again for your help. I would have died back there if it hadn't been for you."

"I am glad to have been able to protect you from injury, or worse." Gabriele stopped and turned toward me. The crowds of people in the street parted around us like a stream around stones. "Though it appears some force other than my own had your protection in mind. When I arrived at your side, the room was aflame and the air full of smoke. You slept, without a single injury—no burns, no blisters, no poisoning of your breath. You have at least one saint protecting you on your pilgrimage."

"How do you know I'm a pilgrim?"

"A woman who lives alone in the Ospedale, speaks with a peculiar accent, has no nearby family to which she would prefer to turn to when offered help by a stranger, and cannot help staring at everything she sees along the streets? With this ample evidence, I hazarded a guess."

"It's not nice to make fun of immigrants," I said sarcastically. Gabriele responded with a puzzled look and an apologetic bow.

Apparently 650 years make a big difference in social convention and my sarcasm wasn't immediately recognized. Plus, he'd probably never heard the word *immigrant*.

"I only meant that your obvious delight in the wonders of the city around you—a city whose beauties I marvel at daily—gives me great pleasure. Wherever you are from, it certainly gives rise to women with remarkable temper and force of will."

He smiled, and I couldn't help smiling back. "Lucca," I said, reflexively.

"I have never visited Lucca but hope to do so; I hear it is a haven for pilgrims as well?" I nodded again, rather than expose my ignorance.

When we reached the Ospedale the smell of smoke still hung in the air. There were puddles of water on the pavement from the bucket brigade, and the place was teeming with people—pilgrims evacuated from the *pellegrinaio*, robed wards, men and women of the lay orders that staffed the Ospedale. A familiar figure appeared out of the crowd, moving quickly in our direction. Umiltà's robes billowed out behind her, making her look like a small sailboat in a high wind.

"Beatrice—it is truly a miracle to see you here, unharmed. May God be praised for his beneficence. How did you manage to escape the flames? It appears that the *scriptorium*'s hearth was the source of the conflagration—you might have easily perished."

She stared at me as if intense scrutiny might give her the answer. *I need some facts to defend you properly*, she might have said. Her eyes went rapidly to Gabriele, who was standing beside me, then back to me.

"I didn't do a thing with the hearth." I didn't mention that I was totally incapable of managing the fireplace. "I fell asleep while I was working." I inclined my head in Gabriele's direction. "Luckily, Messer Accorsi found me."

"Messer Accorsi, we owe you our gratitude twice: once for turning your hand to the beautification of our facade, and again for rescuing this devoted pilgrim and grieving widow." Gabriele shot me a look after Umiltà said the word *widow*.

"It is my great pleasure, Suor Umiltà, to make your acquaintance at last." Gabriele bowed deeply. "I regret that the circumstances of our meeting are so unfortunate. I know Monna Trovato regretted her inability to stay and give aid to the Ospedale, but I assure you that her condition was such that it could not be allowed."

Umiltà nodded, satisfied, then shifted her gaze to me. "Beatrice, you must rest. I shall have Clara attend you in your chamber. Will a physician be needed?"

"No, Messer Accorsi's cousin has taken very good care of me. Was anyone hurt?"

"Fortunately not. And the fire was found early, thanks to Messer Accorsi. This is not the Ospedale's first fire, though I certainly hope it will be our last. Tonight the servants are cleaning the worst of the mess from the *scriptorium*. Tomorrow, though, we will begin to inventory and repair the damaged books." By "we" I knew she meant "you."

"There is nothing more to do tonight?"

"You would do the Ospedale a better service coming to work well-rested tomorrow than getting in the way of perfectly competent servants doing their job today." There was no point in arguing with Umiltà. Before I left, I said good-bye to Gabriele, who was watching my interchange with Umiltà with a small smile on his face.

"Thank you, Messer Accorsi," I said, "for everything."

"It has been my great pleasure," he returned, bowing at the waist. I turned away and headed reluctantly to the Pellegrinaio delle Donne. As I headed up the stairs to my room, my legs started feeling shaky and I admitted to myself that Umiltà might have been right about my need for rest. I fell asleep with the image of Fra Bosi's tear-stained face in my head.

By the beginning of August the *scriptorium* was functioning again, thanks to the efforts of a team of Ospedale wards, led by Fra Bosi. Several documents were destroyed beyond repair, others were damaged but with the text still legible. Bosi set me the task of recopying pages, and Egidio worked around the clock churning out paper to meet the demand.

The day of the fire took on a strange encapsulated quality for me, as if it were outside the normal order of time. I had vivid flashbacks for days afterward—seeing Gabriele's face haloed by sky as I awoke on the Ospedale pavement, and smelling the lavender rising from the bath Ysabella had drawn for me. I stared out the broken *scriptorium* window periodically as I worked, but Gabriele hadn't returned to his post yet. I felt restless and jittery and had trouble concentrating for more than an hour at a time. Ben's mystery seemed like a story I'd once read a long time ago.

After the fire, Umiltà decided to make me an employee rather than a charity case and proposed a small stipend to supplement my room and board as the first-assistant scribe. Earning money for the first time in the fourteenth century hammered home the fact of my existence here—not just a tourist anymore. I had a funny thought of applying for a time traveler's work visa but had no one to share the joke with. I kept the coins in a pouch I carried at my waist, and every now and then I'd pull the pieces of silver out to look at them. Their strangeness reminded me of how impossibly far from home I was, without any obvious route back.

After a week of working dawn to dusk to repair damaged texts, I had time to think again, and thinking led inevitably to anxiety.

Faced with my knowledge of the future, and my growing doubt that I would be able to leave the fourteenth century before the Plague arrived, I had an overwhelming urge to start planning. But how could I plan anything? No one else knew the Plague was coming, so if I tried to warn people, they wouldn't believe me, or worse, they'd think I was a witch. Neither outcome would help eliminate the Plague and both risked eliminating me. I had no illusions about my power to prevent the most deadly health disaster in history from killing more than half the world's population. Even in an electronically connected modern society with high-speed transportation and stockpiled antibiotics it would have been a massive undertaking.

Maybe there was still something I could do for Siena, using my medical knowledge. Quarantine? I remembered reading about Milan's response to the Plague—the communal government's draconian solution was to barricade sick people into their homes to die. It might have worked—Milan was known to have suffered much less than most of Northern Italy—but it was a barbaric solution I wasn't planning to encourage in Siena. Besides, most Plague wasn't transmitted person to person.

I had five antibiotic tablets at the bottom of the bag I kept in my room; probably not enough to cure myself, let alone anyone else. I had a fleeting thought of leaving bread out to get moldy in the hopes that I'd make penicillin by accident, but discarded it as absurd, in part because of my ignorance on the topic. I wished, not for the first time, that Ben were around; a microbiologist would have been tremendously useful. I heard Egidio outside the *scriptorium* and knew I'd run out of thinking time for the moment.

After the fire, Egidio started acting funny. He blushed painfully whenever we met and refused to meet my gaze. I suspected he was feeling guilty for leaving me unprotected in the *scriptorium*. I cornered him, unable to tolerate the tension.

"Egidio, I'm fine, you know."

"Yes, Monna Trovato." Egidio looked so miserable I wanted to put my arm around his shoulders, but I knew it wasn't appropriate behavior for a medieval woman, even a widow.

"Egidio, it's not your job to take care of me."

"I failed in my duty."

"Your duty is to do what people tell you." It was true, my translation of a medieval servant's job. Egidio still looked grim. I had an idea. "Why don't I teach you how to write a bit, and then you can help me sort through this mess. Will that assuage your guilt?"

"You would do that, Signora?" He beamed like someone who'd just been promised a spot in heaven.

Over the next few days, between stints with burned and waterlogged documents, I worked with Egidio on his writing. He knew more than he'd let on and just needed some tutorials before he was able to copy simple documents neatly. I showed his writing samples to Fra Bosi, who grudgingly authorized Egidio to act as my assistant. Egidio was floating on a cloud for the rest of the week.

Teaching was a pleasant distraction, but I soon found myself getting increasingly irritable. At the end of every page of copying I'd wander around the *scriptorium*, shaking out my sore right hand, and end up at the broken window, looking out at the half-finished scaffolding.

On the morning of August 6th, Bosi was off at a meeting of Ospedale officials to discuss a communal subsidy for postfire recovery, and Egidio had gone to buy more pigments for the rapidly diminishing stores of ink. I was so engrossed in repairing a multivolume set of Dante's works that I barely noticed the banging sound at first. Eventually I stood up to stretch, and realized the sound was coming from outside the broken window.

I approached the jagged opening. Outside, I could see the scaffolding, and behind it blue sky with a few drifting white clouds. My view was abruptly blocked by the silhouette of a head.

"I see you are awake this time, in contrast to our last meeting." Gabriele's voice came through the missing panes of the window.

I smiled. "Falling asleep on the job didn't go well last time. I decided not to repeat it."

"I am pleased another rescue is not necessary, as I have only recently recovered from the first one." He smiled to soften his words.

"Do you want to come in? It might be easier to chat."

Gabriele swung himself to the window ledge and stepped into the room.

"How was your time off?"

"To be quite honest, I found it difficult to think of anything else but returning here. A work in progress always compels me powerfully."

I felt oddly disappointed. "So you came back for the Virgin Mary, then."

"Santa Maria holds a place in all our hearts and souls, but humanity has its charms," he replied, his eyes finding mine.

"I'm honored." I remembered the painting of Saint Christopher I'd seen in the gallery just before I left and felt a faint spin of vertigo. Had he already painted me before we'd even met? "What are you painting?" I forgot for a moment that I knew the answer; Donata had told me, in modern Siena.

"The Assumption of the Virgin—ascending to the kingdom of heaven in the company of angels. I had thought to make an angel in your likeness, if that would not offend you." Gabriele tilted his head slightly to one side. I felt the bloom of heat rush upward from my neck to my face. "If it should seem too forward a request, I shall reconsider. . . ."

"No, no, it's fine. I'm flattered."

"Many thanks, Signora." I snuck a look at him, trying to figure out whether this was his version of flirting, or just the mundane efforts of an artist trying to find a model. I wished, not for the first time, that I could use my empathy at will, in this case to figure out what Gabriele was thinking. But for whatever reason, either my inability or his opacity, my attempt to read him failed. He changed the subject gracefully. "Perhaps we should go back to our respective labors until the midday meal? Then we may feel at greater liberty to speak. I would be delighted if you would join me."

"It's a date."

Gabriele smiled, perhaps at the strangeness of my modern idiom, and disappeared again through the open window.

For the next few hours we worked in tandem, with the Ospedale wall between us. By the time the noon bells rang, I'd managed to get through copying the most damaged section of the *Inferno*. The work was absorbing enough that I'd actually stopped thinking about my upcoming meal plans until a shadow fell over the page I was working on.

"The torments of hell are not a good subject to fuel the appetite." Gabriele's voice made me jump.

The door of the *scriptorium* creaked open on its hinges. Clara stood on the threshold, her hand over her mouth and her eyes round with surprise.

"Ser Accorsi, at your service." Gabriele bowed graciously. "It is my great pleasure to make your acquaintance."

Clara's face flushed pink. "Oh, thank you, Ser, our pleasure is to serve you in whatever way we may. Are you hungry? In need of a cool place to rest? May I bring wine?"

"Monna Trovato and I were about to seek refreshment as a respite from the morning's work."

Clara gazed at me as if I had been crowned the queen of England, or the local equivalent.

"Ser, I would be most pleased to bring your dinner to the *scriptorium*."

"We both thank you for your gracious offer." If we ever got to know each other better, Gabriele would have to stop speaking on my behalf, but I did appreciate his medieval graciousness.

Clara backed out of the room with an eager, if somewhat clumsy, combination of a bow, nod, and curtsy. I could hear her footsteps accelerate once she was outside the door.

"Clara seems to be in awe of you, Ser Accorsi."

Gabriele smiled wryly. "I suspect she has never seen an artist before. I am not a particularly remarkable example of the breed."

"Do all artists rescue women from burning buildings?"

"If presented with the opportunity, I am sure many would."

"That's a generous view of your profession."

"I strive to be generous, as I hope others would be toward me."

"You certainly have been—taking me to your house, giving me clothes, feeding me dinner, taking care of me after that fire."

He shook his head modestly. "Ysabella did the caring and the cooking, and the dress is a result of my uncle's generosity."

"I owe all of you my thanks."

"You have suffered many losses, Monna Trovato, and now live without the protection your husband once provided you. My family and I are happy to be able to provide some modicum of the care that you have lost."

I had lost, but not a husband. My lies weighed on me in the face of that pure generosity. "I haven't told you very much about myself."

"Confidences cannot be hurried."

Once again, I was presented with an opportunity to tell someone the truth, and the desire to do so was overwhelming. I wiped my eyes with the back of my hand. "I don't mean to make a spectacle of myself. I'm sorry."

"Your tears reveal a vulnerability not immediately apparent

in your demeanor," Gabriele said softly. Clara was due to come back soon with dinner, and if I was going to say something, I had to do it fast.

"Listen, there is something I have to tell you. I'm not a widow. I've never been married, in fact. But my mother died as I was born, along with my twin sister. I don't know who my father is. My brother was my only family; he raised me after our mother died, and now he's dead too." This time I started to cry in earnest, the tears rolling down my cheeks. I didn't add that I had been wrenched almost seven centuries out of my own time, though it was certainly adding to my loneliness. I hoped Clara would take her time with the food.

"We share a great deal of sorrow, you and I," Gabriele said, bending his head. "I lost my wife, as you have lost your sister and brother, and I too have neither mother nor father. In our shared grief perhaps we shall find comfort." He ended his sentence with an inflection that was almost a question. His hands remained at his sides, but his voice was like an embrace.

"We could both probably use a little comfort." I already knew about his late wife and his orphanhood, from the journal he had written. I wished I could tell him more of the truth in return for that offer of comfort. He handed me a linen handkerchief that I used as gracefully as possible.

"The deep pleasure of work helps, does it not?" He didn't say much, but what he said had a tendency to be unerringly accurate.

"Yes, it does. Quite a bit."

That was the moment Clara chose to come in with our dinner. She seemed too distracted by Gabriele's presence to notice I'd been crying; in fact, she didn't even look at me. From the tray she'd brought, I saw that Clara must have been extra-inspired by feeding the Visiting Artist. I wondered for whom the elaborate meal had been originally intended, since none of it could have been made without advance notice.

Gabriele received Clara's offering with a grace so exquisite, I thought she might swoon. He even asked her to recite the menu. She rolled off the list of dishes with pride.

"Lasagne, Ser, from *pastam fermentatam*, served with cheese and spices, *limonia* of chicken, and *torta di marzapane*. I hope it pleases you, Ser."

"A beautiful meal, brought by a lovely maid with obvious talents in the kitchen." Gabriele bowed at the waist. Clara left beaming.

My first lasagne in the fourteenth century was outrageously good. *Fermentatam* must have meant "leavened," and the pasta was springy and tender. It didn't bear much resemblance to the modern Italian lasagna. The pasta was cut into individual squares about an inch wide, tossed with freshly grated Parmesan cheese, pepper, and a heavenly combination of cardamom, nutmeg, and cinnamon. It wasn't sweet, but was almost rich enough to be dessert, and we ate it with pointed wooden sticks a bit longer than a regular toothpick. The marzipan tart at the end of our meal reminded me of the now-defunct Elk Candy Shop on the Upper East Side in New York City, where Ben would buy me a marzipan figurine every year at Christmas. I'd try to make it last for weeks, taking a tiny bite each day and wrapping it back up in its shiny decorated foil.

When our plates were empty, Gabriele leaned back to speak. "I suppose you are really a scribe. Is at least that part of the story true?"

"I am a scribe, yes. I'm sorry to have deceived you. It's complicated."

"It does appear to be." He said this wryly but without barbs. "And are you a pilgrim?"

"I *have* traveled very far. Is that enough for the moment?" That was as much as I could say while still telling the truth.

He nodded. "I will not interrogate you further and risk spoiling your digestion."

When the door to the *scriptorium* slammed against the wall I expected Clara, but instead it was an unfamiliar boy in a black-and-white tunic and hose.

"Messer Gabriele Beltrano Accorsi?" The boy was out of breath, as if he'd come running.

"Before you," Gabriele said, turning to face the messenger.

"I have been charged to deliver this summons." The boy handed a rolled-up parchment to Gabriele. It was sealed with red wax and imprinted with an official-looking seal: two young boys nursing from a she-wolf, the symbol of Siena's origins.

"I come from the office of the Podestà, Ser Accorsi," the boy said, squaring his shoulders. His voice cracked slightly from high to low. "Your presence is expected on the third day following the Feast of the Assumption." He bowed, and waited for Gabriele's response.

"Am I to be told the matter for which I am summoned?"

"It is explained in the document you hold in your hands," the messenger said. "At least, I think that is what it says. I didn't write it or read it. I assure you, Ser, it was given to me sealed as you see it." He gazed up at Gabriele again, this time looking more like a boy and less like the official he was trying to be.

"I am certain you have carried out your assignment with the utmost honesty, as befits your role." It amazed me how agreeable Gabriele was at the delivery of such an ominous message.

"I shall go then," the boy said, awkwardly, and turned on one heel, leaving as quickly as he had come in. He forgot to close the door. Gabriele and I stared at the roll of parchment.

"Gabriele, are you in some kind of trouble?"

He frowned as he began to peel off the wax seal.

"I sincerely hope not," he said, but judging from the look on Gabriele's face as he read through the summons, I suspected that trouble was coming.

PART IV

WITNESS

The flurry of activity leading up to the Feast of the Assumption precluded more soul-baring sessions with Gabriele. He withdrew into himself—it was a subtle shift, but I felt the difference sharply. He worked outside the *scriptorium* steadily, but his comments to me were more formal and distant.

I was partially relieved to go back to my guarded self. I'd worried about the consequences of discarding my widow-from-Lucca story, since I wasn't in a position to tell the truth. But I missed the brief access I'd been given to Gabriele's internal world—both the honesty of his suffering, and the comfort he might be able to offer me.

In any case, all of the Ospedale staff, myself included, were occupied with preparations for the Feast, which fell on August 15th. I had been given the task of producing the *libri dei censi*: books recording all the tributes paid to the *commune* during the festival. Most came in the currency of candles; wax was expensive, and even ordinary tapers were costly. Under Fra Bosi's direction, I itemized the number and weight in wax of all the candles that had been promised. The *commune* itself was to present a single candle weighing the equivalent of a hundred pounds on the eve of the Feast of the Assumption. The weight of wax to be used in the tributes was actually written into statutory law. I found that funny at first, but there were probably some twenty-first-century statutes that would look just as funny 650 years after being written.

Umiltà took me aside at the beginning of the week to explain. "We come together on the Eve of the Assumption to pay homage to the Queen of Heaven, the source of Siena's strength and solace. We light thousands of candles to honor her, and in doing so, create a fire *so* bright that the Virgin herself, looking down upon the city from her heavenly throne, will see the brilliance of our tribute and the magnitude of our devotion."

The day before the Feast of the Assumption, Gabriele climbed through the window and walked over to my desk. Today he was wearing a white linen shirt open at the neck for his work in the sun, belted over dark brown leggings. His feet disappeared into shoes that tapered to a long point in the front. I had gotten so used to medieval fashion that seeing men in tights no longer struck me as odd. The outfits of fourteenth-century Italy could look pretty attractive, on the right man. Not everyone looks good in tights.

"Are you well, Monna Trovato? I regret we have not had ample time for conversation recently." He was gracious, as usual, but I could still sense the burden of the unresolved summons weighing down on him.

"My hand is tired after five days of writing down every candle, banner, and coin each magistracy and representative of the *contado* territories owes, but otherwise I'm fine. And you?"

"Well, thank you, particularly so at this moment." He smiled at me, a sincere smile radiating outward. It felt like the sun breaking through clouds.

"What have you been doing out there? You can't still be working on the scaffolding after all this time."

"Indeed. Since you express such interest, I was preparing the wall over the entryway to be plastered."

"What does that entail?"

Gabriele looked at me as if he were assessing how much to describe. I'd seen that look on doctors' faces as they prepared to explain something to a patient. *How much does she really want to know, and how much can she understand?*

"Moisture is the enemy of fresco painting—the force against which we painters gird our works to survive the centuries." I couldn't bear the thought that not a single brushstroke of the painting Gabriele was preparing would last, and it was strange to know this when he didn't. My distress must have shown on my face.

"Your reaction is like a painter's," Gabriele said. "One might think you were no stranger to the brush."

"You describe it vividly, that's all. I'm no artist. How do you prevent it?"

"I prepare the surface of the wall with tar, then build drains and gutters to divert the collection of water. Now I am smoothing the surface to receive the *intonaco.*" He looked at me, waiting for signs of boredom.

I smiled. "Please continue."

"I lay on successive layers of plaster, each more fine than the last. The final layer will be mixed with marble dust, and then the wall will be ready to welcome paint." He said the last sentence as if he were describing a long-delayed romantic meeting.

"Do you know what you're going to paint before you start?"

"I spend many days preparing studies before I approach the unpainted wall, and outline my intended image in red-brown *sinopia*, well before I begin to paint. But I can only plan so much. The full execution eludes me until the moment I lay pigment on wet plaster, feeling the brush move in my hand as if a force other than my own propels it. That is the moment I live for, and that I cannot explain. Perhaps this is more than you were prepared to absorb?" Gabriele smiled wryly.

"Not at all." He was describing something I'd felt in surgery—a moment-to-moment knowledge of what to do that transcended planning. "When will you start painting?"

"After the Feast of the Assumption. Am I correct in assuming that you have never been in Siena for the festival of the Blessed Virgin?"

"You're correct."

"I would like to extend an invitation from my uncle Martellino to join our family in the procession of the Civetta *contrada* to the cathedral today, if you are at liberty."

"Of course I'm free, and I'd love to come." I beamed back at him. "Siena has become a second home for me, and visiting your family made me feel more welcome than anything I could have imagined." I remembered Felice draping the Civetta scarf around my neck and putting her soft hand into mine.

"We will all be deeply honored to welcome you this evening, into our family and our *contrada*," Gabriele said, with that killer bow he'd performed the first day we met. I suppressed the urge to say I had prior Civetta loyalties too.

"Thank you so much for the invitation. Where do I go? What should I bring? What time does the procession start?" Gabriele's smile had broadened with each of my queries, and now he looked like he was about to laugh.

"I must ask that you repeat yourself, as my painter's slow mind cannot possibly keep up with your scribe's agile one. Will you indulge my deficiencies?"

"Where I come from, a lot of people talk fast." I was thinking of New York City, but of course he couldn't know that.

"What a dizzying place Lucca must be."

We stared at each other happily until I realized I was supposed to ask my questions again.

"Sorry, I've forgotten my questions too. I guess scribes are no more agile than painters."

"That is a matter for later discussion. I will come to fetch you at the Nones bells, and you need bring only yourself." He bowed gracefully and stepped through the open window onto the scaffolding. The usual glazier had injured his hand and repairs were delayed; I hoped no one would fix the window anytime soon.

The streets were thronged with celebrants by the time the bells rang at midday, and more kept emerging from doorways, dressed in their festival best. Gabriele wore a brilliant red tunic edged in black and white, and a brimmed cap in the same Civetta colors that stood out against the silver of his hair. The family was waiting outside the bakery. Two people I hadn't met before stood between Ysabella and her father. One was a self-satisfied-looking man whose smirk undermined his otherwise attractive features. His arm draped protectively over the shoulders of a woman whose tiny frame was overwhelmed by her pregnant belly. Gabriele introduced me.

"My good cousin Rinaldo Giacomo Accorsi, and his devoted wife, Bianca, it is my pleasure to introduce Beatrice Alessandra Trovato, the assistant scribe of the Ospedale. She has graciously accepted my invitation to join us today, and we are honored by her presence." Martellino beamed at me and bowed. "It is our great pleasure to have you join us, Signora."

Ysabella also welcomed me warmly, then reported on my missing dress. "I'm afraid your green gown is not laundered yet—our preparations for the festival have left many other more mundane tasks neglected. The blue does become you, though." I tried to tell her that delivering it clean wasn't necessary, but she silenced my protests.

Rinaldo stepped forward, releasing his grip on Bianca's shoulders. "A woman scribe, how refreshing," he said, "and from Lucca, little Ysabella tells me. You must tell us how it feels to be in a city so awe-inspiring, compared to what I am sure is a lovely, though modest place to live." His exaggerated bow seemed more like mockery than a sign of respect. I decided I did not like him.

"We all need refreshment on such a hot day. I'm pleased to provide it." I could see Rinaldo's face working to figure out whether I was making fun of him.

Bianca opened her mouth but Rinaldo cut her off, patting her shoulder. "Bianca welcomes you as well. Her condition sometimes makes her slow to speak."

"It's wonderful to meet you, Bianca," I said, addressing her directly. "How are you feeling?"

"I am well, thank you, Monna Trovato." Her voice was so quiet that I had to strain to hear what she was saying.

"Congratulations. It must be a miraculous thing, to be creating a life inside you."

"I thank God for this gift, but I fear for what is coming. May God grant me and our child safe passage." I saw her dart a glance at Gabriele. Next to me I felt a ripple go through him, but his face was unchanged. Instinctively, I tried to read him further, knowing the tragedy that might be at the source of his reaction. He turned to look at me sharply. Maybe I was imagining it, but it felt like he was warning me not to try that on him again.

"I will pray for you both." Had I really just said that?

"Your prayers are most welcome, thank you," Rinaldo answered, pulling Bianca closer to him. I got the feeling he would have put her in his pocket, if pockets had existed in the 1340s.

I've always been a sucker for a good parade, and today's was the best I'd ever seen. Gabriele was buoyant beside me with the power of the holiday, and for the first time I felt I could understand what it meant to believe that the Virgin Mary had ascended to heaven in the company of angels, and now watched her beloved city from above. *I'm getting to be a little medieval,* I thought. The thought made me inordinately happy.

We were surrounded by musicians playing as we walked; the thready high sound of wooden flutes intertwined with brassy sounds from a horn. Above the music the cathedral bells began to ring, calling us to pay our respects to the Virgin. It felt like a small pilgrimage.

In the Piazza del Duomo, we all congregated under a Civetta banner. Ysabella took my wrist firmly.

"Come have a cup of wine," she commanded, and pulled me to a sea of barrels arrayed in front of the cathedral steps, each one manned by someone dispensing drinks to the celebrants. Full cup in hand, I watched while Siena's principal magistrates entered the cathedral. Next came the representatives of Siena's territories in the *contado*, and then the *casati* families, all bearing candles in tribute. Decorated silk banners fluttered above us, and I could see the glint of thousands of candles through the open door of the Duomo.

"The Virgin must see how much we love her." Ysabella, who generally radiated maturity beyond her years, looked suddenly young, her face full of pure delight. It was all so beautiful I almost forgot that I didn't belong here. That thought led to a more troubling one: What if I could not go back to my own time simply because I did not genuinely wish to, and only the purest longing would bring me back? What if losing Ben had loosened my grip on my own reality, allowing me to slip untethered into another century, with insufficient motivation to carry me home again? If I were stranded here forever, it might be my own fault.

As we were waiting in the line to enter the cathedral, a wave of uneasiness swept over me. Near the Duomo's entrance I saw a tall figure in an elaborate red hat trimmed in fur with a matching cloak. It was a hot outfit for August, but that wasn't what had caught my eye. The man, with his dark hair and aquiline nose, reminded me of the scholar who'd made so much trouble for me back in my old time. Ysabella caught me looking, and followed my gaze.

"That is Ser Signoretti," she said proudly, "one of Siena's most esteemed gentlemen, and a great patron of the arts. He has hired our own Gabriele to paint a fresco in his private chapel—the man clearly has impeccable taste." She smiled and I tried to smile back. So Gabriele worked for Signoretti, or at least the Signoretti household. I looked around to locate Gabriele, but he was several people behind us in line, arm in arm with his uncle. I turned back to Ysabella.

"Do you know him?"

Ysabella smiled indulgently at me, the sort of smile kind people reserve for ignorant visitors. "Ser Signoretti? We all know *of* him. Ser Signoretti's patronage is a great boon to Siena."

"Do you know of any connection between the Signoretti family and the Medicis from Florence?"

Ysabella's smile faded. "Ser Signoretti consorting with the Medicis? You may not have realized, living in Lucca, what animosity exists between Siena and Florence. And especially now—the news is already in the streets of the Medici criminal who killed one of our own night watch." I nodded apologetically, letting her blame my Luccan ignorance for the mistake. But I knew something she didn't. I upended my cup into my mouth without tasting what I was drinking.

✳   ✳   ✳

Giovanni was not released from his cell for the festival but had to watch the throngs of other prisoners emerging from the prison gates into the Campo. Perpetrators suspected of homicide, he'd been told by a guard, were not released on feast days. The room's window and high vantage point on the Campo, a privilege Giovanni had paid for dearly, was now proving to be a source of agony. The jailers did however allow him a visit from Iacopo. The narrow room smelled of sweat and fear. Iacopo sat this time without being asked.

"My case will be tried in three days; there is little time to plan.

"Have you been given any details?"

"Only that the witness will give testimony at the trial. Have you found Accorsi yet?"

"There are many Accorsis in the city. . . ." Iacopo winced, expecting his father to lash out in fury at his failure, but instead Giovanni was silent. "Mother is on her way. I told her your release was unlikely."

"Immacolata has all the failings of her sex and none of the virtues. Her presence will not provide any comfort. Get me a lawyer from Bologna for the trial. The best of the *procuratores* are trained at the university there, and renowned for their defense arguments. Go there yourself, find the man with the best reputation, give him fifty florins with the promise of more if he should aid in my acquittal, and bring him back with you."

"Yes, Father." Iacopo didn't reveal what he was thinking—that the trip to Bologna and back could barely be accomplished in time. Experience with his father had taught him such protestations were useless, if not dangerous. "Would Ser Signoretti testify on your behalf?"

Giovanni looked at Iacopo as if he were a thick-headed schoolchild who could not learn the simplest lessons. "Iacopo—do you seriously imagine that our co-conspirator, who is contemplating rising up against his government with the assistance of an enemy *commune*, would take this moment, when I have been imprisoned by that same government and may possibly be convicted of murder, to reveal his allegiance to me by defending my case?" Iacopo winced, hearing his own foolish thoughts taken to their even more foolish conclusion. "Now is not the time. Later, when the matter of my trial has passed, you should approach him to continue what we have begun. You will have the Brotherhood of San Giovanni behind you in this regard, if I should fail in my attempts to defend my innocence." Iacopo knew of his father's meetings with the Brotherhood, dedicated, or so he had thought, to charitable works. Giovanni had not seen fit to involve him before.

Giovanni sighed. His brief flash of anger had subsided, and he looked weary. "Iacopo, I do not expect to leave Siena alive." Iacopo swallowed with effort, tasting bile. "Since your last visit, the guards allowed me no others until today, and the solitude eats at my soul. I try to pray but find my mind racing with unwelcome thoughts. It surprises me to say this, but I have faith that you will carry our name forward and serve Florence." Iacopo held his breath, afraid to break the spell of his father's words.

"You were named Iacopo—*the rival, the one who comes after*. Now you must grow into that name—as my successor, as Siena's enemy, and as the destroyer of the man who has brought me to this ignominious end. You must take up my cause where I have been forced to leave it. I regret that you were born with neither brilliance nor physical strength, neither beauty nor the gift of eloquence. You have not inspired passion in women, nor trust from my clients, and I have doubted your abilities on many occasions."

Iacopo flinched with each cool statement of his deficiencies but made every effort to keep his gaze steady. In contrast to the harsh words, Giovanni extended his broad hand toward his son, a gesture so powerfully seductive and unfamiliar that Iacopo could not resist. He put his hand into his father's for the first time he could remember since he had played with wooden wheeled toys in the palazzo courtyard.

"Now, my son, I entrust this task to you because I know that despite your failings you have the will to succeed, and this will fuel your efforts. You are the bearer of our family name, and I charge you to carry that name into the future, should I be forced to leave this world before my appointed time. Swear to me now: you will dedicate yourself to the cause, and may God give you strength when I am gone."

"I accept this charge, Father."

"Very well, then, Iacopo. You must meet with the Brotherhood, and tell them that I have placed you in my confidence. Here in

Siena there are still powerful men whose discontent with their own government can be turned toward sedition, with Florentine backing behind them. The weakened Sienese regime will be easy picking for Florence when that work is done." Giovanni motioned for Iacopo to come near, so near that he could feel his father's breath upon his cheek.

"If I am hanged for homicide, see to it that you avenge my death, bring this Accorsi to justice, and drive Siena to her knees. I will be beside you, even from the grave, my voice in your ear to urge you on. You will not stop until you have achieved these aims, or die in the attempt. I will go to my death knowing you walk my path after I am gone, and take comfort in that as they put the noose around my neck."

"I swear it, my father, and let God be my witness."

Giovanni's embrace came as a surprise. At first, Iacopo stiffened, but then he threw his arms about Giovanni's back and felt the beating of his father's heart.

*　　*　　*

On the day after the festival Umiltà knocked on the door of my chamber. She found me sitting on the chest next to my bed, strapping on my sandals. I would have to find other footwear if I didn't manage to get back to my world before the end of summer.

"Monna Trovato, you have been with us for over a month, and you have proven yourself as a trustworthy and skilled scribe. Fra Bosi speaks well of you, and that is no minor miracle, as he almost never praises his assistants. God in all his wisdom has seen fit to provide us with your industry and dedication, and to provide you with all that you sought: balm to your soul, a source of livelihood, a safe home, and a trade to keep your hands at work." I had the feeling I was being buttered up for some particular purpose. "We have also had the good fortune to welcome into our midst a painter of extraordinary dedication and talent, who, inspired by his love and devotion to the Blessed Virgin, has been granted a commission to paint the Assumption on this great institution's facade." Of course she knew that I'd been there at her request for funds toward that painter's commission, and had written his contract myself.

She took a deep breath. "Messer Accorsi has been called by our Podestà to speak as a witness in a criminal trial two days hence." That thunderbolt brought me abruptly to attention. "The court's own scribe has taken ill. The Podestà has asked that the Ospedale provide a scribe in his place, and Fra Bosi and I have determined that you should be that replacement." This must have been the summons Gabriele had received.

"I would be honored to provide any help I can."

"Fra Bosi will explain your task at greater length tomorrow to prepare you for your role. I assume you have no prior experience in the courts?"

I assured her that my past did not include any brushes with the criminal justice system other than the time she'd rescued me from the grasp of Stozzi, the sumptuary officer who'd challenged my inappropriate neckline. She nodded to signal the discussion had come to an end, and exited my room with a dramatic sweep of her robes.

*   *   *

On the road to Siena, Immacolata considered the prospect of her husband's death. She was surprised to discover that she felt neither grief nor fear. Instead, her mind slid sideways to other matters—the discomfort of the journey, the flies buzzing about her horse's head, and the appearance of the guard who rode in front of her, wide buttocks and thighs spread across the leather, the flesh shaking like aspic under his leggings. Such mundane thoughts in the face of Giovanni's upcoming trial were reprehensible, but her mind continued to produce them with uncanny perversity.

The two guards behind her talked quietly. Every now and then she could identify a word, usually something off-color. She did not care to comment on their deportment. They were armed and would keep her safe; that was sufficient.

She had leaned into the tasks left behind in Giovanni's absence, finding a rhythmic satisfaction in accounts she managed when he was away. That was the pleasure men spoke of when they disappeared into their work, compelled as if by a secret mistress. As the horses plodded, Immacolata watched the scenery along the road: dense woods with an occasional inn or small town.

Since the arrival of Iacopo's last letter, she had felt detached, as if looking down at herself from a height.

> *Father is still in prison in Siena, and it is said they will hang him. Do you know of an Accorsi in Siena? He may have been an informant, I am looking for him. I will stay in Siena until the trial. Come if you must.*
>
> *On this 5th day before the Feast of the Assumption*
> *Your son, Iacopo de' Medici*

The summary of Iacopo's plan chilled her. *He is planning something, something that reeks of violence*, she thought. A dutiful son should surely avenge his father's death. *But what if Iacopo plans to follow in his father's bloody footsteps, weighting his eternal soul with the evil of murder? I know not what he plots—but even if I did, how could I hope to stop him?*

*   *   *

The courtroom was packed with spectators but eerily silent as Giovanni de' Medici was led, arms manacled behind his back, into the Sala della Pace. From my scribe's seat next to the judge, I watched until he was close enough for me to see the haze of stubble on his unshaven chin, the taut sinews of his neck, the beading of moisture along his brow. When the court official began to speak, I forced myself to look away, dipped my pen in ink, and began to write.

Record of the Trial of Giovanni de' Medici
Commune di Siena

Kalendae Augustus 1347

Giovanni de' Medici, from Florence but traveling for business in Siena, knowingly mortally wounded with a knife a night watchman of Siena, Cristoforo Buonaventura, in the belly. The encounter was witnessed by a citizen of Siena, Gabriele Beltrano Accorsi, who attempted to save the life of Cristoforo without success, and subsequently informed the Podestà of what he had seen and heard. Messer de' Medici was brought before the Podestà, a good man of great prowess and fairness. There being but one witness to the crime, special consideration was made. As the deed was committed late into the night and in secrecy, only one witness was required to testify to the truth of the events that transpired, Ne crimina remaneant impunita—lest the crimes go unpunished. The defendant called upon one procurator, Messer Nicolai di Coppo of Bologna, to represent his case. Objection was raised to holding the suspect in prison for more than one week. Messer di Coppo then denied the existence of adequate incriminating evidence, but this was dismissed by the court. Finally argument was made that the defendant acted in self-defense. Consilia were requested by the Podestà, the most Honorable Guerra Sambonifacio, to establish, through the writings of the most respected jurists, whether it truly met the definition of homicide by legal statute.

After a prolonged discussion, the nature of the evidence proved to be sufficient to establish the crime as homicide with malicious intent, perpetrated by Giovanni de' Medici. The act of violence was deemed most grave not only because of its mortal consequences, but also the nature of the victim, who was acting in his rightful role to protect the Sienese citizens.

On this day, Messer Giovanni de' Medici was thus condemned to death by hanging at the hands of the Podestà and jurists acting on the Podestà's behalf.

Signed by my hand and no other,
Beatrice Alessandra Trovato

August 21, 1347

On the morning of the execution Bartolomeo knelt on the hard floor of his chamber. He wished that this day had not arrived, wished that he had not been assigned to accompany the Florentine to his death on the scaffold. His prayers buzzed in his head like a swarm of hornets, insistent and ominous.

Dear God of Mercy and Redemption, let me do your will in leading this prisoner to his end
Help me guide him to a good and penitent death
Give my feet strength as I walk the path of the condemned
Let my prayers guide the soul from his tortured body.

He paused to make a more personal appeal, hoping the Virgin might be more amenable to the private worries of a young priest lacking confidence:

Please, Holiest Virgin, when it comes time for me to speak, do not let my voice falter.

Bartolomeo closed his eyes, allowing the figure of the Virgin to blossom in his vision. He often imagined her as Duccio's *Maestà*, mysterious and magnificent. Bartolomeo had looked upon that painting so many times that he was able to call up every detail from memory, and the image often calmed him. But today the face of the Queen of Heaven blurred and he could not make out her features, and the more he struggled, the less clear her face became. As Bartolomeo donned his robes he could not tell what unnerved him more: the task before him or the way in which the Virgin eluded him on this day. He hoped it did not presage disaster.

I could have stayed away from Giovanni de' Medici's execution. But the hours I'd spent in the courtroom bound me inextricably to the fate of the criminal whose condemnation I had recorded. I had seen many people die horrible deaths in the twenty-first century— from gunshots to the head, massive cerebral hemorrhages—but I had never seen a scheduled, state-sanctioned, heavily attended execution.

I kept hearing Gabriele's testimony in my head. His lack of visible distress was so familiar to me that I'd found it almost as poignant as outright emotion. Our eyes met as he'd left the Sala, and I saw the gravity in his face, the knowledge of what might happen as a result of the evidence he had provided. On the evening before the execution, Clara came to my room with a cup of wine and a bowl of soup. I motioned her to join me, not wanting to be left alone with my thoughts.

"Do you want some of this food? I'm not hungry tonight." Clara's face fell. "I'm just anxious about tomorrow." I didn't want to say I'd never seen a hanging.

"You have seen the Florentine? I have heard he is the size of a lion with a mane of golden hair and a savage temper. They say Ser Medici bit a prison guard on the arm, and the wound festered so that the guard nearly died." Clara told the tale with alternating breathless horror and relish.

I had seen him, of course. His features were burned in my brain, eyes seething with barely suppressed rage. His elegant clothes and fine grooming proclaimed his nobility—but he had the soul of a murderer. "I've seen quite a lot of him. I can't imagine him biting anyone, but you never know." Clara took the information in, satisfied. I suspected she'd repeat it as soon as she left me. "I assume you've seen hangings before?"

"This is only the second hanging of the year. The last was also for homicide," she said, matter-of-factly. "It might bring a large crowd."

"Do you wish you hadn't seen it?"

"It is a terrible sight, surely," Clara said, furrowing her smooth forehead. "After my first, I had nightmares for weeks. Umiltà had to give me a sleeping draught."

"Why did you watch?"

"Executions are *communal* justice made visible," she said seriously, "and citizens learn best from what they see."

I wondered whether she was reciting something she'd been taught. "Then it doesn't bother you to see your government kill someone?"

"The Podestà, his police, and i Noveschi keep us safe," she said simply, and I saw there was no contradiction in her mind between the government's acts of violence and its peaceful purpose. "Umiltà says the wards must watch the executions, as an example of what befalls those who fail to resist the temptations of the devil. Citizens must see the consequences of crime, so men contemplating evil deeds will instead seek the wisdom of God."

I'd heard these arguments in my old time, though not always with a religious bent. I wasn't sure whether I found Clara's reiteration comforting or disturbing.

"Besides," she added cheerfully, "he's a foreigner."

The following morning I woke to the sounds of a crowd congregating outside. I dressed and went to the Ospedale entrance. Three horsemen wearing the black and white of the *commune* rode into the crowd. Their brass horns blared a harsh fanfare, and the middle trumpeter stood in his saddle to proclaim the news.

"Giovanni de' Medici of Florence has been convicted of homicide by the Podestà's court. His sentence: execution by hanging!" The mood in the crowd was dangerous. Groups of adolescent and younger boys held rocks in their hands, looking ready for a fight. A chant rose up from one side of the piazza: "Death to the Florentine!" Soon it had spread through the mob.

The high bells of the *torre* began to ring. The crowd parted and I saw the somber procession: three priests walking beside a horse-drawn dung cart. Giovanni de' Medici rode inside, hands bound behind him in the grip of a grim-looking guard with a sword at his belt. Giovanni looked straight ahead, swaying with the cart's irregular movement over the stones.

One boy threw a stone that glanced harmlessly off the cart's side. A rain of stones followed the first, one striking Giovanni in the forehead and drawing blood that dripped down to the bridge of his nose. He did not flinch or speak. I recognized the tongue-tied priest from the cathedral, chanting prayers as he walked alongside the cart.

The procession swelled as we headed downhill. "*Penitenza, penitenza, penitenza,*" the onlookers chanted: penitence. But the crowd was demanding something from Giovanni that he refused to deliver. He remained as silent as the guard beside him.

"He will not repent his acts of evil, even as he approaches death," a woman muttered next to me. "He deserves to have his neck stretched, and be thrown to the torments of hell for all eternity." She spat into the gutter.

We passed out of the walled city through the Porta Giustizia. The crowd slowed, and I saw the scaffold rising starkly above us, a gangly monster waiting for its meal. Giovanni was led out to stand before the mass of onlookers while a hollow-cheeked man with a scarred face dropped the noose over Giovanni's neck. The little priest, his hands trembling, pulled a crucifix out from the folds of his robe and held it before the prisoner's face.

"Look upon the cross, that you may die in God's sight." The priest's voice trailed off with a final squeak, but he'd gotten the words out. I heard a collective gasp from the crowd as Giovanni turned his head away from the cross before him.

"Have you not one word to commend yourself to God?"

Giovanni smiled a strange, cruel smile. "Siena will rot for her role in my death."

The executioner kicked the block from under Giovanni's feet in one swift move, and the noose jerked sickeningly with its new weight. The little priest fell to the ground as the crowd pressed forward with a roar.

I now knew why I hadn't found records of an executed Medici when I'd searched before. It was because I hadn't written them yet.

The guards did not cut Giovanni's body down after the hanging but let it dangle, twisting on its rope. "As an example to the enemies of Siena, and those who defy the will of God," a guard proclaimed, to cheers from the crowd. Iacopo watched in horror, crouching behind a thorny bush. He remained there for hours, until a flock of crows came for his father's open eyes. Overcome by sudden fatigue, he closed his eyes against the sight and slept. He awoke to the sound of young boys playing. For a moment he imagined he was sitting in the courtyard of his family palazzo while his little cousins laughed and threw a leather ball around the central fountain.

Iacopo stood cautiously and saw a group of boys scaling the gibbet to cut off fingers from his father's corpse, joint by joint. They gathered, laughing, beneath the hanging body and began to play a gruesome game of dice with the hacked digits. Iacopo vomited into the bushes. He could barely stand for the trembling of his limbs but managed to stagger away from the scaffold, back uphill toward the city gates. He avoided the road, afraid of being seen, but the boys, too absorbed in their game, took no notice of him.

The guards at the *porta* eyed him suspiciously. His clothes were rumpled and reeking, and his hair full of twigs. When the men waved him along he exhaled with silent relief. Iacopo returned to the inn where he'd spent the past week. He'd wisely thought to give a false name there, as the Medici name was being cursed throughout the city. His arrival was met with disgust by the innkeeper Semenzato, who barred the door with his wide body.

"I'll have no drunken brawls in my establishment, I warn you, no matter what you pay for the privilege."

"I became ill upon the road today, and collapsed into a roadside ditch. I trust your hospitality will be as good as it has been these past six days."

"Any word of trouble and you'll be out on your backside, ill or not," Semenzato said with threat in his voice.

Iacopo swallowed the insults he had in mind; the innkeeper's officiousness must be tolerated if he were to find rest. The tavern patrons backed away from him as he passed through the room to the stairs.

In his chamber the despair and horror of the day tore through Iacopo afresh. He lay upon the floor, weeping but without the damp solace of tears.

Hours later, Iacopo woke to a persistent knocking on the door of his chamber. He rose before he called out leave to enter. The black-haired chambermaid stared at him without speaking.

"Have you not seen a man recovering from illness before? Bring me fresh water and a cloth."

"I am here to deliver a message, Ser."

"Well, then, speak."

"Only that your mother seeks you, Ser. She is waiting outside. But she called you Medici. Have you two surnames? I knew it was you by her description."

My mother. "Water first, before I receive my guest," Iacopo said, leaving the maid's dangerous questions unanswered. The girl left the room without another word, returning silently with water and then leaving again. Iacopo managed to wash his face and dress himself in clean clothes before his mother arrived.

Iacopo felt strange looking at her, his sight unnaturally vivid and bright. The fur edging of Immacolata's hood shone white against its dark red wool. Iacopo stared into his mother's face in a way he could not remember doing since he'd become a man. Her eyes were brown and large, with thick dark lashes, and her hair had been braided and coiled beside her ears, entwined with a ribbon of dark red. *She must have been very beautiful once, in the bloom of her youth.* But his words came out harsher than his thoughts, words his father might have said.

"You are too late." Iacopo saw his mother flinch and felt his stomach curl in a mirror of her distress.

"Your father is dead?"

"The crows have come for him, I saw them myself."

"And did he repent before his death?"

"He damned Siena with his last breath."

Immacolata's hands flew to her heart. "Iacopo, I fear for your safety here, now that Siena's citizens may be inflamed to violence. Come back with me to Firenze where our name is celebrated rather than scorned. I have lost my husband, and would not lose my only child."

Iacopo shook his head. "I am no longer the boy I used to be. My father has instructed me to assume his business dealings here, as befits my inheritance. I will fulfill that trust." He sounded as if he were trying to convince even himself.

"Of course, Iacopo." She made an effort not to call him little Iacopo, though at that moment he looked smaller to her than ever. Perhaps now he might grow into his father's power—though, God willing, leaving a measure of his father's cruelty behind. At that moment, the image of crows attacking Giovanni's golden head came into her mind unbidden.

"What was he like in his last days, Iacopo? Did he despair? Did he send a message to those he left behind?"

Iacopo listened to his mother's appeal, and a longing to comfort her rose up in him, like flames coaxed from a fire banked for the night. He could still hear Giovanni's words in his head, and feel the power of his father's arms about him. That power was his now.

"He spoke of his family." Iacopo focused his gaze on the hem of his mother's gown. The cloth was embroidered with an intricate border of leaves and flowers, but caked with dirt from the road. "He charged me to uphold the Medici name after he was gone."

The hem of the dress undulated with Immacolata's movement. "He called you his son, in those last hours of his life?"

"Why would he not?"

"Of course; you are his son. It seems Giovanni learned grace and mercy before he left this world, thanks to the Eternal God we all serve."

Iacopo embraced his mother, breathing in the musky scent she wore, as familiar to him as his own skin. Immacolata departed that afternoon for Firenze, leaving her son to the Medici business in Siena, whatever that might be.

After his mother had left, Iacopo donned a clean robe and round black biretta, and descended the creaking stairs to the great room of the tavern. He had no appetite, but thirst propelled him to seek a pitcher of wine. Iacopo ordered and sat, awaiting his drink. He scanned the room, though he did not expect to find anyone he would wish to speak with. He had made no acquaintances in his week here, but the tasks his father had set him would require some human interaction. His head ached dully and his mouth tasted bitter.

The wine was dark red with a faint scent of blackberries. As he sipped he noticed a group of men against the rear wall of the tavern, heads bent together over the clicking of dice. Iacopo had played a few times in his adolescent years, until his father found him at the game. Iacopo still recalled the sound of Giovanni's voice in his ear:

"What amusements are you pursuing to spend my good money, Iacopo?"

"I thought you were at work, Father."

"I see. So when I am at work, you feel free to go to the devil, taking my soldi with you?" Giovanni had beaten him so fiercely that day that he could barely stand, nor ride, for a week. It was then that his headaches had begun. He had not gambled since.

My father is dead and there is no one to stop me from joining the game now, he thought numbly. He rose and went to the gaming table. One player had a doughy face like an uncooked loaf, and greasy black curls tucked under a felt hat adorned with a bedraggled feather.

"Well, look at the fine gentleman come to watch our game. Friends, is he not pretty in his cap and robes? Perhaps he has some money to lose." When the man smiled, Iacopo could see the gaps of missing teeth behind his fleshy lips.

"May I join you, gentlemen?" Iacopo returned the title, though nothing would have convinced him that these men merited it.

"You can if you're willing to lose." The pale man pulled out an empty stool.

The next speaker was as unpleasantly thin as his companion was heavy with flesh, and spittle flew from his mouth when he spoke. "P'raps we should have a round of introductions. I like to know the names of the people I'm about to beat."

"Matteo di Giunta. I am a wine merchant from Milan, in Siena for trade," Iacopo said. Wine seemed a common enough business to arouse no particular interest. Milan too would not be questioned, known for its superior vintages.

"Guido Baldi," the pale man said, "a great lover of wine." He laughed and slapped his protuberant stomach, making the flesh wobble. He turned to his companion. "And this here is my good friend Fanti. He's too thin for more than one name." The dice players burst into appreciative laughter.

When the guffaws died down, Baldi spoke again. "Your turn then, but let us see your money first."

Iacopo played several rounds, making sure he lost enough to keep the men from changing their mind about his presence at the table. After a particularly bad loss, he feigned distress and slapped his legs appreciatively. "I've met my match among you fellows."

Fanti grinned broadly, but Baldi was a harder man to amuse. "Are you done with us?"

"In fact, I wondered whether you might be of some help. I am searching for a man who's cheated me of a good profit, and if any of you might be able to direct me to him, there will be some money in it."

Baldi grabbed Iacopo's shoulder with his meaty hand. "What's your man's name? Perhaps I can assist you."

"Gabriele Accorsi. Do you know where I might find him?"

Baldi's eyes narrowed into fatty slits. "We should speak in private. I rented my chamber for a woman, but now that she's gone there are two free chairs. It smells of a good rutting, but it faces the courtyard and it's quiet-like."

Iacopo rose and followed Baldi. His source might not be gentlemanly, but he appeared to know something and to want to impart it. The sound of dice rolling did not resume immediately, and he could feel the curious eyes of Baldi's companions fixed on his back.

PART V

THE FOURTH ANGEL

The morning after the execution I got to the *scriptorium* late. Fra Bosi gave me a sideways look, but no reprimand. Someone had repaired the broken window of the *scriptorium*; no more spontaneous visits from Gabriele to look forward to. I had a few remaining *libri* documenting the tributes of the Feast of the Assumption to complete, but every time I picked up a pen, an image from the trial flashed into my head—Giovanni de' Medici, his jaw clamped shut and the cords in his neck prominent above the collar of his robes, watching Gabriele give his damning testimony. A man like Giovanni de' Medici could cause trouble, even after death. I felt the gathering danger, like dark clouds massing before a storm.

My memories of the trial were troubling, but the flashbacks of the execution were worse. I kept seeing Giovanni's legs scrabbling for a foothold as his perch was yanked away, and the slow discoloration of his face. I was sure it would feed my nightmares for months.

I put the final flourishes on the *libri* and put down my pen. I sat still at the desk, thinking. I thought of Nathaniel welcoming me with a recently acquired Henry James first edition and an invitation to afternoon tea. I thought of the coffee date I'd had with Donata, the easy rhythm of our conversation. She must have wondered why I'd left without so much as a good-bye.

I had found pleasure here—my work, new friends and colleagues, and also something intangible, a surprisingly pleasurable medieval-ness. And, of course, I'd found Gabriele. The slow-growing pleasure of that friendship had an undeniable pull. But enough of a pull to compete with my old life? And even if it did, along with pleasures of this new time came the looming Plague and the terrible feeling of powerlessness I felt in the face of the impending devastation, and now the hanged Medici murderer whom Gabriele had testified against, and who might have dangerous friends. I had to get back. But how?

I cleaned my pens and neatened the stack of parchment on the desk. Was there something I'd missed, some key element that might reverse my trip through time? I'd gone back to the Duomo; that hadn't helped. I retraced my steps, mentally. I'd been reading Gabriele's journal when I left—that seemed promising as a bridge to the past, but I could not imagine demanding he show me his private writings. In any case, the journal seemed like a one-way bridge, if it was a bridge at all—the past had come to life for me through his writing, but the present wouldn't. What else? I'd been in the Museo. The Museo . . . where I'd seen Gabriele's painting of Saint Christopher. The memory made the hair on my arms rise. Was it something about the painting, and seeing myself in it, a painting linking our two times? Where could I find another painting by Gabriele with me in it? The idea hit me like a jolt of electricity: right outside the Ospedale. Buzzing with my new plan, I made my way to the entrance. It was time for another art history lesson.

Outside, Gabriele was perched on his platform with a brush in his hand. He had completed the likeness of the Virgin Mary rising to her heavenly reward, and there was a lightness in her body that suggested a pull from a celestial source. But this heavenly grace combined with surprising—for a medieval painting—human emotion. She looked apprehensive, afraid to leave her earthbound existence, but drawn to what awaited her. Gabriele was working on the angels now. They surrounded Mary protectively, wings aloft and shining with gold. Three of the angels' faces were completed and Gabriele was painting the fourth. For the first few minutes his body blocked the image he was working on. When he lowered his brush arm and I saw what he'd painted my heart skipped a beat—I felt the pause, the silence, then a little late, the next beat, blood moving again. I saw the fourth angel's black straight hair, gray-blue eyes, and long-fingered hands. She looked just the way a medieval angel should look, and would have been at home in any fourteenth-century fresco. But anyone who knew me would realize who her model was. I felt the heat rise into my face and the urgency I'd felt in the *scriptorium* faded as I stood there, watching. The idea that the painting might transport me forward in time seemed silly now that I stood in front of it. And not entirely desirable.

Gabriele lifted his brush from the plaster and tilted his head to look down at me, raising his voice loud enough to be heard from above. "Have you been waiting long? I regret my absorption prevented me from noticing you earlier."

"I just got here," I called back, craning my neck to look up at him. "Do I really look like that?"

I heard Gabriele's laugh above me. "You ask the most extraordinary questions. Let us say that you provide inspiration. Will that suffice?"

"For the moment."

"Signora, I would greatly enjoy talking with you at length, but the drying plaster calls to me, and the hot sun demands a rapid pace."

"I should get back to the *scriptorium*," I said, disappointed.

"If you are not excessively busy, I would welcome your company on the scaffolding."

It was an unusually light workday. "How do I get up?" I heard another laugh from above. Gabriele put down his brush and rapidly descended from the platform, landing next to me. Up close, I could see the fine beads of sweat glistening on his tanned face, and the linen of his shirt clung damply to the muscles of his arms.

"I will guide you," he said, "but watch your step. I would hate to lose you to a scaffolding accident so early in our acquaintance, with only a half-painted angel to recall you by."

"I just escaped my first brush with death, thanks to you. I'd rather not risk a second," I said.

Gabriele held out his hand to help me climb, and I managed to scramble up after him despite the interference of my skirts. I settled myself on the platform, trying not to look over the edge. Gabriele turned back to the wall to continue his work.

I sat listening to the muted sounds from below carried up to our perch on the faint breeze. Once, the cathedral bells rang, marking the passage of time, but I was lost in the painting unfolding in front of my eyes—the faint flush on the fourth angel's cheeks, the gentle curve of her neck disappearing into a blue gown, the gesture of her hands guiding the Virgin upward. Gabriele's left hand moved across the plaster as he painted, feeling for the readiness of the *intonaco* to receive the touch of his brush. He painted with a languorous grace despite the imperative to finish the section before sunset. It reminded me of the hushed, deliberate rhythm of surgery. But he was creating beings from paint, or from some mysterious combination of pigment and what resided in his heart and soul. I'd fixed people; I hadn't made them from scratch.

Gabriele stopped and put down his tools. "I must descend for a brief respite. My spirit is satisfied with painting all day, but my body requires attention."

"Sometimes I think it's too bad there's a body at all," I said, wistfully. "Its needs get in the way."

"But the pleasures and possibilities of that limited body keep us marvelously—if painfully—human. Do they not?" He said this so quietly I wondered whether he really wanted me to hear.

Guido Baldi watched Accorsi and that woman scribe descend from the scaffold and disappear into the Ospedale entrance. The painter was with the whore who'd usurped his position in the *scriptorium*. The wine merchant's gold had given him incentive to return to the Ospedale; wine, dice, and flesh required a substantial budget.

How sad it would be if the painter were to fall from his high platform. Scaffolding could be quite unstable—he'd heard of accidents befalling artists often. So very, very sad. Baldi wondered if the scribe would return with Accorsi after their rest. He hoped so. Even if the wine merchant was only interested in one victim, Baldi himself thought it was a tidy way to solve two problems at once. He looked again at the structure rising in front of him. *Nice angels,* he thought, *too bad they won't be finished*. He squinted at one angel, thinking her face looked familiar, but perhaps he'd had a bit too much wine at lunch.

Iacopo de' Medici did not trust his new hire. Why should he—any man so easily convinced to kill could not be trustworthy. It had been easier than he imagined to explain what he wanted done, and to hand over the soldi to Baldi to see that the job was completed. But his father had told him—"You must supervise the work of those you call into service, or they will take advantage of your absence." Some part of him cringed from watching this endpoint of his plan, but he forced himself, finding a spot where he could lean against a building's wall with a full view of the scaffolding, and those who climbed it.

My father would watch with pleasure, Iacopo thought, and though he knew he should respect his father, even in death, the thought made his stomach turn. *I will watch, to be sure it is done, and done well. But I will not enjoy seeing my enemy fall to his death.* And he stood, out of sight, his eyes reluctantly fixed on the scene.

After climbing down from the scaffolding, I headed to the Ospedale kitchens, where a wedge of creamy yellow cheese and a handful of tiny purple plums made a delicious lunch. I peeked into the empty *scriptorium* and decided a few more hours off wouldn't hurt. Outside, Gabriele had already climbed the platform and was working on the angel's hair, somehow making black look like it harbored a thousand other colors in its depths.

I stared up at the scaffolding, watching the clouds drift behind it. The movement made it look like the scaffolding was moving too. I shook my head to dispel the illusion, feeling dizzy. Even looking down, the feeling persisted, as if the ground were tilting under my feet.

A high whine began in my ears, and the aftertaste of the plums intensified in my mouth. When the familiar dampening of sound came, I finally recognized the episode for what it was. I slowed my breathing and forced my eyes into focus. Ordinary strangers were milling about the piazza, doing their business. But when I looked back at the scaffolding, I had a vision of Gabriele falling, limbs outstretched, down past the wooden beams toward the paving stones below. Along with the vision came a rush of satisfaction, the satisfaction someone else would have watching him plunge to his death. But Gabriele was still up there, painting as if the world didn't exist. The wind had died down, but the scaffolding was swaying. I called up to him.

"Are you all right up there?" He was deep in his work and didn't hear. "Messer Accorsi!" He dropped what he was holding— I heard a clatter as his tools fell—and he spun around to look down at me. It felt strange calling him Accorsi when he was Gabriele in my head.

"Is something amiss?"

"Come down."

I saw him hesitate. Most people would have at least asked why, but Gabriele nodded and began to pack up his equipment. The whine in my ears grew louder until I could hardly hear anything else. "Please hurry!"

He left his tools behind and abruptly started his descent. He'd only made it halfway before the platform above him began to tilt. Then I heard the real crack of splintering wood as the joints of the scaffold gave way, and after that everything happened in terrible slow motion. Gabriele gripped one of the wooden supports with one arm, swinging wide of the massive planks as he fell, as the structure he'd so carefully assembled fell apart like a huge, out-of-control game of pick-up sticks. He hit the ground with an audible thud, and the boards of the platform crashed to the ground a few feet from his head.

I found myself standing next to Gabriele, who lay on his back on the pavement. His eyes were closed, and I wasn't sure whether he was breathing. His face was pale. *Look before you act*—years of training had taught me that. The position of Gabriele's head was natural. Good. I watched for a breath. One, two seconds, three. *Come on, breathe.* There: his chest rose and fell once. *A for airway, B for breathing. Circulation next.* I reached out carefully to feel for a pulse at his wrist—strong and even—and felt the reassuring warmth of his skin. I saw his fingers move, then relax again—not quadriplegic. His feet flexed in their soft leather boots. Four limbs working: even better. I watched his face for a sign of alertness. What if he never woke up? The watching might have lasted five seconds but it felt like an eternity. That's when my nondoctor side took over.

I closed my eyes and then I whispered a visceral impromptu

prayer. *Don't take him from me; I can't bear it. I can't.* I thought I might sink down and never resurface, hundreds of years from any familiarity and comfort, without mooring in time and space. I opened my eyes again.

The corners of Gabriele's mouth curled upward. Had I spoken out loud? His eyes stayed closed.

"Messer Accorsi? You can't be smiling."

The gray eyes opened. Equal pupils, round and rapidly shrinking in the light. I couldn't help the quick assessment.

"I am smiling, strangely enough," he said, fixing his gaze on my face. "Why are you crying?" I started to sob then, in earnest. "I do not know how you thought to save me but I believe I owe you my life, Beatrice Alessandra Trovato."

I did not explain. "Then we're even," I said, gasping between sobs that turned into laughter.

Gabriele was whisked to the Ospedale infirmary and I went back to the *scriptorium* to work, but it was understandably impossible. Clara came in periodically to give me updates on the painter's well-being, and by the end of the day she announced that Gabriele had been proclaimed sufficiently recovered to go home. I was glad to hear that, but that didn't eliminate the fact that someone might have tried to kill him, someone whose malicious intent I had experienced firsthand as the scaffolding began to fall. I left the *scriptorium* and went to bed early.

That night I dreamed about my old life. I was in the OR, working alongside Linney on a falcine meningioma resection. The tumor had gotten so large, growing from the tissue that separates the two hemispheres of the brain, that it had squeezed the surrounding brain into a flat ribbon on either side of it. Linney was by my side, competent and quiet. It was a perfectly normal episode from my prior life, but I had a feeling of overwhelming uneasiness in the dream, a sensation of having missed something important. I tried to tell Linney what was wrong, but she couldn't hear me. Then I was awake, panting and drenched with sweat on my narrow bed in the Ospedale women's quarters. For the first time since I'd arrived in the fourteenth century, I was flooded with relief to be exactly where I was, and when.

*   *   *

The following day Clara came into the *scriptorium* breathless with another announcement: Umiltà wanted to see me immediately in the *pellegrinaio*, the hall where I'd seen the man with smallpox on my first day in the medieval Ospedale. I washed the ink off my hands and followed Clara out.

Umiltà explained. "A young priest—one Fra Bartolomeo—is receiving care for his injuries. He speaks in a jumble of confused words, but I believe he is asking for you."

"Why on earth would he ask for me?"

"I am as baffled as you, Beatrice, but in rare moments when he becomes lucid, he calls for the tall woman with raven hair and eyes like the sea." She pulled me along to a cot where a man lay with his eyes closed and a bloody bandage wrapped around his head. I hoped there weren't any brains hanging out under there; even an accomplished neurosurgeon would be hard pressed to handle that in such medieval circumstances. I recognized his face—the tongue-tied man whose mind I'd entered, the priest who had accompanied Giovanni de' Medici to the gallows.

He looked as if he might merely be sleeping, except for the dressing on his head. His flushed cheeks and his faint fuzz of light brown hair made him look like a peach.

"He was trampled by the crowd at the hanging," Umiltà said, "and the guards brought him here." The priest started moaning but didn't open his eyes.

"I shall give him more extract of Papaver, Suor Umiltà." An elderly man in a red robe trimmed with white fur appeared at her side with a long-necked glass flask in his hand. The doctor held the container up to the light to peer at the yellowish liquid within it.

"This is Dottore Agnolo di Boccanegra," Umiltà said, "a most esteemed physician, trained in Paris. We are fortunate to have him here. And this"—Umiltà turned to me—"is our new assistant scribe, Beatrice Trovato." I wondered what fourteenth-century Paris might be like. Dottore Boccanegra bowed briefly before looking up at the flask again.

"The color of his urine proclaims his derangement. Papaver will calm his fevered state and balance his humors."

"Not yet," I said. Everyone stared at me. "It could make him worse, with a head injury. And you won't know how he's doing either, if you keep drugging him."

"Have you experience of physic, Signora?" Boccanegra wrinkled his nose at me as if I hadn't taken a bath in too long, which from my perspective was certainly true. I figured I'd better come up with something plausible quickly.

"My late husband was similarly afflicted," I lied, "and the poppy blunted his ability to speak in his last hours. He was unable to give his final confession." They all looked at me with new understanding.

The physician changed the bandage while I stood there, and I saw a bruise on the young priest's head, with a hint of swelling under the skin. I didn't like the location—right at his temple, over the middle meningeal artery. A fracture there, and he'd be set up for a rapidly expanding epidural hematoma—a lens-shaped collection of blood between the skull and the brain—followed, if not checked, by coma, then death. His color was pale, his breathing irregular. Not good. I stole a hand out to feel his pulse—slow. Also not good. After the dressing was replaced, he looked tidier, but to me, worse. He had stopped moaning, and when I pinched his arm surreptitiously, he didn't withdraw or flinch. I watched the physician examine him, restraining my desire to take over. The priest had the telltale signs of increased intracranial pressure—something was either swelling or collecting inside his rigid, unyielding skull. And if that pressure were not relieved he might never wake up again. How could I intervene? I had no instruments, no anesthesiologist, and perhaps most dauntingly, no authority.

"He asked for me?"

"He described you in a moment of clarity before the third dose of Papaver," Umiltà said. Before I could consider why he might have done so, the buzz of the crowded *pellegrinaio* dampened suddenly and I felt the throb of a vicious headache, unbearable pressure like a vise at both temples. And I knew, with the certainty I now recognized from my hours in the OR, that blood was pooling under the curved table of the priest's skull. A few more minutes, and it would be over. I dragged myself out of the priest's head, still reeling from the remembered agony.

Lack of authority be damned—I had to do something. "Dottore Boccanegra," I said, "have you a . . ." I wanted to do a craniotomy, but that terminology would not fly here. I stretched back to my med school history of medicine course until I had it. "Have you a trephine?"

Boccanegra's eyebrows rose. "This scribe knows more of medicine than most women of her ilk."

I went back to my old excuse. "My husband died thus. But he could have been saved, I was told, had the augur been applied to his skull in good time. . . ." I snuck a look at the priest's face again, wondering whether under one of those eyelids one pupil was dilating now, as the nerve responsible for its contraction was crushed under the advancing edge of brain displaced by blood.

Boccanegra rubbed his chin with one hand. "In some cases

injury to the skull and its tender contents may only be relieved by an aperture such as you describe." I held my breath but my mind was racing. *Come on, make up your mind, Dottore, before we lose him.* "This procedure is, however, more often the purview of the military surgeon." Boccanegra said this in a lofty tone, as if he were placing himself far above the surgeon's lowly existence, but something about his demeanor made me wonder whether all that confidence was real. If I was going to convince Boccanegra to let me take over, I'd need to know what he was thinking. I took the direct route. It was surprisingly easy to slip into his head and find what I needed, and once I could read his thoughts I almost laughed out loud. The man was absolutely terrified. He'd never done a trephination; in fact, he'd never done any surgery at all. Clearly my experience trumped his. If I offered help, he'd have to take it.

"Dottore, my knowledge is, of course, vastly inferior to your substantial expertise . . . but I did, in my husband's last desperate hours, assist the surgeon with the procedure, which might have saved him had it been applied in time. If I assist you, perhaps we could save this young priest from a similar fate." At last, Boccanegra nodded, and I knew I was not imagining the relief in his face. From his case of tools he pulled out a surgical knife, a hand drill operated by a wood-handled crank, and a frightening-looking chisel. Primitive, maybe, but sharp: they would have to do. Sterilization was clearly not an option, but while Boccanegra wiped his forehead with a voluminous sleeve, I surreptitiously grabbed a pitcher of wine from a side table and dipped the tools into it. I hoped the alcohol content in watered wine was high enough to help.

I moved in to position the priest's head. My hand itched with familiarity as I picked up the knife and sliced through the skin at the temple, then peeled away the flap to expose the bone. Boccanegra, amazingly, let me proceed. He blotted the swell of blood from the skin with a cloth as I switched to the drill and made first one hole, then another, the drill's sharp point disappearing into bone. Our patient didn't even squirm as I drilled the tight ring of circles through his skull, then connected them with the chisel, sending tiny shards of bone flying from the wound. When the flap of bone lifted, I almost thought I could hear the hiss of escaping pressure, as if from a tire tested by a handheld gauge. There it was, the fresh clot I'd expected to see, mixed with an ooze of recent blood. I scooped it out and dumped it into a bloodletting bowl Boccanegra had on his instrument tray. Boccanegra, competent despite his unfamiliarity, found the bleeder and stopped its flow, holding firm until the bleeding subsided. I sutured it closed and we replaced the bone, then the flap of skin. Boccanegra closed the wound with a needle threaded with catgut.

I stepped back while Boccanegra turned to find a dressing. I watched the priest, counting breaths. One, two, three . . . more regular now. I snuck a look under his eyelids—pupils blessedly equal.

Boccanegra reassumed control seamlessly. "The good priest must rest now. I will bleed him, then dose him with Papaver. Thank you, Monna Trovato, for your layperson's assistance in this grave matter." I was about to protest—he'd bled plenty already—but I didn't want to push my uninvited medical authority too far. I looked over my shoulder as we left the *pellegrinaio* and saw the *dottore* setting out another tray of evil-looking instruments.

I went back to see Bartolomeo the next day. I'd read about the high survival rate after trephination, which had been practiced since the Stone Age, but I'd had a hard time believing it, until now.

The priest looked up at me wide-eyed as I walked up to his cot. "The cathedral's spirit, come to my aid," he said. "Thanks to the Blessed Virgin for sending you." I didn't bother to correct him.

"How do you feel?"

"I cannot recall anything after leaving my chamber on the morning Messer de' Medici was to be hanged."

"That's not unusual after a blow to the head."

"Truly?" He looked relieved. "I feared a devil had captured my soul. But with the aid of the Virgin who guards us all, and you, her messenger of healing, I have been restored." His brow creased with distress again. "The accused did not repent before his death. I failed in my most fervent prayers and he descended into the pit of hell, damned for all eternity, while I stood by, powerless to bring him to God's side."

"He was a murderer."

"It was my role to guide his soul to the heavens."

"I don't think anyone could have wrenched that soul away from where it was headed. Maybe your efforts spared him some torment."

"Your words bring comfort," the priest said earnestly, and his facial expression changed suddenly with the labile fluidity of a child's. "The Virgin herself holds you in her heart."

"I pray that's true, but I'm just a scribe. Thank you for the compliment."

"It is not a compliment, Monna . . . ?"

"Beatrice Alessandra Trovato. And I really am just a scribe." I smiled at him. He seemed like a very nice, if excessively sensitive, young man.

"Father Bartolomeo the Timid, they call me. With good reason." He smiled wryly. "Ever since the moment I beheld you running through the Duomo, I knew you were a spirit brought to this earth with some heavenly purpose." Before I could ask him what he meant, Boccanegra appeared at his side. I curtsied and made my exit. As I left the *pellegrinaio* it struck me what Bartolomeo had said. Was it possible that he had witnessed the night of my arrival in the fourteenth century?

Every time I went to visit again over the next few days, Bartolomeo was either sleeping or in the company of some caretaker. I allowed myself to hope that he might hold a key to my return to my own time, however innocent he seemed. The last time I went to see him, the cot was empty. Umiltà told me that the priest had returned to the cathedral where he lived and worked.

The following morning I went to Mass in the cathedral. A wizened stick of a priest stood at the pulpit delivering a sermon as dry as his visage. At the end of the service I wandered around, looking into the side chapels. Finally, I recognized Bartolomeo kneeling in prayer. He looked up as I passed.

"I didn't mean to disturb you," I said.

"I am woefully prone to distraction, Signora, and my prayers falter in their constancy. That is why I am here today, rather than in the pulpit." He rubbed the top of his head as he spoke, and his face shifted rapidly. "The sun is so lovely this morning, is it not? I was imagining that I might ride out of this very window upon a ray of light and follow it to its celestial origin." He laughed, a high-pitched, childlike sound, and pointed to a gleaming stained glass panel. Had he been like this before the head injury?

I couldn't help falling into old medical habits, assessing the extent of his amnesia. "Do you remember how you hurt your head?"

"I cannot recall the details. Were you present, Signora?" He was staring off into space now. "Your apparition burns in my memory. I took you for a demon unleashed by the night as I faltered in my prayers to protect our city from evil. But now I understand your beneficent purpose." The hairs on my arms rose as I remembered the sound of a voice chanting the night office, that first night I'd awakened in Siena's Duomo.

"What do you remember about that night?"

"I heard the sound of footsteps in the nave and saw a figure disappearing through the great doors of the cathedral—I know now it was you. Then I prayed harder, in the hopes that my inexpert fumbling had not opened the door to unwelcome spirits."

"I'm not a spirit," I said firmly. But that was an interesting thought. Had his prayers—or a failure of his prayers—allowed a chink to open in the wall separating one time from another? I made up a more reasonable story for him. "I fell asleep in the pews after Compline, and awoke to the sound of the divine office." I still wanted to wring more information out of him, this link to my old time. "Have you ever witnessed such apparitions before, Father?"

"Never, Signora. But my hours spent in contemplation of the Holy Spirit have sharpened my eyes to the world beyond our own, and it was simply a matter of time before otherworldly beings showed themselves to me."

"I'm not an otherworldly being." That wasn't entirely true; perhaps it was better to meet him on his own ground. "Father, do you think the Duomo is a portal of sorts, through which spirits—like myself, for example, might travel?"

"The person is the portal, not the place."

His comment had an edgy clarity that jarred me. "What person?"

The priest spoke in a low melodic voice that was almost a chant. "The cathedral, for all its grandeur, cannot house the love of God without a human element as a vessel, and God must work through the actions of saints and men. Where the heart and soul travel, the divine presence works its miracles. The mystics serve as an entry through which God communicates with our humble world. They harbor the Divine in their hearts and souls at all times and in all places. You, for example, do not appear to be bound to any place. Or any time, for that matter," he added, almost as an afterthought.

With that unnerving statement, he closed his eyes. "I am so

very tired, Signora, I must lay my head down for a moment."
He bowed and left the chapel. After a few minutes I left too. As
I crossed the courtyard I wondered whether he might be onto
something. But if it was the person and not the place that mat-
tered, shouldn't I be able to go home whenever I wanted?

The oddest part of my encounter with the priest was that it had
occurred at all. In my medieval experience to date, intimate conversations between members of the opposite sex were rare. There
was little privacy, and the private places were mostly off-limits.
Gabriele and I had spent time together on his scaffolding, but
that was in front of half the population of Siena, and he'd been
working, not chatting.

I continued to wonder whether Gabriele might be interested
in me as something other than a needy widow or angel's proto-
type, but my ignorance of medieval behavior made it hard to
tell. The biggest challenge was Gabriele himself; I had never
met anyone so difficult to read. My attempts to divine what he
was thinking—either the normal way or my paranormal way—
repeatedly failed. Seeing my own image bloom from his paintbrush
on the facade of one of the most prominent structures in Siena
could have been evidence of his interest, but Gabriele seemed
to pay more attention to his painting than to its model.

By the second week of September, Gabriele's fresco was far along,
and I was working on a business proposal, drawing on notes
from the rector's preferred notary. The document was addressed
to a wool merchant named Girolamo Lugani, whose company
in Genoa would provide new robes for the Ospedale staff and
embroidered altar cloths for the Church of Santa Annunziata.
Lugani was en route to Siena, and the contract had to be ready

before his arrival. I was halfway through the document when I heard the sound of hammering outside—muffled, now that the window had been repaired. I went outside to see what was going on. Gabriele was back outside the *scriptorium*, this time with a team of carpenters.

"I have not the leisure to rebuild this myself, as the Virgin and the rector command my haste," he said when I raised an eyebrow at the three laborers he'd brought to rebuild the scaffolding.

"You don't trust your own work?"

"I suspect, as do you, that my work was not at fault."

I stared at him. "How do you know what I think?"

Just then, a builder tapped his shoulder for attention. Gabriele gave me an apologetic shrug and returned to the reconstruction of his scaffold. I reluctantly returned to my correspondence with the wool merchant.

Over the next few days Bosi glowered constantly and corrected everything I did at least three times. Even the unflappable Umiltà was jittery, talking quickly and forgetting to finish the ends of her long sentences. I started getting nervous myself, wondering whether I'd have the opportunity to meet this Lugani, and not sure whether I wanted to.

I'd closed the door of the *scriptorium* to concentrate. Every error meant rewriting the whole page by hand, which certainly made me try to get it right the first time. The knock on the *scriptorium* door made me jump.

"Who's there?"

The answering voice was muffled by the wood. "Gabriele Accorsi." I leaped up, tripping over my skirt, and opened the door to find Gabriele standing in the doorway with a package. "Good day, Signora. Ysabella regrets the time it took her to return your garment."

Gabriele extended the package toward me. My hand brushed his as I took the dress and I pulled back instinctively. I hadn't touched him since the scaffolding incident, and that time he'd not been awake.

"Thank you—I'll give you back the blue one. Would you rather I washed it first?"

"Ysabella and my uncle asked that you keep it, if it suits you."

"It's a beautiful dress. I wish I could give your family something in return, but nothing I own is of much value."

"Your presence in our lives has been more than sufficient, Signora." I thought of a hundred possible things to say, none appropriate. "May I request a moment of audience, Monna Trovato? I would speak with you about a matter of mutual concern, but I do not wish to keep you from your work."

"I needed a rest anyway. Do you want to sit down?" I pulled a second stool near mine, and we both sat.

Gabriele reached into the pouch hanging from his belt and pulled out something small enough to be hidden in his hand. When he opened his hand to show me, my mouth went dry. Two stainless-steel safety pins glinted in his palm—the pins I'd used to attach my handkerchief to the bodice of the green dress after my brush with the sumptuary police.

"Monna Trovato . . . would it offend you if I use your given name?"

"Call me whatever you like. Can I call you Gabriele then?"

"Of course, please call me Gabriele," he said. "Beatrice, I fear you have not been frank with me. I hold great respect for your privacy, but your silence does not allow me to protect you as well as I might." Once I might have said I didn't need protection, but now I wasn't sure. "My lady, can you speak to me? I will understand if you should choose to remain silent, with only God to hear your prayers."

"I have been praying," I said, quietly.

"As have I." Gabriele would not be deflected. "These implements belong to you, do they not? The work is delicate, and the material unfamiliar to me. I have never seen anything fashioned thus, and would be very surprised if it were found in Lucca."

"They're not from Lucca."

"And are you from Lucca, Beatrice? Or is that part of your story as open to question as your mythical husband?"

Gabriele waited for the answer without a trace of restlessness. It was easier to look at Gabriele's hands resting on the table between us, rather than his face. His fingers were long and graceful and the hair on his arms was bleached golden by the sun, light against the brown of his skin. He had traces of paint under his nails, remnants of angels in progress.

"I'm not from Lucca, no." I hoped all he was imagining was that I was from somewhere far away. Stainless steel hadn't been invented in the 1300s. Maybe Gabriele thought the pins were made of silver, but their shape was nothing like anything I'd seen in the fourteenth century.

"I expect you still have some use for these, since they were affixed to your gown?" Gabriele held out his hand again, the pins innocent in his palm, until I took them from him. "I would be honored to be able to assist you, Beatrice. I may not understand all you have to say, but I will not judge you ill, and I will do all I can to assure your well-being. I am at your service."

I couldn't tell him where I came from, who I was, what I knew. "Thank you," I said instead, and the silence I didn't fill widened between us. Finally, Gabriele rose and bowed his gray head, then left me alone with Ser Lugani's contract and the safety pins in my hand.

Umiltà and Bosi both seemed unusually worried about the transaction I was writing up. Lugani based his business in Genoa, but he had outposts in many cities. He was a prominent businessman whose brocaded and finely woven woolens were known for their quality, and he had enough of a monopoly over the regional trade routes to make everyone anxious to keep him happy. The Ospedale had plenty of arrangements with powerful people of all sorts: wealthy barons and landowners, merchant bankers, patrons of the arts, city officials, high-ranking clergy— and I'd worked on many of their contracts. But Lugani, even in absentia, exerted an exceptional degree of influence. As I wrote out the rector's proposal from my notes, a shadow fell over the page. Bosi stood behind me with a deeper than usual scowl on his face.

"Is my work unsatisfactory?" Bosi hadn't scrutinized anything I'd done this closely since the first weeks of my employment. He'd been busy with his own work copying a book of hours for a weathy patron of the Ospedale, or he'd have taken on the contract himself. Instead, he hovered over me like a stormcloud.

"Not yet," Bosi said gruffly. "But some fault will be found, an opening Ser Lugani will use to his advantage."

"Lugani sounds quite . . . demanding," I said, choosing the word carefully as I finished the last line on the page.

"Lugani obtains all that he reaches for, which may be considered a mark of his success. It is for God to decide whether this success will send the man to heaven when his life comes to a close." With that ominous declaration, Bosi strode out.

Girolamo Lugani arrived before the week was out with an entourage of *fattori*—the medieval Tuscan equivalent of a finance department: ledger keepers, notaries, and accountants—and a pack of well-scrubbed office boys called *garzani*, the lowest rungs on the business ladder. The Ospedale exploded into action. My completed work was whisked away from me after review by the notary. I hadn't met Lugani myself, since there was no reason for me to be put in his path. Clara informed that he had a particular fondness for sweets, and the kitchen went into overdrive preparing sugar-coated almonds, honeyed custards, and jellied fruits dusted with crystallized sugar. When I went near the kitchens I could taste the sweetness in the air.

Every time I passed the Ospedale's main gate I stole a glance at the fresco taking shape. Gabriele had been working extra hours, and he'd been given several assistants from the Ospedale to assist him. They climbed up and down the scaffolding with his meals, and brought the tools and pigments he needed. He was on the platform just before dawn, descending at dusk. I saw him only from underneath when I passed by. We hadn't spoken since he'd brought me the safety pins, and I wasn't sure how to breach the silence, since I'd once again refused his gentle suggestion that I confide in him.

In lieu of direct contact, I watched his *Assumption* taking shape. The four angels gazed adoringly at the Virgin as they lifted her skyward, the sense of movement palpable. Three of the angels glittered brilliantly, their light-colored hair aflame with gold leaf. The fourth angel provided an intense contrast, her hair so black it conveyed endless depth. The dark angel's face gave a suggestion of a hidden mortal secret, something unfathomable and grave behind the serene blue-gray of her eyes. No one said anything directly to me about our likeness, but I felt self-conscious anyway, and avoided looking too long at the painting when other people were around. As a result, I rarely had the luxury to contemplate Gabriele's work for as long as I wanted to.

*   *   *

Umiltà came into the *scriptorium* just after Prime at the beginning of the third week of September. Even at that early hour the sun provided enough light to write, but the heat of summer was fading and the evenings cooled with a breeze that hinted of autumn. That particular change of seasons had always made me a little melancholy, but now, the feeling was intensified, the calendar racing toward the Plague's arrival. I was no closer to a plan to extract myself from this century than I'd been the day I arrived, nor could I protect myself and those around me from the approaching disaster.

When Umiltà walked in, I had just settled down with a new project. Lugani wanted a copy of Dante's *Paradiso*, and my job was to create a new edition in a week. I didn't notice Umiltà until she was in front of me.

"I'm not even close to finishing," I said, looking up from the canto I was transcribing.

"Ser Lugani wants to meet you," she said, grimly.

The shortness of her sentence worried me. "Why?"

Umiltà grimaced. "Messer Lugani's scribe died of flux on the trip from Genoa, and the merchant has need of an immediate replacement."

"You suggested *me?*" I was horrified. I'd been trying to get out of the fourteenth century, but getting out of Siena was no help. There was no point trying to run from the Plague, as it spread through what would someday be Italy and the rest of the world.

"Of course not. But Ser Lugani has discovered your existence, and wishes to evaluate your suitability for the position himself."

"What if I don't want to change my place of employment?"

"Neither of us is in a position to make that decision," Umiltà said acidly, though it was clear her anger was directed at Lugani. "We are loath to lose you. I did appeal to Messer Lugani to consider your employ a temporary position, so that you might be returned to us after his voyage comes to an end."

I didn't like her phrasing. It made me feel like a misdelivered UPS package. "Then I suppose I'll have to meet him," I said, grumpily.

"He requests your presence today after the Sext bells. I will send Clara to escort you."

"I'd rather spend the afternoon with Dante," I said under my breath.

Lugani was not what I expected. The stories I'd heard of his sweet tooth and greed made me imagine an overfed, overprivileged whale of a man. Clara led me into the suite of rooms that had been turned into the merchant's temporary office, and Lugani's force of will hit me before I could even take in his appearance. He'd removed his red biretta and laid it on the table, revealing black hair cut close to his head in defiance of the pageboy style of the time. He wore a scarlet robe, and had a single gold ring on the third finger of his right hand with an inset ruby, but no other adornments. He was a jaguar restraining himself before a kill, and I was his prey.

There was a single guard in the room, armed with a nasty-looking weapon. I stared into Lugani's face, willing myself not to blink. His eyes were so dark I could hardly see the pupils, and his mouth incongruously sensuous.

"Monna Trovato, it is my great pleasure to make your acquaintance. I was told of your skill, but no one warned me of your exceptional beauty."

"My appearance isn't relevant if you want to hire me as a scribe." Lugani laughed, a deep, free sound, filled with mirth. That surprised me too.

"And a sharp wit to match. That will be a pleasure on our voyage together."

"I have an excellent position here at the Ospedale."

"And I will return you to that position when I am done with you. It has been decided."

Since it appeared that refusing was not an option, I got down to negotiating. "What are your terms?"

"Twenty florins to act as my scribe for the duration of the

voyage, the use of a horse to reach the coast, ship's passage, and private accommodations for the duration of the journey. That is far more than you would earn here." He was irritatingly correct about the salary. I supposed he'd found out my stipend before meeting me.

"How long is the trip to Genoa?"

Lugani arched one eyebrow then and smiled in a way I didn't like. "The trip to *Genoa*? That can generally be accomplished in three to five days, if conditions are favorable."

"Aren't we going to Genoa?" Lugani shook his head, still smiling. "Then what is our final destination?"

"Ah, our final destination?" Annoyingly, he didn't answer me. "If all goes as planned, we should arrive by mid-October."

I tried to wait him out. "How will I get home to Siena once the job is done?"

"I see that your many remarkable qualities include intelligence. You are even better than described, and you were certainly recommended highly, if reluctantly. I am certain Suor Umiltà would have sung your praises more enthusiastically had she not feared she'd lose you to my company."

It was nice to know Umiltà valued me, but I didn't like the source of the information. "The flattery is lovely, but doesn't answer my question."

"I will arrange return passage for you at the end of your contracted time in my employ."

"What exactly does the job of scribe entail?"

"You will keep a record of all the materials we carry with us, each item that we sell or purchase, its origin, and its cost. In addition, I expect a daily written log. You will compose any letters that I require, taking dictation from me. The ledgers will be handled by my other staff."

"What if I prefer not to accept your offer of employment?"

"I regret that refusing is not an option."

"What do you mean by 'not an option'? I'm not a slave." I could feel my face getting hot.

"You are, of course, a free woman. However, I have arranged that continuing in your present job depends upon this service in my employ. I'm sure you realize the best outcome will be achieved for all involved if we agree." Free will notwithstanding, I didn't appear to have a choice.

"When do we leave?"

"In one week. I trust you will be able to ready your affairs in time." I waited. "We are bound for Sicily," he said, finally telling me our destination. "I have business with a silk trader from Messina whose goods cannot be matched on the continent."

Sicily. Almost five hundred miles. If Siena held the key to my return home, I'd be leaving it here, along with a life that had begun to feel compelling enough to make leaving hard to imagine. Lugani motioned for me to sit at the table. A contract lay on it, with a space for my signature, and all the terms we'd discussed. Cursing silently I signed my name, and after a brief hesitation, the marker of my scribal identity. That's what I was being hired as, after all.

I had a peculiar dream that night—a fragment without an obvious narrative. A man who looked like Lugani, but dressed in a dark gray pinstriped business suit and black wing-tip shoes, stood outside the Ospedale, staring up at the dark-haired angel. He did not blink, and a small smile played over his lips. Gabriele was painting high on the facade, oblivious to the spectator, putting the finishing touches on my likeness. In the dream I stood on the ground, so close to Lugani I could feel the heat emanating from his body, and I could not move or speak. I woke up sweating. It took me a long time to fall asleep again.

I opened my eyes to see Clara next to my bed, smiling.

"Suor Umiltà has sent me to assist you with your preparations for the voyage. I cannot imagine how marvelous it must be to travel in a great merchant ship! Loaded with gold and exotic spices, armor, dyes . . . wool, of course, since Ser Lugani is a wool merchant. And he's quite a dashing figure, is he not? I have often dreamed of travel but I have lived within these gates all my life. I have never even seen the sea." Clara began cleaning up in a desultory way, as if to keep her hands busy. It was patently unnecessary, as I had almost no possessions. While I got out of bed and dressed, she busied herself with lifting a few objects, dusting them off on her skirt, then replacing them again.

I had a brilliant thought. "Clara, would you like to come with me?"

"Signora, how would that even be possible?"

"I'll tell Lugani I need a personal assistant."

"I cannot read or write! How can I assist a scribe? Perhaps you had better invite Egidio." Her voice trailed off unhappily.

"It would be reasonable to say I needed a servant for the voyage." I was unaccustomed to the idea of having a servant, but it was the norm here.

"Do you really wish it?" Clara's eyes were as wide as I'd ever seen them.

"It would be a pleasure to have your company, and your help. I should be able to pay you something from the salary I've been promised. We'll have to ask Suor Umiltà, of course, and the Ospedale cook should have a say as well, before you abandon her kitchens."

"May I have your leave to ask Suor Umiltà this instant? I cannot bear to wait!"

I nodded, smiling at her enthusiasm. Clara hugged herself and squealed with delight before running out of the room. She'd forgotten the task she'd been sent to do, but I didn't really want her looking through my things anyway. The safety pins had made enough trouble.

Once Clara was gone and I had a moment to think, it hit me. Messina, Sicily: the first landing place of the Plague in Italy. The city where twelve Genoese galleys returning from Caffa, the medieval Ukraine, would enter the harbor with their deadly, microscopic cargo. I remembered the book in which I'd read about the Plague's arrival, could see the cramped words on the page. But *when* had it arrived? If it had been early in 1348, the year that had brought the Plague to Siena by May, then I still had time—a few months at least. Time to do what? That was the bigger problem I still hadn't solved. I had a vision of that paper chart I'd made. But, of course, I didn't have the diagram with me for reference anymore—it was still pinned to a bulletin board over Ben's kitchen table back in modern Siena. I strained at the memory, trying to bring it into focus, but the image grew fuzzier the more effort I made. Memory is like a cat. It comes and wraps itself around you when you least desire it, and the moment you seek it out, it disappears.

*   *   *

Iacopo found Baldi in the same corner he'd occupied at their first meeting, rolling dice while downing a goblet of Messer Semenzato's best wine.

"If we keep going off in private, Ser, someone will think I've taken a liking to men."

Baldi burst into gales of laughter while Iacopo squirmed with disgust.

"Our business is no one else's," Iacopo snapped as they mounted the narrow stairs. Once behind the closed door of his chamber, he turned to face Baldi. "Accorsi is not dead. He is not even hurt."

"Oh no? Too bad. But I've enjoyed your money." Baldi lifted the wine goblet in appreciation.

Iacopo grabbed Baldi's meaty arm. "You have not earned it yet. A little fall and a fright do not do justice to what Accorsi has wrought."

"You want me to try again? I could use a few more coins to line my pouch."

"This time I will pay you only if you succeed."

"Is death by my hand the only outcome you are willing to pay for?"

Iacopo narrowed his eyes. "State your meaning clearly."

"What if your target were to meet an unfortunate end by virtue of the law?"

"I was not aware Accorsi had done anything that merited imprisonment."

"He need not have committed murder to be accused of it." Baldi grinned. "Or to be convicted of it, for that matter."

✳   ✳   ✳

When Lugani announced his intent to remove me from Siena, I felt I had suddenly run out of time. I'd had a silent countdown to the Plague in my head (September now, eight months left), but until then, I believed I would be able to return to my old life before it was too late. Lugani's arrival heightened my predicament: whatever I intended to do here had to happen fast.

I spent several sleepless nights trying to come up with a plan. There was no use evacuating the city or warning people to leave, since I knew the Plague would go everywhere. Preaching doom? Useless, since I was more likely to be imprisoned as a witch than believed. On the morning after my second sleepless night I had a glimmer of an idea, sparked by my own carelessness. The night before, I'd brought a fruit tart to my chamber. Just before dawn I heard a scratching sound, and saw a substantial brown rat making off with what was left of my neglected late-night snack. Then I remembered: *rats. Fleas bite plague-infected rats, then bite humans.* What if there were fewer rats?

As soon as the sun rose I headed straight to Umiltà's *studium* to talk about pest control. She was sitting at her desk, poring over a ledger and frowning.

"Suor Umiltà, may I have a moment of your time?"

"Beatrice, what a welcome respite your arrival has produced from the Biccherna's calculations of our taxes. Do you need my assistance?" she asked, smiling.

"I think the Ospedale should invest in a rat catcher."

"What has prompted your interest in the rodent population of the Ospedale? Has the *pellegrinaio* become infested? If you have been bitten, we must hasten your visit to Dottore Boccanegra, for those bites can fester terribly." She had given me a perfect opening.

"I don't need to see the *dottore*. But I, like you, am concerned about the diseases these rats carry. It is time to take a preventive stance. Immediately."

"Why *now*, just as you are preparing for a voyage across land and sea?"

"It's exactly because I'm leaving—I am concerned for the Ospedale's welfare in my absence."

"Why would you be more worried about the Ospedale's welfare in your absence than when you are still here? I fail to see how your imminent departure might engender such concern."

I cast about for an answer. *When you have to lie, use the available facts.* "I learned of the diseases rats can spread from . . . a text I came across when I was preparing the Dante. Can the Ospedale hire a rat catcher?"

"The kitchen staff already puts out traps."

"That's not enough."

"Beatrice, I am quite baffled by your preoccupation with

Ospedale vermin. It is a business you know nothing about, and an expensive one at that."

"I'll give you everything I've saved if you'll pay someone to kill rats until I get back," I said. Umiltà looked at me for a long time, as if she were trying to read my soul.

"As ill-founded as your suggestion may be, I can see that it springs from a heart bent toward charity, and charity bestows a smile on God's countenance. But you must leave yourself something for the voyage. Charity paired with stupidity is a doomed marriage." I nodded. She was right, of course, about both the specific and the general point. "Very well, Beatrice. Have we settled the matter?" *Barely*, I thought, but maybe it would make some tiny, marginal difference. Umiltà prompted me again. "Is there anything else? I must return to the Biccherna's records."

"There is one other thing. Do you remember that man with the terrible rash, the one we saw that first day you brought me into the *pellegrinaio*? Whatever happened to him?" Umiltà's face clouded.

"He died," she said. "The night you saw him, in a rictus of fever."

"You knew he was contagious, didn't you?"

"Indeed, and I told you as much, as I separated him from his fellow pilgrims."

"But you took care of him anyway."

"Of course. It is my mission to tend the bodies and souls of those poor lost travelers who have no other recourse, and offer them solace and healing."

I thought of what she'd done for me. "Didn't you worry that you might get sick too, being near him all that time?"

"I have lived long, Beatrice, and if I should meet my end in such service, I would count myself among the fortunate." She meant it too; I could see the radiance of her purpose illuminate her features. I had been thinking of warning her—giving her information that might make her turn from her work, in order to save herself. Clearly, though, there was no point trying to convince Umiltà to leave any patient, current or future, and knowing that brought a strange relief with it.

Next, I met Lugani's chief accountant. His brown hair was speckled with gray, and deep lines furrowed his brow. He had most of his teeth, which was unusual in the fourteenth century, and dressed neatly in a dark green tunic belted over a white linen shirt. He leaned close to me as he spoke, closer than I liked. "Monna Trovato, is it not? May God be with you on our upcoming journey, and with us all."

I signaled my agreement with a nod. "Yes, I am Beatrice Trovato." I waited for him to introduce himself.

"Ser Orazio Cane." He bowed his head, but not deferentially. "I hear you will be joining us on the voyage to Messina, and that you were most recently engaged here at the Ospedale Santa Maria della Scala as a scribe. Have you always resided in Siena? The inflection of your speech sounds unfamiliar." Cane smiled thinly, and I wondered whether my answers would be tested against some template for accuracy. I had an image of him as a bloodhound. His last name, Latin for *dog*, suited him.

I stuck to my old story, in case he'd already heard it. "I began my travel from Lucca early this summer, in a pilgrimage I took up after my husband's death."

"You did not continue on to Roma, then. Was that your goal?"

"Siena's Ospedale offered me a haven from suffering." I was about to leave that haven, against my will.

Cane nodded briefly. "And a source of income; no small matter for a young widow such as yourself, and alone too."

"It seems everyone knows my business."

"Ser Lugani keeps me in his closest confidence."

"You must be highly respected, to be held in such regard by a man of his stature." I gave Cane my most genuine smile, but I had the feeling he wasn't easy to mollify with compliments.

My opportunity to meet Ser Signoretti in person came from an unexpected direction. In the last few days before my scheduled departure with Lugani's party, Cane came to the *scriptorium* to announce that my duties would begin immediately. It turned out that Signoretti had international as well as local interest in art, and wished to contract with Lugani to ship panel paintings to a buyer in Sicily. Lugani and Signoretti were apparently longtime business partners, and Lugani didn't need to come along to the meeting. So when I went, armed with a sheaf of parchment and a case of pens and ink, I was accompanied only by the officious Cane.

The Signoretti palazzo was an imposing building with high leaded glass windows and a massive wood front door at the top of a wide flight of steps. A guard stood outside, armed with a short but serious-looking sword. After Cane's introduction, we were quickly granted entry.

Inside the palazzo large tapestries lined the walls, depicting elegantly dressed men and women enjoying themselves in a lush garden against a millefiore background. A manservant led us through the hall to Signoretti's *studium*.

Close up, Signoretti looked less like his modern counterpart than he had at the festival of the Assumption. Ben's scholarly competition was slim and self-aggrandizing, someone who needed to act more important than he actually was. The medieval Signoretti was heavy and sleek with power, an established nobleman with no need to prove anything. His voice was low and certain of its effect.

"Ah, Ser Cane, you look well, as usual. Your employment with Ser Lugani appears to suit you."

Cane bowed. "Indeed it does. He is an excellent employer, and one whose contacts always benefit from the exchange." That sounded to me like a biased assessment, but in this setting I supposed it was appropriate. Signoretti seemed to think so too, as he nodded his heavy head in tacit agreement. He wore a complicated red velvet cap decorated with gold brocade that would have weighed me down, but on him it looked dainty.

When Signoretti's deep-set eyes focused on my face I felt like a specimen ready for dissection. "I presume this lady who joins us today is also in Messer Lugani's beneficial realm?"

Cane nodded. "This is Monna Beatrice Trovato, our new scribe. We have been fortunate enough to acquire her from the Ospedale, which benefited most richly from her services. I regret to say we lost Ser Migliorotti, her predecessor, to the flux on our voyage here."

"Regrettable," Signoretti said, his voice effortlessly shifting into a grave, weighty tone of mourning. "He is with God." Once introductions and respectful silences were done, we got rapidly down to business, which meant my writing out two copies of every contractual agreement laid out in the meeting. Signoretti had paintings to sell but also wished to invest in other materials overseas. Signoretti's family, in addition to being patrons of the arts, were gentleman military officers, and the list of weapons and armor Signoretti required was enough to stock a private arsenal. I made a mental note not to get on his bad side.

When we were done, Signoretti stood up to see us out. Even behind his vast desk he looked enormous. He must have been at least six foot four.

"It has been our pleasure and privilege to work with you, and we are honored by your trust in our *compagnia*," Cane said, bowing.

"The pleasure is mutual," Signoretti replied, with a gracious nod. "And it is a privilege to have met Monna Trovato. I look forward to future business dealings graced by her presence."

A servant saw us out. I did not, of course, hazard a question about Signoretti's acquaintance with any Medicis, and couldn't imagine how I'd ever find out the answer. If Signoretti was talking to a Florentine nobleman, he probably wasn't doing it publicly. Despite the twenty-first-century Signoretti's nastiness, it seemed a lot more dangerous to pursue the question here and now than it would have been in modern Siena.

*　　*　　*

He need not have committed murder to be accused of it. . . .
With Baldi's words tumbling in his head like a pair of dice, Iacopo dressed and splashed water onto his face from the bowl left by the inn's maid. It was a plan that would require powerful witnesses to succeed, and Ser Signoretti was the obvious choice. Giovanni had warned Iacopo not to approach Signoretti from a position of weakness, and certainly, so soon after Iacopo's father's execution, Signoretti might balk. But now was surely the time to meet with Signoretti again, and assure him that the son was worthy of the same allegiance the father had inspired. Iacopo quickly downed a cup of wine for courage and set out for the nobleman's palazzo. He rehearsed his words as he walked, keeping his cap low over his face so that none might recognize him. But just as he reached the *via* on which the palazzo stood with its imposing bulk, he saw two other guests approach the door—a woman with dark hair wrapped in braids around her head, and a man at her side, well dressed, but not nobly—a man of business. Iacopo caught a glimpse of their faces before they were admitted by the guard, and he stood staring at the doors after they closed again. Iacopo ducked into the shadows of an overhanging loggia to think. Perhaps now was not the time after all—not in broad daylight, not without an invitation, not while Signoretti had other visitors, not so soon after his father's death.

The image of Giovanni's purpled face rose in Iacopo's memory like a nightmare. He stood a few moments more, until the terrible image faded enough so he could see the street before him again. *Not now, but soon. Once I have the Brotherhood's support behind me I shall return and seal Accorsi's fate. Signoretti will not refuse me when he knows what we can offer.*

* * *

Clara returned triumphant with permission from Umiltà to accompany me to Sicily. I requested a meeting with Lugani to get his approval and I was directed to bring my maidservant to his office for inspection. Clara complied willingly, but I didn't like the way he looked at her—a cross between examining livestock for good breeding and choosing a girl from a harem. Clara kept her eyes on the ground during the inspection process, even when Lugani walked in a tight circle around her, looking her up and down. At the end of the examination he nodded to me, and waved us out of the room.

The next day, Clara said she'd meet me in the Ospedale kitchens to start packing for the trip. Any misguided visions I'd harbored of sumptuous cruise ship banquets dissipated immediately.

"I have to bring my own food?"

Clara was industriously organizing supplies from the Ospedale pantry in neat piles on the table. "Lugani's assistants assured me that I will be allowed access to the ship's galley. How is it that you know so little about travel, despite your pilgrimage and your advanced age?"

I thought Clara might be joking about my "advanced age," but her face looked no less earnest than usual.

"I'm not that old," I said, grumpily, "and in any case, travel from Lucca to Siena doesn't require a boat." I'd maintained the fiction of my origins and widowhood with everyone but Gabriele. "What makes you an expert? I thought you'd never left Siena."

"I have informed myself of the details from excellent sources," Clara said, haughtily. I suppressed a smile, knowing she'd want to be taken seriously. Across the centuries adolescents seem to share that tendency to excessive gravity and self-importance. She proudly relieved me of my ignorance while helping me pack an impossibly heavy chest of supplies.

"Does it need to be kept in this? I can't even drag the thing."

"We must guard against rats," Clara said ominously, "or worse." I tried not to think of what could be worse than rats. Together we packed dried fruits and nuts, salted meats, onions, and heads of garlic in their papery skins.

"I hope there will be enough to drink on board." I was half joking, but Clara didn't smile.

"So do I," she said. Her head was bent as she worked, her face hidden by the wings of the coif that covered her pale hair. I swallowed, my mouth feeling suddenly dry. The last long trip I'd taken had been the flight to twenty-first-century Siena, and the greatest hardship I'd endured on that trip had been a nine-dollar wilted airport Caesar salad.

Clara added a jug of wine and two metal cups with curved handles. I tried to imagine how long it would last us if there were nothing else to drink.

When she spoke, it surprised me. "How old are you, Signora, if you do not mind my asking?" My response shocked her. "Three and thirty years? And no children yet? What a terrible tragedy to be widowed and elderly with no family of your own. How will you find a new husband so far from home, with no father to provide a dowry?" A memory swept through me: holding little Sebastian in my arms, his indefinably delicious scent, and the pricking I'd felt in my breasts when I'd entered Donata's head, months ago.

"I have heard of women bearing babes into their fourth decade," she continued. "It may not be too late for you."

"But I haven't got anyone to have children with. That's a bit of an obstacle." I'd not considered thirty-three to be an obstacle either, but clearly Clara did.

"I cannot wait until the day I hold my own babe in my arms," Clara said, her voice filled with longing. "I turned fourteen years this past month. And my cycles have just begun; Umiltà says I'm a woman now." She looked younger, and despite her responsibilities, her innocence made her act younger too.

"What did Umiltà say when you asked to accompany me?" Silence. Clara went on packing methodically—a bag of sugar, a flask of vinegar, and a collection of spices in small wooden boxes. "Clara, look at me."

She looked up, smiled blandly, and resumed her efforts to squeeze a small box of salt into an even smaller space remaining in the trunk.

"You did ask her, didn't you?"

"Of course I asked her!" Clara looked horrified at the thought that she might waltz out of the Ospedale without talking to the lioness guarding its gates. "We will have to pack the loaves and eggs closer to the start of our voyage."

"What did she say to you?"

"I wonder whether Umiltà will let us take one of the lambs."

"Clara!"

Clara smiled as if she'd just heard my question. "Yes, Signora. She was pleased that you would have my assistance and company." She paused, uncomfortably. "But that I'd best be cautious traveling across the oceans in a ship run by a . . . a . . . lasi, lusci . . ." She was struggling with the word but finally got it. "Lascivious, venal, power-hungry viper of a man." Her face reddened. "What does *lascivious* mean?"

"It means lustful," I said, carefully.

Clara didn't seem troubled. "Oh, that's what I thought. Lugani is clearly driven by carnal urges."

The smile on Clara's face worried me. "He hasn't spoken to you, has he?"

"No, not at all!" Clara dropped the salt pork she was holding.

"Clara, you look like you've been caught cheating at dice." I wasn't sure whether in the medieval hierarchy of immorality cheating at dice might be a worse offense than having clandestine meetings with a Genoese merchant who was old enough to be her father. It turned out not to be the best choice.

"I have never even touched dice! How could you think that of me?" Clara burst into tears. I put my arm around her narrow shoulders and murmured what I hoped were comforting blandishments until she stopped sobbing.

"Please, Clara, I didn't mean to insult you. You must know how highly I think of you, or I wouldn't have invited you to join me."

Clara wiped her nose on her sleeve and blinked at me with moist eyes. "I would hope never to lead you to suspect me of any dishonesty."

"I'm sure I'll never have a reason to." I patted her arm comfortingly. I didn't think she was a gambler, but she was more entranced by Lugani than I would have liked. I hoped, for her sake, that her interest was not reciprocated.

The week passed quickly. I spent hours bent over the copy of *Paradiso* that Lugani had requested, and in my limited free time assembled a collection of items to take with me. Bosi reminded me that I would have to bring my scribal tools—pens, wax, seals, and inks—adding darkly that Lugani had better spend his own money on parchment.

"Taking you from us was bad enough," he said, gruffly.

I packed the supplies in a velvet-lined box, feeling affection for the tools of my new trade as I nestled them in their traveling case. Other than the obvious problem of being stranded in 1347 with the Plague approaching, I was actually enjoying my job. The peaceful absorption suited me, and the process of recording what transpired had reawakened the historian that my neurosurgical career had effectively put to sleep. *I am Ben's sister, after all.* I imagined telling my twenty-first-century friends what I was doing for a living now and giggled.

"Is there something humorous that I have failed to notice?" Bosi's eyebrows lowered over his eyes, making him look a bit like a Neanderthal.

"No, no, of course not. Nothing funny in the least." I went back to packing and kept my thoughts to myself.

*   *   *

Iacopo stood against the *pellegrinaio*'s wall, watching Accorsi paint. The painting moved Iacopo more than he expected—even unfinished the angels' flight upward, with the blessed Virgin in their midst, was so beautiful Iacopo felt it hard to breathe. So many times he had imagined the moment of the Virgin's ascension to heaven, and now here it was before him, more real than he could have imagined. "Do not waste your time with frivolities," his father had said, when Iacopo, just shy of ten years old, had stayed too long staring at the frescoed walls of the family chapel. "But it is beautiful, Father," Iacopo had replied. "Beauty is well and good, but not if it keeps us from our work," his father had answered, with a firm hand steering him by the shoulder, back to the ledgers he must learn to understand. Iacopo shook his head, as if the memory might be shaken off like water from a wet dog's fur. There was a danger in coming to know his victim too well— he must not allow himself to be tinged by a misplaced sympathy that might undermine his purpose—and he concentrated again on the task before him.

The scaffold was rebuilt, he saw, now stronger than before. The new plan was more subtle, and more certain. Accorsi would be no match for Signoretti's testimony. He would hang, just as his father had, with no one to defend his case. The Ospedale doors opened beneath the scaffolding, and a woman emerged. Her familiar silhouette made Iacopo's heart lurch in his chest. It was the woman he'd seen entering Signoretti's palazzo with the merchant by her side. Before he could slip away, she turned and noticed him. Then he was looking into her pale eyes under a crown of dark braids, and it was too late to hide.

*   *   *

Lugani's large party was scheduled to leave the Ospedale in late September, on horseback until we reached Pisa's port. Lugani had hired a band of armed guards to accompany us, and by the end of the week they were housed in the *pellegrinaio*, looking fierce and unapproachable. From Pisa, Lugani had chartered a ship that would take us to Messina. Lugani, despite his apparent wealth, didn't own a ship; from my new colleagues' conversation I gleaned that most merchants didn't. Lugani's employees were informative but not exactly welcoming, perhaps because of my newness, or gender, or both.

The thought that I'd be leaving Gabriele behind in Siena surfaced frequently, and every time I slammed it down—like one of those kids' games where you use a plastic mallet to hit toy rodents on the head as they emerge from their holes. Suppression worked only partially; I was thinking of him more and more often and with increasing vividness. Sometimes I thought I could hear his quiet voice in the *scriptorium* as I worked, but the sound never left the realm of my imagination.

On the day before my departure for Pisa, I went to watch Gabriele paint again. This time I stood near the entrance to the

Pellegrinaio delle Donne, where I could watch without being seen. For a while I looked at the angels' flight, but then something made me turn. A stranger stood behind me at the *pellegrinaio*'s wall, looking up as I had been. He was small and dark, with a long black cloak that reached nearly to the ground. His lips were moving, as if he were talking, but to no one. His gaze was odd too—toward the painting but not at it, as if there were something else on the scaffold more interesting to see. He must have felt me watching him, because he slowly turned his head until his eyes met mine. They were small, deep set, and shadowed underneath.

"Do you know the artist?" His voice was incongruously high pitched for a grown man.

"I know of him," I said, cautiously. "Why?"

"It is Ser Accorsi, is it not? I have heard of his skill."

Something made me not want to give him information, but it seemed he knew the answer already. "Yes, that's Ser Accorsi. Are you an artist too?"

"Just a patron of art." He looked back at the Ospedale. There was more calculation than wonder in his face, but maybe that's how patrons were.

The bells rang Sext and I jumped guiltily. I had a lot of work to finish before tomorrow. As I headed back to the Ospedale doorway I looked back. The stranger was still there, watching—whether Gabriele or the painting itself, I wasn't sure.

When the woman left, Iacopo remained, the anxiety rising in his chest. She'd seen him, this woman who clearly knew Accorsi and Signoretti both. Perhaps she'd even seen Iacopo waiting outside Signoretti's palazzo. And she appeared to have business here at the Ospedale. Who knew whether that woman might remember his face, should it come to that. She might make trouble, and Iacopo could not risk trouble, not with so much at stake. He would have to find out more about her, whoever she was. And avert trouble before it could arise again.

* * *

The next morning, I woke up before dawn, knowing I had to talk to Gabriele before I left. We hadn't spoken since the safety pin exchange. I dressed in the chilly darkness and fumbled for my shawl.

I made my way to the deserted piazza, which looked flat and surreal in the moonlight. I sat down at the foot of the scaffolding and leaned against the supports. The bells rang for Matins, and the buildings around me became more distinct. A few birds landed on the pavement, pecking for tidbits left the day before. Finally, people started heading to market and the city fountains, carrying baskets and buckets, and leading livestock to graze in the fields beyond the city limits. But no Gabriele. I waited as long as I dared—Lugani was due to leave just after Prime—and finally gave up. *Of all the days to take off work*, I railed at Gabriele in my head. I'd never known him to miss a day. Had something happened? I had an hour left to find out. I walked quickly out of the Piazza del Duomo and toward the baker Martellino's house— Ben's future house.

On the night before Ser Lugani left for Siena, Gabriele awoke, sensing something amiss. Then he heard the faint moaning, so quiet it might have been mistaken for wind whining through the gaps in the canvas covering the windows. Gabriele threw on his shirt and followed the sound to the threshold of Bianca and Rinaldo's room, where Rinaldo's snores bubbled in a lazy counterpart to his wife's muffled cries. In the dark Gabriele could see the pain etched in the line of Bianca's back as she curled on the bed.

Gabriele's mind flooded with an unbidden memory—Paola's pale face as she struggled to birth their ill-fated son, her golden hair damp with sweat. It had been more than a year since the image had returned to him with such force. At the next wave of pain, Bianca rocked so vigorously that the heavy wooden bed shook. Gabriele approached cautiously. The bed linen was stained dark and the air carried the metallic scent of blood. His whispered greeting was barely audible, but Bianca's head snapped up as if he'd fired a cannon by her ear. She grabbed his hand and squeezed so hard he thought his fingers might break.

"Gabriele, help me, God help me!" she whispered, the agony and terror in her voice stirring Gabriele to action.

"I will wake Ysabella, and fetch the midwife," he answered hoarsely. "You will not die here, neither you nor your child. This house will not lose another life." Bianca released Gabriele's hand and closed her eyes.

Ysabella woke quickly. She sprang out of bed, dropped her house gown over her head, and raced down the stairs. Rinaldo was awake now, standing with his back against the wall, as far from the bed as possible. Ysabella bent to feel Bianca's belly, then looked over her shoulder at Gabriele and Rinaldo.

"Don't stand there like fools!" she barked over her shoulder. "Rinaldo, close the windows, and Gabriele, go run for Monna Tecchini."

Downstairs, Gabriele pulled on his *calze* and stepped into the boots at the door, realizing too late that they were his uncle's, a size too small. He forgot the pain in his feet as he ran through the dark streets to the house of the midwife. Gabriele's ferocious banging on Monna Tecchini's front door brought a child's head to the window—Monna Tecchini's young son.

"She's out at a birthing," the boy yelled down. Gabriele despaired when the boy gave an address near the Porta San Marco, but took off running as fast as he could. There he found Monna Tecchini just finishing with a birth.

Monna Tecchini was a comforting presence in the middle of the night—a good quality for a woman of her trade. She had presided over Ysabella's birth; then her hair had been brown, not gray. But she also had presided over Paola's laboring, and she knew Gabriele's summons carried the weight of loss.

"Bianca's time has come?" she said, looking at Gabriele's face. Gabriele nodded mutely. Monna Tecchini began a rapid trot in the direction of Martellino's house and Gabriele followed, trying to keep memory at bay.

On the way to Martellino's house I debated how I would explain my dawn visit, but I didn't have to. When I arrived, the air was pierced by a bloodcurdling scream, long, loud, and full of anguish. As I burst into the kitchen Rinaldo and Martellino were standing awkwardly against the wall.

"Is that Gabriele back with the midwife?" Ysabella appeared at the foot of the stairs, and I could see her consider her options— two useless, cowering men or a visiting scribe? "Monna Trovato, have you any experience with childbirth?"

"Yes," I barked, heading up the stairs after her, desperately trying to remember everything I'd learned in my six weeks of obstetrics twelve years before. My mind raced. *I'm a neurosurgeon. I can't do this. But there isn't anyone else.*

The room was lit by wavering tapers. Bianca crouched on a birthing stool, baring her teeth like a wild animal. The floor was dark and wet, and there was a strange smell in the room—blood mixed with amniotic fluid. So the membranes had ruptured. Was she close? Ysabella pointed me to a basin of water where I rinsed my hands, and she tied a heavy apron around me. I approached the bed cautiously.

"Bianca, I think I can help."

She stared at me, panting and wild-eyed. "Please! God help me, someone help me!" I crouched next to her, put one hand on her belly and the other between her legs. It took me a few seconds to get oriented, but when I realized what I was feeling, my heart sank. Breech—this baby was not coming out headfirst. Bianca was dilated, very far along. I felt a bit more. No cord prolapse, at least not that I could tell. I put my ear to Bianca's belly and listened. Was that a heartbeat? I hoped so.

At the next contraction Bianca began to wail again. I maneuvered her to the bed so she was on her hands and knees to prevent the cord from coming down before the baby. Bianca grabbed my arm hard, her nails digging into my skin. When the pain passed I reviewed what I knew. *Don't rush a breech*—the head can get trapped. I waited, trying to be patient. Bianca screamed and bore down again, and then I saw the buttocks appear. Better than a foot, at least. At the next contraction, the legs appeared at the hip—one then the other—I pushed behind the knees, separating the baby's legs and flexing them into its trunk. The third contraction let me grasp one ankle, and then one foot, then the other. *The umbilical cord is free, that's the lifeline. Come on, baby, let's go.*

One shoulder, the other shoulder, then the arm. *Almost there.* I knew that once the baby's belly met air, I had at most ten minutes to get the head out. *Don't pull. Don't panic.* There were just three of us in the world now: me, Bianca, and this slippery butt-first baby. *Pressure right over the pubic bone with one hand, gentle traction with the other, slowly, slowly.* Bianca was screaming and panting now. Then finally, finally, I felt the baby's mouth and nose emerge into my hand, and then in the next second, the whole head. The sound of a newborn's cry filled the air, lusty and furious.

There were running footsteps on the stairs, and two figures burst into the room. One was a commanding-looking woman who must have been the midwife. The other was Gabriele.

"Monna Trovato," Gabriele gasped, staring at me with wide eyes. "What are you doing here?"

"She is delivering your new cousin," the midwife said and stepped in to take over. I rinsed my hands in a daze and stepped away from the bed, pulling the stained apron over my head. I'd just delivered Bianca's baby in what would someday become my modern bedroom.

"Thank you, Monna Trovato," Gabriele said, his eyes moving from me to the new baby and then back to me again. "Any gratitude I could possibly express falls woefully short."

"You're welcome." I took a deep breath and tried to compose myself. My thoughts were interrupted by the bells ringing for Prime, reminding me of the hour. "God, I have to leave now." Lugani's party would be assembling outside the Ospedale. "Ser Lugani is taking me with him—with his company, I mean—to Messina."

Gabriele's eyes widened. I guessed he hadn't heard. "I will escort you back to the Ospedale."

"No," Bianca said, surprising everyone. "Gabriele must pray for my daughter. He has walked these paths before, and the Virgin herself will hear his prayers." It was light by now, and I could manage the short distance myself. Everyone was still too stunned to ask me what I was doing there.

Gabriele nodded reluctantly. "May God watch over every step of your journey, Monna Trovato. Messina is a long way from Siena." It certainly was.

The midwife tied off and cut the umbilical cord, then washed the baby in a basin and wrapped her tightly in a linen swaddle. I backed out of the room to the sight of Ysabella rinsing the newborn babe's tongue with water and placing a glistening drop of honey in her mouth.

By the time I got back to the women's quarters Clara was pacing anxiously.

"Where have you been? I feared some mishap had befallen you, and that our trip might be canceled." I ignored her question but glanced down at my dress to be sure I hadn't been spattered with anything that would give me away.

Egidio appeared and stood in the doorway. He looked like a child, wide-eyed and uncertain. Because of his competence, I tended to forget how young he was when we worked side by side. I crossed the room to envelop him in a good-bye hug, forgetting medieval norms. When I pulled back, his face was bright red.

"I'll miss you." I smiled into his startled face.

"M-most honored, Monna Trovato. I have come to help with your weight. Your trunk, I mean, the weight of your trunk. There are two of us." He gestured behind him where another boy who worked in the kitchens stood waiting for instruction. The boys struggled with the trunk down the stairs of the women's hospice while I tried to restrain myself from offering to help. In the courtyard my possessions were loaded onto a horse-drawn cart by the burly guards I'd seen earlier that week. I kept my shoulder bag and its contents to myself.

*　　*　　*

When the Medici boy—he was hardly big enough to call *Ser*—had described the woman with the dark hair in braids whom he'd met outside the Ospedale, Baldi knew it was the Trovato bitch who'd taken his job.

"Why don't I just dispose of her for you?" Baldi said, throwing back another cup of the excellent wine Semenzato's provided. The Medici hesitated—squeamish, Baldi supposed he was, about adding a second crime to the first not even done, but he'd finally concurred.

From an Ospedale servant, Baldi had found out that the new scribe would be leaving Siena with a band of merchants that week. Once she was out of the city gates, he told his new Florentine master, it would be a simple task; traveling parties were sadly vulnerable to the threat of outlaws. So dangerous it was, outside Siena's safely encircling walls. None would ever suspect the band might have been . . . *alerted* to this particular party, and the particular scribe traveling with it. Perhaps Baldi could even get his old job back once the scribe had fallen by the road. And he only had to pay the head of the band of outlaws half what the Medici boy had paid him. There'd be plenty of gold left for a whore, and a glass of wine to follow.

The last time I'd ridden a horse I'd been eleven years old, in a tiny stable on the Upper West Side of Manhattan. Ben had given me riding lessons for my birthday. The teacher put me on a massive, placid bay with a back like a table, and my short legs could barely grip his sides. My teacher was a no-nonsense equestrian with no patience for weakness. It was the height of pollen season and as I made the fourth turn around the ring I started to sneeze and couldn't stop. By the time I got home my eyes were red and streaming and my hands were shaking. That was the end of my equestrian career until the moment I got on the big gray Lugani provided for me. I was told her name—Margherita—and had to figure everything else out for myself. I managed to get on her back without hurting myself, and she acquiesced to my presence grudgingly, flicking her ears with impatience as I struggled to adjust to riding sidesaddle. Clara rode beside me on her own mount, looking perfectly comfortable.

Our party left through the Porta Camollia, leaving the paved city behind. The rolling green and brown hills spread around us as we rode out onto the Via Francigena. I looked back at the inscription over the Porta: *Wider than this gate, Siena opens her heart to you*—but we were leaving the protective circle of her arms now.

Outside the gates we passed several small villages that enjoyed the *commune*'s protection and oversight, but as we traveled and the sun rose over the tops of the trees, homes became sparse. We went through an olive orchard, leaves glinting silver-green in the early light. I saw peasants working a large outdoor press, and the fresh green scent of bruised olives made my mouth water.

As we went beyond the city limits the land became more wooded, and the road turned into a stony path bordered by vegetation. Trees blocked the sun, and I pulled my shawl out of my bag, managing to drape it over me without falling off Margherita. Two of Lugani's armed guards led our party, followed by Lugani himself. I could see the red of his cap and gown from our place in line, and the straight arrogance of his back. He rode a spirited black stallion with a powerful neck and flowing black mane. Two guards remained at the rear of the group, making sure no one lagged behind. I peered into the dense woods along the path, wondering what we were being protected from.

A sharp crackle of twigs made me look up. A horned deer ran out suddenly in front of us, making Margherita rear. I slid off Margherita's back, landing hard on the ground. The stag wheeled briefly in his flight to stare at us with huge dark eyes under pale, branched antlers, then abruptly turned and fled, a flash of brown and white disappearing into the woods.

I was still recovering when Lugani's accountant Cane pulled up alongside me on his horse.

"I hope the stag did not frighten you, Monna Trovato."

It had, but I didn't tell him that. I mounted again, sore but fortunately not badly hurt. "It startled Margherita."

Cane smiled thinly. "A stag's bolting may suggest other dangers nearby," he said ominously. I didn't like the sound of "other dangers." "In what company did you travel from Lucca, Monna Trovato?"

"Company?"

"I cannot imagine you undertook the journey alone."

Think, Beatrice, think. "I came with three other pilgrims on their way to Roma."

"And where are your companions now?"

I hid my hesitation in an adjustment of Margherita's bridle. One of the nice things about lying is that you can make things up. "When I stopped in Siena, they continued on the road to Roma."

"Why did you not follow them?"

"Siena made me feel at home." My explanation unwound itself into the air between us; the first words I'd spoken with the clear ring of truth.

"And your journey from—Lucca, did you say—was it uneventful?"

"Fortunately, yes."

"I am glad to hear it," Cane said, smiling thinly. "I do so dislike eventful journeys." Cane nodded to me to signal the end of our conversation in the same way Lugani had in our interview. It was a technique I found irritating, but I kept my eyes straight ahead on the road as he dropped back in line.

"What did he say?" Clara said, as she drew her horse alongside mine. She did not appear to be accustomed to the invisible maidservant role, and had no qualms declaring her interest in my conversations.

"It's possible that he was just trying to be friendly," I said, doubtfully.

Clara nodded happily, not hearing the sarcasm. "It is good to have friends on a long journey." She was right, but Cane, though he wasn't clearly an enemy, didn't strike me as a friend either.

The road began to wind upward along the side of a wooded

hill; the land rose steeply to our right and fell dizzyingly down to the left of the narrow path. As we headed up the slope, I could see the front of our party, where Lugani's scout, Antonio, headed the line. His sweet face was still boyishly plump with an irregular spray of whiskers that looked more like fragments of straw than a real beard.

Suddenly, there was a cracking of twigs and branches, and a band of six men emerged from the gaps between the trees ahead, flashes of metal in their hands. They went first for Antonio's horse, which let out an ear-splitting cry. The horse's legs buckled and the animal dropped to the ground, throwing Antonio and pinning him under its heaving flank. There was no room for the other horses to turn, and no room to pass on either side to escape. Margherita came to a sudden stop, rearing and pawing the air with her hooves. This time, I managed to stay on her back. The outlaws swarmed over us, leaping from above onto the guards at the front of the line; to the left was the cliff edge. The only route of escape was back down the one-horse-wide track behind us.

Antonio lay pinned under his injured horse, his leg twisted in an impossible direction. He shielded his face with his hands but his attacker sliced through the boy's fingers, then his throat. As the brigand bent to cut the saddlebags from the downed horse, one of Lugani's mounted guards drew his sword and swung the blade at the thief. The blow separated the thief's head cleanly from his body, spraying everything in its radius with bright red blood. I sat frozen on Margherita's back as the outlaw's face blanched, as if his disembodied brain were realizing the awful truth of what had happened. I saw Lugani move next, his cloak a slash of red beneath the low trees as he spun his horse to face the next attacker.

Clara started screaming, picking up where Antonio's horse had left off. While I'd been watching the attack on the front of our party, a frighteningly large man in leather armor leaped from the sloping hill above the road and landed between my horse and Cane's, brandishing a glinting knife. Before I could react, Cane drew his own dagger from his waist and drove the blade into the back of the outlaw's burly neck. Our attacker folded slowly to the ground behind Margherita's rear hooves, and Clara's scream abruptly stopped, as if she'd choked on it. Cane motioned quickly to the rear guard, who pulled Clara's horse backward over the body of the outlaw, prone on the path with Cane's dagger still protruding from his neck. When the guard came back for me, our horses half ran, half slid down the narrow, curving trail. The guard led us to an outcropping of granite along the cliff wall with an opening large enough to permit a horse and rider to pass, and we entered a surprisingly large cave. The fighting continued on the path above us, muffled by the thick stone.

"Stay here," the guard barked unnecessarily and disappeared. I looked around at my companions—the back end of Lugani's party. There were two other women besides me and Clara, probably servants judging by their dress, two elderly gentlemen who I thought might be accountants, and two young office apprentices. The last was Messer Cane, who had dismounted and was trying to calm his horse by whispering into her ear. I dismounted too, sending my legs into a painful spasm, but after a minute, I managed to stand again.

I leaned against Margherita's warm flank to steady myself. Clara stumbled as she slid down from her pony, and when I reached out to help, she folded against my chest, burying her face in my neck. I could feel her heart beating fast like a little bird's. Finally our guard came back looking grimly satisfied. He had blood on his cheek, but it did not appear to be his own; I couldn't see a wound on him anywhere.

"The fighting is finished. You may all mount once you are back out on the road."

As we made our way up the hill again I could see two of our guards tying Antonio's slender body onto a pack horse's back. One of Antonio's arms swung with that terrible absence of tone that cannot be imitated by the living.

Lugani's voice was harsh, stripped of its usual finish. "Have respect for the youth—his mother would not want to see him treated like a sack of barley flour." Lugani bent and with surprising gentleness closed Antonio's eyes with one hand, then covered his body with a canvas tarpaulin. Lugani's lips moved silently. I imagined it might be a prayer, but I could feel, with a shiver, that Lugani's intent held more emotion than simple ritual would require. It was the first brush with Lugani's heart I'd had; until now his head had dominated all our interactions. I shook myself out of the unexpected connection and watched him with new appreciation as he remounted his horse.

We passed two bodies by the side of the road as our party resumed its upward path—the outlaws unlucky enough to be in the vanguard of their own band. Their corpses had been stripped of weapons and anything else of value. Cane drew his horse up next to mine.

"How curious that the first journey that includes our new scribe is fraught with danger, though her own pilgrimage along the same road was strangely uneventful."

"Messer Cane, I have no idea what you mean."

"I take special care to send out notice of false routes and times of departure, to avoid potential difficulties. It would be a great shame if any acquaintances of yours should come to know our plans and cause further trouble."

"I have no troublesome acquaintances, Ser."

"I should hope not, but I will be watching you, Signora." I supposed he saw something was slightly off with me, but couldn't know what it was. But perhaps Cane was right—did I have troublesome acquaintances? Could I have made an enemy already after just a few innocent months in the fourteenth century? The rest of the day passed uneventfully, but every bird's flight or rustle of wind in the trees made me catch my breath.

Gabriele arrived at the Ospedale when the sun was already high and found Suor Umiltà standing grimly outside the entrance. He addressed her cautiously, anticipating an outburst about his late arrival. "Is something amiss?"

"Other than the fact that we have lost a scribe and an assistant cook in one calamitous moment?" Umiltà inhaled hugely and seemed to grow larger before Gabriele's eyes as her outrage spewed forth. "Our little Clara left with a face that looked as if she would welcome any threat to her virginity, should it come from that red-cloaked adder, and I have grave doubts that our lambs will be returned to us safely, if at all. Other than that, nothing is amiss, Messer Accorsi, nothing whatsoever."

"Will he not return them to their rightful home after their work is complete?"

"I would not trust Lugani with a sack of grain, let alone a virgin and a grieving widow."

"How long ago did they depart?"

"Too long ago to follow," Umiltà said, looking at Gabriele with narrowed eyes. They stood in a moment of shared distress, listening to the bell tower pealing the midday hour. In his mind, Gabriele began to draw the thin outlines of a plan, like *sinopia* on fresh plaster.

"The rector will want to see you. He is pleased with your work and payment is forthcoming." Umiltà had turned toward the fresco over the Ospedale entry and was gesturing broadly with one cloaked arm. "Your painting is exceptionally beautiful, Messer Accorsi. Have you found a patron for your next commission?"

"The fresco season in Siena is coming to an end, but there is panel work to be found during the colder months."

Umiltà stared up at the wall over the doorway for an inordinately long time before she turned her gaze back to Gabriele. "The dark angel is quite different from the other three. She seems almost mortal, juxtaposed against the heavenly demeanor of her companions. And there is something curiously familiar about her face." The dangerous direction of their interchange was conveniently rerouted by the arrival of a boisterous juggling troupe in parti-colored red and white, accompanied by two musicians playing a flute and small drum. By the time they had finished their performance, Umiltà had either lost her train of thought or deliberately chosen to abandon it.

Umiltà paused to inspect a loose thread at the edge of her sleeve. "The rector of the Ospedale of Santa Maria Alemanna in Messina is seeking to commission a set of altar panels for the chapel. Messina's Ospedale is not equal to ours in scale or grandeur, but perhaps that opportunity might be of interest. You are almost finished with the *Assumption*, are you not?"

Gabriele felt the heat rise to his face. "I shall complete this fresco within the next two days, with God's help, and I would be honored to be considered for the Messina commission."

"That is excellent news. I have, in fact, already suggested to our rector that he bend his considerable influence toward your candidacy. A letter praising your work is on its way to Messina. It is an excellent time of year for travel south." Umiltà smiled briefly and turned to enter the Ospedale. Gabriele lagged slightly behind to stare up at his painting. He had never spent much time examining it from below, and the novel perspective made it look unfamiliar. As he watched, his focus blurred, and he saw the fourth angel incline her head slightly to meet his gaze, her hair streaming out behind her like a dark flame.

PART VI

THE CONFIDANT

It took three days of steady riding to get to Pisa, but we had no more unpleasant surprises along the way. We traveled north to reach the Arno, then west toward the coast where Lugani's ship would be waiting. At the first nightfall, we stopped at a roadside inn. There I made the unhappy discovery that Clara snored. I could stop the noise by kicking her under the covers of the bed we shared. She'd snort once and resume breathing more quietly for a while. I'd try to fall asleep before she started snoring again, but I rarely succeeded.

Along the road we passed a few imposing abbeys and castles that made me stare—I had seen photos in guidebooks, but instead of ruins they were alive and active. Imposing soldiers guarded the castle gates, and turrets bristled with brightly colored pennants. Abbeys were surrounded by fenced gardens or pens of livestock tended by robed monks. Lugani insisted we avoid the major towns, including San Gimignano and Poggibonsi, and after the first night in the inn, we found lodging with *contado* landholders. Apparently the wealth of Lugani's party softened our arrival— several gold pieces exchanged hands to mutual satisfaction. The armed guards probably helped too. And each night of the trip, a guard kept watch outside our door.

We rode into Pisa as the Terce bells were sounding. Two guards at the gate lowered their weapons to let our party enter the walled city. A street lined with bustling shops ran along the gleaming curve of the Arno, and flags fluttered in the early fall breeze, displaying a white cross on a red ground. I could see two curved bridges spanning the water in the distance; one was an arcade, lined with small businesses. The broad walkways along the river teemed with pedestrians. As we crossed the Ponte Nuovo and faced north across the river, the great bell tower appeared, not yet finished but clearly already leaning. I suppressed a laugh at the tower that would become one of the most well-recognized buildings in history because of an architect's mistake. Cane pulled up beside me after we crossed the bridge.

"Is there something you find amusing, Monna Trovato?"

He caught me off guard. "Oh, just the tower. It's funny to see it in person finally, leaning already. One little error can make an architect famous—or infamous."

"Have you seen paintings of the tower before?" Cane looked at me sharply and I realized I'd made a dangerous slip. "Or perhaps you have been here on an earlier occasion? Meeting your companions, the ones you said 'moved on without you' when you chose to stay in Siena? Ones who might, for example, be inclined to accost travelers en route to Pisa, and divide the spoils of the attack with you?" Now I saw what he suspected me of. It wasn't anywhere near the truth, but it was a dangerous suspicion.

"I've been told about the tower," I said, "that's all." It wasn't clear he believed me.

Our first stop was Pisa's Romanesque cathedral, where Lugani, with the same compassion he had shown at Antonio's death, arranged the burial with the cathedral canons. He had me write a letter to the family Antonio left behind.

"Young Antonio was a short distance from home when he lost his life," Lugani said quietly. "But the brief time he spent in our company proved his worth. We must express our gratitude to his family, along with the sad news. Would that we had instead news of his success." He sighed as I transcribed his words onto parchment. I couldn't figure the man out—so brusque but also unexpectedly sympathetic. The combination was strangely compelling.

It took almost a week to arrange our passage. Lugani had wanted to find a modern carrack to charter, faster and more efficiently rigged than the *nave* we eventually acquired—a flat-bottomed, but stable cargo vessel.

"Old-fashioned tub," he said, with obvious irritation, but there was no other vessel of appropriate size available. At least it was watertight.

I knew Latin and Italian, but now I had to learn medieval nautical language; my head hurt from all the new vocabulary. Fore, aft, lateen sails, rigging . . . *pyxis*.

"*Pyxis*, isn't that the round container used for Communion wafers? Will we be giving Mass on board?"

Lugani's laughter was genuine. "Your questions never cease to amuse me. Your value in that regard far exceeds that of your predecessor. And he was considerably less attractive."

"I would do an even better job if you would answer my questions directly," I replied.

Lugani looked into my face with the surprise often engendered by my straightforward approach, but answered without comment this time. "*Pyxis* is a compass, named for the small round box which houses it, similar to the Host's receptacle. We will all be as glad to have the direction afforded by that instrument on this voyage as we would be from the guidance of our Lord himself."

I nodded. "Ideally we will have both."

Lugani laughed and put his hand briefly on my shoulder. "We've work to do, though I do enjoy the exchange of wit, Signora. Back to writing."

After the ship's charter had been arranged, Lugani kept me

busy writing contracts with local and distant merchants. The medieval wool trade included every part of the process, from the raw materials required—sheep's wool, dyes, alum for fixing the dye—to finished woven cloth. I loved the names of the dyes—*tintore di guado, indigo, madder, robbia, burnet, saffron, oricello*. Strung together, they rang like an incantation of color. The most extraordinary was *grana*, a vivid and particularly long-lasting red made from the *Coccus ilicis* insect. It was used to color the bright and elegant scarlet cloth from which Lugani's cloak was fashioned, appropriate to his power and wealth. The thought of making a dye by crushing thousands of Mediterranean insects was daunting.

I also recorded transactions for the purchase or transport of silk, medicinal herbs, olive oil, wine, leather, wax, armor, weapons, and some of the veined marble unique to Siena. Some contracts promised goods sent "*salvi in terra*"—delivery guaranteed, but at a price. A cheaper option was "*at risicum et fortunam Dei, et gentium,*" freeing the transporting merchant of responsibility for any unforeseen acts of God or men. It reminded me of the modern insurance business.

We were ready to sail before the end of the first week of October. By then we'd eaten all our perishables, and I decided I wanted to visit the city's marketplace to restock. The day was cool, but the sunshine softened the autumnal edge in the air. I'd have to find a cloak before long. I bought a small woven basket and wandered through the stalls. I succumbed to piles of hazelnuts and earthy mushrooms, and a few fragrant bundles of the herbs that still grew outside at this time of year. The last of the season's pears beckoned golden brown; I chose a few as a treat. I eyed some black and white hens squawking in wood-slatted pens, considering how nice fresh eggs would be. But then one let out a loud squawk and a spurt of avian excrement that made me reconsider. Instead I bought two dozen eggs, without the hens.

Fish wouldn't keep for a long voyage, but I stopped for a moment to watch their undulating bodies and flicking fins, letting the fall sunshine warm the back of my neck.

Something made me look up. I saw a glint of silver hair, like an echo of the fishes' metallic brilliance—and then a swing of a dark cloak. The figure disappeared into an alley between two buildings flanking the marketplace. I pushed through the crowd as quickly as I could and stumbled into the alley but found the little street empty. I made my way back through the market, clutching the basket in my hand, and with an ache in my chest.

Pisa's port was a few hours' ride from the center of the city. I stood beside our ship in the bustling port, recording the cargo in a logbook as the company loaded bound trunks, casks, baskets, bolts of cloth, and clay jars into the hull. The load made my enormous trunk look insignificant. The *nave* didn't appear particularly fast with its stubby proportions and blunt prow, but Cane, appearing at my side, pointed out that stability would be more important than speed. There's no point in a fast ride if you don't survive it.

Our ship, *Il Paradiso*, was large, with triangular fore and aft lateen sails and a double rudder for steering. The two rudders were so far apart two people would need to operate them, which didn't seem like an efficient use of nautical personnel. But I assumed medieval shipbuilders knew what they were doing.

Five shabby pilgrims joined Lugani's party. We also took on a group of eight female slaves under the command of a trader who was taking them to sell in Sicily. The slaves looked barely old enough to be called women and sounded like they were speaking Arabic. Cane marshaled the human cargo down a hatch in the aft of the ship. I started to follow them, but he stopped me with a motion of his hand.

"Slaves and pilgrims will take the lowest accommodations in

the storage hold. You and your servant have quarters near the aft hatch." He made sure I acknowledged his command.

A crew of weather-beaten sailors moved about the deck working the sails and lines. Lugani checked the passenger list and the tabulated steerage fees I'd compiled for him.

"There is room in the storage hold for a few more, and we've need of the gold," he said with a frown. "I shall send Cane out to find other parties seeking passage. You may retire to your quarters with your *able* servant." His slight emphasis on "able" made me suspicious, and I got even more suspicious seeing the rhapsodic look on Clara's face as Lugani left us.

"He called me able—he is so manly, is he not?"

"He's certainly a man," I said, edgily, but Clara didn't notice my tone.

Clara quickly found our tiny windowless cabin with its narrow berths one above the other, and got one of the burly sailors to lug my trunk into it. It took up most of the floor space but provided a convenient way to get to the upper bunk. I was glad Clara took the top; the only time I'd ever slept in an upper bunk I'd stayed up all night worrying I might fall out.

In the cabin, Clara insisted that she redo my hair, which hadn't ever had this much attention in my thirty-something years of having hair. I let her rebraid and coil it all around my head, enjoying the gentle tugging. We were still belowdecks when I heard the squealing of the anchor rising on its winch. Clara and I went up to the deck to watch as we sailed out of the harbor with an auspicious breeze at our backs.

On our second day, the waves got choppy, and I learned Clara was prone to seasickness. The side-to-side sway combined nauseatingly with vertical motion each time we crested a wave and came down hard on its other side. A cold driving rain pelted the decks, making attempts to seek fresh air bitterly unpleasant. Clara was not alone in her misery; wooden buckets provided for motion-sensitive passengers were soon in use. She took one of them downstairs and used it steadily in our tiny, increasingly rank accommodations. I climbed the ladders to the deck to empty the bucket between bouts. Somehow, I managed to avoid joining Clara at the bucket.

After two more days, the wind died down and the sea settled. The sun rose watery and pale, drying the wet decks and rigging. Clara had a gray tint to her skin, but she was able to sit up and drink. When she was done, I tucked her under a cleanish blanket to sleep off the previous day's misery and I escaped for a welcome breath of air.

The change in weather helped the motion-sick passengers, but it did not please Lugani or the crew. The seamen had trimmed the sails to get the most out of the breeze, but it was barely strong enough to ruffle anyone's hair, let alone drive a fat-bellied *nave* to Messina. Lugani paced the deck like a caged animal, and Cane prowled the ship, keeping an eye on the passengers, who were cautiously starting to appear. I found a secluded nook on the starboard side behind a row of olive oil barrels and sat, listening to the creaking of the ship's boards and the clanking of the rigging.

Something about traveling—when I'm suspended between what I've left and where I'm going—transcends time. At sea that sense is magnified—the water stretches to a flat horizon where the dark water meets the lighter blue of the sky. The ocean goes on and on with a relentless, rhythmic power, as it has for centuries, and people sail their little boats on it, thinking they are getting somewhere. Leaning back in the sun I had the sensation that if I closed my eyes for a few seconds I might open them to find myself on the deck of a modern ship instead of a medieval one. But I wasn't on a pleasure cruise to Sicily—I was a hired scribe bound for a medieval trading port. My imagination wasn't strong enough to move me forward six or seven hundred years; I had yet to figure out what combination of factors might do that.

And now I was heading away from the home I'd found in this century, leaving behind almost everyone I knew as the Plague's arrival loomed larger and larger. And even worse, I was headed straight into its path.

After a few hours, the wind picked up again. Lugani stood grimly on deck, deep in conversation with the ship's captain. I made my way to where they stood and pulled up alongside them to listen.

"A bad storm is on the way; I can taste the bitterness on the wind." The wizened captain, who looked like he'd seen more than his share of bitterness, spat onto the deck.

"Keep us off the bottom of the sea, shipmaster, and you'll have extra gold for your troubles."

"If gold could gentle the storm, sailing would be a different business," the captain grunted, "but I'll take your promise as extra incentive." He smiled, showing a small number of peg-like teeth. "You see the dark clouds massing there on the sea's edge? They'll be here soon, and we'll see how your gold holds up against them." His laugh was humorless.

I stayed on deck as long as I dared, horrified and fascinated by the approaching storm. The sky grew dark, with a greenish tint that made it feel like we were underwater. The ship cut through the fierce wind, our starboard-side railings close enough to the water to be wet with spray. The merchant ship seemed impossibly tiny against the rising waves.

I wasn't sure whether my ignorance made me feel better or worse. Were the sails in danger of tearing? Could a mast break? I doubted life jackets had even been invented. Was there something that could serve as a flotation device? I'd cataloged every item on the boat and couldn't think of anything. The sailors swarmed on deck, pulling and tying lines. The most agile shimmied up the masts to handle the sails as the captain barked commands. The first raindrops spattered on the deck, and then within seconds the clouds opened up and a wall of water swept over the boat, soaking me and everything else in its path. As the captain sent two sailors to relieve the spent rudder men, he saw me at the rail.

"Get down below, madwoman, before the waves take you!" I took his excellent advice without arguing. The wind was so strong I could hardly make my way across the deck to the hatch. I slammed the trap above my head against the rising wail of the storm and descended to the cabin, bracing myself against the walls for support. There I found Clara hunched in a ball in the corner, knees to her chest and hands over her head. She looked up at me as I came in, tears coursing down her cheeks.

"Are we going to perish, Beatrice?"

"I hope not." I stripped off my wet clothes, shivering. I found our warmest blanket and draped it over Clara's shoulders, then got another blanket for myself and sat next to her. She wrapped her arms about me as if I were a raft that might carry her to safety. We clung to each other in the dim cabin, feeling the shuddering of the ship each time a wave crashed against it, and the vibration from the pounding footsteps above. Every few minutes one end of the room rose up nauseatingly, then slammed down hard, throwing us against each other and the wall. The sickening rhythm continued for hours, like a horrible amusement park ride gone out of control. Clara and I reverted to a primitive state of waking and sleeping. We shared the bottom bunk, cocooned in each other's arms and rocking together in a mirror of the water's frenzy. What would happen if I drowned in this medieval ocean, hundreds of years from my own time? I fell asleep imagining my lifeless body appearing in Ben's guest room bed, soaking wet with seawater-filled lungs, lying still as the linen curtains blew in the orange-scented breeze from the window.

A change in the ship's movement woke me. Clara was still asleep—her head nestled between my head and shoulder.

The rocking had subsided, and I hoped that meant something good. I had no idea what disaster might feel like. Would it be ferocious, a spinning, violent descent under the waves, or would it be swift and silent as the craft gave up its battle with the water? I gently disentangled myself from Clara. My dress was still too damp to wear, but my chemise had dried enough to put back on. I drew the blanket around my shoulders and pulled it closed. I picked up the bucket and Clara woke, her eyes wide in the dim light.

"Are we dead, Signora?"

That, at least, I was fairly certain about. "No, we're very much alive."

"I should hate to die, with my life just beginning," Clara said. *Just beginning.* It was an odd turn of phrase, and her rhapsodic tone made me suspicious.

"Just beginning? You mean because you're leaving Siena for the first time?"

Her response was surprisingly flustered. "Oh, I meant nothing. Yes, as you say, the voyage, a new beginning." She laughed awkwardly. There was a long pause that she eventually broke. "Monna Trovato, what is it like to be married?" I didn't say that I had no idea, since in theory I was a widow.

"I'm sorry it ended. Why?" I didn't mean to be snappy, but it was a peculiar topic for discussion, at this grim, malodorous moment in a ship sailing through a deadly storm.

"I cannot keep it to myself any longer!" She beamed broadly and continued. "I am so glad to be alive today, with the promise of bethrothal before me."

"Betrothal? To whom?" She hadn't been out of my sight for more than a few hours—how had she managed that?

Clara looked heavenward and sighed rapturously. "Messer Lugani has shown me the ways of love."

"He *what*?"

"He assured me that once we were safe on land, our intimacy would be blessed by the Church."

My suspicions were unfortunately well founded; Lugani had seduced Clara, and even promised her marriage—this adolescent orphaned Ospedale assistant cook. There were many things I didn't know about Lugani, but if he carried through on his promise I'd eat my logbook.

"I'm going above, Clara. Stay here." I headed up the stairs with the bucket.

The sun had set while Clara and I were clinging to each other belowdecks, and a crescent moon rode high between rapidly moving clouds. A network of dark shadows cast by the masts crisscrossed the deck with lines. I emptied the bucket over the side rail and stood there, trying to calm my anger before acting on it. I had a vision of walking up to Lugani and slapping him—I could hear the sound of my hand hitting his smooth, self-satisfied cheek. If I'd had no respect for the man it would have been easier, but the way he balanced his power with gentleness made it harder to tolerate what he'd done. A little girl—that's all Clara was, an innocent, impressionable girl who'd been saved once from an uncertain future and was now thrown back into uncertainty by a man who used his power to take everything he wanted.

"The moon does you justice, Monna Trovato." I spun around to find Lugani standing a few feet behind me. "What brings you on deck tonight, Signora? I would hate to see you pulled overboard by an errant wave." I wrapped the blanket more tightly around me, unpleasantly aware of how little I had on underneath it.

"I needed air."

"I too, Signora. I trust you have no objection to sharing the air with me?"

"I certainly do." I kept my voice quiet to keep the sailors from hearing, but there was nothing sweet about my tone. I saw Lugani's left eyebrow lift quizzically. "You seduced my maid."

"Would you rather it had been you, Signora? She is a flickering candle to your gleaming presence."

"No!" My indignation made me reckless. "Clara thinks you're going to marry her." I hated the look on his face—as if he were indulging my chatter.

"She's quite a lovely thing. So eager, but with the bloom of innocence upon her." He smiled, remembering. "Motherhood will grace her nicely someday."

I wanted to kill him. "Not as your wife, though."

"Of course I have no intention of wedding a servant girl. You though, Signora, might be a better match." Persistent bastard. He took my arms and leaned into me until my back pressed against the wooden barrels. The blanket fell from my shoulders, and I could see the gleam in Lugani's eyes as he realized what I was wearing.

"Remove your hands from this woman, Ser, before I remove them for you." The new voice made my head spin.

Lugani dropped his hands and turned to face my rescuer. "Do you fancy yourself her bodyguard? Monna Trovato and I were in the midst of a private conversation."

Gabriele stood on deck, holding an unsheathed knife. "Signora, am I intruding, or can I be of assistance in protecting your honor?"

"I am chilled, Messer Lugani, and wish to return to my cabin. Thank you, Messer . . ."

"Accorsi," Gabriele said, without a change in his expression. "Gabriele Accorsi, at your service."

Lugani's easy smile did not falter. "It seems your charms have attracted more than one man's attention." He wrapped his cloak about him. "We can resume our conversation in the morning. Please, do stay warm, and inform me if there should be any way I can facilitate that . . . *warmth*." He gave a low laugh and walked away, matching his step to the *nave*'s swaying.

Gabriele sheathed his knife at his belt. The sight of him made me want to throw my arms around his neck, but I didn't.

"What on earth are you doing here?"

He did not answer my question. "Was I correct in rescuing you, Monna Trovato? Messer Lugani's parting words suggest the interruption was unwelcome."

"Of course I wanted to be rescued." I smiled, but he didn't smile back.

"Your embrace, and the familiarity of Messer Lugani's words, suggest you found a more compelling confidant than those you left in Siena."

I imagined how it must have appeared to him—me wearing my underwear and a blanket, Lugani pressing me close against the wall of barrels. "Gabriele, he's my employer, making inappropriate advances. What do I have to do to make that clear?"

Gabriele stared at me for a few seconds. "He should not have dared to lay his hand upon you."

"How funny, I was thinking the same thing."

Gabriele finally smiled—a sweet smile that made me feel like the sun was rising just for me. "Your capacity for humor in grave situations astounds me, Monna Trovato."

Not back to first names but definitely an improvement. "I haven't seen you smile in a very long time."

"I have not had occasion to until now."

It felt so natural to be talking with him again that I'd almost forgotten how strange it was that he'd appeared on *Il Paradiso* in the middle of the open sea. "So what exactly *are* you doing here?"

His smile broadened. "I have secured my next commission, in Messina, by the grace of the rector of Siena's Ospedale. An artist travels at the mercy of his patrons."

"Oh, so you just happened to get your next job in Sicily? What a remarkable coincidence."

"I could find no other way to follow you here, Signora."

My heart gave an extra beat. "Follow me?"

"I had the good fortune to find Messer Cane seeking additional passengers just before *Il Paradiso*'s departure. It was not until I boarded that I realized he was Messer Lugani's colleague. That may have been chance, as you say, or the hand of God acting on my behalf. I had planned to search for you in Messina, but did not imagine we would travel on the same ship."

"Why didn't I see you before tonight? The boat isn't that big."

"As I am sure you know, Messer Lugani keeps strict rules on board. I was not encouraged to show myself on deck, or to disturb the more esteemed passengers. I have accommodations of a sort, in the forward storage hold."

I remembered Cane's command to me to keep my place. "But you came up tonight."

"I have attempted, within the limitations imposed upon me, to assure your safety."

"So you traveled five hundred miles to be my bodyguard?"

"Beatrice, have I been so opaque?"

"You're as clear as a brick wall."

He laughed out loud. "Do you really have no idea of the regard I have for you?"

"I guess I'm as dense as you are opaque."

"No other living woman has found her way into my art."

I let that sink in, recalling the painting of Saint Christopher that had sent me stumbling into the Duomo, in my last few minutes in the twenty-first century. Had he painted it before we'd met?

"I'm very happy to see you," I said simply, not finding any more energy or reason for artifice.

"As am I."

I stared at this man who had pursued me across Tuscany and then onto a ship bound five hundred miles from his home. I had seen Gabriele many times since my arrival in medieval Siena and had imagined him for weeks before I left my own time. But I found something in his face now that I'd never seen before. A current of emotion ignited him, just under the surface.

THE SCRIBE OF SIENA

"You look different," I said, not quite capturing all I'd been thinking.

"I am the same man." Something had changed—was it him or me? Gabriele looked at me carefully. "Monna Trovato, the wind is cold, and you are shaking. May I help you to your accommodations?"

I couldn't imagine returning to my cabin. "I don't want to disturb Clara. She's been horribly seasick and is probably resting." Gabriele was quiet for a few seconds, as if gauging how to proceed. There were faint lines at the corners of his eyes I'd never noticed before. I knew from his journal's dates that he was a bit older than me: born in 1311, and this was 1347, so he was thirty-six, give or take six-hundred-plus years. I allowed myself to study the angle of his jaw, the way a few days' growth of beard had begun to darken his chin during his travels. I could see the dip at the base of his throat where his cloak parted. He watched me as I studied him, and I wondered what details he was taking in with those otherworldly gray eyes. Finally, he reached out his hand to touch my shoulder.

"Come below with me, then. I have a spare cloak, and another blanket to ease your chill." I nodded, not trusting my voice. He turned, guiding me gently with one hand. "My accommodations are not as comfortable as yours. But they are warm, and quiet."

"It sounds perfect," I said, and followed him, leaving the bucket on deck.

Gabriele struck a flint and lit a candle, placing it carefully in an iron wall sconce. He'd led me to a storage space in the bow where bolts of woven wool and raw sheepskins were kept. The hides were stacked in high piles, and where they ended the rolls of fine cloth began, making a makeshift chamber. It smelled like sheep but it was warm and private. Gabriele wrapped me in his cloak and then in a coarse blanket, and we were quiet until I stopped shivering. He sat across from me on a low pile of sheepskins.

237

"Beatrice . . . may I call you Beatrice? It seems we are on good terms again, enough to merit less formality." I nodded, happy to hear my first name. "What led you to be in Messer Lugani's presence on deck at midnight, if I may ask?"

"Lugani seduced Clara, and now she's under the false impression that he plans to marry her. The man is a"—I remembered my conversation with Clara before we left for Pisa—"lascivious wolf. I wanted him to take responsibility for his unscrupulous behavior."

Gabriele raised one eyebrow.

"You went up on deck in the middle of the night in your shift and blanket, confronted your employer, and accused him of deceiving your maidservant?"

"Pretty much." It did sound unbelievable.

"How extraordinary."

"Can we start this conversation over? This isn't how I'd envisioned it." I cleared my throat. "How are Bianca and the baby?"

"Bianca is very well, and so is Gabriella, whom you helped bring into the world. "

"She named the baby after you? Rinaldo must have loved that."

Gabriele laughed again. "In a short time you have come to know my family well."

"It must be nice, having a baby in the house."

Gabriele sighed. "I was hardly there long enough to benefit from her arrival. But Gabriella's tiny presence has blessed my uncle's home with a sweetness that had been long absent." Gabriele paused expectantly while I gathered my courage.

"I suppose you're wondering why I was there, in your house at the crack of dawn, delivering Bianca's daughter?"

"I was grateful for your presence. But I did wonder."

I said it fast, before I could lose my nerve. "I came to find you."

"I am deeply flattered. But how did you manage to acquire such skill as a midwife, while also training to be an accomplished scribe?"

I hesitated. Lie yet again, or try him with the truth? I imagined my old life: the cool blue of the operating room, the warm hideaway of Nathaniel's bookstore, the feel of Donata's daughter's hand in mine.

"Gabriele, I'm not from Lucca."

"You did tell me that."

"I'm from somewhere so far away, it's unimaginable."

"I will do my best to comprehend."

"It's worse than not being from Lucca." The truth couldn't be restrained any longer. "I'm not even from your time." I heard my own words in a vortex, the truth spinning out into darkness, incomprehensible and dangerous.

"What time are you from then, Beatrice?" Gabriele looked perfectly normal despite what I'd just said.

"From the twenty-first century. About six hundred and fifty years from now, two thousand years after the birth of Christ . . . our Lord," I added, for clarity.

I waited for the worst. I had to wait quite a long time—Gabriele stood up and began to pace, alternately looking at me and looking at his feet. When he finally responded I was cursing the idiotic impulse that had led me to confide in him.

"I admit that many thoughts moved through my mind at your revelation, Beatrice. I wondered—had you perhaps injured your head in the storm, and were you suffering from the effects of an injury? Had you been given some draught unbeknownst to you, perhaps even by Ser Lugani, in preparation for the seduction that fortunately did not transpire? But then . . ."

I realized I was holding my breath, and my hands and face had started to tingle. I reminded myself to continue breathing.

"But then I reflected upon the oddness of your language and bearing, peculiarities that ought not to arise simply because you come from Lucca." He stopped in front of me and paused to collect his thoughts before he finally spoke again. "How lonely you must be . . . how terribly lonely." The poignant accuracy of this response, the only right response he could have made, struck me at the core.

"It's been an awful burden, having this secret that I can't possibly tell, one that has kept me separate from everyone around me. I don't know what I thought might happen when I finally told the truth—the last thing I'd imagined in return was sympathy."

"Empathy, Beatrice," Gabriele said, wiping the tears from my cheeks with the sleeve of his shirt.

Without the sound of church bells I had no way of marking the time, but I know the truth poured out of me like a river through a breaking dam. Gabriele weathered it all without flinching, sitting across from me in our woolen chamber below the ship's deck.

His first question surprised me. "Why did you come to this time and place?"

"Why? I have no idea." I'd never even stopped to ask why—the question of *how* had occupied most of my thoughts and I hadn't made much progress on that.

"Perhaps as you talk we will be able to make sense of it?"

We. I felt a warmth in my belly as the pronoun sank in.

"I've always reacted to other people's experiences intensely— in a way that sends me into the heart and head of the person I'm with." I'd never articulated this before. "I think that's why I became a doctor. I wanted to do something constructive with that access and information. But I didn't realize how strange it was until very recently."

"And did you move into the head and heart of someone from this century? Is that what brought you to us?" I was stunned by his concise and accurate summary of my nebulous suspicion, but wasn't ready to tell him whose head and heart.

"It's possible," I said, weakly. "You're good at this."

He smiled. "Do you miss your home very much, Beatrice?"

"At first that was all I could think of: how to get back."

"And now?"

"Now? I'm not sure." When I imagined home now, I saw my little room in the Ospedale, the scarred surface of my desk in the *scriptorium*. It seemed I was accumulating homes to be sick for. "I was set adrift when my brother died. I'd been certain for so long—about where I lived and how I spent my time, about surgery, about everything. Now I'm certain of nothing." I had to pause here to explain the modern version of surgery, since the medieval one was more like first aid.

"You entered people's heads in more ways than one—with your hands, and with your heart?"

"Right." I remembered the feel of the curve of cortex under one gloved hand, the cool weight of a scalpel in the other. Did I miss that? "Medicine was becoming a dangerous job for me—I couldn't protect myself from my patients' suffering anymore. And once I started doing research for Ben's book . . ." I stopped talking, thinking of how I'd felt discovering documents that gave me a window into the past. "Then I found other work to fall in love with." It had felt like love too, that heady absorption and exhilaration.

"I know that love of work," Gabriele said gently. "Ben was your brother?"

"Yes." I pushed down tears. "He wrote about Siena in this time. I immersed myself in the world he'd re-created, and began living it more intensely than my own. And now here I am, stuck in it." I wished that I didn't know what I knew, and that I wasn't in a position to tell Gabriele where his history was headed. "Siena magically manages to exist in more than one time at once. Maybe that's why I was able to move from then into now."

Gabriele nodded. His acceptance of what I said was startling, given the subject matter. Was it something about the medieval mind, or was it unique to him?

"I don't know whether it's more frightening to realize that I might rather be a scholar of Siena's history than a neurosurgeon or . . ."

"Or?"

"Or to realize that I might feel more at ease in the fourteenth century than my own."

"Why is it so disturbing to you that you should find yourself happy here?" The gravity of his question did not escape either of us.

"I'm afraid that if I get too content I might lose my ability to go back. Not that I have any idea how to do that. Maybe it's not possible."

Gabriele studied my face with concern. "Do you wish to return to your cabin? I am afraid I have fatigued you with my probing."

I didn't want to leave yet. I was thinking of the first time I'd read Gabriele's own handwritten words. "I read about you. Back in my time, I mean. Not just about you—I read what you'd written."

He looked puzzled. "I am no writer, Beatrice, I am a painter. What words can you possibly mean?"

"Don't you have a book where you record your thoughts?"

He paused, then reached behind him and brought out a leather shoulder bag, placing it between us. Opening the flap he drew out a small, familiar little book, simply bound and tied with a leather thong. It looked weirdly new, incongruous in its bright-ness. I stared at the book anxiously, wondering whether it had the power to throw me forcibly through the fabric of time.

"This? This of all things will survive me?" His voice sounded incredulous.

"You never know what's going to end up as history." I smiled cautiously. "May I touch it?"

"Of course," Gabriele said, holding it out to me. The book

felt perfectly ordinary, and when I opened the pages nothing happened. But of course it was where it belonged, settled in its own time, as was its author.

Gabriele stood up abruptly. "We will be plunged into darkness if I do not replace the candle." I watched him use the nearly spent taper to light a new one. The new candle burned brightly, limning his features with gold, and my desire for him suddenly sharpened, astonishing me with its force. I had to lower my eyes, and sat there wrapped in the cloak and blanket, feeling the heat rise in my chest. The only sound in the room was our breathing until he spoke.

"Look at me," he said gruffly.

I let the journal drop into my lap. Gabriele knelt down on the floor until our heads were on the same level, forcing me to meet his gaze. "Beatrice, I would be deeply honored if you would allow me the pleasure of taking your hand."

I felt like I was falling, like I had forgotten how to breathe. In the OR my hands never shook, no matter how urgent or deadly the problem might be, but now I watched my outstretched hand tremble.

His long fingers closed around mine, startling in their warmth. I felt every joint, every inch of skin, each tiny nerve exclaiming at the contact. One part of my brain rebelled—*I can't possibly be holding hands with a 700-year-old fresco painter*. The rest of my brain was, mercifully, silent.

After a few moments Gabriele smiled. "Perhaps that is all that we can manage." He released me, pulling his hand back reluctantly. "At least for now." He touched my chin and gently raised my head toward his. "Do you concur?"

I could feel my heart pounding. "Stop *now*?"

"There is nothing I would like more than to continue, Beatrice, truly."

"You're refusing me?"

"Do not mistake my restraint for lack of desire. I am only asking for a postponement, Beatrice . . . until you are my wife," Gabriele said simply, "if that is a palatable consideration."

"Your wife?"

"Is this as shocking to you as your suggestion that I proceed to ravish you was to me? What a strange world you must come from." He was smiling now.

"Totally shocking." My heart was racing, and I felt like I might pass out.

"Beatrice, I must confess that since the earliest days of our acquaintance, I have thought many times of asking you to be my wife. But your revelations tonight have made my thoughts more urgent, as I fear the time we have remaining together may be shorter than I could have imagined. Is it so difficult for you to believe that I might know, without doubt, that I wish your life to be entwined with mine?"

I thought about my answer. When I was a child, Ben told me the story of our grandparents, Sofia and Luca, whom I'd never met. Luca first saw Sofia behind the counter at her father's grocery store in Brooklyn. "That's the girl I'm going to marry," he'd said. Sofia ignored him for six months while he courted her doggedly, and then she realized she was in love with him. They were married for fifty-two years, until they died within a week of each other in their respective sleep.

Gabriele cupped my face in his hand and put his thumb against my lips, silencing and caressing me at the same time. "Do not answer me now," he said firmly. "A husband is a difficult enough matter to decide upon; a century is another choice entirely. I will understand if the creation of a tie that would bind you to this time might make it impossible for you to accept my offer. But if you do choose me, and the time I inhabit, I will make your wait worthwhile, I promise you." He leaned forward to put his lips to my forehead. "No part of you will be spared when you are mine."

I wanted him so much I would have attacked him in the storage hold of the ship, but I could tell he wouldn't bend. "May I offer you an escort back to your cabin now? It would not be seemly for you to be found here at daybreak."

"I'll take the escort," I said, feeling like my voice wasn't in my control. "And . . ."

"And?"

"Don't propose marriage to anyone else in the meantime, all right?"

"I will restrain myself," Gabriele said, bowing. He saw me to the door of my shared cabin with Clara. My legs were trembling from fatigue and desire, but I managed to get myself into the room and fall into bed.

PART VII

MESSINA

I woke to the sound of waves slapping against the hull. I stretched out under the weight and warmth of the wool blanket. Blankets? I found two piled over me, and a third layer came from a dark wool cloak. I buried my face in the cloak and the scent——a faint tang of plaster and paint and the almost herbal muskiness that I now recognized as Gabriele's own——brought a full-fledged memory of the night with it.

Finally, someone knows the truth. The exquisite liberty of that realization, dispelling months of fearful silence and deceit, coursed through me. Had Gabriele really asked me to marry him? I tried to imagine what a medieval wedding might be like. Feeling suddenly hot, I threw off the layers of wool, dressed quickly, and went up on deck.

Clara accosted me within seconds of my appearance, bubbling with excitement.

"Signora, have you heard the news? The sailors say the storm gave our ship great speed, and we should enter Messina's port sooner than expected! I can hardly imagine what Sicily must be like." Clara stopped effervescing and peered at me with concern. "Monna Trovato, are you seasick?"

"I'm well enough, thank you, Clara," I managed to say. But

my thoughts answered silently—*where we are headed, no one will be well again for a long, long time.*

Clara raced off to tidy our cabin while I remained on the deck of *Il Paradiso*. Three months had passed since my arrival in the fourteenth century, months during which I should have done more to prepare for this looming disaster. I scanned the horizon for the first sight of our deadly target, the port of entry to Europe for one of the greatest public health disasters in the history of the world. I had modern knowledge but no modern tools to change the path of the Black Death through Europe. No city, village, or tiny hamlet would be spared the assault, and eventually there would be nowhere to go.

I walked back to my private space behind the barrels and sat down on the deck. My reading hadn't often veered into fantasy, but obviously any story about time travel, mine included, posed difficult logistical and philosophical problems. Had my arrival already shifted the fabric of history to accommodate my appearance? Would any attempts I made to alter the course of events be rolled into the relentless forward motion of time's wheel, picked up and scattered like gravel from the tires of a car? Or perhaps small changes could go unnoticed while the great ones hurtled along—deaths, births, battles, peace treaties, the building of cathedrals, all a massive backdrop to the mutable tiny movements of daily life. Could I get in the way of the forces that doomed Siena to her particularly brutal losses? I had no idea. I thought of Gabriele's painting, the one with me in it, painted before July of 1347. Had the past made space for me in preparation for my imminent arrival—or had I always been here to be painted? The deterministic pondering gave me a headache. I didn't even know whether I could die here. And Gabriele—I hadn't seen any entries in his journal that were dated after the arrival of the Plague. Was there a terrible reason for that silence? Or had I simply not read far enough?

Once we got to Messina my job would be done, and I could leave, ideally with Clara and Gabriele—before it was too late. I'd go talk to Lugani now, to clarify the terms of the end of my employment. After we landed, I could return to Siena, where at least I'd have more time.

As I left my refuge, I saw Lugani conferring with the grizzled captain at the ship's prow. The captain sounded smug.

"I have word, Ser, from a small ship sent to meet us this morning, that the Genoese galleys have dropped anchor in Messina. Your contact will be glad to see you've arrived so early."

I felt a wave of dizziness and held on to the barrel at my side to steady myself. If the Genoese galleys were here, the Plague was too.

"Excellent news. I shall pay you well for the quick journey." I drew up behind Lugani, trying to keep my expression neutral.

"Good morning, Ser."

Lugani turned to face me. His face was cleanly shaven this morning, his cropped dark head topped with a red biretta, his scarlet cloak brilliant against the gray-brown of the weathered ship.

"Good morning indeed, Monna Trovato. You look well rested, which is for the best, as we will all have much to do today. We shall arrive in Messina earlier than expected."

"I heard."

"I sent your maidservant—Clara, is that her name?—to arrange your possessions. If you will excuse me, I have business to discuss with our captain."

You bastard. You know her name as well as you know the rest of her.

"I need to speak with you immediately. Privately."

"How intriguing." He seemed to be considering whether he'd have time for a few minutes of pleasure before we dropped anchor. "Captain, we will resume our discussion shortly."

"As you wish, Messer," the captain said with a leer.

I followed Lugani to his chamber, hoping I'd be able to defend myself if his misunderstanding went too far. His accommodations were relatively luxurious: a wide berth with a blue velvet coverlet, and a wooden desk affixed to the wall. A *portolan* chart was spread out on the desk. I'd seen them in the Ospedale *scriptorium*, printed with black and colored inks on whole lambskin, depicting the coastlines of the Mediterranean and Black Sea.

"I am delighted to see you've changed your mind," Lugani said, motioning me into the room. He closed the door, then positioned himself between me and the exit. I didn't like that maneuver at all.

"We must not disembark at Messina."

Lugani raised his eyebrows. "How did you arrive at such a peculiar conclusion?"

"The pilgrims on board have news about a terrible pestilence brewing in the south, with Messina at its heart."

"How might these shabby pilgrims have better information than I? And if they had such information, why would they seek passage to the city that harbored sickness within its walls?"

I struggled to make the story more convincing. "One told me that in his prayers, he was struck by a vision." I searched for words from the chronicles I'd read. "A vision of a black dog, devouring everything in its path and leaving a trail of death and darkness behind it."

"And why, Monna Trovato, would they ask you to be the mouthpiece for their prophecies of doom, rather than speak to me or the captain themselves?"

"They are afraid of you," I said, knowing he would believe me.

He nodded slightly. "That may be the case, but I am not inclined to follow the ravings of a group of shabby pilgrims."

"I request permission to stay on board then, until the ship departs again for the north."

"You are a persistent woman," Lugani said with a chuckle,

"but I am afraid I cannot indulge your wishes. At least not in this matter."

"Why not?" I tried to keep the desperation out of my voice.

"You are still in my employ, Monna Trovato. I will assure your passage home when your job with me is done, but not before." He eyed me critically. "You have been quite useful, but Messer Cane has cautioned me to watch your behavior closely. He seems concerned about the ambush on our trip here, and your possible role in it. There are those who make agreements with bands of outlaws—or other undesirables—and benefit as a result, while seeming to be innocent victims. Your consorting with ragged pilgrims who ought to be of no interest to you, and now, your insistence on a change of route, are concerning in light of Messer Cane's suspicions. I have urged him, because having you in our *compagnia* has been a great boon, to keep his suspicion at bay, but his interests are rightly meant to protect me and my business. It is also troubling that two passengers from the same city—by which I mean yourself and Messer Accorsi—might arrive separately on the same ship, seek passage at the same moment, and yet not reveal their knowledge of each other. Should I take Cane's advice in my dealings with you? Perhaps I offered you more freedom than was warranted, or wise."

"I have done nothing to betray your trust."

"That remains to be seen. When we land I will ensure that you are not in a position to endanger my business, in the event that Cane's suspicions are justified. I will enjoy your close company until you are finished with the work I require of you in Sicily. And we will be watching you, Monna Trovato. Now, are we finished?"

Clearly we were. He opened the door to let me out in front of him, following close behind. He left me to consider what his mistrust might mean for my future as he returned to the foredeck to plan our route into the Messina harbor.

Even with the shipboard breeze, the air held a promise of warmth, heralding our proximity to Sicily. I stared in the direction of our destination until my eyes watered. No degree of scrutiny could tell me what was happening there. Everyone on deck was too busy to notice me as I made my way down to the storage hold where Gabriele stood with his back to me, bent over his belongings.

"Gabriele." He whirled around quickly.

"Beatrice! Can it be that you have decided in my favor so soon?" His smile faded as he saw the serious expression on my face.

I wished we could talk about his proposal instead of what I had to say. "I've remembered something about Messina. Something I know because of where I come from."

"You are determined to tell me of the future?"

"I have to."

"Speak, then."

I chose my words carefully. "A terrible pestilence awaits us in the city. A deadly disease that will someday be called the Black Death."

Gabriele studied my face as if the details were written there. "I wish I could doubt your certainty."

"So do I."

"Is there any hope in fleeing Messina? Can this pestilence be outrun?"

I had an image of the two of us running, with a dark and roiling evil at our heels. "Maybe temporarily, but not forever."

He didn't question my authority on the subject.

"Have you spoken to Messer Lugani?"

"Yes, but now he thinks I'm plotting something dangerous, possibly even something with you. Cane has been raising suspicions about me, and Lugani is starting to believe him."

"He would do better to trust you. I imagine that my support of your efforts would only increase his suspicion of both of us?"

I nodded grimly. "I suppose this is what Cassandra felt like."

Gabriele smiled at the ancient reference. That history at least we shared.

"Is there no cure for this pestilence?"

"Not now." I envisioned the victims riddled with festering buboes, doctors with beaked masks bending over patients in their agony. "Your time does not find a solution, and the disease will rage through the world."

"Is there a cure in your time?"

I thought of the few tablets of antibiotic I had left over from my old life, a tiny symbol of my century's ability to fight disease. Those pills might save one person, but probably not two, and certainly not a shipload, or a city, or a nation. I wasn't even sure whether it was the right kind of antibiotic.

"Even in my time, people still die of this disease, but less often." I took the tablets out to show him. He reached out to touch the small white ovals in my hand.

"How beautiful they are. Like you, Beatrice, strange and beautiful." He took my hand in both of his, closing it around the tablets. "I did wonder, as I came to know you, whether you might be saint or spirit, or perhaps a mystic who had dedicated her soul to God's service. Your unusual manner of speech, your otherworldly air, your visions, and your ability to delve into the hearts of men set you apart. But now that I have discovered you are simply mortal, I am happy to regard you as a woman. No less marvelous, but human."

I had a fantasy of kissing him that was so vivid it bordered on hallucination. I've always been amazed at the way happiness intrudes on misery, with no regard for the seriousness of the situation.

"Not being mortal would be useful right about now," I said.

"Indeed it would, though you might become terribly weary, living forever, with everyone dying around you."

I wondered whether we were thinking the same thing. Immortality with the right company might not be so bad. "I've been struggling to think how my knowledge might be useful. Here I am, under oath to dedicate myself to human health. I see death coming, but all I can do is wait. It's a doctor's nightmare." I could feel the sharp edge of panic again.

"Surely everyone does not die, else how would men and women exist in your time?"

"No, not everyone."

"And what is it that allows some to survive, if not this magical medicine you bring from your century? Can you tell me that?"

"No one, even in my time, understands the answer to that question, except that those who have survived it once cannot be infected a second time. And"—I racked my brain for something I'd read that might make a difference—"isolation of the well from the sick may help, and avoidance of rats and fleas."

"Rats and fleas? Do they carry a miasma of filth that makes men succumb?"

I paused, trying to decide how to describe the life cycle of the parasite and all of germ theory in as few words as possible. I gave up. "Something like that."

"Will it make its way to Siena as well?"

"Eventually, yes."

"Then there is no purpose in flight."

"It might save us a few months, that's all."

"In that case I will do what I am capable of, and what I love, until the time should come when I fall prey to this pestilence or survive it. I will pray to the Virgin to keep us and others safe. I will pursue my commission in Messina so that I may pick up my brushes again. I will paint, and as I paint, I will dream of you, and of the day that you accept my offer." I closed my eyes for a few seconds, listening to him.

"There is one more thing," I said.

"I assume it refers to Siena's fate, and not our betrothal," Gabriele said wryly. His comment made me smile despite the grim topic.

"Unfortunately, yes. Siena will suffer, perhaps more than other cities, at the Plague's onslaught—but I don't know why. If I did, it could be something to act on."

Before we could go any further with that inflammatory topic, the sound of footsteps coming down the ladder behind me made me jump.

"Monna Trovato," Cane said in a low voice. "How surprising to find you here, with Messer Accorsi himself. Your fellow Sienese, if I am not mistaken—have I interrupted some private matter?" He looked at me, calculating. "Messer Lugani will be most interested in hearing where I found you today, and with whom. Let us return abovedecks together, Monna Trovato. I prefer to know the whereabouts and purposes of my master's employees."

"I don't need scrutiny."

"But scrutiny is necessary for the well-being of our *compagnia*. I am certain you will agree." He took me firmly by the upper arm. "And see that you restrain yourself from further contact with your compatriot, so that I need not intervene in his business in Sicily. Understood?" I nodded bleakly. Cane escorted me out, leaving Gabriele behind. I did not dare turn around to look at him again, and I hoped Cane and Lugani would leave him alone.

I had little of my former liberty for the remainder of the trip, as Cane had warned; Lugani kept me occupied from dawn until dusk with scribal tasks. I did not catch a glimpse of Gabriele again until we dropped anchor in the Messina harbor at the end of the second week of October, 1347.

From the *Chronicle* of the Franciscan Michele da Piazza:

At the beginning of October, in the year of the incarnation of the Son of God 1347, twelve Genoese galleys, fleeing from the divine vengeance which Our Lord had sent upon them for their sins, put into the port of Messina. The Genoese carried such a disease in their bodies that if anyone so much as spoke with one of them he was infected with the deadly illness and could not evade death. The signs of death among the Genoese, and among the Messinese when they came to share the illness with them, were as follows. Breath spread the infection among those speaking together, with one infecting the other, and it seemed as if the victim was struck all at once by the affliction and was, so to speak, shattered by it. This shattering impact, together with the inhaled infection, caused the eruption of a sort of boil, the size of a lentil, on the thigh or arm, which so infected and invaded the body that the victims violently coughed up blood, and after three days of incessant vomiting, for which there was no remedy, they died—and with them died not only anyone who had talked with them, but also anyone who had acquired or touched or laid hands on their belongings.

The people of Messina, realizing that the death racing through them was linked with the arrival of the Genoese galleys, expelled the Genoese from the city and harbor with all speed. But the illness remained in the city and subsequently caused enormous mortality. It bred such loathing that if a son fell ill of the disease his father flatly refused to stay with him, or, if he did dare to come near him, was infected in turn and was sure to die himself after three days. Not just one person in a house died, but the whole household, down to the cats and the livestock, followed their master to death. Because of the scale of the mortality, many Messinese looked to make confession of their sins and make their wills, but priests, judges, and notaries refused to visit them, and if anyone did visit their houses, whether to hear con-

fession or draw up a will, they were soon to die themselves. Indeed the Franciscans and Dominicans, and others who were willing to visit the sick to hear their confession and impose penance, died in such large numbers that their priories were all but deserted. What more is there to say? Corpses lay unattended in their own homes. No priests, sons, fathers, or kinsmen dared to enter; instead, they paid porters large sums to carry the bodies to burial. The houses stood open, with all the jewels, money, and treasure in full view, and if someone wanted to enter there was nothing to stop them; for the Plague struck so suddenly that at first there were not enough officials and then there were none at all.

As we pulled into the busy harbor I saw the long row of galleys flying Genoese flags like our own *nave's*—twelve hulls lined up along the shore. What was the lag between arrival of the vector and the first deaths—weeks? How long would it take before the rat fleas, hiding in clothing, chests, hair, and animal hides, found new hosts and infected them with deadly bacteria? How long would it take before those bacteria multiplied by the thousands, then millions? How long before the first victim would succumb? I didn't know how much time I had to get Clara, Gabriele, and myself out of here.

The industrious bustle of the port seemed painfully innocent. Merchants hawked huge baskets of gleaming silver fish, the sun shone, and our sailors furled the sails and shouted to one another, assured of good drink and fresh food and water on land. I felt the way I did when I looked through old photo albums with Benjamin, seeing pictures of our mother in kneesocks and a calico high-waisted dress, knowing the future that she couldn't know—the birth of her three children, and the death of two. It was hard to picture the disaster I knew was coming in the face of such busy normalcy.

I saw Gabriele as we were preparing to disembark, his bright hair partially covered by a green felt hat and his cloak fastened with a metal clasp in the shape of two overlapping leaves. He was elegantly dressed for his first visit with Messina's rector. When Cane stopped to direct the guards to load our belongings onto a cart, Gabriele moved in a step behind me. Clara was engaged with the trunk and we had a few moments unobserved.

"Do not turn to regard me, Beatrice," he whispered. It was all I could do to prevent myself from doing just that. I strained my ears to hear his voice over the din of the harbor.

"I am bound for the Ospedale to present my letter of intro-duction to the rector. After I have established myself there, I will attempt to find a way in which we might leave the city quickly, if it should come to that. I will come for you. Can you nod to ac-knowledge you have heard me?" I lowered my chin subtly, wishing I could see his face. His breath was warm on the back of my neck.

"May the Virgin keep you safe, my sweet Beatrice," he said. I watched him walk away from me and melt into the crowd of the harbor.

Clara finished supervising the loading of our belongings and came to my side. "What are you looking at, Signora?" She fol-lowed my gaze. "Is that Messer Accorsi, the painter? Whatever is he doing here in Messina?"

"I'm told he secured a commission here."

"Was he on our ship? He must have been, to arrive at just the same moment. And the entire voyage we had no knowledge of his company! Or did you know and hide it from me?" She smiled conspiratorially.

"I've only recently found out myself," I said, avoiding her question.

"Isn't that extraordinary, Signora?"

"Quite," I said, and I watched Gabriele's disappearing figure as long as I dared, blinking to keep his image from blurring.

We made our way from the ship to Lugani's Messina outpost, up the slope from the curve of the harbor and through the city's narrow streets. The most established merchants often operated branches of their business—*fondaci*—in other cities. I knew from my scribal assignments that Lugani had *fondaci* as far flung as Barcelona and Mallorca in addition to Sicily. Lugani motioned me to stay with him while Clara dealt with our baggage under Cane's direction. I was relieved to be free of Lugani's right-hand man for a while.

The Messina *fondaco* was in the plump hands of a man named Provenzano degli Uberti, who was, I quickly learned, a Genoese transplant reluctant to be sweating it out in Messina. He ran the Sicilian headquarters of the trading business, which included a warehouse, an office, and a small storefront. The shop was stocked with jars of spices, blocks of creamy beeswax, spools of brightly colored silk thread, and small dense cakes of solid dye. Bolts of cloth—silk, linen, and wool, in a range of colors—lined up below the lowest wooden shelf on each wall of the shop. There was a strong smell of sandalwood in the air. Provenzano—I thought of him by his first name because Lugani used it—smiled from behind a large wooden desk when we entered his office. He struggled to extricate himself from his narrow armchair. Bursting free, he bowed in greeting.

"Messer Lugani, what a great pleasure to have your company at last. We suffer for lack of culture in this unsophisticated town. The Messinese like to call it a city, and we do indulge them for the sake of business, of course." He mopped his forehead with a handkerchief that looked too damp to absorb anything more.

Provenzano waddled around the desk and squinted at me. "And who is this lovely creature you've brought back from your travels? Our plain sparrow feathers are dull in comparison to her resplendent plumage." There was something so sweetly comical and self-deprecating about him that I found myself smiling in response.

"This is Monna Beatrice Trovato, my new scribe. She will be joining us at the *fondaco* until the shipments we have brought are fully inventoried, and our next ventures firmly under contract." Those were the first details I'd heard about the endpoint of my employment with him. I hoped I could finish in time to escape the Plague.

"Delightful, delightful," Provenzano said. "We are in great need of a scribe just now."

"Indeed? Please elaborate," Lugani said.

My heart sank as Provenzano explained that the contents of the entire warehouse needed cataloging; I wasn't going anywhere soon. Lugani and his Sicilian *fattori* wasted no time before getting down to business. I spent the rest of the day in the warehouse with the two of them.

Wool, dyes, alum, raw hides, silk, velvet and leather, oil, wine, salt, ceramics, carved wood, and even some minor artworks were piled up in Lugani's warehouse. By the time the light through the high small windows dimmed and we could no longer see the products we were cataloging, I was exhausted and starving.

Lugani asked Provenzano to show me to my quarters, which were conveniently part of the *fondaco* complex. The whole business was behind a high stone wall with a locked gate, keeping people in as well as out; any thoughts I'd had of escaping unnoticed withered at the sight.

Clara was already ensconced in our shared room when I arrived. It was dominated by an enormous bed made of carved wood, hung with a brightly painted canopy and surrounded on three sides by a low footboard that served as both a step up and a bench. The enormous bed would have easily fit two of me and three of Clara, but there was a small trundle bed next to it, clearly intended for a servant. A walnut table and chair, a commode, and a small stand with a pitcher of water and basin completed the furnishings. The windows were not glazed but fitted with wooden shutters that swung outward. At that moment they were open to the warm Sicilian breeze.

I allowed myself to appreciate the small pleasure of a welcoming bedroom despite my worries. Clara helped me strip my clothes and rinse off with water from the pitcher and basin, then left and returned with supper—roasted pike stuffed with raisins and a side dish of small mushrooms that smelled deliciously of fall. Clara had a knack for making friends with the people responsible for cooking, and she had clearly already worked her magic on Provenzano's cook. We ate together, at my insistence.

"Did you speak to Messer Lugani on my behalf?"

Clara's question made me choke on my fish. "I did, Clara, yes, indeed." I tried to smile.

"What did he say when you spoke to him about our future?" I sifted through my memory of Lugani's words to find something positive.

"He said motherhood would grace you nicely." Clara blushed and smiled through her bite of mushrooms. My heart sank. "Clara, I don't mean to make trouble, but have you considered that he might not marry you? There is a dramatic difference in your social stations."

"He has placed a guard at our door to protect me, and our future." She sighed happily. "What more proof of his devotion is necessary?"

Her certainty of Lugani's devotion was almost pathologically innocent; he must have talked a good game when he seduced her. The image of the two of them together was more than I could stomach during supper and I let her finish the meal.

"Shall we prepare for bed, Signora? The candles are nearly spent." Clara closed the shutters and we went to bed. She fell asleep long before I did and I listened to her snores coming from the trundle bed as I lay propped up on pillows—the first I'd seen in the fourteenth century. I wished I had Clara's capacity for false security.

I spent three solid days on the work Lugani assigned me, traipsing around with the odd trio: Lugani, smooth and elegant; Cane, sharp and suspicious; and Provenzano, plump and jocular. The aroma of spices clung to my clothes and hair, and the bright hues of dyed silk and fine wool shimmered behind my eyelids when I closed them.

Everything reminded me of Gabriele. The bolts of wool recalled our private meeting place, and the spices made me think of his elusive scent. Most often I imagined him preparing panels for painting in Messina's Ospedale. Sometimes in my imaginings he ignored me as he worked, his focus pure and narrow. Late at night, I imagined his attention turned toward me, as it had on the ship. I wished I could send Gabriele a letter but it was impossible under Cane's intense scrutiny.

As a break from making a list of everything in the warehouse, I drew up contracts for Lugani's business associates. The men varied from elegant noblemen to weather-beaten traders, but they all had one passion in common: money. I saw Clara only at meals and when she helped me undress at night. Cane had her assisting with food preparation and housekeeping for the *fondaco*, so we were both too worn out to talk by the end of the day. At night, I dreamed of Plague-infested cities, and woke up gasping in the dark. Clara snored on.

On the evening of our fourth day in Messina, Cane came to my chambers after Vespers. I was so exhausted I'd fallen into the huge curtained bed, so Clara answered the door.

"Is your mistress indisposed?"

"She has retired, Ser."

Cane cleared his throat. "Be sure she rises early tomorrow, for a trip to Messina's port."

"Yes, Messer. How should she prepare?"

"She will accompany Messer Lugani in a meeting to discuss the purchase of cargo from Caffa. Be sure she brings materials for creation of contracts. We will be waiting at the *fondaco*'s front door at the Terce bells. You need not accompany your mistress."

"Yes, Ser. No, Ser."

I listened to Cane's retreating footsteps. If we were planning a trip to meet the sailors that brought the Plague from Caffa, I wasn't sticking around for it. Maybe Clara, Gabriele, and I could be on a ship at dawn—or if not, hide until a ship was available. But I had to find Gabriele first. I waited until I heard Clara snoring, then rose and dressed in the dark. A guard slumped in a chair in front of our room. It was all easy until I reached the *fondaco*'s gates. There, just as I was reaching out to slide the bolt, a hand gripped my arm, and then there was something cold and hard against my throat.

"I see our trust was ill-placed, after all," Cane hissed, his fingers digging into the flesh of my forearm. "The hour is late, Monna Trovato, and this knife is sharp. Would you care to inform me of your purpose, opening our front door at this late hour? It is, you must realize, ill-advised to wander about the streets alone, well after curfew."

"I needed air."

"There is plenty of air inside your chamber. In fact, air is plentiful even in a prison. If it is only air you seek, perhaps your chamber should be a bit more . . . prison-like? It would be so unfortunate to lose our valuable employee before her contract is fulfilled."

"Yes, Ser." The knife moved against my throat when I swallowed.

"If you consider leaving again, Monna Trovato, I shall not hesitate to use this weapon for its intended purpose. Perhaps I should consider maiming your little maidservant if I don't find you where I expect, the next time I look." With that horrifying addendum, he turned me by the arm, propelling me back down the hall to the door of my room. "Whatever little trust Ser Lugani bid me have in you, I have now lost. Do not bother to attempt to leave your room again. It will be locked—from the outside, Signora. And I shall keep the key." Before he closed the door in my face, he leaned in close and whispered, "Enjoy your air, Monna Trovato."

Cane's suspicion, until now inconvenient, had turned dangerous.

This time, the port seemed sinister. A dark cloud hung low over the harbor, shrouding the tips of the masts. The red and yellow flag that had whipped briskly in the breeze the day we'd arrived lay limp on its pole. Two sailors stood along the quay whispering to each other.

Lugani approached the men with Cane and me in his wake. "Where are your masters?"

"There is a sickness aboard our ship." The taller of the sailors chewed his lower lip anxiously. "It has struck both the captain and the merchant, Messer." The tall sailor looked at his companion for help, but none was forthcoming.

"Were they ill yesterday when the meeting was arranged?" I knew Lugani well enough to realize that the mildness of his voice did not reflect his mood.

"No, Ser." The sailor swallowed, and his protuberant Adam's apple bobbed.

Cane stepped forward menacingly. "Speak up, before my master loses his patience." He and Lugani had a smooth bad cop/good cop routine, probably perfected with years of practice.

"The captain is raging with fever. He gives off an odor so foul, from every fluid that emanates from his body, that none but the ship's doctor will attend him. The merchant is with the angels, Ser. As of dawn today." The young man shrank from Cane's glare.

"How could he have been well at sunset and dead by the morning? We received his message yesterday before Compline."

"Ser, begging your pardon, but I don't know."

Lugani looked at me, his lips narrowed into a thin line, then back at the cringing sailors. I wondered whether he remembered my warning. "Return to your ship, boys, lest you are carrying some contagion upon your person. Cane, notify the port officials that there may be a pestilence aboard the Genoese galleys. Monna Trovato, return to the *fondaco* with me. We shall discuss this further."

The galleys were anchored a short distance from the shore, and the sailors struggled to untie the rowboat they'd used to make their way to the port. A taut line stretched from the ship's stern into the water, disappearing under the smooth surface of the harbor. Along that line traveled a small, sleek shape with a curved, upraised tail. The shape was joined by another just like it. I watched the rats as they dove into the water and made their way to the shore.

"Monna Trovato." I heard Lugani's voice from a great distance, through the roar in my head. Everything spun around me, and I felt a searing pain under my arms and in my groin, with the fierce heat of fever. My knees buckled and I fell, dimly aware of landing on the pavement.

I awoke to the sight of a group of horsemen stabbing a wild boar until his flanks ran red. I closed my eyes again, hoping when I reopened them the scene would make sense. I wasn't hallucinating—it was the painted canopy above my bed in the *fondaco*.

"Signora, are you awake?" I thought about lifting my hand; it was a thousand miles away from my body and impossibly heavy. "My lady, can you answer?"

I forced my mouth to move. "How did I get here?"

"Messer Lugani brought you in his arms. At first, I thought you were dead! I am so very glad you are not." Clara burst into tears and buried her face in my chest. I put my hand on the back of her head as she sobbed. The warm wetness seeped through my chemise—someone must have undressed me. I hoped it had been Clara.

I sat up. The pain and fever, or whatever I'd felt at the port, were gone. I must have had an empathic version of the Plague. I definitely didn't want the real thing. "We have to get out of here. I'm going to talk to Messer Lugani. Where is he?"

As if on cue, there was a knock on the door. Clara wiped the tears off her face with her sleeve, and got up to open it. Lugani stood in the doorway, his height filling the entrance. He was hatless, and his dark short hair stood up from his head in spikes, as if he'd been running his hands through it repeatedly. His cloak was pinned off center. I had not seen him look so like an ordinary man before, vulnerable to the vagaries of life. And, I was happy to see, Cane was not with him.

"Monna Trovato, it seems you were right. The pestilence has come." His admission of the accuracy of my warnings and his failure to believe them made even more of an impact on me than his appearance. "Messer Cane and I plan to leave the city immediately. You should prepare to leave with us."

There was nothing I wanted to do more than accept. Nothing, that is, except find Gabriele and leave with him. "Ser Lugani, I wish to leave the city as much as you do. However, I must find my Sienese acquaintance first, Ser Accorsi, the artist who now resides in Messina's Ospedale, where he has a commission. I wish to leave with him."

Lugani's face darkened. "There is no time. We leave before the next bells."

"Surely you can wait a few hours for the possibility of saving one more life?" We stared at each other openly, and I saw the battle inside him—his own life balanced against the life of someone else.

"There is a ship—*La Serena*—leaving Messina in two hours. If you are not on it, you will have to find your own arrangements."

I made a quick decision I hoped I wouldn't regret. "Well, then, you may leave without me." Lugani nodded.

"You may find your gold in Messer Provenzano's hands. May God protect you." Lugani turned and left. I thought I could feel a cool wind stirred up by his cloak, but it might have been fear. Clara made a small noise at my side.

"Clara, you can go with him." She looked up at me, and I saw the longing in her eyes. It wouldn't be as his betrothed, but it might buy her ten months of life. I watched her conquer that longing, and replace it with something else: a fierce, young resolve.

"No, Monna Trovato. I am staying with you." I hugged her quickly, feeling her limbs tremble. I hoped we both wouldn't regret our decisions. We were now likely to be stranded five hundred miles from Siena in a city about to be overrun by Plague. I stood up, pulled on my dress, and tied my hair into a loose knot while Clara fumbled with my buttons. Then I went to find Provenzano. He greeted me in the *fondaco* office with his usual combination of good humor and friendly grumbling. I suspected Lugani had not told him what was coming, since without him, there was no one to run the *fondaco*. Lugani was a businessman after all.

"Signora, it is always such a pleasure to see your radiant face in this dim little shop. I rue the sad day when you depart, leaving me bereft in this godforsaken post." His fat face creased with a smile. He either didn't notice the wild look in my eyes and the unusual state of my hair, or was too polite to mention anything.

"Provenzano, I'm told you have something for me."

"Is it just your wages that you seek? How disappointing."

If I had to choose someone among Lugani's administrative staff to be stranded in Messina with, this was definitely the guy. "I hear that Messers Lugani and Cane are leaving Messina," I said, trying to gauge how much he knew.

"Oh, they often leave on short notice. Busy men, busy, busy men." He wiggled his hands to connote business.

"They didn't say anything about a pestilence at the port?"

"Messer Lugani said that his Genoese contact had fallen ill, but nothing more than that."

"Provenzano, there's a deadly contagion brewing at the port that endangers all Messina. You should leave town as soon as possible. After, of course, you give me my money. I'm resigning, effective immediately." I held out my hand.

He looked at me uneasily. "What sort of contagion exactly?" He coughed once. "I'm quite susceptible to illness. I am always the first to fall ill, and the last to recover."

"Swellings in the groin and under the arms, raging fever, coughing up blood, delirium, and rapid death."

Provenzano's forehead took on a sweaty sheen. "Perhaps I will take this opportunity to retire to the countryside. Would you care to come with me?"

Yet another offer I had to refuse. If I knew I could promise Provenzano passage somewhere, I'd take him with me too.

"I need to go to the Ospedale, to find my . . . my cousin. He is an artist, with a commission there, and we plan to find passage to Siena together. Can you tell me where the Ospedale is?"

Provenzano provided me with directions, then pulled a key from a ring at his waist. He bent over a large chest, fumbling with the lock, then drew out a leather pouch of coins for me. "Ser Lugani will be most displeased if I leave my post."

"You won't care if he's displeased if you're dead."

He blinked twice.

"Or get to your country place as soon as you can, and don't worry about what your boss will say. And avoid rats and sick people." No matter where Provenzano went, he wouldn't escape the Plague. But if he survived here, at least he'd have a job.

Provenzano seemed accustomed to following directions from those who spoke with authority. "I wish you God's protection in your travels, Signora."

"I will make my way home," I said with more confidence than I felt, "with this to assist me." I lifted the bag of coins, hearing them clink against one another. As I left the *fondaco* office, I realized what I'd said: in returning to medieval Siena, I would be heading home.

I unlaced the pouch and shook its glittering contents into my hand. I hoped it would be enough to buy three berths on the next boat out. If there was a next boat. Clara was sitting on her trundle bed. "Let's get packing."

"Where are we going?"

"First, I'm going to find Messer Accorsi. Then, a boat out of here."

Clara's eyes widened. "The painter? I will begin assembling our possessions this very moment." She curtsied and left.

Outside, I pushed past crowds, wondering if any were already infected, and infectious. The bubonic version was common, with its hallmark lymphatic swellings in the groin and armpits, but the pneumonic manifestation of Plague—rare and rapid—attacked the lungs first, and might be transmitted through the air. All forms were deadly. I held my breath every time I passed someone.

I didn't need paranormal abilities to sense that things were starting to go wrong. A woman stood wringing her hands in the entrance to her home, talking to a grave-looking cluster of robed and hatted physicians in long scarlet wool robes with collars of white fur. There were more physicians around than I was used to seeing, and more priests.

The chilling sound of a funeral bell heralded a procession of clerics followed by pallbearers dressed in black. They were burdened with a wooden coffin, and a group of lamenting family members walked behind. At the end of the train a bunch of curious oglers wound their way up the hill toward Messina's cathedral—the bell tower loomed over the buildings surrounding it. No one knew enough yet to flee the dead or to shun the grieving families who had tended the sick until their deaths.

In a side street, a row of large wooden bins overflowed with rotting vegetables, a pile of white and pink turnips at the top of the closest one. But the heap was garnished with a final touch—the carcasses of three crows, their feathers black against the turnips' pallor. Here was the leading edge of the great pandemic. A narrative spun out in my head, though not from any source I'd ever seen.

> First the birds died in large numbers. Flocks dropped to the earth in mid-flight, stricken with the advancing pestilence, and then the people followed, one by one and then in human flocks to match their winged predecessors, until the cities were stripped of men.

I ran the few remaining blocks to Messina's Ospedale.

Other than a tired-looking guard, the entrance hall was ominously empty; my steps made a dull echo as I crossed the room. The door at its other end opened into Messina's version of the *pellegrinaio*. It was much smaller than Siena's, and packed with misery from wall to wall. Some patients lay on cots, but most were in piles of straw on the stone floor. Two black-robed *mantellate* moved about the room, attending to the sick. Near the door a young man on a cot writhed in agony. He was bare to the waist, and the swellings beneath his arms and at his neck proclaimed his illness. His skin was speckled with purplish spots, and he gasped with every breath. I imagined the miasma of the Plague making its way into my body through my mouth, nose, even the pores of my skin. Every itch sent me swatting at an imagined flea carrying certain death. Nothing I had ever encountered before in medicine or elsewhere could compare to the stench of *Yersinia* claiming its victims.

My task kept me moving through the maze of bodies until I was sure Gabriele was not among them. The exhausted sisters had not seen or heard anything of a gray-haired painter. I stumbled through the doors at the opposite end of the *pellegrinaio*.

I'd entered a gemlike, empty chapel. Tall stained glass windows topped with pointed arches let beams of colored sunlight into the room, slanting red and blue. The air smelled sweet—seasoned wood and the tang of paint. I walked farther into the chapel, past rows of wooden benches carved with twining leaves and flowers. Every detail stood out in this strange, quiet place. At the far end of the chapel was the altar, a large stone table with a crypt underneath, and above the altar, a partially painted altarpiece.

I stared at the unfinished panel. Was it Gabriele's? In some places, gold leaf had been applied on a background of reddish brown clay and gleamed in the light from the windows. At the top of the panel were four saints: Christopher, Luke, Placidus, Nicholas. I dropped my eyes to look at the unfinished *predella*. It portrayed the Annunciation; Mary arched away from the angel Gabriel's intrusion, her arms warding off the frightening news that she would bear the Son of God. If this was Gabriele's painting, the model might have been Paola—his late wife. Her fears of childbearing had been justified, I thought grimly. But where was Gabriele? What might be keeping him from his work in the middle of the day—illness, or worse? The wall behind the altar was covered by a blue velvet curtain that I pushed aside with one hand—there was another room behind it, darker than the chapel.

As my eyes adjusted, I saw brushes in clay jars on a table along with the raw materials to mix tempera-based paints—pigments, a basket of eggs, a mortar and pestle, sheets of gold leaf. Then I looked down. Gabriele lay on the floor on a makeshift pallet with his eyes closed. He was curled on one side, mirroring the arc of Mary's body in the moment of the Annunciation, warding off suffering to come. I could see every detail of his face as if it were illuminated—his long curved lashes, the slant of his closed eyes, the faint shadow of new beard growth on his cheek. He had to be alive—wouldn't I have known otherwise? He opened his eyes and his hoarse voice made me jump.

"I am not dead yet, Beatrice, if that is what you are wondering." He coughed once, a harsh sound.

I would have laughed had I not been so afraid. I moved toward him, but Gabriele raised his hand in a gesture of warning.

"Stay away." I dropped my hands. "You were quite right about Messina, it seems." His words trailed off in a spasm of coughing. I wanted to lie next to him and cradle his body in mine. I could almost imagine how his long slender back might feel under my hands, and the rasp of his unshaven cheek against my own—but that was irrational and deadly.

"Please leave me, Beatrice. Your presence endangers your life."

"I can't." I stood frozen, drinking in the sight of his face and the sound of his voice. "Can you walk?"

"I cannot."

I imagined picking him up and carrying him out of the tiny room, the chapel, the Ospedale, through Messina's streets and out into the surrounding *contado*, as he had carried me, once, from the burning *scriptorium*. But even if I could, then what?

"Beatrice, you must leave the city. It will do neither of us any good if you too should fall ill with this malady." He stopped to cough once more, holding his hands over his face. "I will find you, if I recover. Some do, do they not?"

Some do, some must. Gabriele looked up abruptly, an odd expression on his face, as if he had heard my unspoken words.

"Do you know, given your possession of my journal and your place in time, what befalls me? Is it written somewhere in the century you once inhabited?"

"Oh no, I have no idea what happens to you. I wouldn't be considering your marriage proposal so seriously if I'd knew you were about to die." Gabriele smiled weakly. "I accept," I said, my voice breaking.

"Not now," he said. "I cannot bear to think of your precious vows given to a dying man, if that is what I am. I know what it means to have my promise follow someone to the grave." He looked toward the doorway that led to the chapel and his unfinished painting.

I reached into my bag and found the five antibiotic tablets I'd brought from my old home. They felt curiously heavy, as if their power had lent them weight. I placed them into Gabriele's palm without touching his hand.

"Take one of these now," I said to him. "Can you swallow?"

He brought one tablet to his mouth and chewed it, grimacing. "Is your century this bitter, Beatrice?"

"I usually swallow them whole." I didn't know how to answer his bigger question. "Take one every time the bells ring the hours, until they are all done."

"I shall, sweet Beatrice, until either the tablets are gone, or I am."

"Gabriele?" He raised his eyes to look at me. "Please don't die."

"I will do my best," he said, "and I hope you will do the same." I nodded. "Leave me now, Beatrice."

"Can I touch you first?"

"You are the physician. You know how the disease passes from one body to another."

This was probably the pneumonic form, with all that coughing. Both of us were probably doomed. Fifteen years of training die hard—I couldn't bring myself to touch him. But my head filled with unexpected images—burning gold and red and blue, a shimmering sweep of fabric, the glitter of outstretched wings. He'd let me see the visions in his head.

"If we survive, I will call upon you to keep your promise," he said, so quietly I could hardly hear him. "Now, for the love of God, please leave me."

I left the tiny room and began to run. I ran around the unfinished painting, ran through the bright gleaming chapel, ran out of the Ospedale. I kept running, running while crying, until my lungs burned and my legs ached, running without knowing where I was going.

Clara finished packing, but her mistress had not returned. She went to look for Messer Provenzano, who was loading trunks into a cart behind an irritable-looking horse. He was going to the country, he said, and she'd be wise to do the same. Feeling desperate, Clara watched Messer Provenzano hoist the last of his belongings into the carriage.

"Can you help me find my mistress, Ser?"

"I can't imagine how I could help, Signorina," he said, not unkindly. Clara put her face in her hands. "Now, now, don't despair. I do hate to see a young girl cry." He patted her shoulder awkwardly, apparently unaccustomed either to young girls, or crying, or both.

Clara attempted to calm herself; she hadn't survived as an orphan this long without learning to make her rescuers feel at ease. Her throat ached, but she managed to produce a smile. "Will your travels take you past the Ospedale?"

"I'm bound for my lodgings in the *contado*. But I can take you on my way."

Clara was not even certain of her mistress's whereabouts—perhaps she was wandering through the streets, lost or ailing. Clara looked up at Messer Provenzano's round face and felt the panic in her throat.

"Monna Trovato is so wise, and so kind. What if I cannot find her? What will become of my poor mistress, alone in this terrible place?" Clara's voice broke in a wail, the sound of the child she had so recently been.

Provenzano reached out and brushed the tears off her cheek with his plump fingers. "I am sure she will be found. How hard could that be? She stands out in any crowd like a Moor among maidens. Or no, that is not quite right, more like a maiden among Moors. Never mind the comparisons. And I shall leave a note here with directions to where we've headed, should she return and find us gone."

When Provenzano was done writing, Clara took the piece of parchment and, as they left the *fondaco*, affixed it to the front gate. It looked forlorn there, pale against the dark iron. Clara climbed up with Provenzano into the cart, and leaned up against his ample side, finding comfort in his bulk and constant conversation. But as they headed into the city streets she heard the cathedral tolling funeral bells, and the sound made her shudder.

When they reached the Ospedale piazza the sun was nearing the horizon. At the Ospedale entry, the guard did remember a woman with blue eyes and black hair who had come and eventually gone, toward the city gates. There was nowhere else to look.

"I must be on my way," Provenzano said at last, "before the roads become too dangerous to travel." Clara imagined being left here, alone in Messina with a pestilence raging. Desperate, she reconsidered her approach. An idea came to her with sudden clarity: food, of course. His width proclaimed his propensity to give in to that temptation, one Clara was well-equipped to deliver.

"If, heaven forfend, we fail to find my mistress, and it is to your liking, I will serve you in the capacity of cook and maidservant in your country home. Perhaps you have tasted a bit of what I have to offer?" She held her breath, watching his face.

"Ah, yes. You are the author of that lovely breast of pheasant." He closed his eyes and she prayed the memory of the pheasant would do its work. To Clara's great relief, Messer Provenzano's face softened into a smile, and as he opened his eyes he patted the seat beside him. "Jump up here with me. I daresay there's room for your small self, and perhaps we will find your mistress on our way. If not, I will welcome your company and talent in the kitchen."

"I shall come," Clara said, relieved but also despairing at the thought of leaving her mistress, wherever she might be. She climbed back up beside Provenzano, closing her eyes with fatigue. When she opened them again she saw the high walls of the city with the hills looming beyond them. She said a quiet prayer for Monna Trovato and herself as the cart rumbled out of the gates.

They had traveled no more than a few minutes before she saw a woman dressed in blue, slumped under a tree by the side of the road.

"Stop your horse!" she cried shrilly, feeling her heart begin to pound. Clara clambered down from the high seat, nearly falling in her haste, and ran across the grass to the base of the tree. Small brown pears still hung from the branches.

Her mistress leaned against the tree's trunk, her eyes closed and face flushed. Was it heat or fever? The blue eyes opened, grave and deep, those remarkable eyes that made loyalty inevitable.

"I thought I'd lost you! Why are you here? Did you find the

painter? Why is your face so red?" The hint of a smile briefly curved her mistress's lips.

"I found him, yes. You have so many questions." Her answer was unusually short. "I had to leave him there—he's sick."

"Will he recover?"

"I don't know, Clara, I don't know." Her voice trailed off. "Clara, I'm so incredibly thirsty . . . can you please find me something to drink?" Her mistress closed her eyes again. This was very strange— in all their time together Monna Trovato had never stayed still while asking anything of her. And she never complained of anything affecting her own self—decidedly strange, and troubling.

"Are you ailing, Signora?"

"Ailing? I hope not. I don't know." She did not look at all well; sweat had started to collect at the line where her black hair met her smooth brow.

"I shall go and fetch you water straight away," Clara said breathlessly. "Don't go anywhere."

"Where would I go?" Signora Trovato opened her eyes again. "The water bottle is in my bag, there." Clara reached into the bag and found a peculiar flask, perfectly cylindrical and made of a hard, shining metal—could it be silver? Her mistress had never shown it to her. It felt cool in her hands.

"I will be back soon. The fountains are not far from the city gates." Her mistress nodded listlessly. Clara said another prayer, imploring all the saints she knew, and the Virgin, to protect them both. Provenzano stepped down from the cart.

"She's thirsty, have you any water, Ser?" Clara asked anxiously. Provenzano shook his head.

"I've just finished the last bit of wine. May I offer you an oat cake, Monna Trovato?"

"No, thank you. I'm too thirsty."

Provenzano's horse whinnied loudly, frightened by a few wild dogs who had come too near. As he lumbered back to his cart to deal with the beasts, Clara walked back to the city gates. The guards remembered her and let her through. By the time she'd found the fountain, filled the curious vessel, and passed through the gates again, the light was fading. Provenzano and his cart were still waiting. He'd pulled off the road, and he and his horse had both fallen asleep. But when Clara returned to the base of the pear tree, her mistress was gone.

PART VIII

THE RIVAL

Giovanni de' Medici's confraternity, the Brotherhood of San Giovanni Battista, met in an underground chamber of the Medici palazzo. Iacopo sat uncomfortably in his father's chair and gripped the wooden armrests until the decorative scrolls etched themselves into his palms. The scribe beside him penned the date on a sheet of parchment, quill scratching audibly. Iacopo watched the black letters spidering across the page: *In the year one thousand three hundred and forty-eight, this month of February* . . .

The light from golden sconces flickered on the walls, illuminating tapestries that depicted the life of San Giovanni Battista. Named for Firenze's patron saint, the Brotherhood included some of the wealthiest and most powerful men in the city. Eight of them sat around the long table, and to Iacopo they seemed to evaluate and dismiss him with one communal glance. His breastbone barely cleared the top of the massive table in the center of the room.

"I have a matter of grave import to discuss today." Iacopo's voice squeaked, and he paused to collect himself.

"What graver purpose can we have than to serve God through charitable works?" Ser Acciaioli bore his devotion like a badge as vivid as his family's crest, spouting a relentless flow of piety to all within earshot.

"Do you not have an answer for Ser Acciaioli, *young* Medici?"

The objectionable adjective came from Ser Albizzi, a prominent member of the Arte di Lana—the guild of wool cloth-makers.

"All in God's name, and with God's help," Iacopo intoned. The eight other men nodded, apparently pleased by his answer. But the day's agenda was long, and Iacopo's business was postponed until after Ser Acciaioli completed a discussion of a program to supply bread to the urban poor through a subsidy to local bakers. The room was cold, and all the men kept their cloaks drawn about them. A fire in the hearth warmed mostly Ser Acciaioli, who, despite his preoccupation with the afterlife, always managed to sit closest to the earthly source of heat.

Finally, it was Iacopo's turn, and he cleared his throat. "I grieve my great father still." A good beginning, he saw, as several of the Brotherhood nodded gravely.

"As do we all," Ser Albizzi said, but Iacopo felt a stab of worry—was Albizzi implying that the son was a poor substitute?

"His plan should live on."

Albizzi's gaze sharpened. "Ah. So your good father did take you into his confidence before his untimely death?"

Iacopo swallowed, a lump in his throat. "He did, Ser." The other members of the confraternity exchanged a shared, knowing glance. *They do not trust me as they did my father—not yet.*

Albizzi gestured at the scribe, who was scratching dutifully away at his parchment. "Buonfiglio, you may leave now. Thank you for your service this evening." The scribe bowed, gathered his papers, and left.

"Tell us what you know, young Iacopo, and we will see how you might be useful to further our plan," Acciaioli said, unfolding his long legs and leaning forward. "You are not your father, but perhaps you have enough of him in you to accomplish something of worth."

Iacopo wrestled with competing impulses: the desire to prove himself worthy of the Brotherhood's trust, and rage at the fact that they had relegated him to this position of service, rather than recognizing the leadership he ought to have inherited. Caution, perhaps better called subservience, won out.

"You will find me dedicated to the cause, as my father was, and capable."

Acciaioli's narrow lips twitched doubtfully. "Your capacity will have to be demonstrated."

Iacopo sat as tall as he could in his father's chair. "My father told me of the gentlemen in Siena who might support our cause against i Noveschi. I alone know the matter of his latest meetings, those which he arranged in the few days before his arrest and death. I joined him at the house of one of our conspirators in Siena, who now trusts me as he did my father, to further our shared cause." *The fact of the meeting with Signoretti was true—though the trust, in truth, had not yet been proven. But it would come.* Iacopo saw Acciaioli nod, a hard-won, if subtle, sign of his approval.

"I see. Do others of the Brotherhood see as well?" The eight concurred. "Then let us turn to the plans we have for Siena, our self-important little neighbor. There are many *commune* now in Siena's grasp whose loyalty—and taxes—might be ours. The arable land that Siena holds could feed the citizens of Firenze— that grain could fill the mouths of our children with bread, and those grapes our goblets of wine. Since Montaperti the Sienese have paraded their victory, even now, when those who fought have turned to dust. Now it is time to put Siena in her place." There was a rumble of aquiescence from around the table. Acciaioli took a deep breath and resumed. "There are, as the young Medici says, men in Siena whose dissatisfaction might make them easy to incite to rise against their own government. Brienne's plans went astray, but with all we have rebuilt, the next attempt against Siena's Nine should proceed more smoothly." *Nine,* Iacopo thought—*our nine pitted against theirs.*

Albizzi nodded. "Perhaps, then, we should begin by hearing what the young Medici has to say."

Iacopo told the Brotherhood of the plans his father had made, of Signoretti, and other men of noble families in Siena who might be used to overthrow the Nine, and thereby unwittingly deliver their own *commune* into Florentine waiting hands. As he spoke, he searched the faces regarding him from around the long table— some speculative, some withholding judgment, some opaque. It was not a ringing victory, but at least they all listened until he was done.

The men were rising to leave when Iacopo lifted his hand again to speak. "One more thing, good Sers."

The scraping of chairs stopped as the men turned to face him again.

"I have found the informer who brought my father to the hangman's noose."

Ridolfi di Borgo raised one eyebrow. He held an influential position in the Arte di Calimala, the cloth-finisher's guild. "Have you, Iacopo? Well then, do tell us what you have done with him."

"Done with him?"

"Now that he has been found."

He is mocking me now. "I know his name, and his identity."

"And his whereabouts?"

"I am not certain."

"How inconvenient. And what will you do when you find him again? Strangle the offender with your own hands and get yourself strung up by the same hangman who took your father's life?"

"I have a trustworthy man who is willing, for a reasonable fee, to bring this informer to justice."

"And do you know *his* whereabouts, this trustworthy man?"

Iacopo's vision swam, distorted by a spray of bright lights and an arc of geometric lines. Soon, he knew, the nausea and headache would follow. "He resides in Siena."

Ser Ridolfi grunted. "Indeed. Why don't you start by telling us the informer's name, and how you managed to lose him? Siena is not such a great city that a man can hide in it for . . . what has it been now? Six months? A full winter of disappearance."

Iacopo winced, recalling the failure of the sabotaged scaffolding, and then the months lost before he discovered the painter had left Siena on commission. He had spent the hard winter in Firenze struggling to take the reins of his father's business, sifting through papers he could hardly understand, meeting with bankers who realized that the son was a poor substitute for the father. But as the winter's hold began to break, a letter had arrived from Baldi, who had at last managed to discover where Accorsi was headed when he'd left Siena the previous fall. "His name is Gabriele Accorsi, a painter of no particular renown, one Siena would not be likely to mourn, or defend."

Ridolfi made a guttural sound.

"My man discovered Accorsi's departure from Siena just before the leaves began to turn. He was headed to Pisa," Iacopo added.

"And is he still in Pisa?" Ridolfi scowled. "That would be a manageable distance."

Iacopo's head was throbbing; even the wavering candlelight pained his eyes. "I believe he followed a commission to Messina."

Ser Ridolfi laughed unpleasantly. "Messina. I see. So are you proposing that we pursue this third-rate painter across land and sea in an attempt to bring him to justice? And for what crime?"

Iacopo flinched. "With his last words my father commended me to our confraternity's good grace and support. My man in Siena has a plan to denounce Accorsi, and whatever crime he is accused of, I shall find witnesses, my father's allies, who will testify against him."

"A denunciation for an invented crime, and calling false witnesses to trial? Iacopo, this is revenge, not justice, and with a criminal bent. Give it the name it deserves." That was Albizzi now, his face grave.

"Revenge and justice are here intertwined," Iacopo insisted.

Ser Ridolfi leaned back in his chair. "Your head is too small, Iacopo, for the grand thoughts within it."

"I have prayed fervently these past months for a manner in which to serve my father's dying wishes. I appeal to you all to join me in my prayers."

Albizzi spoke, his voice soft but forceful. His wisdom and clear judgment lent him unofficial authority within the group. "Prayers we can promise. We value your filial piety, Iacopo, and your words are eloquent. However . . ."

There was always a however.

". . . your plan is as yet ill-formed. You know the informant's identity but he is too far from Firenze to pursue, and his whereabouts are not confirmed. In faith, I have heard news of a pestilence that has landed in Messina, borne from Caffa on merchant ships. For any of us, the dangers of travel to Messina are too great. In all likelihood, this informant of yours has already succumbed to the illness." Iacopo swallowed, his saliva sour in his mouth. Albizzi was clearly not finished with his summary. "You plan to indict this Accorsi for some unnamed crime he has not committed, and bring him to trial. This might succeed were he in Siena, but his absence prevents any forthright action. Your proposal is too vague to merit further discussion."

Albizzi rubbed his hands together slowly, as if he were molding his thought between his fingers. "I propose that we adjourn for today. Iacopo, should the whereabouts of your Accorsi become clear, we will hear your plans in greater detail." The seven remaining elders of the confraternity variously expressed their agreement, some in words, some with nods, Ridolfi with a grumble.

Albizzi stood, the dark blue of his overmantle falling straight around him. All the rest rose in turn, bowing to one another and making their way up the stone steps and out of the palazzo, leaving Iacopo alone in the chair that dwarfed him. *If they will not support me in my pursuit of Accorsi, then I must act alone.* He sat silently, watching the fire burn down until it was only a faint orange glow of ashes in the hearth.

After the meeting of the confraternity, Iacopo penned a letter to Baldi in Siena, demanding news of the painter. Baldi's response took nearly a month to arrive, coming at the beginning of March, and he reported neither word nor sign of Accorsi. Was a bit more gold forthcoming? He was certain that would advance his search. The Duomo was being enlarged—did Ser Medici wish to know? A crew of workers had been hired to make Siena's cathedral greater than Firenze's own duomo. Perhaps Accorsi would be called back with a commission to decorate the new transept? Iacopo saw the offhand news for what it was—a Sienese barb directed at his Florentine pride. He composed a letter in response:

> *When I return to Siena, we will discuss your fee. In the interim seek out the Accorsi household, to find word of the painter's whereabouts. If he should set foot in Siena again, proceed to set the wheels of justice against him, in the manner that we have discussed. You will denounce him, and I will procure witnesses to testify against the painter. I will send word when I arrive.*

Iacopo found reason to return to Siena in mid-March; the confraternity had agreed it was time to revisit the Signoretti household, and determine whether the *casati* gentleman's collaboration could be assured. "See how you manage this meeting," Ser Acciaioli had said, loud enough so that the confraternity could all hear that the mission was a test of his capacity. "And if you deport yourself well, perhaps other responsibilities will be forthcoming." Iacopo felt like a lone pawn on a chessboard, weak and easy to sacrifice. Though a pawn could, if it advanced far enough, rise higher than its origins—even to become a queen.

Ser Signoretti received Iacopo, if not with warmth, then at least with acquiescence. In Signoretti's *studium* where Iacopo had once proudly accompanied his father, now he entered alone, and the room that had been warm that previous summer now was drafty, dark, and cold. Iacopo stood in front of Ser Signoretti's desk, feeling the nobleman's scrutiny like a knife scraping across his skin. At last, after an unbearably long silence, Signoretti spoke.

"You have come, I assume, to resume where we left off? You must know many things have changed since then."

Iacopo had rehearsed this moment a hundred times on the journey to Siena, and the words, he was relieved to find, came smoothly.

"Ser Signoretti, times change like the weather, but those with a firm purpose stay the course despite storms, with a strong hand on the tiller. Our purpose is as strong as it ever was; perhaps stronger. And the benefit you stand to gain remains just as desired."

Signoretti made a guttural sound. "I would like to trust that the son who stands before me can promise what the father of-fered—the father who was hanged as a criminal by our own courts—and I would like to be as certain as possible that no taint of that crime should stain our family name, which we guard, as we well should, with great care and pride."

Iacopo nodded gravely. He felt, at that moment, his father's mission weighing on his shoulders like a heavy cloak. "My father died for this cause, and I am his successor. He sent me to meet you with that aim in mind. I come with the strong support of the Brotherhood of San Giovanni, and we shall, of course, do all we can to keep your family's position secure in this time of change." Iacopo knew, by the set of the nobleman's head, that he had spoken well this time. Now there was one more item to be discussed: Accorsi.

"In return for our support, Ser Signoretti, both political and financial"—Iacopo with some deliberateness adjusted the pouch of gold coins at his waist, letting them clink audibly—"in return for our support, I would ask one small favor in return. . . ." Ser Signoretti leaned forward to listen, seduced by the promise of power and gold. *I have him now*, Iacopo thought exultantly, *I have him now*.

When Iacopo returned to Firenze with a letter signed by Ser Signoretti's hand confirming his allegiance against i Noveschi, even Ser Ridolfi acknowledged Iacopo's success. The winter cold subsided and the trees began to bud. And with the spring came the weapon the Brotherhood could use to strike Siena at her heart.

This time, Ridolfi and Acciaioli met with Iacopo at night, and alone. The fire was lit but the corners of the cavernous chamber were dark and seemed to Iacopo to be filled with malevolent shadows.

"You have shown your dedication to the cause," Ser Acciaioli said, showing his teeth in a cold imitation of what might have been a smile on someone else, "and competence in dealing with a man your father called an ally. He would be pleased."

The praise made Iacopo uneasy, coming from Acciaioli.

"Ser, I welcome the opportunity to serve my *commune*, and bring my father's plans to fruition."

Ser Acciaioli's teeth flashed white in the firelight. "It is good to hear such a renewal of your purpose, Iacopo, particularly now, when loyalties are tested, and success depends on the devotion of men who do not waver from the path. Would you not agree, Ser Ridolfi?"

"Indeed. These are trying times." Ridolfi had positioned himself so that Iacopo could not look at both men at the same moment, but had to turn his head from one to the other as they addressed him. "It seems our Iacopo might rise to the challenge, given the chance. Would you concur, Ser Acciaioli?"

Acciaioli nodded gravely. "It does appear so. I am encouraged that in the young Medici we have found our man."

At last, my time has come. They will acknowledge my birthright, and my contribution to the plan against Siena. Iacopo sat up straighter in his chair. "You shall not regret any task you set me."

Ridolfi's next question was a surprise. "How fares the search for your painter—Accorsi, did you call him?"

Why do they ask me this now? Is this some test, and if so, what must I do to pass it? Iacopo felt his face flush and welcomed the dark of the room. "I have not found him yet. But I know now where he lives, and the house is watched. And Ser Signoretti has vowed to stand against him in the Podestà's court. I am well positioned to achieve my father's aims."

Ridolfi's eyes flickered toward Acciaioli before settling on Iacopo's face again. "Iacopo, we have a plan that would bring your father's informant to justice, and also serve the larger purpose—to bring Siena under Florentine control."

"Certainly I would be proud to be its instrument." Instrument, *I should not have used that word.* Instrument *is a word they would use.* But Ridolfi and Acciaioli both nodded gravely, cementing his pledge.

"That is excellent news, most excellent news, Iacopo de' Medici." Thus, Iacopo swore fealty to the cause before he knew the extent of what he would be required to do. And once he had heard, once the two members of his father's confraternity set out the plan before him in its chilling detail, it was too late to refuse.

Iacopo had heard news of the malady, brought by traders from the Orient, newly arrived in Firenze. Those infected died an agonizing death, bulging with purulent buboes at the groin and under the arms, and drowning in their own bloody vomitus. When it began to spread from one member of a household to the next, then to the doctors who came to minister to the sick, and finally to the priests who gave the dying their last rites, word spread faster than the disease itself of its rare, rapid contagion. The Mortalità, men began to call it, the great death, for with it came a certainty of destruction far beyond any illness known. Ser Acciaioli, righteous in the pursuit of the piety he declared was his shield against contagion, addressed the full meeting of the Brotherhood in the chamber beneath the Medici palazzo. "Our efforts to raise a rebellion among Siena's *casati* have been too small, and too slow." There, he announced the plan that he and Ser Ridolfi had formed against Siena. And Iacopo, Acciaioli said with a grim smile, would be the one to carry it out. "God has provided us with a weapon, in this Mortalità," he said. "Iacopo, having proven his dedication, and his worth, shall be the one to wield it." Iacopo watched the faces around the table mouth their assent, but he could not hear the words for the roaring in his ears.

It was then that Iacopo became acquainted with the Becchini, the city's pallbearers. The Becchini roamed the city, robed in black or dark red cloaks that fell nearly to the ground, and wore hoods and masks so that only their eyes showed. They would enter a house touched by the Pestilence when no others would, extorting exorbitant sums for their services, and demanding those under threat of violence. Few would do their job, and they could set their own price. Some said the Becchini were unhinged by their proximity to death, and the consequences of their contact with the festering bodies of the victims. They acted as if they had no fear of purgatory. Bands took to entering homes where none had yet died and demanding gold before they would leave the premises, for they were known to carry the contagion with them, bringing destruction wherever they went.

"Iacopo, where are you going?" The undercurrent of fear in Immacolata's voice was audible, and with reason, for a man who left his house to walk Firenze's streets might die before the sun rose on the following day.

"Il Ponte Vecchio, Mamma." The lie came haltingly off his tongue. "I have business to resolve with a goldsmith there."

"Your father never did business there before. Why should you start now, when the smiths have begun to abandon their shops?"

"My father's business is my task, not yours."

But Iacopo's mother read him as well as she had when he was a child, catching the thread of a lie easily. He closed his eyes to an old memory—he had spilled a jug of wine climbing up on the supper table, then blamed the cat. Immacolata had recounted the improbable story to his father at the supper table, protecting him from a beating. When Iacopo opened his eyes again he was startled by his mother's aging face.

"Iacopo, you need not shoulder your father's burdens alone."

He was silent, longing to confide in her. Since his father's death she seemed to have grown in size, filling in the space left by her husband's departure. Iacopo's solitude and his twisted thoughts made him yearn for the promise of her comfort. But he was past that possibility. "My father charged me to carry on his work, here in Firenze and abroad."

"You are still my son, though fully grown in both stature and purpose. Tell me what you are about, *caro* Iacopo."

He could in no way reveal his dark purpose: this planned partnership with the Mortalità itself. "I cannot." When Iacopo left the palazzo, he knew his mother watched him.

Iacopo had arranged to meet a leader of the Becchini, steeling himself against revulsion and fear. He'd been assured that the man showed no signs of illness, but the Pestilence might be boiling invisibly in a man's blood, waiting to burst out into the buboes that heralded certain death. The appointed meeting place, an abandoned *calzoleria* whose owner had perished in the Mortalità, was unlit and musty. Unfinished hose and patterns for shoes lay on the table in the center of the workshop with no one to resume their making. The pallbearer called himself only Angelo, and he kept his face hidden. Angelo—*the Angel of Death.*

"I have a proposition for you," Iacopo said, dropping a bag of gold onto the table between them.

"Tell me of your plan, and I will tell you the price," Angelo said.

Iacopo, overwhelmed by the enormity of the task he had been set, found his mouth trembling so violently he could barely speak. "I would have your men travel to Siena," Iacopo said, "and bring your contagion with you."

"We will need more gold than this to travel the distance you require," Angelo's voice rasped.

"You will have it in allotments as you perform what I have bidden. I know better than to pay too much in advance of the task."

"We will need full names, and places of residence and work, if we are to visit your acquaintances in Siena."

Targets, rather than acquaintances, would be nearer the mark. "You will have those as well." The Accorsi household first, and after that, the cathedral builders, who dared to make Siena's duomo "the greatest church in all Christendom," the Lorenzetti brothers, whose paintings decorated the palazzo, civic leaders, judges, architects, members of the Biccherna, i Noveschi: all those whose industry, art, power, and renown graced Siena would be struck down by a blow too savage to withstand. He imagined a swarm of Becchini fueled by the Brotherhood's gold, winging toward their targets like deadly birds of prey.

Iacopo's step felt lighter with the gold gone as he left the abandoned shop and reemerged into the sun. But soon doubt, his familiar companion, came back to accompany him on the walk home.

When he arrived at the family palazzo, one of the chambermaids had drawn a bath for him. Immacolata would not let any member of the household back inside without cleansing the dirt from the street, for who knew how the illness spread? He lay in the tepid water, but when he closed his eyes he saw the pallbearer's bony hand extending to grasp the pouch of gold.

Two disembodied voices warred within him now, one questioning his purpose as the other spurred him on.

Now, I shall follow in my father's footsteps.
-You are not your father, Iacopo.
I shall prove myself to be his equal.
-And is that what you desire, to be your father's equal? To walk his violent path?

Iacopo was not sure whether he uttered these words out loud or whether they stayed silent in his own head. It had become difficult for him to tell the difference.

*   *   *

Ysabella took up her apprenticeship with Monna Tecchini just as the long winter began to release its grip on Siena. She accompanied the midwife at every hour of the day or night, learning to coax new lives into the world. One particular birth, twin babes each vying to be first to take a breath outside their mother's womb, kept Ysabella late. Both infants survived, but there were moments when, struggling to untangle the wet limbs, Monna Tecchini had feared they might lose not just the babes but the mother as well. When Ysabella left the house, all three were safe at last, two wrapped tightly in linen, the third holding her miracles against her chest.

The streets were dark when Ysabella began her walk toward home. As she passed the house of the Lorenzetti brothers, she saw an odd sight and slowed to watch. Two men cloaked in black stood at the grand house's front door, lit eerily by the lamp at the top of the entrance stairs. It was odd enough to see a visitor at this late hour, but these gave her a chill, for she recognized the distinctive garb of the Becchini, the pallbearers' faces hidden under their wide hoods. Their presence always meant death, a body waiting to be carried to its grave. Tonight their sight sent fear snaking through Ysabella's chest and into her limbs. She had seen the Lorenzettis only that morning when she'd passed the house as the bells were ringing Prime, on the way to the twin birth she'd spent half the night attending. Had one of the brothers sickened and died in just that short time? And if the pallbearers had not come to pick up the dead, why had they come at all, in this secret dark after moonset?

When the door opened and the two figures disappeared into the doorway yawning black against the stuccoed walls, Ysabella slipped from her post and headed quickly home, trying to erase the image of the grim twin silhouette that shadowed the Lorenzettis' door.

Two days later, she heard that Pietro first, then Ambrogio, had died, the new Pestilence from the Orient raging in their blood like demons let loose from hell. Ysabella did not understand what she had seen, for certainly the Becchini came to take death from a household, not to bring it. Afterward, though, her dreams were haunted by the image of two cloaked men, angels of death bringing despair in their wake. In the weeks that followed, when the Becchini passed in the street outside the bakery, she barred the door against them, but that did not protect their home from death's entry.

Gabriele had not returned to his uncle's house by the time the dying began in Siena. Ysabella prayed at first for her cousin to return to them, but as each day brought new horrors, she began to wish he would stay away. Her father, Martellino, went first—one night in May, he took to his bed early complaining of a mighty headache. The next dawn, when he failed to come down to stir the coals in the bakery oven, Ysabella sought him out.

They no longer shared a room; since Gabriele's departure for Messina, Martellino had offered the top floor *camera* to his daughter. "You are nearly a woman now, though it seems only a few days ago that you wore a child's long-hemmed gown. Might the space serve as a *studium* for preparation of your herbs and tinctures?" He had smiled, touching her cheek with a hand that smelled, as it always did, of fermenting yeast—but he would not smile again, and her herbs could do nothing to save him. Ysabella found her father in bed that morning, shivering so violently she could hear his teeth clacking in his mouth, and the boils stood out florid against the pale skin under his arms. The doctor would not come, fearing for his own life. Ysabella tried to nurse her father back to health, bathing him in her own urine mixed with fresh water from the Fonte Gaia, for the urine of a virgin was said to hold exceptional powers of purification. She surrounded his head with bundles of sweet-smelling rosemary, and burned lemon leaves and juniper until the smoke filled the room and she could hardly see her father's face.

When he began vomiting blood, staining the linen coverlet rusty red, Ysabella went out into the streets to find a priest. Even the parish priests remained behind locked doors, unwilling to pave their own roads to death by smoothing their parishioners' paths to the afterlife. Within the day Martellino was dead, and Rinaldo had begun to weaken, unable to rise from his bed to help. Ysabella wandered the streets, where bodies were piled alongside buildings, trying to find a gravedigger to bury her father.

None would help, at least not for a reasonable fee. The Becchini requested an exorbitant price, far more than she could ever amass. When Ysabella blanched, the leering pallbearer suggested her body might serve as currency. Ysabella shrank back from the hands extending from the long, black Becchini cloak, and ran back home, where the closed shutters hid the once-fragrant bakery. She washed her father as best she could, though the stench of his body resisted all her efforts. She dragged his heavy corpse down the stairs legs first, head bumping on each step, but she could get no farther than the doorstep of the bakery. She left him there, covered with a linen shroud.

Rinaldo died a day later. His final hours were much the same, but the last weeks of his life had been vastly different from his father's. When the Mortalità had first begun to wreak its madness upon Siena, Martellino had turned to penitence, prayer, and simplicity of living—eating little, and that which he ate barely seasoned, kneeling to pray at each peal of the bells. Rinaldo had turned instead to debauchery, carousing with bands of men in the streets, drinking in taverns, gambling, and brawling. He returned home long after dark, often with a new cut on his cheek or a blackened eye. Ysabella, when she had a moment to think at all, reflected upon the two men's souls and the opposite ways they chose to meet the looming threat of death.

Ysabella burned the bedding and clothing Rinaldo had worn, and Bianca sequestered herself with little Gabriella in what had once been her marital chamber, covering the baby's face with cloths soaked in aromatic oils. Ysabella did not ask for her assistance in managing Rinaldo's corpse. She dragged his body just far enough outside so she could shut the door. This time, she found a beggar willing to carry the bodies in a cart for a few soldi, and she followed her brother and father to a huge ditch in the parish churchyard where their bodies fell with a soft thump and a scattering of flies upon the heaps of corpses layered there. The house was thus stripped of its men.

Ysabella fully expected that she would succumb, but after a month of watching those around her fall ill and be carted away, she feared her own death less. Bianca and Gabriella were also spared, perhaps because of their isolation—they never left Bianca's bedchamber. The baby slept in a cradle suspended by ropes from a beam in the ceiling, and each time she cried out Bianca leaped up from her bed, with heart pounding. But miraculously, the babe stayed well and cried out only for ordinary reasons: hunger, thirst, or a soiled cloth. Gabriella was taking a bit of *poratta* now from a wooden spoon, and Ysabella brought that and all Bianca's meals to their *camera*, and made sure the oiled cloth and wooden shutters barred the miasma entry.

Every few days Ysabella left the confines of their house in search of food. The *mercato* had shut down and nearly all the businesses were shuttered against traffic that might bring the Pestilence with it. Those that were left sold their goods at exorbitant prices because so few dared to stay and sell at all. Ser Tornabuoni put forth eggs and capons for three times what they had brought before the Pestilence came, and sugar was beyond reach, as it was used for bolstering the diet of the sick. Many shops were left unmanned. Ser Buonacorsi, from whom Ysabella's father had always purchased the wheat and barley for his loaves, had fled to lodgings in the *contado*, along with many of the more prosperous merchants. Some houses lay empty because all within had died, and looters had stripped the buildings bare and left the front doors ajar, creaking on their hinges.

Ysabella could not imagine reopening the bakery after her father's death, but the remaining family must have some livelihood. Monna Tecchini had died in the first few months of the contagion, but she had taught Ysabella well, passing on her knowledge of herbal lore and training Ysabella's hands to coax babies from their watery homes into the perilous world. Ysabella drew upon her knowledge of midwifery and healing, and made a livelihood of it, supporting the three of them. Few doctors would attend to the sick in these times, and those that did often died in the attempt. The beak doctors—armed with birdlike masks against contagion—walked the streets, ominous in their disguises, trusted less and less as the scourge ground on. Ysabella's aim to comfort even when she could not cure made her a welcome visitor. It seemed to Ysabella that each birth was evidence of God's desire that the race of men should continue to inhabit the earth. These thoughts gave her some comfort that the Divine still smiled upon Siena, even as the Pestilence ravaged the city.

One incongruously bright day, a visitor came to the door. Ysabella nearly leaped out of her skin at the knocking, so unfamiliar was the sound. In these times of terror and contagion no soul would enter a house marked with death as theirs had been. She raced down the stairs from her *studium* where she had been drying herbs for a poultice. The smell of lemon balm and rue followed her to the front door.

She did not recognize the visitor. His neck lay in thick folds above his dark wool tunic, and the pallor of his skin reminded her of maggots that multiplied in meat left too long in the sun of the market. Ysabella held the door partially ajar, barring the entrance with her body.

"I am seeking Gabriele Accorsi, the painter. Does he reside here?"

Ysabella started at the name of her cousin; it had been many months since she had heard it anywhere other than within her own head. "He is not here."

"But this is his residence?"

"He is away on a commission." Ysabella's response was just within the boundaries of propriety. It would not do to anger this unknown gentleman, with no man in the house to protect her. But she took an immediate dislike to the caller and could not bring herself to be civil.

"And is he expected back soon?"

"Who are you, to come with probing questions, but no introduction?" Ysabella had never been timid, and her months of survival in the face of overwhelming death had strengthened her already substantial will.

"I am a friend to Accorsi. Giovanni Battista is my name. Your kinsman and I became acquainted during his time at the Ospedale where I am a scribe, assistant to Fra Bosi."

Ysabella narrowed her eyes. He had not counted on her knowledge, and it betrayed his lies now. But she let him continue, gathering information by listening.

"I and the other staff of the Ospedale are concerned for his whereabouts, and hoped there was no news of his demise at the hands of the Pestilence."

Ysabella could see the man's small eyes shift to the left, then right, as if he were reading the next untruth from an invisible page in front of him.

"It is a boon to know that my cousin still has friends, despite the friendless times in which the Mortalità has left us. But I know as little as you, Messer Battista." The man was dangerous. She would have known it even had he not invented a story she knew to be untrue, having met Fra Bosi's scribe herself. And what *had* become of Monna Trovato, after she left Siena under the Genoese merchant's employ? Gabriele had told the story the night before he left for Sicily himself, his pleasure at the new commission tempered by worry for the scribe's welfare. Ysabella hoped Messina had provided a haven for both travelers.

"Your expression of concern is gracious, Ser Battista. Where can my messenger look for you, if I hear any news of my cousin?"

Battista, if that was his real name, hesitated before he gave his address, further raising her suspicions. What sort of man is it who does not swiftly recall his own place of residence? When the visitor took his leave, Ysabella made certain he was well out of sight before she closed the door again.

By the height of spring, the Becchini had turned to looting and pillaging, and the mere sight of a dark-robed figure at a distance would send gentlefolk rushing home to bar themselves behind locked doors. But Iacopo continued to meet with his messengers of death, slipping out of the palazzo late at night to avoid his mother's gaze, and sending them on continued trips to strip Siena of her greatest men.

The first of the Brotherhood met his death at the hands of the Pestilence in May, speckling the walls of his bedchamber as he sputtered his last breaths. Within a month, half the Brotherhood was gone. Albizzi, Ridolfi, and Acciaioli survived, as did Iacopo himself, crossing one name after another off the list of Siena's most respected citizens that he kept hidden close to his heart. There were moments Iacopo half wished the Mortalità would take him as well, and allow him oblivion. But through some odd perverse good fortune, it spared him, to bear witness to all that he had wrought.

PART IX

ROUND TRIP

Afterward, I was known as "that neurosurgeon who came down with Plague on vacation."

"It wasn't exactly vacation," I usually said, though that didn't get at the nature of the inaccuracy. I was well enough by Thanksgiving to celebrate with Nathaniel and Charles at their sleek Upper West Side apartment—always a banner event, especially when Charles was cooking. Linney would have been there but had the flu. Not Plague, she'd made sure of that. The three of us studiously avoided the topic of my illness until dessert. I'd been gone since June—five months, though for me it was more than five centuries.

"So, about that trip you took," Charles said, grimacing wryly as he brought in the final course of the meal, "just tell me where you stayed so I can avoid it. And next time consider a flea collar, okay, honey?" I had to laugh, and the dessert Charles plopped down in front of me kept me smiling—pumpkin crème brûlée, the top browned with a handheld torch. The scents of vanilla and nutmeg filled the room, and the espresso Nathaniel served had a perfect flourish on the *crema*: ferning dark brown on white that would make any barista proud. But even the delicious smells were dull compared with what I had become used to—the headiness of freshly ground spices, the jammy aroma of fruit picked from a *contado* orchard, a loaf baked in Martellino's wood-fired oven. When my eyes teared up, the boys misunderstood why I was crying.

"Sweetie, I'm sorry, it's not right to tease. We almost lost you." Charles was always more voluble with his affections than Nathaniel, but I knew from the look on Nathaniel's face that he had feared for my survival. So had I.

The oldest memories, from before Messina, were crystal clear; I could replay them like a vivid film in my head. But my recollections fragmented as they drew closer to that moment when I jumped centuries for the second time. Maybe because the sickness had been brewing inside me already, distorting my consciousness. Or maybe clarity was impossible at the border of the two worlds I had bridged. Whatever the reason, those last few hours I spent in the fourteenth century assembled themselves like a collage of pictures pasted loosely together on a page.

I remember sitting under a pear tree outside Messina's walls. Feeling thirsty—terribly thirsty. Clara is bending over me, her eyes overly large and glistening with tears. But I send her away— to find water? Then the headache starts, a strange, dull, evil headache, like a warning. How long has she been gone? I am not sure.

I remember the flies buzzing around a squashed fruit on the ground—an autumn pear. I look up to see fruit still on the tree, too high to grasp. I remember the ache in my legs, my run from the Ospedale, then backward, a bit clearer, the brilliant colors of the unfinished *predella* in the chapel. What transpired there—my mind shies away from the memory.

Under the tree, I am lying on something lumpy and uncomfortable: my bag. I look for the water bottle, but it's gone of course. I gave it to Clara. My hand goes to the very bottom of the bag and touches a corner of paper. It's a letter, a modern handwritten letter. I can see the watermark on the page when I hold it up to the light filtering through the fruit tree. Did I already try to reach the fruit? Yes, I think so. I see it's the note from Donata I've been carrying around since June, but a different June. The page is creased and grubby. My eyes are out of focus now; I have to strain to make the words clear. I have the beginnings of a fever, and every seam of the dress I'm wearing grates against my skin.

The letter looks familiar to me; of course it does. There is my name at the top of the page, *Beatrice*. Even in my head I say it the Italian way now.

Cara Beatrice,

How silly to write to you when you live next door, but it seems we never have a moment to talk when I am surrounded by my sweet distractions.

Sweet distractions. I once knew what that meant, but now I can't recall.

If you can spare a few hours from your research, perhaps we might attempt an adult outing together? There is a place near the Fonte Gaia—Caffè Rossi—that the tourists have not yet discovered. And Signora Rossi makes espresso like none other in the Western Hemisphere.

Espresso. I used to drink espresso—the bitter rich taste blooms in my mouth like a hallucination. I think I am crying because now I taste salt, and I remember the feeling of standing next to Donata so acutely it's almost real.

Perhaps tomorrow afternoon?

—Ciao,
Donata

The fever is rising, I know, because the chills are coming, and the shadow of the tree twists and bends on the ground. As I read, I can hear Donata's voice, the intelligence and humor vivid in her words.

And that was when it must have happened, because I don't remember anything after that. I think I rode that letter home. All this time, I had it in my bag, and could have used it. Or could I? What released me from the time I'd become attached to? The Plague taking root in my body and scrambling my sense of place? Or was it the loosening of ties that held me there, with the knowledge of Gabriele bent in suffering in the workroom behind Messina's chapel? I still don't know. But when I awaken, I am staring into a worried, pale face. At first I think it is Clara, then Donata. But then slowly I become aware of the beeps and whines of machines around me. I am in a hospital bed, and the face is Linney's, surrounded by her dark red hair.

I pieced together what happened from what I was told. A group of Russian tourists on a bus tour of Sicily found me lying on the ground, delirious and sweating a half-mile outside the Messina city perimeter. They'd called an ambulance that took me to the local hospital. It seems it wasn't much of a hospital, because it took them nearly twenty-four hours to figure out I didn't just have heatstroke. It had been a record hot day for Sicily in October. Fortunately, Dottoressa Elena Ricci, an infectious disease specialist from Venice, was visiting Messina's main hospital to give a lecture on in-hospital staphylococcal infections. On rounds with the ICU team she heard about the mysteriously ill woman who'd been found passed out in an orchard outside the city gates, wearing medieval dress-up clothes. A few tests later I was in isolation on high-dose intravenous antibiotics.

When the nursing staff went through my bag, they found my

name written on a piece of parchment and were able to figure out where I worked. It didn't take long for the massive clunking Machine of American Medicine, with some help from the U.S. Embassy, to have me flown back home on a medical plane, once I was stable and not contagious, and deposited safely in my former workplace—in New York City. With *Yersinia pestis* safely put in its place, I managed to recuperate fairly quickly, although I'd lost a lot of weight and my legs trembled when I stood up for too long. Still, for a few weeks after, the sight of one of those big buzzy indoor flies that show up in the late fall made me shudder. It would have been more accurate to fear fleas than flies, but my visceral reaction didn't differentiate. I had a lot of unsettling dreams. Sometimes I wondered whether my time in the fourteenth century might actually have been a dream too. The only evidence that I'd traveled hundreds of years into the past was the Plague I'd brought home with me. But, since it had not been eradicated completely even in the twenty-first century, that was not proof enough.

Before I was discharged from the hospital, I'd asked Nathaniel to go through my mail. He brought the most pressing items, including a letter from Ben's lawyers, but after just a few seconds of reading a stabbing headache started between my eyes.

"Just tell whoever wants to know that I'm alive, I'll deal with the rest later," I croaked, "and Ben's neighbor, I mean *my* neighbor . . . Donata . . . ah, what is her name . . . Donata Guerrini—write her too. Just tell her I'm OK." I drifted off to sleep again, for the hundredth time. More often than not I dreamed about Gabriele, and awoke reaching for someone who wasn't there.

Once I was well enough to leave the hospital, I was well enough to think about Ben's mystery again. At first my thoughts were vague, without any impetus to action, until the second letter from the lawyers came.

Dottoressa Trovato:

We hear from your colleague Signor Nathaniel Poole that you became ill while traveling in Sicily, and hope you are on the road back to health. Signor Signoretti, whom we are sure you will recall as the well-regarded Plague scholar, has approached us in your ab-sence—most reasonably requesting your brother's notes so he might complete the work you left behind. We imagine you will need time to recuperate, and that a return trip to Siena may not be forthcoming in the near future. We look forward to your approval, which will allow the most expedient publication of what appear to be important matters of great historical interest.

My first response, which I did not commit to paper, was full of profanity. Instead I wrote:

Dear Sirs:

Thank you for your concern for my welfare. I do not authorize the transfer of any materials to Signor Signoretti. I intend to resume the project, and I appreciate your protection of my late brother's doc-uments. I trust you will continue to exercise the same caution should any future requests arise. Please inform me of any matters regarding the maintenance of my brother's house in my absence.

Best Regards,
Beatrice Alessandra Trovato, MD

I wasn't going to hand over any of Ben's papers to his un-scrupulous competitor, even if he was descended from a fourteenth-century nobleman I'd met in person. But feeling proprietary about Ben's book didn't necessarily translate into actually resuming work on it—at least not immediately. My concentration wavered and I tired easily, napping at every opportunity on the faded pink couch in my apartment. Plus, I was still in New York City. Everything I'd done in Siena, even before my life was split between two times, seemed impossibly far away, and medieval Siena, even farther.

Once I was strong enough, I went back to operating: part-time at first. It might have been easier to work all day than to rest. Resting meant thinking, and thinking meant remembering.

Five weeks after I'd been discharged from the hospital, I decided to go to the Met for the visiting exhibit of medieval Italian art from the Uffizi in Florence. I found a room full of panel paintings from the 1300s and settled myself on a low bench in the middle of the gallery to bask in the images. It was late on a Wednesday afternoon and I was nearly alone in the exhibit; all the senior citizens were probably at half-price Broadway matinees. A blue-uniformed museum guard stood unobtrusively at the doorway, adept at watching for trouble while letting museumgoers commune with the art around them.

I stared at the elongated face of a Madonna with almond-shaped eyes, at the curving plump hand of the Christ child reaching toward his mother's cheek. I had a sharper eye for these images now—I could see emotion in faces I would once have found impassive. I looked at the date: 1320. *Gabriele was nine years old when that was painted*. I suppressed the thought and the sharp sudden pain it created in my chest.

The clothing now looked familiar to me too, and when I closed my eyes I could feel the brush of a long skirt on the tops of my feet, and the smell of wool rose strong and almost sweet around me. But when I opened my eyes again I was still sitting on the upholstered bench in the middle of the gallery. I stayed for two hours, getting up periodically to stare at the paintings at close range. It was the small background details that felt most real to me—a nightingale in a cage hanging under a covered second-floor loggia, a glimpse of sheep dotting the rolling green hills through an open window, pages of a book, illumination in progress, on a scribe's desk. The last one moved me most of all.

I was operating at full swing by the beginning of December. Linney and I worked side by side, and sometimes I'd catch her watching me from under her cap, as if convincing herself that I was really there. I didn't know how to reassure either of us. My mind was occupied with what I'd left behind, a silent parallel narrative that intruded on whatever I was doing. And although I felt competent cutting, cauterizing, and suturing, the undercurrent I'd come to expect during surgery had gone quiet. In fact, since I'd returned nothing had elicited the rush of empathy that had come so frequently before. Sometimes I'd attempt to open my mind to someone else's perspective, or I'd wait expectantly for a passage from a book to elicit a wave of pure emotion. I supposed it was safer to be free of it, if safety was my goal.

The next letter from the lawyers finally jolted me out of my post-Plague inertia. Someone had tried to break into Ben's house—my house. The attempt had failed, but the lock needed to be replaced. I authorized the expense and asked the Albertis to put everything related to Ben's research into a safe-deposit box at the Bank of Siena.

Would someone commit a crime to get at the information I'd collected? And if so, why—to publish it, or to suppress it? What had Ben been on the threshold of discovering that anyone would want to steal? Could the modern Signoretti have had something to do with the break-in? I couldn't sit pondering in New York City anymore. My convalescence was officially over.

The next day I finished a thorny spinal stenosis case early enough for a visit to Nathaniel's bookstore. I hadn't been there since the day I'd announced Ben's death; it felt like seven hundred years ago. Nathaniel was standing at the front of the shop, sorting newly arrived books from a large wooden crate.

"New shipment?"

"An estate sale. There's a complete set of Dickens first editions, and that's just the beginning. Care to help?" Nathaniel beckoned me over and I happily joined him. We spent the next hour peacefully unpacking and cataloging. Finally, I put the book I was holding down on the table between us. Nathaniel put his down too and regarded me steadily.

"Nathaniel, have I ever told you that you have nice eyes?"

"Thank you for the lovely compliment." He smiled so sweetly I wanted to kiss him. Chastely of course. I sighed loudly. "OK, Beatrice, tell me what's eating you. It's not every day you rhapsodize about my facial features."

I was quiet for a minute, trying to figure out how to explain.

"I'm not quite right here."

"Here?" He caught the key word hidden in the sentence. I chewed my lower lip before answering, realizing as I did that it was a habit I'd gotten from Gabriele. I still could barely think about what might have happened to him, let alone discuss it. But what did I mean by *here*? Here and now? There would be no way of discussing *now*.

"Back home. In New York, being a surgeon, all of that."

"Was it so wonderful in Italy, despite what happened?"

He meant getting sick, of course, but that wasn't what I was thinking. "When I'm operating now, part of me is somewhere else. That's not ideal for a neurosurgeon."

"Maybe a full schedule is too much for you right now."

"No, that's not it." I closed my eyes and saw the *scriptorium* the way I remembered it on the last day before I'd left for Pisa. I'd finished the Dante, and it lay in front of me with the ink still drying. The sun came through the thick panes of the tall windows, dappling the stone floor with rippled light. But in my vision one window was still broken, and through it stepped Gabriele, haloed by sunshine. I knew he was dead now, more than six hundred years later. But had he died of Plague in his time?

"You're not sure you belong here anymore?" It was Nathaniel who said it first, my thoughts from months in the fourteenth century finally given voice.

"There are things I have to deal with back in Siena. I left pretty suddenly."

Nathaniel reached out his hand and folded my smaller hand in his. I felt in danger of floating off, away from everything I once knew and wanted.

"What will you do—finish Ben's book?"

I nodded, not saying the rest.

"Well then, we'd better throw you a hell of a going-away party."

"Yes, you'd better," I said, and, suddenly moved, I kissed his hand.

"Should Charles worry?" Nathaniel said, smiling.

"Why should he worry? I'm leaving, right?" I smiled back. We finished sorting through the books from the estate sale, then sat down together to make the guest list.

Packing was harder this time. I didn't know how long I'd be in Siena, and in how many seasons—or centuries. I didn't know whether that thought produced dread or desire.

I packed everything from my medicine cabinet. I hesitated when I got to my diaphragm—bringing birth control seemed presumptuous. But it might be as lifesaving as antibiotics, given the risks that accompanied pregnancy in the fourteenth century. I threw it in with everything else. I called in prescriptions to the neighborhood pharmacy for myself: two weeks of several antibiotics—ciprofloxacin included. I should be immune to Plague by now, but others might not be, and there were plenty of other infections to worry about. I justified it as being like packing mefloquine for a trip to a malaria-infested country.

Next I packed my few pieces of jewelry. Folded into a velvet envelope was a heart-shaped pendant that had been my mother's, inset with small rubies. I'd often taken it out to look at but hadn't worn it since my high school prom. I put it on now, feeling the gold warm against my skin. I moved on to clothes, putting as much as I could fit into a vast yellow duffel bag I'd had since medical school. It smelled funny but worked fine.

The bottom drawer of my dresser was full of surgical scrubs. Looking down at that pile of blue and green gave me a more explicit pang than saying good-bye to any live person. I closed the drawer quickly without touching the contents.

I flew to Siena on Christmas day. This time my keys fit the lock. There was no bakery—no yeasty smell from Martellino's ovens, but it still felt like home, or halfway home. I fell asleep in my clothes on the little guest bed.

I woke up to the sound of Felice's voice mingling with the twitter of winter sparrows in the courtyard garden. It was almost noon. I stumbled downstairs to find Felice perched in the orange tree. At this time of year there were no blossoms or fruit to pick. In true childhood fashion she launched into conversation without awkward preliminaries.

"You're back. Where did you go? You missed Christmas. I have a new doll. She has red hair. And you missed my birthday. Mamma made me pear cake. I like pears. Do you?" She scrambled down from the tree.

"I went home to New York," I said. "And I'm sorry I missed your birthday. I love pears." My Italian felt rusty, but she nodded, satisfied.

"Is your *mamma* home?" I'd sent Donata a letter as soon as I'd gotten out of the hospital, sketchily explaining my three-month disappearance. I wondered what she'd thought.

"She's making risotto." The memory of the first time I'd seen Donata cook risotto came back to me. Sebastiano must be walking by now. As if to prove me right, the back door to the garden opened, emitting an unsteady but determined Sebastiano, who squealed with pleasure at his escape and toddled toward me.

"Sebastiano, *caro, vieni!*" Donata's head appeared in the doorway, following her voice.

"Beatrice! What a pleasure."

It had been a long time since I'd heard my name out loud in Italian. Donata's face was flushed from the heat of the stove, and tendrils of golden hair escaped from a loose bun at the base of her neck. Even in a faded flowered housedress she looked like an angel.

"I didn't know you were back."

"I got in last night, too late to say hello."

"Come for lunch," she said. I didn't need to be asked twice.

Risotto in December is very different from risotto in July in a place where the seasons get the respect they deserve. In Italy winter is dried mushroom time, and I walked into the Guerrini kitchen to the intense aroma of porcini. The family welcomed me without any questions, letting me eat before I talked. I was hungrier than I'd been in weeks. When I helped myself to thirds, Ilario, who'd only had seconds, laughed.

"Do they starve you in New York City? Or is the food not worth eating?"

"Nothing like this." The creamy rice, the glass of Montalcino red, the astringent bitterness of the arugula salad dressed sparingly with olive oil, lemon juice, and salt, all combined to make a heavenly meal. *Maybe I'll be all right now that I'm back in Italy,* I thought; *it doesn't have to be medieval.* But I wondered.

After lunch, Felice and Gianni reluctantly cleared the dishes, then disappeared upstairs to play with their new holiday toys.

Donata and I washed up, and Ilario retreated into the bedroom with Sebastiano. When I peered into the room a few minutes later they were both asleep, son blissfully splayed out on his father's slowly rising and falling chest.

"Now tell me the whole story, Beatrice," Donata said, wiping her hands on a kitchen towel and pulling out two chairs for us. I took my time settling, needing a few moments to strategize.

"I went to Sicily, for research. I'm sorry I didn't tell you where I was going; things happened more quickly than I'd expected." Still true, if deceptively so.

"A spur-of-the-moment trip to Sicily sounds very adventurous. Your research must have been successful, to keep you there so long."

"Well, I met someone." *When you have to lie, use the available facts.*

"How romantic—in Sicily?"

"We ended up in Messina. My work got a little derailed while I was there. He's from Siena though."

"*Cara* Beatrice, how fairy-tale marvelous that sounds. Was it?"

"It was until I got sick."

"So you said in your letter." She paused expectantly. I didn't answer right away, and the silence grew uncomfortable. "Nothing from him, I hope?"

"Oh, no, nothing like that!" I laughed with relief. She'd thought I had some rip-roaring sexually transmitted disease. "Donata, I need coffee. Can I make some for us?" I needed alcohol more than caffeine to tell this story, but the preparation would buy me more time than pouring a glass of San Rafaele.

"No, no, sit, *cara*. I'll do it." I loved the way she called me "*cara*." When Donata says "dear" she really means it. She made espresso and we both sipped in appreciative silence for a while.

"Now that you have your coffee, you must repay my hard work on lunch with the story." She smiled encouragingly.

I took a deep breath. "Plague. I got the Plague."

"Plague? How?"

"I was exposed somehow, then I was airlifted to New York. But I survived. Unscathed, I think." I tried to smile but it came out feeling lopsided. My hands were shaking and I put my espresso cup down, but too hard—coffee spilled over the rim and onto the table. The mess shocked me. I'd made plenty of mistakes in my life but my hands rarely were the problem, fortunately for my patients. I looked up at Donata and saw her eyes fill with tears.

"*Carissima* Beatrice, how glad I am to have you safe with us again." She rose suddenly from her chair and came to my side of the table, putting her hand on my shoulder. "I was so terribly worried about you, not hearing for months like that. I imagined the most awful things. Why didn't you tell me?"

"I'm sorry." What could I possibly say as an excuse—*I couldn't write to you because I was stuck in 1340s Siena?* The difference between my story and the truth hung between us like a curtain. I pushed my chair away from the table and stood up next to her. Before I could figure out what to say, Donata wrapped her arms around me and buried her face in my neck. She smelled like porcini mushrooms and coffee, and more faintly, lily of the valley perfume. I stiffened, startled by her sudden embrace, but then the sweetness of it overwhelmed me and I let myself soften in her arms. It had been forever since anyone had pushed past my physical restraint like that, and a wordless relief swept over me. But it was more than that. My ears were humming, my vision darkened, and then I felt Donata's emotion firsthand—the affection, the fear of loss, the stark relief. *It's back*, I thought with a stab of joy. *It's back, and so am I.*

In the next few days, I met with the lawyers, retrieved Ben's notes from the safe-deposit box at the Bank of Siena, and clarified that I'd be resuming work on the manuscript without the aid of any meddling scholars. The Albertis were tight-lipped with what I suspected was disapproval, but they remained polite. The gas and electricity had been turned off while I was away, and I had to spend several unpleasant days getting my utilities back. This made me not only cold and dependent on candles, but also unable to make coffee—a bigger disaster. A few days after I'd arrived in Siena the weather hit record low temperatures, and the pipes froze in the top-floor kitchen. Not having running water reminded me of the less pleasant aspects of medieval life. I went to the corner bar for espresso to stay caffeinated, but while I was waiting for the heat to come back on a frozen pipe burst upstairs, damaging one plaster wall. Donata recommended a plumber and contractor for the repairs and offered me hot meals and showers until I could resume modern life at home again. Then I dove back into research. I had firsthand information about medieval Siena now, but I wasn't sure how my intimate knowledge of the fourteenth century could help me with Ben's mystery.

Ben's unanswered question was as much a part of his legacy as the house he'd left me. Since the break-in, I had imagined the lengths to which someone might go to interfere with the work I was doing, and my resolve to finish it had grown even stronger. But beyond the modern-day academic threats, I had a personal drive to know. The evil that Ben had uncovered wasn't just an academic question for me anymore—it might have killed people I loved in a time and place I had once called home.

On the morning of December 28, I woke up just after dawn. Out the window, a bitter freezing rain was falling and the street was empty except for a woman bundled against the cold, leaning into the wind. What was I looking for? Did I want to take up where Ben had left off and make a new life of scholarship? Or did I want to find a more direct route to the past? *Read about it or live it?* And who knew whether I could control my reentry to the past anyway? It had happened by accident the last time, as far as I could tell. Now, in this city that straddled a millennium with uncanny grace, the past pressed in on me.

Gabriele's journal could be the key to my return to his time. But where could it be? The book hadn't followed me into the fourteenth century—I'd lost it on my trip, perhaps because Gabriele had it then himself. So where should I be looking instead?

I thought through the twisted logic. When did I last have it? The time Gabriele had handed me his freshly written diary to hold didn't count—that wasn't the right version of the book I'd lost. I traced my path backward in my head. I'd been reading it in the Duomo when I first traveled to July of 1347. That book, if I could find it, might tell me whether Gabriele had survived the Plague. Gabriele's handwritten lines stood out when I closed my eyes, like a bright afterimage:

> *I find the mysterious figure hovering at the edge of my paintings, watching the events unfold in the scenes I depict. It is as if she were seeking a path through my paintings and into this world.*

Seeking a path through my paintings and into this world.

Here was something even more compelling and terrifying: maybe the journal, far from its time of origin, would again open a gateway to the past, as it had before. *You'd better be sure you know what you want before you look for it, Beatrice.* But even as I thought those words, I rose from the bench and walked out of the room.

I arrived at the Duomo in time for Mass. It was almost possible to pretend, listening to the Latin, that I was back in the 1300s. Until I looked at the boy next to me, fiddling with his mother's smartphone. After the service, I made my way over to a gray-haired docent at an information desk near the entrance. She turned to me with a practiced smile and perfect English. "How can I help you, Signorina?"

"Do you have a lost and found?"

"Of course. What have you lost?"

"It's been a few months."

"You're coming back for the first time now?" Her pleasant demeanor cracked a bit.

"I didn't realize I'd lost it." It sounded lame even to me.

"It's quite unlikely we'll be able to help you, but why don't you give me a description of the item and I'll ask the other staff."

"It's a book."

"What sort of book? At this point you might just want to buy another copy."

"It's irreplaceable, actually." I had a terrible thought about how much trouble I'd be in with the Siena library for losing the book, and with the inappropriately trusting Fabbri.

The docent raised her eyebrows but pushed a small piece of paper and a pen over to me. "Please write a description here, and your contact information. You must realize how unlikely it is that we will find it after all this time."

I wrote a few lines, and she put the description into a manila envelope. I took a walk around the cathedral, going back to the pew where it had all started. I even checked the floor but found only a discarded monthly Siena Attractions pass and a plastic barrette decorated with a yellow daisy.

Foiled in my attempt to find Gabriele's diary, I resorted to academic pursuits. I considered my evidence: firsthand knowledge of Giovanni de' Medici's execution, and the poignant letter written by Immacolata Regate de' Medici about her grieving, increasingly inaccessible son. If it somehow related to Siena's extreme devastation by the Plague, then it might implicate the Medici family—but the connection was still obscure to me. I had Immacolata's letter with me now, carefully packaged in a waterproof archival envelope. Once I got to the library I took it out and read it again, the words familiar now.

> Since the death of his father I fear my little Iacopo has been full of strange and troubled thoughts. . . . But ever since the misery that has befallen his father, my beloved husband, the execution that has become the tragedy of our noble family, Iacopo . . . broods alone and writes endless pages in a small cramped hand. . . . It does not appear to be a letter. . . . I pray to see the joy return to my son's face, and lighten the shadow that weighs upon all our hearts.

Iacopo de' Medici. Giovanni de' Medici had to be Iacopo's father. How many executed Medicis could there have been in 1347? It was enough to get me started.

A quick Internet search for Medicis in the 1300s came up with a Giovanni, executed for an unknown crime, but in 1342—too early. Could the website be wrong? My best living source was Donata, who, over coffee that I managed to make competently enough to please her, suggested I try the crypt. The crypt was the university library's underground archive, which I'd missed on my first trip to Siena. Built in the catacombs of one of the university's original buildings, it housed some of its oldest documents in a dimly lit space with low arched stone ceilings. The humidity was tightly controlled by a regiment of humming machines along the wall.

I spent the rest of the day there, assisted by the now familiar and untiring Emilio Fabbri. I smiled my most Gabriele-like smile and told him how helpful the journal had been thus far in my research, omitting the fact that I'd lost it. I hoped he didn't mind if I kept it a bit longer? He bowed his assent and left me to the documents he'd assembled.

Fabbri suggested I start with tax records, a good way to find medieval people, assuming they'd paid their taxes. Since it was unlikely that any Medici would have paid his taxes in Siena, I didn't expect that approach to be useful. However, through an odd twist of fate, it was. A former graduate student at the University of Siena had done her thesis on contrasts between Sienese and Florentine financial record-keeping in the fourteenth century, a topic that would have once bored me. As a result of her work, though, a good chunk of Florentine tax records was available in the library's archives. It took me hours to read through the pages of faded writing despite my unusual firsthand experience as a medieval scribe.

It was almost closing time when I finally found his name: Giovanni de' Medici, and the rest of his household too—Immacolata (wife) and Iacopo (son). Fortunately for me, the family had been good about paying taxes, and the records were from 1345. If this was the executed Giovanni, he'd lived past 1342. Just as things were heating up, Fabbri appeared and regretfully asked me to gather my belongings, as he needed to close the archives to visitors. I looked at my watch—ten minutes to five. I could do a lot in those ten minutes. I headed for the steel cabinet that housed execution records from Siena's medieval prison. With Fabbri's increasingly anxious assistance, I found the year I was looking for. And then, just like that, there it was. The parchment had yellowed with age, but of course I knew the handwriting and the signature—an owl and knife like a branch beneath the owl's feet.

> On this day, Messer Giovanni de' Medici was thus condemned to death by hanging at the hands of the Podestà and jurists acting on the Podestà's behalf.
>
> Signed by my hand and no other,
> Beatrice Alessandra Trovato

This of all things survives me? I had been there, then, after all. *If anything should send me back in time this should*, I thought, waiting for the thunderclap. But I felt nothing out of the ordinary, other than the combination of thrill and shock I might be expected to have, seeing a document I'd written centuries before.

The repetitive throat clearing of Fabbri at my shoulder brought me back to my own time: 5:00 p.m. exactly. I put the documents I'd found together in a file box allocated to me for that purpose, and left my discoveries to sit overnight (in a locked carrel) while I went home for dinner, a shower, and an early bedtime.

That night, I dreamed about Gabriele. We were in the elevator of the building I'd grown up in; it smelled like Mr. Clean. I knew in my sleep that an elevator was a place where people from two different worlds could meet, because it hung suspended between places, with no real location of its own. Gabriele looked pale, as if he hadn't fully materialized. He didn't speak, and when I reached out toward his face, my hand touched the paneling behind him. He didn't notice my intrusion on his physical integrity.

"Are you alive?" I asked, but it seemed he couldn't hear me, or maybe I hadn't phrased it right. "I mean, are you alive in your own time?" He smiled, as he often had when I'd said something amusing. "Did you take all your pills?" *Medication compliance—what a ridiculous thing to waste my otherworldly encounter on.* But Gabriele had already turned away. Slowly he took on the colors and patterns of the objects around him—the brass railing that ran around the elevator's perimeter, the false wood grain. Gabriele would love that, I thought, remembering how much he delighted in the portrayal of inanimate objects in his work, but before I could finish the thought he was gone, and the elevator opened onto the bright fluorescent light of the tenth-floor hallway.

———

The next morning I woke up with a headache. I made a cup of coffee and sat at my kitchen table sipping until the pain receded, but my larger problem could not be solved by coffee. I had told only one person the truth about what had happened to me, and he was centuries old. I briefly imagined explaining time travel to Donata. The thought made my head ache again. Instead I did what I had done in 1347. I wrote a letter that I had no intention of sending.

Dear Nathaniel,

You were so close to the truth, I almost told you. I didn't simply go to Siena last summer; I went to Siena's past. And there I found myself in the middle of the mystery that Ben had started to unravel. But I found more than that. I found colors brighter than I had ever seen, and flavors more intense, and a way of life that centers around the pealing of the bells. I glimpsed the edge of that existence a long time ago, before surgery wrote its name in capital letters on my future. Now I've read Dante in the medieval Italian vernacular, and copied it myself. I've played a part in the law and business of a place where contracts are still written by hand, and faith is a profound part of daily existence. I've dedicated myself to the practice of history rather than medicine, and in the process I've learned a new way into people that doesn't require slicing them open with a scalpel. It has all been surprisingly satisfying, and sweetly, terribly beautiful.

You know me well enough to see I'm leaving something out. As you predicted I've met my match. It makes me cringe but there it is. The inaccessible Dr. Trovato, you must be thinking, hooked at last. True to form, I've picked a person who is so staggeringly inaccessible (or he has picked me, or some other force has picked us both, but now I'm sounding medieval!) that there's no chance—well, almost no chance—it will succeed. Because, you see, not only is he dead, he's from another century. He was dying the last time I saw him, dying of the Plague, the way I almost did. But he didn't have modern American medicine to pull him through. I gave him a taste of it, but was it enough? The obvious thing to do would be to try to find out whether he survived, and if he did, to go back for him. And if I went back to find him and he was dead, then what? Would I wish I had stayed in my own time? I'm not sure, believe it or not. I felt more at home there and then than I've ever felt, but I can't tell how much of that was him. Maybe I'm crazy, but this particular insanity revolves around the truth, as improbable as it may be.

When I finished writing, the page was wet from tears.

The next morning I went back to Fabbri again. He seemed inordinately happy to see me; it was possible I was the only person he'd seen in months.

"I'm looking for a Giovanni de' Medici," I said, "who paid his taxes in Florence in 1345 and died in 1347. What other sources might be useful? I'd like to know more about his family."

Fabbri's pale forehead furrowed with thought. "You might search for birth and death records from Firenze's archives."

"Can I get the information without leaving Siena?"

Fabbri looked pained that his resources were insufficient for my purposes. "We can arrange an interlibrary loan if you'd like."

I liked, but unfortunately it would take three or four days to get a copy of the pages of interest. Now that the question of Giovanni de' Medici's family was on hold, I was free to pursue the answer to the question I'd been afraid to ask.

Donata's office was on the sixth floor, and there was no elevator. By the time I reached the top of the last set of steep marble steps, I was panting, and when Donata opened her door to my knock she looked alarmed.

"Beatrice, you look gray."

"Out of shape," I gasped.

"Oh, the stairs." Donata smiled with a trace of impishness. "They separate out students who have something important to say from those just looking for a better grade on the midterm. The pretenders give up."

I collapsed into a leather armchair and sat for a moment, recovering. "I'm a well-meaning visitor but I need a beverage." Donata laughed and went to fill a glass of water from a hand-painted pitcher on a credenza behind her desk. She watched indulgently while I gulped.

"Now that you are well-hydrated, please tell me, Beatrice: to what may I attribute this surprise visit?" Donata sat down in a comfortable chair across from me. I imagined that with her students she might sit behind the desk.

"I'm trying to find out about a painter who lived and worked in Siena in the 1340s. His name was Gabriele Beltrano Accorsi." *Lived. Was.* Speaking about him in the past tense made a wave of sorrow rise up in me so acutely I had to pause for a few seconds. I could feel Donata scrutinizing me.

"Accorsi? He was a pupil of Simone Martini, in the years before Martini left for Avignon." She pulled a massive text from the shelf and flipped through it quickly. "Yes, here he is. He was born in . . . 1311. Would that be the same Accorsi you're thinking of?"

My heart was pounding. "That sounds right."

I came into the world three years to the day after Duccio di Buoninsegna's Maestà was carried through the streets to the Duomo by a great and reverent crowd. . . .

Donata interrupted my thoughts. "Now, date of death, let's see." I held my breath. She was still looking down the page.

. . . not October 1347, please not October 1347 . . .

"Hmm, no date of death. I guess it's not known. This book would include it if it were."

I exhaled.

"Few of his paintings have been found, but we assume that more were painted than survived. Do you want to read this? There's a bit more." She handed me the heavy volume and I pored over the one-paragraph entry. Born in Siena. No mention of his marriage, but a list of a few paintings attributed to him. The Saint Christopher painting I'd seen in the Duomo's museum was on the list, the one in which I, or my look-alike, stood on the river's edge. There was no mention of the painting I'd watched Gabriele labor over, the four angels on the Ospedale facade guiding Mary's Assumption into heaven. I searched for a note about the Messina Ospedale altarpiece but didn't find it. Did that mean it hadn't been finished? Donata's voice made me look up.

"I'm happy to do some additional research on Accorsi—one of Siena's own, little-known painters—that's my sort of subject. But it will take me a few days—I have a manuscript due to a publisher this week. Can you hold out until next Monday? The Guerrinis' next meal may depend on this advance."

"Research on a medieval fresco painter can hardly be considered an emergency," I said, trying to sound lighthearted, "compared to feeding a family of five."

"Why is Accorsi so compelling to you, if you don't mind my asking?" Donata leaned back in her chair. She looked charmingly academic with her wire-rimmed glasses pushed up on her head, caught up in her golden hair. She wore a tweed skirt suit of muted pumpkin-colored wool and high brown leather boots. The outfit would have made me look like a Dunkin' Donuts fall special, but on her it was gorgeous.

"He testified against a Florentine murderer and got himself into trouble."

"And you think this relates to Siena's failure to recover after the Plague, and her eventual loss to Florentine rule a hundred and fifty years later? I'm missing the connection."

"So am I, but it may have something to do with the murderer's family. He was a Medici. An early Medici, but still."

Donata raised her eyebrows. "You would certainly make a splash in the academic world if you could prove it," she said thoughtfully, "and most things don't even cause a ripple. Medieval historians like to pretend we know everything there is to know when of course the reverse is true."

"Well, I'm very grateful for your help."

"Of course. But what am I looking for?"

What was I looking for? *I want to know whether he'll be alive if I go back to find him.* I came up with a more sensible version of the question for her.

"I want to know what he painted after the Plague arrived in Siena, if he painted anything at all. Those post-Plague years, until the fall of the Nine in 1355, seem key to the story." She looked at me curiously. I didn't say, of course, that I wanted to know whether he'd survived the Plague.

"I'll do what I can. But . . ."

"But?" I smiled brightly.

"You seem awfully passionate about this topic, for a neuro-surgeon." What did she hear or see in my manner that made her wonder?

"Former neurosurgeon."

"So it's gone that far?"

"I don't have a return ticket."

"Welcome to starving academia," Donata said cheerfully. "At least you don't have a family of five to feed. Yet."

Now I had three projects on hold waiting for someone else's help—finding out about tax records from the clerk, the missing journal at the Duomo's lost and found, and Gabriele's fate from

Donata—and I felt restless and irritable. The heat was on in the house now, but wind got in through the old wood-frame windows. I felt a strange sense of déjà vu, imagining the house as I'd seen it in Gabriele's time superimposed on the modern version I lived in now. I stayed home for New Year's Eve, and spent New Year's Day in a flurry of housecleaning just to make myself feel better. I took a look at the damaged wall in the kitchen. Getting someone to fix it over the holidays was hopeless; Donata had recommended a contractor who said he could start mid-January. Looking at the chunks of loosened plaster, I thought I might be able to do some of it by myself, and, using one of Ben's ancient metal kitchen spatulas, I started chipping away at the fragments. One big piece fell off, and I backed up, saving my toes. But when I looked at the hole I'd created I stopped and stared. On the wall underneath, the much older plaster wall, were lines in a faded brown—not mildew, but *sinopia,* the pigment used to draw out frescoes before they were painted. Suddenly I heard the bubble and hiss of my espresso boiling over and raced back to the stove to rescue it. With my heart pounding, I went back to chipping. After an hour I'd cleared a few feet of space, and could see I was right—it was a sketch of a man. It was not a perfect likeness, but the man's features reminded me of Giovanni de' Medici. I kept chipping until I'd bared most of the wall down to the original plaster. It wasn't a coherent single painting, but a series of sketches. It must have been Gabriele's studio—who else would have drawn on the wall on the top floor of Martellino's house? Knowing that his hand, hundreds of years before, had touched the plaster, made the past seem suddenly closer. I wanted to touch it too, to narrow the centuries that divided us. Then I realized I'd been hacking away at a centuries-old work of art with a kitchen tool.

The man with the Giovanni-ish face was one of two talking outside a birthing room where a newborn was being bathed in a basin. The sight of the second man's face made my heart skip a beat. This face reminded me of Signoretti—the medieval Signoretti. Why did they keep showing up side by side, this unlikely pair of noblemen? Was it just a coincidence? Was Gabriele just using the faces he knew? I wished I could ask him myself. I put down the spatula, which was now hopelessly bent, and went back to my coffee. It was cold but I drank it anyway, staring at the sketches.

A memory of Gabriele painting, holding a brush like an extension of his arm as he chewed his lower lip thoughtfully, filled my head. The thought that he might have died in the chapel where I'd left him in Messina was unbearable. I had to have that journal.

That evening, exhausted from my day with a plaster wall, I decided to go out for a drink. I sat down on a stool at the worn marble bar and ordered a sherry, feeling decadent. As I waited, I saw a familiar figure walk in the front door. His pale hair was flattened to his head when he took off his winter hat, and his slim stooped build reminded me of a parenthesis. For a few seconds I couldn't place him out of context, and then I realized it was Fabbri from the university library. He saw me and waved, surprising me with his enthusiastic smile. People are sometimes very different when they're not at work. I motioned to an empty stool and he joined me after shedding several layers of wool onto a coatrack by the door. I like to play a game of trying to guess what people are going to order and made a quick assessment. *A gimlet*, I thought as he gestured to the bartender, *or something else quaintly old-fashioned*. But he surprised me again by asking for an Absolut Citron kamikaze. You just never know.

"Dottoressa Trovato," he said with a polite nod. He didn't mention Gabriele's journal, fortunately.

"Beatrice, please."

"You know, it's a funny coincidence I've found you here. I have your papers, copies from the library in Firenze. They came late today, but as I was on my way out the door I put them in my bag. The mailbox is so far from my office I didn't want to go all the way back." He handed me the sheaf of papers and then took an appreciative sip of his drink. I looked around me to make sure no one was watching before reading—I'd started to imagine Signoretti was following me everywhere, waiting for a misstep. But as I read through the pages, I forgot both my paranoia and my sherry. I saw Giovanni and Immacolata de' Medici's names immediately but found no mention of Iacopo's birth, just a record of Giovanni and Immacolata's only daughter, baptized Cristina.

"That's odd."

"Dottoressa?"

"Beatrice, please," I said reflexively, reading over the pages again.

Fabbri had another sip of his drink, which was disappearing fast. I hoped he would be able to stay on his stool.

"I can't find the person I was looking for. Just a different child, who died shortly after birth." Could the tax records be wrong about Iacopo? I had that letter from Immacolata, about her son in the aftermath of his father's execution. Maybe he'd been born later? The records extended several more years, but there was no mention of the birth of any Iacopo de' Medici.

"Are the documents helpful?" The clerk had finished his drink and gestured to the bartender for another.

"Yes, quite. Thanks so much. I'm glad I ran into you." I slid off my stool, forgetting the sherry.

"Your drink?"

"Oh, I've had plenty," I said distractedly, leaving some cash for the bartender. I was about to leave, but remembering Gabriele's skill at making everyone feel special, I stopped.

"You've been an enormous help," I said. "I feel fortunate to be able to work with you." He beamed—the Gabriele magic worked.

I walked home in the dark, wondering where Iacopo had come from, if not his parents. If they were his parents.

With an empty weekend looming, I decided it was time to repay the Guerrinis' hospitality and invite the whole family over for brunch, American style. Grocery shopping was challenging. It took me three hours to find a bottle of maple syrup, and six ounces cost the equivalent of twenty dollars. Bacon took less time, though I wasn't familiar with the packaging and almost bought prosciutto by mistake. The ingredients for pancakes were easy.

Brunch was a huge success, if a messy one. I sat everyone in the dining room, out of sight of the kitchen. I wanted to show Donata what I'd found, ideally privately, after we ate.

Felice and Gianni were allowed to pour their own syrup and overdid it extravagantly. Sebastiano had a fistful of pancake in each hand and syrup on nearly every item of his clothing and all his exposed skin by the end of the meal. Donata and Ilario oohed and aahhed appreciatively about the unknown delights of American cuisine. We finished a triple recipe, and I was gratified to see the slim Ilario surreptitiously unbuttoning his pants under the table.

Ilario had promised the kids a trip to a medieval Christmas pageant in the Campo, and bundled them all up and out my front door. It was inordinately quiet after they left.

"Did you submit your manuscript to the publisher?"

"Thursday, just before deadline. Our next few months of dinner are secured." Donata swirled the last little bit of coffee in her cup, then set it on the table.

"Donata, can you come in the kitchen for a second? It's a mess, I'm warning you."

"You are not the first person to have a messy kitchen, Beatrice."

"Well, it's unusually messy, actually, since the pipe leak. But I want to show you something."

She raised her eyebrows. "Now I'm intrigued." Once we were in the room together, I was satisfied to hear her gasp.

"Beatrice, this is extraordinary."

I nodded. "Who do you think painted it?"

She narrowed her eyes. "It's difficult to tell from sketches, but there are qualities of the drawing that remind me of Accorsi's work. That would be a peculiar coincidence, to have your favorite painter's frescos on your kitchen wall." I snorted. She had no idea what a coincidence it was. She looked for a long time, close up, and then backed up a few steps. "It looks like studies for the birth of the Virgin. Apparently the Signoretti Chapel, here in Siena, has remnants of a fresco depicting the birth of the Virgin, though not enough survived to determine the painter. I have never seen the work myself; it's not routinely accessible to the public."

The Signoretti Chapel. It certainly wouldn't be accessible to me, not if it required convincing the twenty-first-century Signoretti, my current archenemy, to let me see it. The slice through almost seven hundred years made me so breathless I couldn't even respond. And what would I say if I responded anyway? I couldn't tell Donata that I knew Gabriele had painted the Signoretti fresco, and I certainly couldn't say I thought I recognized the models. I would have been very surprised if Gabriele had actually used these same faces in the final painting anyway, putting a notorious Medici in a Sienese nobleman's house. "Do you know someone who could figure out what to do with these? I feel like my house has suddenly become a museum."

Donata laughed. "Welcome to life in Siena—we all feel that way. Yes, I'll have one of our restorers come take a look and see what we can do. I suppose it's a blessing, your burst pipe."

We both stared at the wall for a while, seeing different things. Finally, she turned back to me.

"Beatrice, I asked a curator I know at the Museo about Accorsi. You know that he has paintings here in Siena?"

"The Saint Christopher one? Yes, I've seen it." I wondered whether Donata had. My likeness was glaringly obvious to me, but maybe an outside observer could miss it, among all the people he'd painted at the water's edge.

"There are two actually. The second wasn't painted here but was transported sometime in the 1800s from Messina, Sicily." I felt the hair on my arms rise at her explanation. "Would you like to go see it?"

"What, *now?*"

"The Museo opens at eleven on Saturdays." Donata called Ilario to alert him to her plans, and at my insistence, we left without washing the dishes.

We walked to the Museo. After a week of nasty weather the sun had finally emerged, and everyone was outside, enjoying the break from winter. In my head I was in the tiny chapel of Messina's Ospedale again, walking through the slanting beams of sunlight. Donata read my mood and didn't break the silence. I was aware of her at my side, matching my pace, and was happy to have the quiet company.

After consulting the museum floor plan we went straight to the right gallery. I saw the altarpiece right away, hanging on the far wall of the room. I crossed the length of the gallery slowly, as if I were walking through water. As I stood in front of the painting, I started to cry.

"Beatrice, what's the matter?" Donata put her hand on my shoulder.

"It's not finished."

"Is that such a tragedy, *cara?*"

I looked at the painting through my tears—four saints in the panels above: Christopher, Luke, Placidus, Nicholas—and the *predella* below, recounting the life of the Virgin. And there was

Paola-Mary with her fearful face and outstretched hand, still warding off the news of the Annunciation. But as hard as I stared, I saw nothing that had not been there before. If he'd finished it I would have known he'd lived. I was crying too hard to look any longer, and I felt Donata lead me by the hand to a padded bench in the center of the gallery. I sat there with my head bent, sobbing steadily.

"You must care quite deeply about this painter to be moved so by his work." Donata spoke quietly.

"Crazy, isn't it?"

"Perhaps not."

"I'm glad you're an art historian," I said finally, my throat aching. It must have struck her as bizarre that I was sitting here in anguish over an unfinished altarpiece.

"You mean so that I can understand your grief?"

That made me start crying again. I took a deep breath. "Donata?"

"Carissima?"

"If I can't finish this book of Ben's, do you think you might be able to help finish it, and get it published?"

"Post-Plague recovery isn't really my area of expertise, Beatrice."

"It wasn't mine either, until recently. But what if you had all my notes, could you do it?"

"Is there something that might keep you from finishing? I hope not an illness, God forbid."

"No, nothing like that." I took a deep breath. "If I disappear again, please don't worry about me."

She pulled back and looked closely at my face. "What are you planning? You can't be suggesting you want to end your life because of an unfinished painting."

That made me laugh, even through tears. "No, I'm not that theatrical, but if it happens, don't worry about me."

She sat silently for a moment. "You want me to accept this without understanding why?"

"Please," I said. "I can't explain."

She nodded once, looking troubled. "I'll try."

I hugged her then, the warmth and solidity of her body rooting me, at least for that moment, in the present.

My Gabriele-inspired gallantry to the archivist paid off; the phone rang just as I was walking into the house. Emilio said he'd found another Medici document from the period, and perhaps I'd want to take a look? I hadn't even taken off my coat, so I turned around and walked back out the door.

The crypt felt colder today—maybe my imagination, since it was probably climate controlled to within a nano-degree. Emilio welcomed me with new warmth; we were drinking buddies now. He went to fetch the document, encased in the usual archival swaddling. It was a ledger, and as I extracted it carefully my ears hummed. Emilio's voice came to me muffled, as if from a distance.

"I thought I might look through Siena's records for any other mention of fourteenth-century Medicis. As I'm sure you know, the family did not rise to prominence until the sixteenth century and there is relatively little from this earlier period. I went through the transcribed proceedings of the Biccherna, Siena's financial governing body. It's mostly ledgers, the sort of thing one might not look at . . . unless one had a *particular interest*." With the emphasis on his last words he smiled a conspiratorial smile. "This ledger is interesting because it's not Sienese at all; I think it was misfiled—it is not from the Biccherna. The accounting is more typically Florentine, as are the names. And there are a few mentions of the Medicis."

I opened to the first page and read:

Monies owed to Giovanni de' Medici for safe transport of luxury goods on behalf of a client with interests in Avignon—70 fiori in gold—

And the date was right—1347. I slowly went through the entries on the next few pages, struggling to read the faded lines. Then I found a familiar name—Signoretti. A lot of money went to Signoretti—first in 1347, but more in 1348 and 1349. And not only Signoretti—I recognized other names of noble Sienese families listed in this Medici ledger, with big numbers next to them—now that I understood medieval currency I knew how big they were. I looked up at Emilio, who was smiling strangely at me.

"I hope the mention of your late brother won't upset you, Dottoressa, but it seems Signor Trovato was quite interested in the same book you have in your hand. I found his name in the call records."

It was upsetting, but exhilarating too. I *was* on the right track. And my hands were touching a book Ben had probably held just before he died. "Thank you for letting me know," I said. "I'm proud to be following in his footsteps." It sounded trite, but I meant it.

"Why don't I leave you alone with it for a while," Emilio said gently, and moved away between the shelves. I looked back down at the little book. "Ben," I whispered, "help me out here. What am I supposed to be seeing?" I don't really believe in communicating with the dead, but there was something eerie about the way the book fell open to a new page. The handwriting here looked driven by some extreme emotion or pressing need. On the page were more payments, this time in fiorini d'oro—gold florins—to a man with only one name: Angelo. The payments went on for many dates, exorbitantly high amounts, but the reason for the payments wasn't noted. Then, on the next page, a list started, and it didn't look like a ledger anymore. It was a list of names, all in that pressured, tense handwriting. I read through the names, recognizing some, including Pietro and Ambrogio Lorenzetti, the famous Siena brothers who painted the Sala della Pace. Emilio came back as I was puzzling over the rest, and I showed him the list. He read through it silently.

"I would have to check to be certain," he said, frowning. I held my breath. "Some of the names on this list include those lost to the 1348 to 1349 plague in Siena. Though it might be something else entirely that links them, of course."

What on earth was a list of Siena's most prominent dead citizens doing in a Medici ledger? I felt suddenly cold, thinking of some Florentine nobleman bent over the names, gloating.

"I need a lot more time to get through this book," I said, hoarsely. Perhaps assuming I was overcome by sisterly emotion, which was only partially true, Emilio nodded kindly. He wrapped the ledger carefully for me, and I tucked it into my bag and apologized silently for yet again taking advantage of the archivist's trust. I headed out of the library, my mind reeling.

I had a voice mail from the Duomo visitors' center waiting for me when I got home. They had a book that matched my description, found in early July. I could come in tomorrow to retrieve it.

I sat down at my kitchen table, feeling shaky. I closed my eyes and imagined the *scriptorium* at the Ospedale, the feel of fresh parchment under my hand, the scent of Egidio's paper-making rising in the steam from a kettle in the corner. I heard the sounds of morning prayer and the pealing of the Prime bells. Did Clara and Provenzano escape the Plague? Did Ysabella become a full-fledged healer? Had she even survived? The Black Death would have torn its way through Siena by now. By then. I opened my eyes again to the cream-colored walls of the little kitchen.

I remembered the ledger from the crypt and went to retrieve it from my bag. It was clearly the Medici family's, with Giovanni's name earlier, and Iacopo's in some of the later entries. I scanned a page tallying shipping tariffs, and as I turned to the next set of entries two loose pieces of parchment fell from the book and drifted to the floor. They were letters—two different letters—and the handwriting on both pages matched the earlier ledger entries.

> *I am being held in a cell awaiting trial for the dispatch of that night watchman who presumed foolishly to block our way. If he had known that it is wiser to let a businessman go about his business undisturbed, he might still be alive today. . . .*

I turned to the next page, my heart skittering.

> *I find that the unexpected Confinement and restriction of my Liberty has made me long for the company of my Family, those in whom love and loyalty for the commune runs as deep as the blood that links us. . . . I bid you to come with the Greatest Haste . . . to stand at my side so that I may have some Reminder of a life outside these walls. Keep this letter to yourself, my son, a silent knowledge between us.*

I was holding letters Giovanni de' Medici had sent to his son in the few weeks before his execution. His son, Iacopo, of uncertain birth. I put the ledger aside but not what I'd discovered hidden in it—*that* I was going to keep, at least for a while. I silently apologized to Emilio in my head.

Next I dove into Ben's collection of books; it might be my last opportunity to learn about Siena's past through modern eyes. I skimmed through titles and opened a few, not knowing exactly what I was looking for. I reminded myself of the Plague's timeline and I read quickly through several texts, trying to memorize as many useful facts as I could.

I left Ben's bedroom for last. Books were still piled on the bed table and the floor, all covered with a layer of dust. I'd looked through them on my first visit, but this time I found something I'd missed. At the bottom of one pile, hidden in the pages of a dog-eared copy of *Asterix the Gaul*, was a nondescript-looking manila envelope. Inside that was another envelope, unmistakably archival. Ben must have hidden it here, maybe because he was suspicious of his rival scholars. Having had my own experiences with their willingness to go as far as was necessary to achieve their aims, I was not surprised.

The document inside was a fragment of a single letter. The recipient's name and the signature were both missing, but the text made my skin prickle with fear.

Conception of the Blessed Virgin, 1348

Now that Accorsi is back in Siena, you must seek him out and go forward with the plan we have discussed. The painter must pay the price for his testimony. Send me word when it is done.

And so I learned two things, in one wonderful and awful moment. Gabriele had survived the Plague, and someone was planning to kill him. I could not continue to read crumbling documents in my own ineffectual century for a minute longer. I took the papers with me and closed the door on Ben's dusty room.

It was time to pack. Assuming I could get back, I needed a lot more than I'd come with the first time. First, I dumped the contents of my medicine cabinet into a bag, including my new self-prescribed antibiotics. Then I moved on to clothing. The blue dress I'd come home in had been destroyed during my hospitalization for fear of infected fleas, but I found a nice medieval replica in a historical reenactment boutique, along with a warm wool cloak with a hood. I added two pairs of wool tights and then assembled a pile of bras and underwear. It wasn't as crucial as antibiotics, but I'd missed modern lingerie on my last trip. In Ben's closet I found an old camping canteen that looked vaguely medieval. I searched in the pantry: a package of whole wheat crackers, dried currants, almonds. What else? I still had the necklace from my mother and added whatever jewelry I could wear; I wasn't certain the bag would come with me. I'd return Fabbri's ledger but I kept the papers I'd found inside it.

I still had the letter from Donata inviting me for coffee, the one that had brought me home. I found it in a drawer of my desk, creased and grubby but still legible. I folded it carefully and packed it too. *The person is the portal, not the place* . . . maybe I would need it again someday.

I put my last letter to Nathaniel in an envelope, addressed it, and added a stamp. I left it on the kitchen table, then brushed my teeth and went to bed. I needed sleep before my appointment early the next morning with a 650-year-old journal.

It was Gabriele's book, looking old again, the way it had when I'd first seen it. My hands shook when the docent handed it to me. I thanked her, and she looked at me oddly, probably wondering what kind of idiot would leave something so obviously important, then wait six months to retrieve it. Fortunately, no one seemed to have opened it and discovered what it really was. I curtsied by mistake, a medieval habit, and fled before I could make any more errors.

I wanted to be in the Ospedale to read the journal this time, someplace that felt like home. I followed the route I'd learned in two different centuries until I was looking at the blank space over the entryway where Gabriele's *Assumption* had once been.

Instead of entering through the front door, I headed for the Cappella delle Fanciulle—Young Women's Chapel—that led into the Pellegrinaio delle Donne, my first medieval home. Inside I hardly recognized it—the chapel was decorated with fifteenth-century frescoes—the Trinity, a scene of women praying at Christ's tomb, the Crucifixion, and a fourth labeled the Madonna of Mercy. I moved closer to see the angels holding the Virgin's mantle, and the worshippers at her feet, praying for protection. I imagined myself among them, looking up into the Virgin's radiant face. There was no one else in the room. I opened the journal to the last page of writing, and began to read.

I cannot paint now, as I am too weak to stand, and I can barely wield a pen. I have taken the last of your bitter tablets, Beatrice. The bitterness reminds me, by contrast, of the sweetness of your face. After you left me, I felt a sudden tear in the fabric of my knowledge of you, as if you had gone a great distance, beyond the reach of my soul. I pray that this is not a sign of your departure from the world of mortal men—and women.

I know now, because of what you have told me, that this book will survive me. It may therefore serve as a medium through which I can speak with you in your own time. With that knowledge I write now, imagining that your eyes might gaze upon this page, and through it, know my thoughts. I hope, for both our sakes, that you have gone far enough to be free from the grip of the dark beast that claws now at my lungs and burns my skin with fever. Perhaps you have found a path back to your own century, and if so, and if it is a haven for you, I bid you stay, free of danger. But if I survive this terrible ailment, and the way for you is safe, I pray, with all the strength that remains in my body, that you will come back to me, and to our Siena, where we may intertwine our lives before my family and in God's name.

With all my love and prayers for your safety, and your return,

Your Gabriele

Messina 1347

It was the last entry. I felt the little book slip from my hands, but I never heard the sound I expected—there was no thump of the journal as it met the ground. Instead it fell soundlessly, endlessly, as if it were traveling a great distance, into a chasm rather than to the marble floor beneath my feet.

PART X

TESTIMONY

It was much worse this time: maybe because I knew how far I might be going, and how much I was leaving behind. As I fell, I imagined the ties to those I loved stretching to the breaking point. I saw Donata stirring risotto, Nathaniel smiling at me over a dusty book jacket, Linney pulling off her blue surgical cap on the way out of the operating room. I could hear a high-pitched whine, and felt a thump of pressure in my ears.

I don't know if I could bear to do this again, I thought as the pain in my head reached an agonizing peak. When the pain stopped, I stood in a candlelit room staring at blank plaster; the painting of the Madonna was gone. That meant I'd arrived before 1500. It struck me, too late, that I had no certainty that I'd landed in the right century. The chapel had a small wooden altar, and a few unadorned benches lined up in rows. Fat wax candles in iron sconces were spaced around the walls, their flames flickering in the darkness. It was cold—an unremitting medieval cold with nothing but a banked hearth to warm the room.

My bag had made it through with me, but not the journal. Maybe that was a sign that I'd come into the time when it belonged to a living Gabriele? It could also mean the journal didn't exist yet because I'd come too early. I heard footsteps outside the chapel; they stopped just short of the door, giving me time to think. If it were someone I knew, that would confirm the time I'd come into. If it were someone I didn't know, I'd have more problems than just not knowing the date. A light flared outside the doorway. I could see a shadow thrown by the newly lit lamp, but not the shadow's owner. The footsteps receded and I breathed again. As I made my way toward Umiltà's *studium*, the city bells began to ring for Prime.

Church bells ring all the time in New York City, but their impact is weakened by all the other noise competing for attention—cell phones, car horns, sirens. Here the campanile's bells spoke with undiluted power, and for me the call to prayer sounded both a welcome and a warning: *Siena holds you tightly in her arms now, and this time you will stay.*

As the last peal faded, I knocked at the door of Umiltà's *studium*. Even if it was the right year, I didn't know whether Umiltà, or anyone else I knew, had survived the Plague. When the door swung open, revealing Umiltà herself, I almost burst out crying with relief.

"God be praised, and the angels in heaven above us, thanks be to Saint Christopher patron of travelers, holy Maurus and Placidus who brought you forth unharmed from far-off Messina, Ansanus, Savinus, Crescentius, and Victor, who protect the devoted citizens of Siena, and Santa Maria herself, who must in truth hold you in the palm of her hand." Umiltà, bless her, hadn't changed a bit. I threw myself into her tiny, wiry embrace and stayed there, my face buried against her wool-covered shoulder.

"Beatrice, whatever happened to you? It is more than a year since you left with that scoundrel Lugani." She went on before I could formulate a response: "We all worried terribly after you left. First that you might have fallen prey to the evils of the road, second that Messer Lugani might have kept you from leaving his employ, and third, once we heard of the devastation emanating from the south, that you had succumbed to the Mortalità. Beatrice, in truth, to see you whole and well on this bitter January morning is truly a miracle."

It was, though she couldn't know the extent of the miracle that had saved me. More than a year, she'd said, and nicely provided me with the month. So it was January 1349.

"I was so afraid that everyone had died. It must have been awful here, from what I saw in Messina."

"The Great Death struck Siena with a ferocity that knew no equal," Umiltà said, pounding a fist into her open palm. "I shall never forget the terrible scenes I witnessed. The images come back to me at all hours of the day, visions of death and decay, and the wails of those who remained to mourn their losses haunt my dreams. Our own Fra Bosi, who kept the Ospedale alight with the fire of the written word, is gone. The Mortalità took him before the first frost, along with half of Siena's souls. Those of us who remain have so many to mourn we have no space left—neither in our graves, nor in our hearts."

My former boss, the irascible but generous guardian of the Ospedale library, was gone. I remembered Bosi sitting on the Ospedale steps weeping for the fate of his burning books, and I felt the tears start in my own eyes.

"Beatrice, I have asked God many times why some were taken while others were left to witness what felt like the end of the world. We lost the Lorenzetti brothers—their brushes halted forever—and countless others whose souls gave life to Siena. Those who planned the enlargement of the Duomo also fell prey to the Mortalità, leaving us with the shell of our hopes for the great new nave that would proclaim our devotion throughout Christendom. Many have suffered across many lands, but at times it has seemed to us here in Siena as if someone aimed directly at our heart, our art, our aspirations, and our beliefs, and tried to snuff us out not just by death but by despair, with great and evil deliberation."

I felt cold. What if she was right and someone did have it in for Siena? Was that what Ben had been on the verge of discovering, with his letter from a grieving Medici wife about her troubled son? With ledgers listing payments to Sienese noblemen and someone mysteriously named only Angelo? Did it have anything to do with the connections I'd discovered between the Signoretti and Medici families? Was there a nefarious reason why a Medici ledger would have a list of Siena's plague deaths tucked inside it, and that the modern Signoretti would try to stop me from finding out more? The pieces of the puzzle shuffled themselves in my head but failed to make a coherent picture. Even if a conspiracy had existed—how could conspiracy translate into pestilence? People conspired, but diseases didn't.

While my mind raced, Umiltà continued. "You must tell me your story at length, Beatrice, but there is little time now. The painter Accorsi is called to trial today, for homicide. Are you prepared to testify? The Ospedale is assembling witnesses on his behalf."

"Homicide?" Gabriele was alive, but accused of murder? "How could he have killed anyone? The last time I saw him he was dying in a chapel in Messina."

Umiltà raised her eyebrows so high they disappeared under her wimple. "Indeed? You left him dying in a chapel? How unchari- table. The Pestilence has brought its share of regretful behavior in its wake, but I would not have imagined it from you. This trial is your opportunity to atone for your callousness—praise God who allows us to repent. And all this happened more than a year ago? Whatever have you been doing since? Were you in Messer Lugani's employ all this time? Egidio feared you had died, as did we all." It sounded like Egidio was okay then, or at least alive. I opened my mouth to answer, but Umiltà held up her hand to stop me. It was just as well, since I hadn't come up with anything sensible to say.

"Beatrice, we shall have to leave these troubling questions for another occasion. I will tell you what you need to know for the trial, and you will vouch for the painter's character. The defamation is surely false, but we must convince the court so that the case will be dismissed. I would hate to see Ser Accorsi hang." Umiltà ushered me out of her *studium*.

So would I, I thought, trying not to panic.

"Thanks be to God we are not governed like France, where two citizens speaking ill of a person is enough to prove guilt. This *fama* must be put to rest for what it is: rumor, or worse, deliberate lies." I too was glad Siena wasn't like France. "Messer Accorsi had just returned from Messina when the Podestà's police force paid him a visit. He was brought up on charges and imprisoned until the matter could be brought to trial."

Why didn't he finish the painting? How did he get back? Did his family survive? I envisioned Gabriele pushing open the front door of his uncle's house to meet the untended corpses of his relatives, the fragrance of Martellino's baking bread replaced by the stench of death. But it was just fear, not empathic vision. More than half of Siena's inhabitants had died in the Plague of 1348—what was the chance that Martellino, Bianca, Ysabella, Rinaldo, and little Gabriella had all survived? And Clara? Umiltà hadn't mentioned her, but she might have died in Messina where I'd left her.

"Ser Accorsi was denounced by an informant," Umiltà continued grimly as we stepped from a narrow street into the thin winter sun of the Campo, "an anonymous informant. The painter was accused of killing Cristoforo Buonaventura, of the night watch."

This was blatantly outrageous. "Giovanni de' Medici killed him! I was at the trial when he was convicted and hanged."

"The informant seeks to overturn the verdict and clear the Medici name. He avers that Ser Accorsi made his accusation to deflect suspicion from himself."

"And one anonymous letter to the Podestà is enough to throw

the whole process of justice on its head? That's ridiculous!" Fear laced my indignation.

"I have heard there is a witness prepared to confirm that Ser Accorsi brought Ser Buonaventura to his death." A witness. What witness? I saw the net drawing tight, with Gabriele at the center. And here I was, heading straight into it.

Umiltà put a hand on my shoulder to calm my obvious anxiety. "I am certain it is a false charge; our painter is no murderer. The details will be revealed at the trial, and there, you will testify and, God willing, all will be well again and Accorsi released from prison." All I could do was nod. It was a relief to be back in Umiltà's presence again, where things always got taken care of. Maybe this is what it would have been like to have a mother.

"Well, then, your arrival is well timed," Umiltà said briskly. It was surprisingly difficult to keep up with her. I couldn't see her legs beneath her gown and robe, but I imagined them spinning around in a blur, like the Road Runner's in old cartoons from my childhood.

"Where are we going?" I panted as we headed out of the Ospedale.

"The Iudex Maleficiorum likes to hear the most serious crimes—treason, homicide, blasphemy—before dinner. He leaves the minor offenses—petty thievery, defamation, and such—for later in the day."

That's a nice orderly approach to the administration of justice. I always preferred to have my most complicated OR cases early in the morning too. We were out in the Piazza del Duomo now, and turning onto the street that led to the Campo. Something from my bag was digging into my back but I couldn't stop to readjust.

"What is the Iudex Maleficiorum?" It sounded nasty in Latin.

"The criminal judge appointed by the Podestà. Is Lucca's system of justice really so different from ours here in Siena?"

"Oh . . . we just have a different word for it." Umiltà accepted my explanation.

"Now, Beatrice," she said, steering me by my elbow, "are you well enough acquainted with the painter to speak in his defense?"

I floundered, not knowing how much to reveal. "He did save me from the fire, you know that, of course. We met periodically after that. Accidentally, of course, when he was painting the Ospedale fresco. It *was* right outside the *scriptorium* windows."

Umiltà stopped walking, and I stopped next to her. She was looking at me with a penetrating stare.

I felt my face get hot. "Messer Accorsi and I also happened to be on the same ship to Messina. You know he had a commission there?"

"I helped him secure that commission," Umiltà said.

"Oh, really? That was nice of you." Clearly it was best not to underestimate Umiltà. "I was certainly happy to find him on board. I mean, his presence was most welcome, since he took it upon himself to protect me. Messer Accorsi is quite chivalrous."

"Indeed, I can see the painter has made an impression upon you." I wasn't sure whether Umiltà looked amused or disapproving.

The Palazzo Pubblico occupied the low point of the sloping piazza; it felt like we were succumbing to the pull of its gravity as we approached. I remembered Giovanni de' Medici's face, his features leonine and merciless. He'd been hanged for a murder Gabriele was now accused of committing. A murder to which Gabriele had once been the sole witness, though now another witness had appeared for the second round. Someone wanted revenge for Giovanni's death.

. . . *The painter must pay the price for his testimony. Send me word when it is done.*

Back in modern Siena this was an absorbing academic question worthy of publication; now it meant Gabriele's survival. Which of the surviving Medicis wanted revenge—his wife, Immacolata? His putative son, Iacopo, absent birth records notwithstanding? I was thinking so hard I didn't hear Umiltà's question.

"Can you speak on his behalf? You have not answered me." Umiltà stopped at the main entrance of the Palazzo. The white stone of the building's first story was bright against the red brick above, and the castle-like crenellations on the top of the Palazzo looked like they were moving, silhouetted against shifting clouds. I pulled my eyes away to look at Umiltà.

"Of course. But what sort of questions will I be expected to answer?"

"If you knew the facts you might be asked to provide them, but in this case you will simply vouch for the painter's character."

Character I could do. But I had more than character. If the documents I'd brought from the twenty-first century had made the trip through time with me, then I had hard evidence too. And I'd have to figure out how to use it, fast.

The Sala del Mappamondo, the Council Hall of the Palazzo Pubblico, was jammed with people. I scanned the room but couldn't find Gabriele. A massive wooden wheel attached to the far wall of the *sala* was painted with a map that had given the room its name, and that I knew wouldn't survive the centuries. On the opposite wall a fresco depicted a Madonna enthroned, surrounded by angels and saints. *Donata would know the artist*, I thought, but I had someone else to ask now. I leaned down to the level of Umiltà's ear.

"That *Maestà*, who painted it?"

"Why, Simone Martini, of course, our own departed master, and Accorsi's teacher. I hope the Maestro's work above him will give him strength in his own defense."

"Where is Ser Accorsi?"

"He will be kept under guard until his name can be cleared." Umiltà's voice dropped a few decibels. "Do not despair, Beatrice. He will not be harmed in any way before the trial. Afterward, depending on the outcome, I may not be able to protect him. But I will do everything in my power to see him acquitted." I wanted to believe her power would be sufficient.

Back in my own time, I had often tried to remember Gabriele's face. But I'd always failed, and the further I got from my break with the past, the harder it had become. I'd stored a shorthand description of his features, but those made a catalog of details, not a coherent picture. So when I saw Gabriele again in person, I was not at all prepared.

He was escorted by two menacing armed guards wearing parti-colored tunics of Siena's black and white. I saw him from behind, but even that view of him cut through me with an intensity that was almost painful. I took in the way his arms rested against his sides, the measured grace of his steps. There were no jeers from the crowd, or even whispered comments; the assembled citizens felt his gravity, and respected it. As Gabriele entered the *sala*, he lifted his head and tilted it to the side in that gesture I knew, like a falcon listening. I could see part of his face now, his right ear, the slope of one cheek with several days' growth of beard, the straight profile of his nose, and in seconds, the real Gabriele took the place of months of inadequate imagination.

A court official began the proceedings with a bow to the judge. "Gabriele Beltrano Accorsi, a citizen of the Commune of Siena, has been accused of the murder of Cristoforo Buonaventura, a guard of the night watch. We are assembled to hear the testimony of witnesses, and to resolve the question of his guilt."

I shot a look at Umiltà, whose eyes were narrow with anger. "Someone has accused him of the selfsame crime for which he bore witness. It reeks of *vendetta*, Beatrice," she hissed. *Vendetta*. The word sounded just like what it meant—vengeful and dangerous.

As the first witness was called my heart sank: Ser Vitalis Signoretti. He wore a belted red velvet tunic embroidered with an intricate pattern of diamonds in gold, and over that, a dark blue cloak lined with fur. Was I really going to go to bat against this powerful nobleman with only a scrap of time-traveling parchment to support Gabriele's defense? And if I won, what would Gabriele's and my future be like with Signoretti as an enemy, in addition to a vengeful Florentine?

As Signoretti was led to the witness stand, my head went in another direction. Why was Signoretti testifying now, against an innocent man? Did Signoretti actually think he had information linking Gabriele to the crime, or had he been bought? I thought of the Medici ledger, with its columns of payments to this member of Siena's *casati*. Gabriele's denunciation of Giovanni would have made him a Medici target, and it was possible that some remaining Medici was using Signoretti as a weapon.

"On the night in question, I overheard an argument through a window facing the street—of course my family and I were well inside by curfew." He spoke with the infuriating confidence that comes with being born into privilege. "I opened the shutters and saw Ser Accorsi, who stands before you today, in conversation with the much-mourned Ser Buonaventura. I overheard Ser Buonaventura demanding an explanation for Ser Accorsi's late-night wanderings. Their words became heated, and the crime for which he has been detained followed." It was all going to rest on the force of one witness against another, one a marginally solvent fatherless painter and the other a powerful member of the aristocracy. Unless I could tip the scales.

I leaned over to open my bag. A clerk was reading the denunciation verbatim now. I felt the desperation that comes when you suddenly realize, at your doorstep, that you might have lost your keys. Was it still here?

There, squeezed between my jewelry case and five bras, was the envelope I was looking for. I said a silent prayer to the god of primary sources and time travel as I pulled out the letters from Giovanni to Iacopo, written during Giovanni's imprisonment. They looked new again, back in the century where they had been written.

The Iudex Malificiorum, a big-jowled, appropriately ominous-looking administrator of justice, spoke from his great wooden chair. His low voice rumbled out over the crowd. "As there are no further witnesses to corroborate the accusation, we will now hear from Messer Accorsi himself, in defense of his position. This is an unusual matter, since to indict the accused would require overturning a prior conviction of a man executed at the hands of the Commune."

Gabriele stepped up to speak, and I finally saw the rest of his face. He had lost weight, and his skin was paler than it had been when I'd met him in the summer of 1347. But his eyes were the same, and today, taking on the color of an angry sea. He spoke briefly.

"I confirm my prior testimony. I witnessed the murder of Cristoforo Buonaventura by Giovanni de' Medici. I am innocent of the crime in question." His voice wasn't loud but I could hear every word.

"Messer Accorsi, have you nothing further to add in your defense?" The judge leaned forward.

"Nothing, Your Honor. It has been said before, and recorded. I will not trouble the court with repetition of the truth."

"Very well, then. Are there further witnesses who would speak on behalf of the accused?"

Umiltà's piercing voice rang out into the room. "To Your Honor

I recommend the witness Beatrice Alessandra Trovato, chief scribe of the Ospedale. Monna Trovato transcribed the trial in which the Medici murderer was convicted, and was thereby privy to the original account of that fateful night's events. Furthermore, she is a grieving widow and a pilgrim, holy in God's sight, and Ser Accorsi's intended. Her word is to be trusted on matters of character, and fact."

Chief scribe and Gabriele's intended? A job promotion and an engagement, all in one sentence. I would have to speak to Umiltà later on these two points.

"Monna Trovato, step forward to give your testimony."

I moved through the crowd, which parted to let me pass. Everything around me took on a strange distorted quality, like an image seen through a kaleidoscope—faceted and flecked with color. At the end of the path through the assembled people Gabriele faced me. Even across the room, and despite his obvious efforts at composure, I could see the shock register on his face. A force emanated from him like heat from a furnace. I stopped at the spot directed by the judge's clerk and held up the letter.

"I am in possession of a document that proves the role Giovanni de' Medici had in the death of Ser Buonaventura. I present it respectfully to the court." The clerk delivered the letter to the judge, who spread it out on the table in front of him. He read silently.

"Monna Trovato has produced a letter written by Ser Giovanni de' Medici during his imprisonment." The judge directed his next words to the clerk. "Please read the document aloud, so the assembled may hear the evidence presented therein."

The clerk read into a silence so complete that I could hear him swallow. *"'I am being held in a cell awaiting trial for the dispatch of that night watchman who presumed foolishly to block our way. If he had known that it is wiser to let a businessman go about his business undisturbed, he might still be alive today.'"*

Everyone started talking—the clerks, the spectators, even the guards flanking Gabriele. The judge had to call for order, and it was several minutes before the room was quiet again.

"Monna Trovato, please explain how you came to be in possession of this document, and why it was not previously brought into evidence at the Medici trial." The silence in the courtroom felt like the lull before a hurricane hits, when the sky turns green and trees are weirdly still.

How I came to be in possession of this document? I had not prepared for that question, so extemporized.

"I discovered it in the pages of another book, Ser, unexpectedly. A tax record collected for an entirely different purpose. When I laid eyes upon the letter, its relevance to the case in question became clear, and I brought it with me today, for examination by the court." *I brought it further than you could imagine, Mr. Iudex, in your wildest dreams.*

The judge put the tips of his fingers together and regarded the shape he'd made with his hands, as if it were the most fascinating structure in the world. "The nature of the evidence presented suggests that the denunciation must be reconsidered, and the indictment held for the present. I will review the matter after we adjourn today. Is there any further testimony you would care to provide, Monna Trovato?"

My opinion of Gabriele's character seemed superfluous, but I didn't want to miss any opportunity to keep him from hanging. "I would like to affirm Messer Accorsi's honesty, gentleness, and good character, if it would have bearing on the case."

The judge nodded once. "Noted. This session of the court is now adjourned. Messer Accorsi will remain in prison until the verdict, which will be announced at Terce tomorrow." Gabriele filed out between the guards. He had an odd look on his face, halfway between wonder and amusement. It was remarkable that I could have come hurtling through the centuries, arriving just in time to provide evidence to support Gabriele's innocence, and then, having done that, not even have the opportunity to say hello.

When Umiltà and I were reunited, she grasped both my hands in her powerful grip and looked up at me. "We have matters to discuss, Beatrice," she said firmly. "Come with me now to my *studium*." She held my sleeve as we filed out with the crowd. As we headed down the stairs, I answered under my breath.

"Matters to discuss? That's the understatement of the four-teenth century." Umiltà didn't seem to hear.

PART XI

THE CHIEF SCRIBE

As Umiltà and I crossed the Campo, my mind moved toward critical overload. *Was some Medici responsible for Gabriele's false arrest, with Signoretti as part of the plan? If so, which Medici? Did Umiltà really just offer me a new job? And what did she mean by calling me Gabriele's "intended"?* I stopped walking. The slight hill of the Campo looked much steeper than I remembered.

"I have to sit down," I said to Umiltà, who never had to sit down.

She sighed and appraised me as if I were a lame horse some swindler had tried to sell her. "I suppose we can postpone further discussion until you have rested. Where shall I send a messenger to collect you?"

"I'm not staying anywhere," I said, and hearing how forlorn that must have sounded, amended slightly. "I just got here. I don't even know where to lie down."

Umiltà's eyes widened. "You mean to say that you sought me out within minutes of entering the city gates, with minutes to spare before your testimony was required on Messer Accorsi's behalf? God must certainly have set these events in motion."

The timing had turned out awfully close. "Suor Umiltà, if I don't find a place to rest soon, I'll have to lie down in the middle of the Campo."

"Of course, of course." She sounded more solicitous, now that she didn't think I'd returned to Siena without letting her know. "Your former chamber is still available. Once you begin your new role as chief scribe, in place of Fra Bosi, bless his departed soul, you will need more suitable lodgings, but this will serve in the interim." It was not so much a job offer as a statement of fact. In that way, Umiltà reminded me of Lugani. I wondered what had happened to him, and his suspicious second in command.

"I'll take it," I said, not clarifying which "it" I was taking—job or lodgings. I managed the walk back to the Ospedale and to my familiar little cell.

I'd forgotten to ask what had happened to Clara. Back in the room where I'd first met her, the sharpness of her absence made my chest ache. Nothing had changed since I'd left on that September morning. There was the wooden chest, the bed, the *inginocchiatoio* in the corner where I'd attempted my first medieval prayer, and the small wooden table. But now the room was bitterly cold, the closed shutters doing little to mitigate the draft. I eyed the bed I'd threatened to lie down in, but now that I was alone, the urgency for sleep had subsided. I put my bag down on the floor and started unpacking.

All my possessions fit easily into the chest. The *inginocchiatoio* beckoned silently and I walked over to kneel at it, familiar with the motion after my months of medieval life. I closed my eyes and imagined my first-grade catechism teacher, Sister Amelia. I'd come to her once for help crafting a prayer to ask for a dog for Christmas. I remember the way she lowered herself to my six-year-old level until her eyes met mine.

"Prayer is not currency, Beatrice. We pray to God not to bargain for favors. Prayer is an act of praise. We pray to express our devotion to God." It wasn't exactly what I was looking for, but I sat with her and tried to learn what she was trying to teach me. I never did get that dog.

It was not an easy task to praise rather than ask, under the circumstances. I couldn't help the thoughts that crept in, particularly one refrain that was clearly more plea than praise. *Don't let them hang him. PLEASE don't let them hang him.*

I felt the cold draft as the door to my room swung open.

"Is that truly YOU?" The high-pitched voice pulled me onto my feet.

"Clara?"

She looked much as I remembered her, round face flushed pink under the white of her coif. She stood in the doorway with her feet planted wide and her mouth wide open to match.

"Monna Trovato? I thought you were dead!"

She raced over and threw her arms around my neck. She smelled of woodsmoke and cloves, and as we embraced I felt the roundness of her belly filling the space between us. Pregnant. We emerged from our hug and I tried not to stare at her midsection.

"Clara, how did you know I was here? I've just barely arrived."

"I heard from the other Ospedale wards that a woman—a former scribe—testified at the painter's trial. I came right away, hoping it was you." She must have seen my surreptitious glance, because she put her hand on her belly protectively. "Yes, I have been blessed with the promise of a new life." Asking who the father was didn't seem appropriate. "Have you just arrived in Siena?"

"Yes," I said, trying to decide what story to tell her.

"Where did you go? When I came back with the water, you were gone."

"I'm told I was found by a group of travelers who nursed me back to health."

Clara's eyes grew wide. "Praise God for miracles," she said, and embraced me again, her face nestling at the hollow of my throat. We held each other quietly, like two survivors of a shipwreck.

When she emerged from the hug, a familiar look appeared in her eyes.

"You must be hungry."

I had to smile. "Clara, I can wait to eat."

"No, you must be famished after your travels—and you look thinner than I like to see you." I wasn't sure how she could tell anything about my weight under all the clothing I had on. "I shall visit the kitchens right away to find something nourishing and warm."

I did feel hungry, despite the violent disruption of hurtling back in time and the drama of testifying at a murder trial. "Is there any *poratta*?" I remembered the fragrant soup that had been my introduction to medieval Italian cuisine.

"*Poratta*, Signora? I can find something better than that."

"No, please, *poratta* is just what I'd like. It will be the best welcome home I can imagine."

Clara smiled. "I am so glad to have you with us again, Monna Trovato."

"I'm glad to be back," I answered. Before I could say anything else, she was gone.

* * *

When Iacopo left again for Siena on business he would not explain, Immacolata had had enough of the Medici men's secrets. After supper she went into Giovanni's *studium*—in her mind Immacolata could not think of it as Iacopo's—and began to look through the papers her son had left behind. The room was dark and cold, and smelled of melted wax.

Iacopo had become even more secretive when the *magna* Mortalità arrived in Firenze. The city went mad with terror and mourning, and with the fury of priests proclaiming the arrival of God's wrath upon the earth. But there was something else, something hidden and dangerous in her son that seemed to have been spawned by the Mortalità itself. Iacopo left the palazzo heavily cloaked and hooded, and returned from his forays long after curfew. He burned candles at all hours writing in the drafty *studium*, and managed to find messengers to take his letters despite the horror sweeping the city, paying the carriers in gold. Immacolata was grateful that she and Iacopo had been spared the touch of the Pestilence, but it was as if she had lost her son to another incarnation of the beast. Iacopo had grown a long straggling beard and mustache, and became even thinner than before; the bones of his face reflected the light.

Immacolata paged through the ledgers, her eyes blurring over the columns of black ink. With Giovanni dead and Iacopo in Siena, the accounts were her domain again. This time, Immacolata went back to the days and weeks before her husband's death. As she read the entries, she felt a chill at the back of her neck, as if a window had been opened to let in a winter's draft. Several names repeated themselves next to increasingly large sums, names of Siena's powerful *casati* families, well known even outside that city's walls. Signoretti led the list but was not alone. Vast sums had gone to these men of Siena, men whose families angled for power in the *commune*. Next to each of the sums was a set of initials, the same letters each time, in Giovanni's sharp, angular writing. The initials spoke to her, calling up a name she had heard many times in Giovanni's conversation. *He thought I was not listening, or if I listened, thought I could not understand.* But she understood now: it was not the name of an individual, but the Brotherhood of San Giovanni Battista. Pouring florins into the coffers of Siena's most powerful noblemen. *What were you about, my dead, conspiring husband?*

Now, with this new knowledge, Iacopo's assumption of his father's work, his silence, and his increasingly frequent trips to Siena took on even greater menace. But it was not enough to

understand what drove Iacopo now. There must be more, something recent and urgent. Shivering, Immacolata turned to the
cold hearth. And there she found what she sought: a half-burned
letter, edges curling brown and streaked with ash.

For Messer Iacopo de' Medici:

*I have done your bidding. The painter Accorsi has been imprisoned
by the Podestà's police and will stand trial within the week. That will
pay him back for bearing witness at your father's trial. With success
your family name will be cleared of any taint and the painter will
hang from the gallows. Ser Signoretti granted me audience once he
read the letter of introduction you sent, and has agreed to take the
witness stand in your favor.*

*I will find you after the trial to collect my due. Will you be staying
at your accustomed place? This time we have him.*

*With God's help this letter will move you to ride quickly to Siena
and bring my gold.*

Penned by my hand on this last Day of December, 1348

G.B.

Siena

Immacolata held the letter tightly and closed her eyes. What
was her child planning, her son who carried the taint of his father's violence in him? She recalled Iacopo's last letter, before
her husband's hanging.

*Father is still in prison in Siena, and it is said they will hang him.
Do you know of an Accorsi in Siena? He may have been an informant,
I am looking for him. I will stay in Siena until the trial.*

Accorsi must be the informant who had brought Giovanni
to trial for murder. Immacolata closed her eyes and saw Iacopo
as a swaddled infant, his dark eyes, so unlike his father's pale

ones, large in his tiny face, in those first days when the sound of a babe's cry blew the stale air from their home. Her body had failed her, but her husband's gold had bought them the child they had desired. He wanted an heir, she wanted a son. In Iacopo they both had their desires, mutual or not. And Iacopo would never know his true origins.

The fragile parchment crumbled in Immacolata's fist as she gripped it. Iacopo had promised to return by the week's end, and when he did she would speak to him. She would take him to their family chapel, and there the truth would be known at last, as it must, between mother and son. She left the *studium*, closing the door tightly behind her.

*   *   *

Umiltà's messenger came to fetch me just as I was wiping the inside of the *poratta* bowl with a slab of bread. I'd hardly gotten through Umiltà's doorway before she started talking. "First we shall address the matter of your employment." Umiltà sat at her high desk behind a stack of parchment, an account book, and, incongruously, a small wooden spinning top. I wondered whether she played with it. "It has been extraordinarily difficult to manage the *scriptorium* in your absence, and Egidio, though able to copy a few lines now and then—thanks to you, he tells me, remarkably, whenever did you have the opportunity to teach him?—is no equal to you, nor to our Fra Bosi, may his soul rest in eternal peace. Your payment will of course be commensurate with your new level of responsibility. Before the Mortalità your appointment might have been questioned, for reasons not limited to your sex and your origins, but in these sparse times with so many dead or fled to the *contado*, few complain when anyone steps forward to do a job that needs doing. Do you concur?"

"Of course." Chief scribe of the Ospedale? My medieval dream job.

Umiltà began straightening items on her desk. I wondered whether this might be the time to bring up the subject of *vendetta*, Signoretti's testimony, and the Florentine threat. Just as I was formulating a sentence, Umiltà took a deep breath and thumped her hands on the desk loud enough to make me jump. "Now, let us speak of Accorsi." Her words made me blush.

"What about him?"

"With the document you produced, Accorsi's case was much strengthened. I am hopeful they will pardon and release him."

Amen, Sister, I thought silently. "The person to whom that letter was addressed—Iacopo, Giovanni's son. How difficult would it be to find him?"

"Why would you seek out the son of a twice-confirmed, once-hanged, Florentine murderer?" Put that way, it was a tough question to answer sensibly.

"What if Iacopo de' Medici had something to do with Gabriele's arrest?"

Umiltà narrowed her eyes. "Are you so quick to heap the father's ills onto the son, knowing nothing about the man other than his parentage? And why would Messer Signoretti consort with a Medici criminal? Accusation is a dangerous business, Beatrice, and oft goes awry. You might be punished yourself for false denunciation, particularly against such powerful individuals, and might lead me to be suspected as well. Have you evidence to support your suspicions?"

Evidence? There was the other letter, the one from Ben's room. But with no signature.

. . . send me word when it is done . . .

I would have to figure out another strategy.

"Thank you for your wise advice, Suor Umiltà," I said meekly. She looked at me closely, knowing my rapid compliance should be viewed with suspicion, but I gave her a deferential smile. She accepted the gesture at face value.

"Now, let us move on to betrothal," Umiltà said.

My heart sped up suddenly. "Betrothal?"

"To Messer Accorsi, of course. Marriage to an honest woman can save a condemned man from the gallows. Have you no such procedures in Lucca? You are a widow, not a virgin, but your virtue has no taint upon it, so the effect ought to be similar." That was an interesting legal argument. "Do you find the match beneath you? You are the former wife of a notary, and he an itinerant artisan."

"He's an artist, not an artisan. And he travels for commissions. There's nothing wrong with that."

"You defend him very prettily."

"I'm just being accurate."

"Indeed." She looked at me again with that penetrating gaze. "Beatrice, please be seated. My neck tires from staring up at you." I lowered myself onto an uncomfortable bench, wondering whether it was especially designed to put claimants visiting her *studium* at a disadvantage. "Do you agree to the match, should Messer Accorsi's innocence be confirmed by the court?"

"You think he'll be released?"

"The evidence is in his favor."

"He'd marry me just because I served as a witness in his defense?" My nervousness, as usual, made me resort to sarcasm, which Umiltà, as usual, missed.

Umiltà leaned forward over her desk. "Beatrice—the painter has proclaimed his love for you on the facade of the Ospedale. Are you not his dark angel?" For a few seconds, all I could hear was my own pulse in my ears. I couldn't respond. "Ah, well. You need not answer now, Beatrice. Your words will not change the truth."

Umiltà picked up the little wooden top on her desk, rolling it between her fingers. "The practical matters are of some concern, since there is no paterfamilias to arrange the marriage." Umiltà placed the top on the desk and spun it briskly. "The painter's mother died in childbirth, and his father followed less than a year later." The top slowed and toppled onto its side. "His uncle, alas, was buried in the early days of the Mortalità, when there was still someone to record the deaths." I imagined Martellino's broad smile and floury hands. Umiltà was unaware of the blow she had delivered. "And have you no father, nor other family to offer your hand in marriage, even in Lucca?" I shook my head. "Then I can stand in the stead of family you have lost."

I absorbed the simultaneous news of Martellino's death and Umiltà's offer to act as my adoptive parent. "I'm very grateful. But Ser Accorsi may not survive to marry anyone."

"I agree it is premature to consider Messer Accorsi seriously as a bridegroom until his release. Report to me tomorrow after Terce when we will know the verdict and can act accordingly. I trust you will be well rested by then."

"I'll be there," I said and turned to leave. It appeared that I had just discussed letting Umiltà arrange my marriage to Gabriele, who might be convicted of murder tomorrow unless my evidence could save him. I staggered back to my room in the women's hospice. This time I collapsed fully dressed on the narrow bed and sank into oblivion.

On the morning of the third of January, 1349, I made my way to the Campo to hear the heralds announce the verdict. The Mortalità had gone quiet when the cold weather began, and the few who were left in the city came out for the spectacle. Heralds raised gleaming horns and filled the piazza with their high, bright sound. Gabriele was not the first to have his fate proclaimed that day, and I waited, shivering. One indictment for homicide, another for theft. I could hardly breathe. Then Gabriele's name rang out across the assembled crowd, his ancestry, the crime for which he was tried, and finally the news of his acquittal. I am not usually a fan of noisy public demonstrations, but this time I yelled myself hoarse.

I had hoped to see Gabriele again at the proclamation of his verdict, but none of the reprieved were present for the announcement of their innocence nor were the indicted. I left the Campo and headed back to the Ospedale to keep my meeting with Umiltà. She smiled at me as I entered her *studium*.

"Your painter will be released later today; God works wonders through those who serve him." I loved how the medieval mind could seamlessly intertwine belief and fact. "Have you thought about my proposal?"

"Yes. And my answer is yes."

Umiltà beamed. "In that case, I shall execute the necessary steps."

"Steps?"

"I remember you as more quick-witted than you now seem. Whatever happened to you on your voyage to Messina? It seems to have affected you adversely."

"I fell ill in Messina." Umiltà's smile vanished abruptly.

"What sort of ill?"

"The Mortalità *magna* sort."

"You did not say." Umiltà inhaled once; I saw her shoulders rise and fall under her cloak. "Both you and Messer Accorsi were touched by the grim hand of the Mortalità, but escaped its grasp. You and the painter must have been watched over by the same protecting saint." *Or we took similar antibiotics.* And Umiltà had survived too—maybe helped by my attempt to set up a rat-catching operation before I'd left for Messina? "I will dedicate myself to the furthering of your betrothal. In the wake of these miracles there is no more fitting way to honor our savior."

"Excellent," I said. So long as she was heading in the right direction, I didn't care how she got there. "When can we visit Messer Accorsi?"

"We?" Umiltà laughed for the second time in my memory of her. "Now that I know the cause of your dimmed wits, I shall excuse you a bit more readily. You will stay at the Ospedale, demonstrating the piety of your widowhood and the industry of your scribal duties. I shall approach the Accorsi household. It would not be seemly for you to meet at this early stage, and all must be conducted without a breath of impropriety. I shall take my role as protector of your honor quite seriously, have no doubt about that."

I had no doubt whatsoever, looking at Umiltà's belligerent stance and jutting chin. She reminded me of a petite bulldog. "In any case," she said, leading me to the door of her *studium*, "in your new role as chief scribe, you will be far too busy to do anything else." Umiltà, as usual, was right.

When I entered the *scriptorium* I saw a man bending over the paper trays in the corner. At the sound of my entry, he turned to face me. Little Egidio was no longer little. His transformation over the months I'd been gone had an Alice-in-Wonderland quality—his body had elongated and his small round boy's head sat on top of his new height awkwardly. When he saw me he dropped the tray he was holding. It hit the stone floor with a clatter.

"Egidio? You've grown into a man since I left, I hardly recognized you."

I saw more evidence of his new adulthood as he looked at my face, then body, then rapidly back to my face again. He flushed to the roots of his hair. "Signora, to see you well is a great blessing."

"I'm very happy to be back." Egidio bent to retrieve his work; the rag pulp had scattered onto the floor. "The Virgin herself must surely have you in her hands. I know of no one else touched by the Pestilence who lived to tell of it."

I could think of one other person. "Can you show me what needs doing? I'm sure much has changed."

"Gladly," he said simply, and we went to work.

I had explicit instructions not to go looking for Gabriele, so I applied myself to scribal tasks, glad for the distraction. I fell back into the rhythm of the *scriptorium* as the familiar movements reasserted themselves: smooth the parchment flat, weight it with lead, lay out inks, select a quill, set the lines to rule the page. But my preoccupation with Ser Signoretti's role in Gabriele's near conviction, and the possible Medici threat to his welfare, kept me on edge. I felt like I had to do something—but what?

*　　*　　*

I had an opportunity to interrogate Clara on Sunday evening after Vespers. I had not experienced medieval January before, and I discovered that there was no effective way to get warm. Fireplaces warmed only one side of me at a time, and were banked before bedtime. As a result, I became obsessed with the idea of having a hot bath. I wouldn't let Clara fill the tub, despite her protestations, so a kitchen maid and I lugged the buckets of steaming water upstairs to the women's baths. I was the only person desperate enough to bathe so late, so Clara and I were alone in the room. I sank into the water gratefully. Clara took a seat on a wooden stool behind me and began washing my hair with a fragrant mixture of dried winter herbs. The feel of her fingers on my scalp made my words come easily.

"Clara, where did you go after I left Messina? A penniless orphan in a city overrun with pestilence?"

"I had the good fortune to find accommodation with Messer Provenzano in the *contado*," she said crisply. I sat up out of the water to look at her face. A small smile played at the corners of her mouth. "The good man gave me a place in his household as a cook. At first."

"At first?"

"We found ourselves quite well-suited. I was without recourse, as you said, and he did not like to be alone. His staff was much reduced and many of his acquaintances perished in the Mortalità." Her voice trailed off, and we were both quiet for a while. I sank into the bath again, and after a few moments she resumed scrubbing.

"Where is Provenzano now?"

"He is on a business voyage at present. Do you mean where does he reside?"

"Yes, please, enlighten me."

"Why, here of course."

I sat up again, splashing water out of the tub. "Here? In Siena? But isn't he from Genoa?"

"Why would I not leap at the chance to find passage back home?"

"Provenzano brought you here? That was generous of him."

"Yes, I am fortunate to have found such a generous husband." Clara said it without a trace of drama, but to my ears the word *husband* hit the air like an explosive.

Wow, nice work, Clara. "Congratulations on your marriage," I said, too stunned to say anything else. That explained the new baby, though I was beginning to realize that it was never quite safe to make assumptions about Clara. I sank back into the bath, done with questions. But after she was gone, I wondered whether she'd stay with me, since she was, amazingly, a married woman now.

By the end of the first week of January I was too restless to sit in the *scriptorium* writing all day. The thought that Gabriele was out of prison and chatting with Umiltà about my future made me frantic. On top of that, I still had no plan to ferret out a possible Medici troublemaker. I put on my cloak and headed out the door, not knowing where I was going.

As I walked, I started to have the feeling I was being followed. Now that I'd provided evidence in court contradicting a powerful member of the Sienese *casati*, I might be a target. I thought of the ambush en route to Pisa, and walked faster.

I turned onto the Via di Fontebranda; on the wide busy street I felt safer. Soon I saw the fortress-like building that housed the *fonte* itself. This was the dyers' neighborhood. Even in the cold weather, evidence of their trade was in the air: the acrid smells of mordants used to make cloth hold the dye. The scent reminded me, not pleasantly, of my trip with Lugani. The *fonte* had three basins under its arches. At the first, women filled their vessels for cooking and watering wine. At the second, two horses stood shivering as they drank, their masters looking colder than they. The runoff into the third was for washing clothes.

I stepped inside, out of the wind. Light came through the archways under the vaulted roof, but at the far edges the pools were dark. I watched the light playing over the water's shifting surface, the patterns ruffling then resetting as the few bundled women bent to fill their vessels.

"Depicting the mysterious union between water and light is a life's work, even for a master."

The voice startled me out of my reverie. Gabriele stood a foot away from me, in a hooded cloak that hid all but his face.

"What on earth are you doing here?"

"Regarding you, as you regard the water: with wonder at the beauty of God's creation." Artists certainly give beautiful compliments—at least this artist did.

"Aren't we not supposed to meet?" Medieval propriety kept my hands at my sides.

"We are not."

"But now Umiltà can't blame us for meeting by accident."

"This is no accident. I followed you."

"You *what?*"

"I came to the Ospedale to meet with Umiltà, and saw you leave by the gate. I stayed a few paces behind you all the way."

"You had me feeling paranoid."

"*Paranoid?* Another of your own time's words?"

"It means thinking people are plotting against you when they aren't. Sorry, I keep forgetting to talk properly."

"You talk beautifully, if mystifyingly at times. But certainly I am not plotting against you." He tilted his head and the familiarity of that gesture gave me a full-body rush of warmth. "Why were you afraid of being followed?"

"Haven't you been afraid, since the trial? Wondering who denounced you, and why Ser Signoretti testified against you?"

"I have been grateful for your testimony, which saved my life."

"My pleasure. But escaping conviction doesn't mean there isn't someone out there who meant you harm."

"I cannot see a purpose to living in fear. I have lost a wife and a son, survived the Mortalità, and now escaped this false accusation. I am free to walk the streets of the city, to paint, and, it seems, to marry. I prefer to enjoy my hard-won freedoms."

"What if he's still out there somewhere—the man who had you falsely arrested for murder?"

"Is there something you might know, Beatrice, from your unusual vantage point?"

"I might."

"Tell me then."

"It's suspicion, not fact. Don't go out and break someone's legs."

Gabriele smiled. "Humor in the face of disaster, Beatrice; your singular skill."

"Thanks. Giovanni de' Medici has a son."

"The one to whom he wrote the letter you miraculously produced in the courtroom."

"His name is Iacopo de' Medici. And I suspect he's out for revenge." The name tasted bitter in my mouth. "But I don't know whether I'm right."

"But you may be. So we must find him."

"Sure. I could go to Florence and ask everyone I see whether they know a guy named Iacopo. Or maybe I could write a letter to his mother; I think her name is Immacolata. It could go something like this: 'Dear Florentine Noblewoman: your son is trying to kill my future husband. Would you mind telling me where I can find him?'"

"Do you jest, sweet Beatrice?"

"Can you think of anything better? We can't send a message to him directly."

"I shall think upon how we might find this man, or at least prevent him from further mischief—if he is in fact the origin of the mischief. I should hate to accuse someone falsely, having experienced false accusation myself. And a young man who has lost his father has suffered amply as it is." I'd never thought of it from Iacopo's perspective. "For now," he said, "we have escaped our rival's wrath again, whoever he may be."

A woman came to fill her bucket, curtseying and smiling shyly at Gabriele. I shook my head, amused. "You seem to charm everyone, Gabriele."

"Do I charm you? That is all that matters."

"Absolutely."

"Then you are likely to accept, if Umiltà should present my proposal of marriage? I would be comforted to know my chances of success."

"Your chances are one hundred percent."

"Does that mean certain?"

"Exactly. Are we betrothed now?"

He laughed quietly. "There are procedures to follow, as you will see. Now that I know your origins, I understand your peculiar gaps of knowledge."

"You'd have some peculiar gaps too, if you were transported centuries out of your time."

"I am certain of it." Gabriele paused. "Beatrice . . . what befell you?"

"After I left you in Messina, you mean?"

"After you left me dying, or so I thought."

"You told me to leave you!" My voice echoed, too loud, under the vaulted roof. Only one horse and his master were left—they raised their heads to look at us.

"I meant no offense. But please tell me what transpired."

"I got sick too," I said. "The same sort of sick."

"Ah," he said. "I feared as much."

"I thought you would die. For a while I thought I might die too, during the rare moments that I could think at all. But I had a letter written by a friend from my own time, and I believe that letter took me back. I traveled on a current of longing for what I'd left behind." This was the first time I'd articulated it, the strange story of my return.

"I hoped you had found your way to somewhere safe."

"It was safe, yes. My time is good at taking care of sick people."

"Then why, if you had safety in your time—why would you choose to return?"

I was silent for a few seconds before answering. "The beauty of this time called me back." Gabriele nodded, as if he knew exactly what I meant. "I saw what you wrote."

"So my words found you, Beatrice?" The last horse had slaked his thirst at the fountain, and his owner led him out.

"They did."

He smiled slowly. "As I hoped they would."

"And what happened to you?"

372

Gabriele pushed his hood back, and the sun slanting through the entryway fell across his bright hair. "Your strange medicine saved me. But it was many months before I could stand, and more before I could travel home again. When I came home, Martellino and Rinaldo were gone. Thank God the Pestilence spared Ysabella, Bianca, and little Gabriella."

"Thank God, indeed." I imagined the two women and a baby, alone in the city as thousands died around them. "Gabriele, may I please touch you? I know it's not allowed but I can't bear it anymore."

"Please," he said.

I put my hand to his face. His cheek was warm. "You *are* real."

"I might have wondered the same of you, but your reality is evident. And your hands are very cold." Our laughter echoed under the arches. "Beatrice, we ought not to risk further impropriety. Soon our embrace will be sanctioned by God."

"Amen," I said. Neither of us made a move to leave. "But I want to risk further impropriety."

Gabriele stared at me as if I'd spoken a foreign language. In a way, I had. "Do you?" Gabriele's voice dropped to a whisper. "At this moment?"

"Please don't say no this time."

Gabriele gathered my hands between his, tightly. "You tempt me, Beatrice."

"I'm trying to."

In one swift move, Gabriele leaned in, pinning my hands between us. Then his mouth was close to my ear, his breath hot on my cheek. "I shall give you a taste of what this marriage will bring, Beatrice, but just a taste. And then I shall make you wait. For there is sweet torment in the waiting, and the relief will be all the more delicious when it comes at last." He kissed me at the tender spot where my ear and jaw met, where my pulse raced under his mouth. Heat shot to a precise location between my legs. I heard myself moan, a sound I didn't know I could make. The next kiss was lower, at the base of my throat. He pushed my cloak aside and his lips brushed the bare skin just above the neckline of my gown. He raised his head to look at me.

"You are a dangerous woman, Beatrice," Gabriele said, breathing hard. "Spectacular and dangerous. I shall imagine you like this, open and wanting, until the night when you are mine at last."

"God, please don't stop now, please." I was almost crying.

He pressed his body into mine so that our hands, caught between us, pressed into the tender spot at the base of my belly, where I could feel the ache building. "I am sorry, Beatrice, but I shall have to stop. When we are wed, you shall have what you deserve. And so shall I."

I managed to get the words out. "You still want to marry me, even though I use incomprehensible words and touch you when I'm not supposed to?"

Instead of answering, Gabriele kissed me on the mouth. Through that point of contact, his insistent mouth on mine, I could sense the rest of his body and his will: the tension and power in his limbs, the fierce desire held barely in check. It was only a kiss, but he was right—through it I knew what I was in for. He drew back, freeing my hands. Then he closed my cloak gently and solicitiously around my neck.

"Despite, Beatrice, and indeed because of that."

After my meeting with Gabriele, I was useless for the rest of the day. I had to toss three bungled pages, I spilled a pot of ink, and I couldn't add a column of numbers. By evening, I was so agitated that I made my way to the chapel for Vespers. I knelt in one of the pews, trying to let the Latin fill my head, but instead I found myself staring at a young nun whose dress marked her as a novitiate. I watched her kneeling in prayer, the shape of her body hidden by her habit, and wondered what it must be like for her to anticipate a celestial bridegroom instead of an earthbound one. She looked like a paragon of serenity, but who knew what was going on beneath that veil. I gave up on prayer and returned to my chamber. I spent most of the night staring into the opaque darkness of my room.

I woke to the cathedral bells pealing for Prime. Instead of wasting another day in the *scriptorium* making mistakes, I went for another walk. I'd sold some of the jewelry I'd brought back with me from the twenty-first century, and spent the proceeds on warm winter clothes. I had a pair of soft leather boots, a long linen *camica*—a chemise—a simple housedress called a *gonella*, and over those I wore the gown and the heavy gray cloak from my century.

Outside, the biting wind made me wish for the down coat I'd left hanging by the front door of Ben's modern Siena house. I put my hood up and started walking quickly toward the *mercato*. The stalls were just opening and I made my way to a pastry seller's display.

"What's in those?" I pointed to a high pile of glossy hand-size pies brushed with egg and dusted with sugar.

"Pumpkin, Signora, spiced with cloves. They are still hot—can I tempt you?" I bought two and held one in each hand, eating as I walked and scattering flaky crumbs onto my cloak. The pumpkin was sweet, baked into a custard with a rich mixture of egg and cheese, and it warmed me from the inside. Throughout the market the winter vegetable offerings were sparse—dried herbs, root vegetables, a few squash, and baskets of onions and garlic shedding papery skins. Whole dead rabbits hung trussed by their ankles, furred ears stilled and pointing toward the ground. The crowds were not as dense as I'd remembered—*it's winter*, I thought at first, *not the best time to be browsing in the market.* But then the truth made the pie heavy in my stomach—*it's not just winter. Half the population is gone.*

The bells had just rung for Terce when a familiar voice startled me. "Monna Trovato?" The voice came from a figure heavily bundled against the cold. When a small hand emerged to push the hood back, I recognized Ysabella, Gabriele's cousin.

"Beatrice, please," I said, smiling. "I'm so glad to see you again."

"And I to see you." She smiled back. "For a time we thought you had died in Messina."

"I almost did. I heard about your father, Ysabella, I'm so sorry."

Ysabella's smile faded. "I will mourn him until the day I leave the earth. And Rinaldo is gone too. But they are with God." She stopped speaking, collecting herself. "Let us not dwell further in despair—now, I hear, it is time for celebration, and Gabriele can speak of nothing else." Ysabella's smile was back.

I could feel myself blush. "I'm trying to pass the time without losing my mind. That's why I'm walking around here in the freezing cold." It was surprisingly easy to confide in her.

"Time does stretch when we wish it would shrink, and the reverse," she said, sagely. "Will you accompany me to the *calzoleria*, where we may speak in greater comfort? I have a pair of repaired shoes to collect." We entered the shop, which was warmed by a fire in its hearth.

"Bianca's shoes were worn nearly through," Ysabella told me as she greeted the shopkeeper. He disappeared into a back room. "I am the only source of income in the house, with my father and brother gone, and it has not been easy to feed three mouths on the earnings of a new midwife. Gabriele, once he has a commission again, will help, though an artist is no baker." She passed a few coins to the cobbler when he returned and tucked the shoes into a basket. "Ser, may we speak for a time in the warmth of your shop? My cousin is blue with cold." It was nice to hear her call me cousin. He nodded, and Ysabella motioned me to join her on a bench along the *calzoleria*'s wall.

"Beatrice, I've wanted to talk to you about something. Not as happy a matter as your betrothal, I'm afraid."

"Please. If you need money I can certainly help."

"No, thank you for your offer, but we are managing thus far." She dropped her voice. "We had a strange visitor last spring while you and Gabriele were away. He called himself Giovanni Battista, but when he said he was the Ospedale scribe I knew he was lying. He said he was Gabriele's friend too, but I didn't believe him."

"What did the man want?"

"He was looking for Gabriele," she said. "I didn't like it at all."

"Did you tell him anything?"

"I told him Gabriele was not home—at that time we had no idea whether he'd survived the Mortalità in Messina—and I turned the man away. But when Gabriele was accused of murder, I began to wonder whether this visitor had some evil purpose."

Giovanni Battista—neither Umiltà nor Egidio had mentioned a Battista scribing at the Ospedale since I'd left. "It does sound suspicious. Did you see him again?"

"No, never. You don't know anyone by that name?"

"I don't. Would you recognize him if you saw him again?"

"I certainly would—a more unpleasant-looking man would be hard to imagine." Ysabella made a face. "He did give me an address, though it may have been as false as his name."

"That's as good as any other piece of information I've got." Ysabella nodded and told me the street name and landmarks. It was in a part of the city I didn't know well.

"Please be careful, Beatrice. The visitor looked like trouble."

I nodded, not wanting trouble either. But I suspected, as Ysabella did, that any man bent on making trouble for Gabriele would probably not have given his real name and address.

The Torre bells rang, marking the hour. "I must be off, Beatrice.

I promised milk for little Gabriella." Ysabella embraced me before we left the *calzoleria*. "Welcome, cousin," she said into my ear. Her words warmed me as I made my way back to the Ospedale. But the thought of the visitor who'd claimed to be a scribe lodged itself uneasily at the back of my mind.

PART XII

DUCTIO AD MARITUM

wrote my own marriage contract. Umiltà dictated and Gabriele watched silently.

> *On this ninth day of January, in the year 1349, I, Gabriele Beltrano Accorsi, pledge to take Beatrice Alessandra Trovato as my wife, under oath and in the presence of God and witnesses. And I, Beatrice Alessandra Trovato . . .*

Once the ink was dry, Gabriele and I signed. At the threshold Gabriele paused to look at me. In this atmosphere of medieval restraint, meeting his gaze directly felt shockingly intimate. He bowed his head and then let Umiltà lead him out. I'm not the first person to feel the weight of two names paired on a marriage contract, but seeing our oaths documented so clearly under the date did more than cement my connection to Gabriele. The numbers embedded me firmly, inescapably, in this place and time.

✳   ✳   ✳

> *You bade me seek news of your quarry. He has returned from Messina. The denunciation did not stick, despite our witness. That upstart bitch*

of a scribe saved her painter from the gallows—the Podestà's court has granted him his freedom. And now Accorsi will marry the object of his lust, for their betrothal was announced in the Campo a few days ago.

I am still at liberty to forward your cause, at the right price. Shall I call upon you tomorrow? I did like the wine you got last time so find me more of the same.

Guido Baldi

After the failed trial, Iacopo stayed up into the night transcribing lists of Siena's dead. His belly churned with nausea, and his head buzzed. *Now that the Brotherhood can see my dedication to the cause, and my capacity, I will rise to lead them, as my birthright demands. I have carried out the first of your commands, Father: Siena, weakened by the Pestilence, is ripe for the taking. Are you not proud of your only son?*

There was, of course, no answer.

But Iacopo's success was hollow, for Accorsi had eluded him again. This persistent failure was a torment, keeping Iacopo awake night after night in his solitary room. Desperate for sleep, Iacopo visited an apothecary for a draught to make the nights endurable. With the bitter taste of poppy in his mouth he slept at last, and then for days awoke only to take a bit more mixed with watered wine. He resurfaced once the vial had been drained to its dregs, with foul breath and a gnawing hunger in his belly. Finally, he penned a response to Baldi, his hands shaking.

Messer Baldi,

I have grown weary of your schemes that fail so unerringly. Gather all the information you can about the painter, those he lives with, the hours they keep. This will assure greater success in achieving my aims. On this occasion I shall plan and you will execute my wishes. I expect to hear from you in several days—see that you are well prepared the next time.

In the name of God, Amen.

While he waited for Baldi's response, Iacopo visited the Brotherhood's allies in Siena to assure their continued allegiance. There were still *casati* families in Siena who harbored hope that with Florentine help, i Noveschi might soon be overthrown. Siena, a shadow of her former self, should fall easily to a well-laid plot from within her gates. He avoided Ser Signoretti, once his father's strongest supporter in Siena, fearing the outcome of the trial had turned the man against him. He had not told the Brotherhood of the failed trial, nor his use of Signoretti as a key witness. God willing they would not learn what he had done and blame him for the loss of this crucial ally.

Iacopo managed, in his meetings, to keep the voices in his head at bay, though afterward his headaches raged, pulsing in his temples and sending a vicious stabbing to lodge behind one tearing eye. At the end of a week, when Baldi's answer had still not arrived, Iacopo made his way back to Florence, where he waited for news and tried to avoid his mother's watchful gaze.

Iacopo expected an invitation for the confraternity's next meeting, where he might be rewarded for the success of his mission, but no message came. As the days passed, he grew anxious, inventing dark possibilities in his head—perhaps the plot had been discovered, and they all risked death by hanging. One afternoon when the wind blew cold off the Arno and through Iacopo's heaviest cloak, a messenger at last arrived, requesting that Iacopo call upon Ser Albizzi at home, rather than in the Brotherhood's usual meeting place. Albizzi bid him enter, for caution's sake, through the servant's entrance where he might not be seen.

Ser Albizzi welcomed Iacopo in his *studium* and motioned him to sit. As Albizzi waved his manservant out, Iacopo's head filled with the triumph of all he had done. *Now, finally, I will have my due. I have proven myself worthy beyond any expectations, and the leadership of the Brotherhood shall be mine, as it was my father's.*

When the servant was gone, Albizzi cleared his throat to speak.

"You have done well. Remarkably well."

"Thank you, Ser. Your praise is most welcome." Iacopo waited for what would surely come now, the announcement of his new role within the group, and plans for tightening the conspiracy against Siena under his leadership. But instead, Albizzi was silent. The fire in the hearth crackled, and a log fell suddenly with a small shower of sparks. One errant ember landed on the slate before the hearth and glowed briefly before going out, fading red to black.

Albizzi leaned forward, narrowing the distance between them. "Iacopo: I shall speak quickly and briefly. When I am done, we shall not mention anything that transpired here again. Nod your head to show me you have understood." Iacopo nodded mutely. "I speak to you in honesty now because I respected your father, and now that he is gone, he cannot protect you." Iacopo's heart began to pound with apprehension, as if it were trying to exit from his chest. *Protect me from what?* Albizzi dropped his voice to a whisper. "Your knowledge is dangerous to the Brotherhood now."

Iacopo could not restrain his response. "Dangerous? The remaining brothers, thank God for their survival, know as well as I what plans were formed, and how they were realized. What has changed?" Iacopo's voice rose in pitch as his fear did, breaking on the last word.

"Your failure with Ser Signoretti is known to the confraternity, and its leadership no longer trusts you. I fear they will make it certain that you will not reveal the conspiracy's secrets—permanently. You are not safe here any longer, Iacopo. Am I understood?" It was all Iacopo could do to keep silent while his mind raced. *All that I have done, for them and for Firenze, has come to this?*

"When we are finished here you will leave as you entered. Keep your hood up, and do not let yourself be seen on your return home. I have done all I can for you. Is this clear?" Iacopo rose, his legs trembling. It was clear—frighteningly clear.

* * *

Of course I knew nothing whatsoever about medieval weddings. Since I'd already theoretically married the imaginary notary from Lucca, I should have been better informed than your average newlywed. I just kept my mouth shut and let Umiltà and Clara take over.

The next step was the delivery of the receipt for the dowry in the presence of the notary.

"I have arranged your dowry with Ospedale funds," Umiltà said, briskly. I was itching to find out my bride price but couldn't bring myself to ask. "Now we require a notary."

"What about the Ospedale notary?"

"Dead," Umiltà said, grimly. "Since the Mortalità few remain, and many are charlatans. Transactions came to a near standstill in this awful year, and those that transpired were terribly mismanaged. God be praised that the winter has brought some relief from the contagion." I had a nasty thought about what the spring thaw might bring. Gabriele and I should be immune, but that wasn't true of most people.

"Compose an announcement to be read by the criers in the morning. I shall choose among the candidates," Umiltà said. I went back to the *scriptorium* to write out a medieval classified ad.

Three days later Clara came to my room before dawn and shook me out of sleep. I rolled out of bed and onto the floor, which was freezing cold. When Clara set her lantern on the table I could see she was smiling broadly. "He's sent your ring."

"The wedding is *today*?"

Clara laughed. "I do wonder how a widow like yourself can be as unknowing as a babe sometimes." I knew she was not as innocent as she looked. "The notary presides over your mutual consent and exchange of rings. The painter had this made for you, but Umiltà worries that it may not fit your hand." Clara held out a small velvet pouch. I took it from her but didn't open it. "Though I don't doubt the painter knows every bit of your body perfectly, at least, the parts he can see." She giggled. Definitely not innocent.

I opened the pouch and looked inside. "Oh, Lord."

"Is it not lovely? Messer Accorsi had the goldsmith work yours especially." The ring was engraved with a pattern of intertwining vines and flowers, the center of each flower a polished unfaceted dark red stone.

"It is lovely." I slipped the ring on my finger—it went from cold to warm. I hesitated before giving it back to Clara.

"You'll have it back soon enough, Signora, and before you know it, more than a ring will be wrapped about you."

"Clara!" I'd never heard her like this.

"You are no stranger to the joys of marriage, nor am I," she said pertly. "Now, let me help you with your gown and hair." I didn't mention that my familiarity with those joys had nothing to do with marriage.

The notary looked at least ninety years old. His features were surrounded by a sea of wrinkled skin, and when he wrote, his hand and the excess flesh of his face and neck trembled with the effort. Umiltà presided over the event, as usual. Gabriele arrived with a young man as witness, someone I'd never met. Gabriele introduced him as Tommaso Barocci, a fellow painter and friend from Martini's workshop.

I didn't know you had any friends, I thought silently. But of course there was a lot I didn't know about Gabriele. Tommaso greeted me graciously, and I returned the formal greeting. When Clara entered she was not alone—a familiar bulky shape followed her through the door.

"Provenzano!"

He bowed, his wide face creasing with pleasure. "I would have come sooner to see you, but I've been in Arezzo on business. I owe you a great debt of gratitude, Monna Trovato, for your advice that sent me to the *contado*, away from the lash of the Mortalità. And an even greater debt for lending me your lovely maid. I've kept her, to our mutual pleasure." He put his arm around Clara, who was approaching his width as her pregnancy advanced.

"It's wonderful to see you," I said, meaning it.

"And you as well," he said, "particularly on such a happy occasion. I've allowed little Clara a few more weeks in your service—until the wedding. She begged me, and of course I could not refuse her. The wife of a merchant should not be a maidservant, especially one who is with child! But you are no ordinary maid to serve." There was no more time to talk. We all held our breaths as the notary labored to scratch out the receipt.

Once the dowry was duly recorded in the notary's shaky handwriting, Gabriele and I stood to face each other. The notary's voice trembled but he got the words out.

"Do you, Gabriele Beltrano Accorsi, take this woman, Beatrice Alessandra Trovato, to be your wife?"

"Messer, *sì*," Gabriele said.

"And do you, Beatrice Alessandra Trovato, take this man, Gabriele Beltrano Accorsi, to be your husband?"

"Messer, *sì*."

Gabriele produced the ring I'd tried on that morning.

"I trust this fits your hand, Signora?" Gabriele gently slid it onto my fourth finger. I saw Tommaso draw his arm up and back, as if he were about to throw something, and then he slapped Gabriele on the back, hard enough so that the sound made us all jump. By the time I realized it must be customary, everyone was laughing.

"*Mariate*," Umiltà said, and we were, just like that.

Mariate, but not, as I soon learned, *ite*: married but not gone forth. That would be the final step, the *ductio ad maritum*—the installation of the bride in her husband's home. Umiltà selected an auspicious day at the end of February for the ceremony: just a few weeks away. The Ospedale still had a few drapers and seamstresses at its disposal, and a team went to work to sew me a wedding dress. Within a week I was able to try it on for final adjustments. It was deep blue with a long skirt that reached the ground behind me, and it came with trailing sleeves and an underdress of pale yellow. I wore a linen chemise underneath—the layers rustled against one another when I moved.

"Blue for purity," Umiltà said, and the blue was embroidered with golden lilies. Umiltà told me she would keep it in her *studium* for safety. I let it go reluctantly.

On my next afternoon off, I went to check out the putative Giovanni Battista's address. I ended up at a dive-y wine shop that reminded me of a few places in New York's Bowery district before all the drunks had been cleared out to make way for trendy clubs. I got a lot of quizzical looks from both the ragged clientele and the wine seller, who smelled like the floor of a bar at closing time. In the short three minutes I was in the shop I had to escape two gropes and one offer of payment for more than a grope. But it was clearly no one's residence, and no one there had heard of a Giovanni Battista. Not surprised, I escaped with relief into the fresh air again.

Next I had to pursue the Medici question. Unfortunately my empathic tendency didn't work like a tracking device, though it would have been convenient if it did. Iacopo must have come at least once to Siena, knowing his father was imprisoned here, and he must have stayed somewhere. I could start asking at local inns, but I didn't want a repeat of my last attempt, and I needed a trustworthy man whom I could ask for help. Gabriele was off-limits until the wedding, but Provenzano would be perfect. He was big enough to avert trouble, and unsuspecting. Somehow this would have to be done without putting my friends in danger; the best strategy would be to keep them ignorant. When Clara delivered my midday meal, I set my plan in motion.

"Clara, is there a good place nearby with lodging for travelers?"

"Semenzato's is the best, and best known," she said, putting down the tray carefully without bending at the waist, since her waist had vanished. "Do you have a guest coming from another town for the wedding?" She looked at me with interest. "I thought you said you had no family." She'd conveniently provided me with an excellent cover.

"All sorts of family come out of the woodwork when a wedding is announced." I smiled brightly to match hers. "My late husband's cousin may come for the festivities."

"One must ask in advance to be sure of accommodations. There aren't many rooms, and they are in great demand."

"Whom shall I send? Ideally someone articulate, well established . . . someone . . ." I paused, pretending to consider the options. "Do you think Provenzano might be able to go?"

"I am sure he'd be delighted! I shall ask him this very moment." So far, so good.

Clara's husband was inordinately happy to see me. Our conversation inevitably turned to what had happened to him in Sicily, and from there to what had become of his former employer. I was surprised to see Provenzano's face turn a deep, embarrassed pink.

"Ah, Monna Trovato, an excellent question, to be sure, an excellent question." He pulled out a handkerchief to mop his brow, though it wasn't at all warm in the room.

"What is so excellent about the question exactly?"

"You may be happy to know that he did survive the Mortalità."

I didn't hate anyone enough to wish them death by Plague. "Good news indeed."

Provenzano was even pinker. I waited for clarification. "Messer Lugani actually sent you a letter, *via* me." He trailed off unhappily.

"He sent *me* a letter?"

Provenzano rummaged in his large bag and handed me the folded parchment with an apologetic look. "I hadn't wanted to bother you, but since you've asked, I can't very well keep it to myself." I unfolded the letter and began to read.

Vigil of Epiphany, January, 1349

In the Name of God, Amen.

I have heard the good news from Messer Provenzano, that he has found both excellent employment, and a lovely wife whom, I believe, used to be your faithful servant?

My Messina fondaco, as you must realize, now lacks competent staff to keep its operations running smoothly. I know, from the time you spent in my employ, that you have skills adequate to the task. I would certainly find time to pay frequent visits when you take up the post, and would enjoy resuming our prior acquaintance. Your professional competence is the least of what I would look forward to, in my visits south.

You will be happy to know as well that Messer Cane has survived, and he has promised to supervise you as you learn what is required of the post. I feel certain, given your meager salary and lack of family ties, that this offer of employment will appeal to you.

I look forward to your acquiescence.

Messer Girolamo Lugani, Genoa

The man was truly unbelievable. I looked up at Provenzano, who was cringing, waiting for my response. I folded the letter back in thirds and handed it to him calmly.

"You can tell him I'm otherwise engaged," I said, "in more ways than one." And with that out of the way, we turned to discussion of the local inn.

Provenzano, fortunately, was as unsuspicious as Clara. I shifted the story slightly—my cousin was considering places to stay in Siena, could he ask about availability at Semenzato's? And while there, it would be of particular interest to find out what other visitors were staying at the tavern—and where they came from. This cousin had a peculiarity about Florentines, I said, embellishing—his grandfather had died at Montaperti and he'd detested the *commune* after that.

Provenzano took my request without question. "Any family of Monna Trovato is a friend to me," he said, a smile on his plump face.

Provenzano came back the following day with his regrets: the inn was fully occupied by a group of wine merchants from Poggibonsi who were in Siena for a long stay. "Perhaps it's just as well your cousin avoid the place. It seems Florentines do frequent his establishment, at least one does. Messer Semenzato said there was one Florentine fellow—thin and ill-looking, who kept odd hours and stayed for a while. The man has come several times, the first more than a year ago—just before the Medici trial. He's gone again now, but your cousin would be better off finding a place less likely to house such people, given his concerns."

"Thank you so much, Provenzano," I said. "I'm sorry to have wasted your time."

"Not at all, not at all. Semenzato's wine was certainly very good, particularly with the eel tart that came with it." He patted his belly happily, remembering. As we parted, I wondered how this new information might help me. Could the repeat visitor at Semenzato's be Iacopo de' Medici? If so, he was gone now. It still wasn't enough to go on.

*   *   *

Iacopo planned his immediate return to Siena, with the knowledge that the Brotherhood lay in wait for him. Now when he walked the streets he once called home, every sound made him start and look over his shoulder for an imagined assassin hired to assure his silence. *So this is how they repay my loyalty, these men whom my father called brothers.*

Would that it had been only in his imagination. As Iacopo walked back to the Medici palazzo after a late meeting, he turned into a long narrow street—a short route rather than a populated one. His choice proved nearly deadly. At the far end of the *via*, a hooded figure appeared from a dark doorway and began to move quickly toward him. When a second joined the first, Iacopo's heart began to pound in his ears, drowning out the sound of the men's feet on the stones. He turned and ran with his breath like a knife in his chest until he reached his family palazzo. Firenze, once home, was no longer a haven.

The morning Iacopo left for Siena, Immacolata took her son into the chapel, where they knelt and prayed together as they had not since his boyhood.

"Iacopo, I know your father's business troubles you."

The way his mother looked at him made Iacopo fear she knew more than he had said. "Business is best kept out of the home," Iacopo answered, attempting to keep his voice steady.

"Not if the business endangers the home, and those who live in it. Your father died in the pursuit of this same business." Iacopo shook his head and did not answer. *If I am quiet, she will stop asking.*

His mother sighed. "I fear this business has gone beyond accounts and ledgers, and weighs now upon your conscience. If you will not speak with me, at least speak with God. Will you promise me that?" He nodded, and only half to placate his mother, for he longed for relief from the terrible things he had seen and done. When she took his hand in hers he willed himself not to melt into her familiar embrace.

"I must return to Siena," he said finally, and she could get no more from him. When he left on horseback, his mother watched gravely from the palazzo's entrance.

Semenzato's was full of merchants, requiring him to seek other accommodations. It was inconvenient, but perhaps for the best; it would keep his movements difficult to trace. He met with Baldi in the small tavern on the ground floor of the new inn he'd chosen.

Baldi's face shone with sweat in the flickering light from the inn's hearth. "The painter and his wench are getting married. The Ospedale is busy with preparations and no one will expect anything. It will be as easy as taking a rattle from an infant."

"A wedding means many witnesses," Iacopo said, scowling.

"A wedding means no one will see me coming," Baldi replied, "and the painter will be so busy taking his new wife to bed he won't know what hit him. When I hit him, that is. And I'll throw his new wife in, for the same price." Baldi laughed at his own humor, too loud. Patrons a few tables away raised their heads at the sound.

"I told you to keep quiet," Iacopo hissed angrily.

"They are too drunk to care. Now show me those lovely florins you promised. I know where the painter lives and the house is otherwise all women and girls now. He'll be between his new wife's legs and the rest will put up no obstacle."

"See that you get it right this time," Iacopo said grimly, "or you will pay for your mistake." Baldi laughed again, and picked up the florins in one thick-fingered hand.

*　　*　　*

The night before the wedding was cold and bright. Clara came to find me staring out the unshuttered window of my room at a cluster of brilliant stars. How much would it change in the centuries between now and the time I used to inhabit—how many stars might be born or die, and in dying, give rise to new stars?

"If you die of cold, your bridegroom will never forgive me," Clara exclaimed, sealing the window. "Now come, it's time for your bath." On our wedding eve, Gabriele and I were each to take baths, separately of course, and then bathe with childhood friends. But I had none—not here. I wondered whom Gabriele would be bathing with. Tommaso? It was hard to imagine. As Clara unlaced my dress, I felt her hands pause.

"Clara?"

"Signora, I'm sorry. I was . . . thinking."

I turned to look at her. "Thinking?"

She blushed faintly. "Well, perhaps wondering is more the word."

"Wondering what?"

"Whether we would see each other often, once you are in your new home, and now that I am wed. Provenzano will keep me as befits my new station, but I don't like to leave you."

"My new home." My mind had wandered in a direction she couldn't follow, in which my new home meant my new century.

"I would be happy to find you another maid to take my place." Clara took a deep breath and started to talk quickly, as if to comfort herself. "Of course it would make more sense for you to have someone unencumbered, for I have a babe nearly born, and a husband as well. Will you allow me the honor of choosing a worthy replacement?"

"Clara, we'll still see each other."

"You are sure of it?"

"Of course. I'll be miserable to lose you."

"Oh, Signora, you are the most wonderful mistress imaginable," Clara exclaimed, and she embraced me, her bulk awkward between us.

As she pulled away I caught a glimpse of the steam rising

invitingly from the bath into the chilly air. A small fire was lit in the hearth but could only do so much to temper the February wind seeping through the shutters.

"Will you bathe with me, Clara? I hate to waste all that hot water on only myself."

"Me? You want to bathe with me?"

"Yes, please." She smiled broadly, and didn't argue.

When we undressed together in the cold room I couldn't help staring at her. Her swollen belly and breasts gathered the candlelight, shining as if they had light of their own.

"I'm sorry, I don't mean to stare. You're beautiful."

"Thank you for saying so," she said, dipping her head shyly. "My Provenzano tells me the same, but I don't see the beauty in all this bigness."

"Your beauty is in the bigness," I said, and held her hand to steady her while she stepped into the high-sided tub. We both sank into the warm water, sighing in unison as the scent of thyme and verbena rose into the steam. I closed my eyes and into the silent warmth came an unexpected sound, the sound of a beating heart, and with it a rush of foreign consciousness—bright, quivering, and alert. It must be coming from Clara, I realized, as my head spun with the knowledge that I was sensing a life nearly ready to emerge into the world. We sat and bathed, two of us luxuriating in the warmth of the water and the third in the warmth of its mother-to-be, preparing for the days ahead.

On the day of the *ductio ad maritum*, I woke up feeling not entirely normal—as if I were looking through a kaleidoscope, the images fractured and glittering. The chitter of a winter sparrow outside my window made my throat catch, and the smell of oranges filled the air like a hallucination. I felt I was everywhere at once, still in the bath with the sound of a heart beating in my ears, looking through an open window at the spinning stars, and living through this day in Siena, in late February of 1349. After saying our vows in the Ospedale chapel, Gabriele and I walked out into the courtyard to the sound of trumpets, the horns fluttering with forked pennants in Siena's black and white.

"*Sono onorato di presentarvi Beatrice Alessandra Trovato è Gabriele Beltrano Accorsi . . .*"

I imagined the words spinning far and fast through the city, to the walls that should have kept us safe, past the gates to the winter gray and brown of Siena's *contado,* and beyond—to the wild continent that would one day become the home I used to call mine. But Siena was my home now.

It was warm enough to celebrate outside, one of those perfect days that happen in late February, a promise of relief from winter. The Ospedale's courtyard streamed with colored ribbons; banners and tapestries hung from the windows and high stone walls. Everything moved around me except Gabriele himself, steady at my side, his hair bright against the deep blue and red of his tunic and robe. When the horns stopped, there was music—pipes and a drum—and dancing. Across the circle I spotted Bianca, and in her arms a little girl with a head of brown curls—*little Gabriella,* I thought, remembering her harrowing entrance into the world— she looked old enough to walk but maybe not to dance, so her mother held her, laughing, as we moved across the flagstones.

Someone handed me a cup of *clarée* and I drank the spiced white wine, feeling the heat of cloves and ginger. I sat at a table with Gabriele at my side again, tall and straight in his chair. A servant passed us a bowl of tiny oranges; the sections burst sweet and tart in my mouth, and Gabriele leaned over to brush a drop from my chin. Trays of roast pheasant appeared, decorated as if still alive with their magnificent plumage, and acrobats in red and black made everyone gasp. We began dancing again to the music of lutes and singers rising in the darkening air.

We headed out of the courtyard. The guests followed behind, cheering and singing, holding torches and candles against the gathering night. We stopped at the doorway of Martellino's house; the house that had once been Ben's—and mine—would be my home again. The missing scent of baking bread was a void of sorrow where there used to be a sweet, yeasty comfort. But we crossed the threshold, arm in arm. When the crowds followed us through the bakery and up the stairs, I gripped Gabriele's arm and put my mouth to his ear.

"Gabriele, are these people going to leave soon? I hope to God it isn't part of your tradition to have the consummation of a marriage witnessed by a cheering crowd."

He laughed once, and the sound warmed the house the way the cold oven no longer did. He leaned down to whisper back. "They will leave as soon as they are assured we are settled. Then we can indulge in the pleasure of our seclusion." *Pleasure of our seclusion*. I liked the sound of that very much.

*　　*　　*

After his meeting with the Medici boy, Baldi assembled the supplies to carry out his task. The carpenter he hired, happy to have any commission at all in such sparse times, had worked quickly, fashioning a ladder that could reach a second-floor loggia, and Baldi found a blacksmith outside the city walls and purchased a small dagger, easily hidden.

From an alley across the *via*, Baldi watched the wedding party approach the newlyweds' home—just as he'd predicted, with the guests drunk on the Ospedale's fine *clarée*. He moved into the shadow of the alleyway and sat down to wait until moonset, wrapping his cloak around him.

PART XIII

NOS MODERNI

The guests finally filed out, calling out good wishes and bawdy suggestions. But when they had left we were still not alone. Clara had insisted on attending me this one last time. She removed my cloak, then began to unlace the back of my overgown. Gabriele strewed fresh rushes on the floor and added wood to the fire until it crackled and gave off a wave of heat. What if Clara's presence wouldn't be considered company, from the medieval point of view? I hoped the wedding night would not include her settling in for the evening.

Gabriele lit candles and placed them in the wall sconces. In the wavering light, I could see the faint outlines of the sketches Gabriele had made, the ones I'd found in my kichen. The bed loomed ominously large, draped with a heavy dark red canopy. Clara removed my overgown, leaving me in the long-sleeved dress beneath it. Finally, she curtsied, and left with a small smile dimpling her cheek.

I moved against the wall, conscious of the cold plaster against my back. Beneath the dress I had a long linen chemise, the sort of thing I once would have walked around in unabashedly—but now, even in two garments, I felt undressed.

"You are shivering," Gabriele said.

"The wall is cold."

"Come away from it, then, and to the fire."

I heard sounds from the kitchen below—Gabriella laughing, Bianca, quieting her daughter in a tone that sounded like bedtime. I couldn't quite make out the words.

"Do I live here now?"

"Indeed you do. With us. With me."

"Just like that—boom—this is my house, and I'm your wife?"

"*Boom?* Does that mean all at once?"

"Basically." My new ring pinched the flesh between my fingers.

Gabriele smiled gently. "Just a few weeks ago you bemoaned the slowness of our many-stage betrothal process, did you not?"

"It's just strange—one minute I live in the Ospedale, the next minute I'm standing here married to you."

"There must always be a moment when before changes to after; just as there is a division between unborn and born, or life and death."

I was finding it a bit hard to breathe. "It's kind of stuffy in here, can we open the window?" I could see from the look on Gabriele's face that I'd made an outrageous suggestion, to open up the tightly sealed window of a medieval bedroom in February. But before I could retract it, he had pulled over a chair to stand on, and was opening the shutters to remove the parchment.

"I am here to serve your wishes, my lady and wife," he said, "though I begin to wonder whether that will prove difficult."

I felt my face get hot and welcomed the breeze from the open window. "I'm nervous."

"Do you think you are alone in that? Beatrice, look at my hands."

I stared at his long fingers, the gentle curve of his knuckles, the surprisingly delicate bones of his wrists. I wanted to reach out and touch him, but couldn't. I'd just married a man centuries older than me and committed myself to his place and time. Had I really once held that hand?

"Gabriele, you're shaking."

"How could I not? It is incredible that we have bridged the centuries that separated us." He put his hands down.

"Maybe we should just talk for a while," I said. He nodded his assent. There were two chairs by the fire, and we sat. "Why don't you start?"

Gabriele drew his lower lip into his mouth to consider his answer. "Would you care to tell me of those you have left behind?"

"What, you mean my friends?"

"*Famiglia, amici, consorterie*—in whatever order pleases you."

"I don't have family." It sounded harsher than I'd intended.

"Would you like to speak of the family you once had?"

"I might get upset."

"What is a husband for, if not to comfort you?" I smiled for the first time since the door had closed behind us. But I wasn't ready to talk about Ben. A few seconds passed while we listened to the crackling of the fire in the hearth. "Beatrice, I have never known you to be so hesitant to speak."

"Sorry. I'm not quite myself."

"You are your *new* self."

"You're always so gracious, no matter how difficult I am. That's a nice quality."

"It bodes well for our marriage," he said.

"Don't you ever get upset?"

"When necessary."

"Efficient of you."

"I prefer to reserve my energy for what is to come. The night is long."

My face got hot again. "I'll tell you about Nathaniel."

"Please." Gabriele looked at me expectantly.

"Nathaniel owns—or will own—a bookstore in New York City—it doesn't exist yet, of course. Across the ocean from here."

"What is the basis for your friendship with this . . . gentleman?" Gabriele's tone of voice had changed—more formal.

"Gentleman? I guess he's a gentleman. He does have excellent manners. And he takes, I mean took, good care of me."

"Good care, you say?"

"Oh, not that kind of care, he wasn't my boyfriend or anything."

"Boy-Friend?" We were on different planets. This was not going to be easy.

"Er . . . lover? Is that what you are thinking? No, he was just a great loving friend."

"Such friends are good to have."

"He's gay, anyway, and basically married."

"I see," Gabriele said stiffly, but clearly he didn't see.

"*Gay* means . . . he loves a man named Charles. Charles is a doctor, but he deals mostly with dead people."

"Beatrice, I do not mean to judge you and your time ill, but your closest friend is a sodomite who loves a man who deals in dead bodies?"

Things were not going well. I felt my patience ebb, strained by the demands of cross-century transplantation and marriage coming to a head all at once—over Nathaniel. My Nathaniel, who understood me without explanation and would never recommend a book to me again.

"Who are you to criticize my friends for being 'unsavory'? In your world they hang criminals by the neck while a crowd cheers the hangman on." I glared at him.

"No criminals die at the hand of the government, in your time?"

"Well, no, they do sometimes. Just not visibly."

"Then your government does it in secret, so the people can have no part in their communal justice?"

"It isn't the way you make it sound."

"How then do you kill your criminals?"

"This is an even less romantic subject than Nathaniel," I said, and then unexpectedly I was crying.

"Beatrice, I am sorry. I should not press you thus." Gabriele produced a handkerchief from somewhere in his tunic. "May I dry your tears?" I leaned forward, and from his seat he reached out to touch my cheek. It was such a relief to feel his hand on my face, breaking through the centuries that divided us, that I started to cry harder.

"Sweet Beatrice, is there a safer topic? We seem to be traveling the chasm between our worlds quite perilously."

"Tell me about your wife."

"That is not a particularly safe topic either."

"This time *I'll* listen while *you* explain."

"You are a challenging woman, Beatrice."

"You didn't know that? You'll be in for nasty surprises over the next few decades, then."

"I hope to be surprised for decades, as you say. Boredom is a poor reward for fidelity."

I had to smile. "I still want to hear about your late wife, if you are willing to talk."

He sighed. "What do you want to know?"

"Did you love her?"

"That is a difficult question to answer."

"Is that what you would say about me to your next wife, if I died?"

"No." He answered simply.

"What would you say, then?"

"I would say that I loved you more than painting, more than the air I breathe, more than my own life. I would say that the void created by your parting was so great as to be unfathomable, and that I feared I might fall into its bottomless abyss, from which I would never find the light again."

It was almost a minute before I could speak. "I shouldn't have made you answer that question."

"It is your prerogative to know my thoughts, as I would know yours. But perhaps we can learn more gradually?"

"Good idea." I got out of my chair and stood next to him,

unsure why I was standing. The candles flickered unevenly in the wind from the open window. Gabriele looked up at me.

"Will you tell me your thoughts now, Beatrice?"

I considered his question. "My mind is blank."

"Excellent," Gabriele said, rising suddenly. In one swift movement he took my face in his hands and kissed me on the mouth. His lips were warm, and shockingly soft. He caressed the back of my neck with one hand, and his other traveled down my back.

"Gabriele, I have to tell you something."

He looked at me indulgently. "I suspect that this will not be your last topic of the night."

"I'm not a virgin. I hope you didn't think you were marrying one." I had an image of him walking out of the room without another word.

"Nor am I," he said simply.

"I know you aren't, obviously. But . . . you don't care that I'm . . . sullied, or anything?"

He smiled. "Why should I? I hope to benefit from your experience."

The implications of his answer made me flush. "You just think I'm amusing because I'm from a different century."

"You have spoiled me, Beatrice. No woman from my own time could ever equal you."

"But another modern transplant could do it?"

"There will never be any woman, from any century, to move me as you do."

"You haven't met anyone else from my century."

"I do not need to," he said. "Now I hope I have convinced you sufficiently of my devotion to allow another kiss."

I stopped arguing. After a few minutes we both pulled back, breathless.

"Beatrice, please turn around."

"Why?"

"If I try to remove your gown without unlacing it, I am likely to tear it to pieces. Do you have any further questions?"

"I might, later," I said over my shoulder, hearing him chuckle.

The time and effort required to get a medieval bride undressed could drive anyone's anticipation through the roof. By the time Gabriele got me out of the chemise, more than my hands were trembling. Behind me, I heard Gabriele's intake of breath.

I started to turn to face him but he stopped me with one hand.

"Wait." His breath was warm in my ear. "It is a great luxury to look at you this way." His fingers followed his words, and my skin warmed under them. "The sweet arch of your neck, the curve in your back, just here." He touched the base of my spine, briefly, and I shivered. "I must admit, Beatrice, that at this moment I am not thinking about painting you. Not at all."

I held my breath, feeling his eyes on me.

At last he turned me gently to face him. "Beatrice, you are shaking again. Ought I to close the window?"

I wanted him so much it made my knees weak. "Gabriele, haven't you ever taken a hungry woman to bed before?" I saw the answer in his face, the sudden shift in his expression.

"No, I have not. We are each virgins in our different ways, Beatrice—you to marriage, and me . . . to reciprocated desire."

For a moment I was embarrassed for us both, but then my body won out over my mind. "Well, if I'm going to deflower you, you've got to undress too. Otherwise it's not fair."

"By all means we must be fair," Gabriele replied hoarsely as I reached for his belt.

We stood in front of each other, surrounded by our piles of clothes. I was not prepared for the sight of his body. Nearly every inch of his skin had been hidden for the months I'd known him, under fabric from neck to ankles. But beyond the pure shock of seeing his beautiful, breathtaking nakedness, I'd never felt the marriage of emotion and desire as I did now.

"Come to me, Beatrice," Gabriele said. I took a step to narrow the space between us, then matched my length to his—chest, belly, thigh—and buried my face in the heat of his neck. His pulse beat fast under my mouth, the incontrovertible evidence that this man, born more than six hundred years before me, was alive in my arms. My head spun, the world tilting. And it was more than desire that blurred my vision and filled my head with sound—my extra sense kicked in as the physical barriers between us came down at last. But unlike all the unsuspecting others whose minds I'd visited, Gabriele was aware of my arrival, and unlike the others, could resist it.

"May I?" I said, hoping he would know what I meant.

"You may," he said, looking down at me gravely. "But beware, for I will reciprocate, in my own way."

"What do you mean?"

"Beatrice, you must know what I mean."

"I want to hear you say it."

He kept his hands firmly on my arms. "I have waited as long as I can bear to have you. I may not be able to be gentle."

"I don't want you to be gentle."

His eyes narrowed. "I am a great deal stronger than you."

"Prove it, Gabriele."

And then he let me in his head. And I learned, in that shocking moment, what it felt like to be a man—this man—my sweet, articulate, chivalrous Gabriele, driven by a need so sharp and hungry that it blinded him to everything else. I saw myself through his eyes, saw what he intended to do with me, felt the passion behind that intent. It was exhilarating and dangerous.

"You want *that* from me, Beatrice? Are you certain?"

I didn't answer out loud. We stumbled across the stone floor to the edge of the huge canopied bed, which welcomed us with a loud creak of boards and the sharp smell of wool.

When Gabriele made space for his body between my legs,

I learned just how strong he was, and he proved it without restraint. I had given him leave, and he took me at my word. After that, I lost the boundary between my mind and my body for a long time.

Gabriele woke me a few hours later, his fingers stroking my leg under the piled blankets. The candles had burned down, and a faint silvery moonlight came through the open shutters. For a moment I did not know where I was. Then the reality of my dislocation overwhelmed me, the expanse of centuries separating me from my own time. I grabbed onto Gabriele's shoulder and he put his hand over mine.

"Beatrice, did I frighten you?"

"No, of course you didn't. But wouldn't you be frightened if you woke up in the middle of the night in a strange bed, more than six hundred years from everything you've ever known?"

"Do you regret your decision, Beatrice?"

"No." It wasn't regret, it was the truth laid bare in the dark. But my heart was slowing down as I listened to the sound of his voice. "It's hard to believe I'm here."

"I too awoke, fearing that I was alone again with only a memory to keep me company." Gabriele's hand warmed my fingers, and I relaxed into the certainty of that simple contact. "Beatrice, may I hazard a guess that we both need the same sort of reassurance?"

"What sort of reassurance?" He put his mouth on mine. "Oh, that was an excellent guess. Please do that again." Gabriele proceeded to reassure us both quite thoroughly of my physical reality until we were damp with sweat, despite the open window.

"I almost wish I could be a man for a few hours," I said to him afterward, still feeling the thrill of being carried along by that concentrated fury of want.

"It seems you will be, if you continue to enter my thoughts this way. And if I continue to allow you to do so."

"I hope you will," I said, truthfully. "I'd miss it if you didn't."

"I will—under one condition," Gabriele said, his voice shifting. "What condition?"

He cleared his throat. "This time, Beatrice, you will tell me, as I make love to you, what it feels like to be in your body. I do not have the powers you possess, but I would know the experience of being . . . taken."

"I have to talk?"

"Yes, Beatrice. And if you need me to pause for you to catch your breath, I will do so, before I resume. And you must be frank, and thorough. It is only fair, is it not?"

"It is fair," I said, shivering with the prospect.

"Then turn onto your knees, Beatrice; it will be easier for you to speak." I did, and felt his chest against my back. "Now, start speaking," Gabriele said, "and do not stop until you are beyond speech." And I did as he asked, until I couldn't.

For hours we moved in and out of sleep as the moonlight slanted across the bedcovers. Sometimes I woke first and reached for him, sometimes he reached for me, sometimes I could not tell who moved first. I could not have enough of him, and he was as gently relentless as I was hungry. We pushed each other beyond the line of reason, until we stopped talking at all. The night smelled of spent candles, and somewhere I heard the hoot of a lone owl. The moon had set by the time we disentangled ourselves from each other and the bedcovers. Gabriele propped himself up on one arm.

"I'm not going to be able to walk tomorrow," I said, looking up at him.

"You can stay in bed, Beatrice. Although it may be more tiring to stay in bed than to rise, if things continue as they have thus far."

I laughed, but his breathing had changed, and when I reached out to touch his face, it was wet. "Gabriele, why are you crying?"

"I, like you, am afraid."

"Afraid of what?" He was safe in his own time, unlike me.

He took a deep breath before answering. "I fear this passion I have for you will give rise to new life."

I'd thought of it more than once, what it might mean to bear a child in the fourteenth century, stripped of modern medicine's reassuring presence. "We've survived a raging inferno, a collapsing scaffold, a storm at sea, your murder charge, the Plague. Don't you think we can survive a baby?"

Gabriele's shoulder shook, and I worried for a moment that he might be sobbing. But instead he laughed, a bright, sweet sound in the velvet dark. "If you continue to make me laugh, thus, even in the midst of my tears, then we are destined for a marriage blessed by God."

"Amen," I said, and this time, we slept.

PART XIV

THE CONFESSOR

I woke again without knowing why. Then I felt it, the internal hum I knew so well. I untangled myself from the blankets and slipped out of bed, then fumbled in the dark to find my chemise. Now the hum was louder, and with it came a flash of vision—a dark night with no moon, a makeshift ladder, the jutting edge of a loggia. Danger, I could feel it. But from what?

In the narrow alleyway, Baldi assembled the ladder. It nearly escaped him, swaying in his hands as he pivoted it sideways, then upward. The free end hit a ceramic pot resting on the loggia's edge, and the pot teetered dangerously but did not fall. Breathing hard, Baldi braced the ladder against the building across the way, wedging it firmly, and began to climb.

He tested the first rung with one foot—it held. As he climbed, the ladder bowed under his weight. His foot reached the eighth rung, the ninth, the tenth. Then the jutting edge of the loggia was in reach, and he grasped it, his fingers scrabbling against rough plaster, until he was high enough to clamber over the wall. The shuttered doors opened with a hoarse creak as the hinges complained.

The room was darker than the alley. No matter, he'd have his quarry—especially drugged with spent lust after rutting with his new wife. Baldi began to make out the outlines of the canopied bed. There was one elongated shape draped with a patterned coverlet, or were there two? He fingered the dagger at his waist. Accorsi's new bride was black haired, but it was hard to see anything above the blanket's edge.

Then he saw a second head, a small one, in the bed with the large. Before he could make sense of what he saw, the child opened her eyes and let out an ear-splitting shriek. Baldi leaped to the bed to clap one hand over the screaming mouth, but as he did so, the babe, hellspawn that she was, bit down on his finger hard.

Gabriella's scream sent me running. As I burst into the room Bianca's yells joined her daughter's. It was dark, but I could tell there was a stranger there, a large stranger who did not belong. I saw the flailing of limbs—Gabriella's small ones, Bianca's white and wild as she pounded the intruder with her fists. He was fumbling at his waist for something while trying to keep Bianca's blows from landing. I knew, from a combination of common sense and my uncommon one, that a dagger was next. I threw myself at the bed, aiming for the attacker's arm before he could find what he was fumbling for.

The man was heavy and smelled of sweat, and gave a grunt as I hit him. Then his force turned on me: he flipped me onto my back, pinning my arms to the bed with one hand, and drove his knee between my legs. Bianca pounded at his back with her fists but he barely flinched. I could see the dagger now, glinting as he drew it from the scabbard at his waist. Then there was a crack, the sound of metal hitting bone, and the intruder's huge body collapsed onto mine, squeezing all the air from my lungs and blanketing me in dirty wool.

"That's Giovanni Battista, the man who claimed he was an Ospedale scribe," Ysabella declared, brandishing the bloody candlestick that she'd used to bash the intruder on the head. We all stared at the beached body of the unwelcome visitor. The man lay on the floor with blood oozing from a head wound. Bianca had retreated to the wall, holding the wide-eyed Gabriella in her arms, when Gabriele burst into the room.

"We shall find out more when he awakes," Gabriele said grimly, "imminently. Light the wall sconces so we can see his face."

Ysabella took a glowing ember from the fire to do that while Bianca disappeared, taking Gabriella with her to safety.

Our attacker began to groan and move his limbs. Gabriele took the dagger from the bed, and he bent at Baldi's side, holding the blade near his throat.

"To forestall any difficulty," Gabriele said, and we all waited until Baldi's eyes opened.

"Bastard," he said.

"Perhaps, but that has no bearing on this situation," Gabriele responded. Humor in the face of danger was his specialty too. "Tell us your true name. We know you are not the Ospedale scribe you claimed to be."

"I was the scribe until this upstart bitch took my job from me."

So this was the Guido Baldi I'd replaced, the one Fra Bosi had told me about on my first day of work.

"Trying to kill your replacement is a pretty extreme reaction to losing your job," I said, still shaking from the adrenaline of the attack.

"I was hired," Baldi said, cringing away from the dagger's point.

"By whom? I should very much like to know," Gabriele said evenly.

Baldi's eyes went to Gabriele's face, then mine. "What might the information be worth to you?"

"Your survival might be of some worth," Gabriele answered evenly.

Baldi grunted. "I will tell you if you don't turn me in."

In the candlelight I could see the sheen of sweat on Baldi's face and the small, deep-set eyes. Gabriele and I exchanged glances. The information might be worth it.

"You should be in prison, Messer Baldi," Gabriele said.

"It's my master you want, Accorsi. I'm done with him now."

"Very well. Tell me who hired you, and I shall not turn you over to the police," Gabriele said, "but if I find you are lying, or if any trouble arises that could be attributed to you, I shall make it my business to see you arrested. Or worse."

We all watched, waiting for Baldi's answer.

"Iacopo de'Medici, of Florence."

*　　*　　*

Immacolata moved about her rooms with a new sense of freedom, now that the men of her household were gone. Giovanni's death had receded from the most acute place of shock, replaced by a disturbing contentment. When she stretched out in their large connubial bed, she no longer worried she might accidentally brush one of her husband's furred limbs. Once, waking him in the night would have brought at best a day of angry words, and at worst, a beating; now there was no one to wake.

But Iacopo's absence gnawed at her. A week after her son's latest departure for Siena, Immacolata woke from a dream with her heart pounding. In the dream, Iacopo sat immobile in a flat-bottomed boat without oars, a boat that skimmed rather than parted the water. His craft headed inexorably toward the narrow line of horizon, and though she tried to call him back, he faded from her reach, shrinking to a pinpoint.

Awake in bed at dawn, Immacolata rubbed her eyes to dispel the nightmare's afterimage. When she went downstairs for a cup of something warm to drink, her manservant appeared from the gloom of the hall.

"A letter for you, Signora," he said, handing her a folded parchment, sealed with wax.

In the Name of God, Amen

Cara Mamma,
    Business keeps me here longer than I planned and I do not know when I shall return. Do not expect word from me.
                                                    Your Iacopo

Immacolata clutched the letter as if it were Iacopo's own hand, rather than his words. The message, bare of any detail, unnerved her. She placed the untouched cup of hypocras on the kitchen table and walked slowly back upstairs.

She found the old letter she had hidden in a drawer, and unfolded it to read again.

I have done your bidding. The Painter Accorsi has been imprisoned by the Podestà's police and will stand trial within the week. That will pay him back for bearing witness at your father's trial. With success your family name will be cleared of any taint and the painter will hang from the gallows. Ser Signoretti granted me audience once he read the letter of introduction you sent, and has agreed to take the witness stand in your favor.

    I will find you after the trial to collect my due. Will you be staying at your accustomed place? This time we have him.

With God's help this letter will move you to ride quickly to Siena and bring my gold.

Penned by my hand on this last Day of December, 1348

G.B.

Siena

The initials brought no one to mind. But those words—*this time we have him*—told of other times and failed attempts. Failed attempts at what? She hoped to God Iacopo had stopped, would stop, at false denunciation—a heinous enough crime. But what if he had worse evil in his heart? What if he planned murder, the ultimate vengeance?

What use are the secret plans of men if they only bring death and destruction? I will not let my son follow his father to the gallows with blood on his hands. The words reverberated in her head like a Compline prayer.

Immacolata arrived in Siena by carriage in the last days of February. She went first to the inn where she'd visited Iacopo in the terrible days after Giovanni's death. Messer Semenzato himself answered her knock.

"Do you have a guest here by the name of Iacopo?" Before she used his last name, a name that might not be well received here in Siena, she paused to let the innkeeper answer.

"We don't see many women looking for a man without a family name," he said, narrowing his eyes. The bells in the Torre rang for Vespers. Immacolata had not intended to arrive so late; a dangerous time to be a stranger in any city.

"He travels under several names," Immacolata said, the answer rolling easily off her tongue. It might not be a lie. "And he comes from Firenze often on business."

"He might have been here before, but now my rooms are full

of Poggibonsi merchants." The innkeeper looked more closely at Immacolata. She had dressed carefully for the journey in a high-necked gown of dark red wool edged with green and embroidered with a pattern of vines. There were advantages to being an aging woman—few would suspect trouble from her. Messer Semenzato opened the door wider when he saw the florins glinting in her hand.

"What makes you think he might have been here before, Ser?"

"A Florentine has stayed here several times, but never called himself Iacopo. He came recently to rent his usual room, but I had no rooms to let."

"Was he dark, and slim?"

"Could be," the innkeeper said, "though many are."

"Do you know where he might have gone, if not here?"

"I'm afraid I do not," the innkeeper said, and she had no luck prying any more information from him, other than a recommendation for a place where she might rest her horses and herself for the night. She hoped the dawn would bring more help, as finding a single man with an assumed name in a city of this size would be a daunting task.

When Baldi did not appear at their appointed place and time, Iacopo knew this last plan too must have gone awry. Accorsi was still alive, and exonerated from the murder charge. Was Baldi dead or captured, and what secrets might leak out of him if he were pressed? Iacopo returned to his chamber in the new inn as the day's light was fading. This latest failure sat in his belly like a stone.

Iacopo stared at the scarred wood of the desktop, seeing imaginary figures emerge from in the pattern of scratches. He must devise a new plan against Accorsi, and this time, act alone, and quickly. His days were surely numbered, if the Brotherhood now saw fit to dispose of him. *I cut down a thousand men with the Mor-*

talità as my blade—surely I can kill one more with my own hands? But when he looked down at those hands now, those smooth untried hands of a nobleman's son, he wondered.

Iacopo awoke to a thumping on the door of his room. The light slanting through the *camera*'s single window told him he had slept long and late. The knocking grew louder, followed by a familiar voice.

"Iacopo, open the door." *Mamma.* Iacopo leaped out of bed, looking for another exit, or a place to hide. There was only the door behind which his mother stood.

"Iacopo, I shall not leave without speaking to you." The handle rattled but the lock stayed firm. Iacopo stood silent, not moving lest the sound alert her to his presence. The noise at the door stopped. Could she have gone? He waited a minute, two, barely breathing. Then he heard the rasp of a key in the lock, and the door swung open, letting his mother in.

He stared at her face, so familiar and yet so unwelcome. He was beyond her comfort or aid now, though he longed for the solace she might once have given him. *My heart is an alien thing, barbed against any confidence or warmth.*

"How did you find the key?" His voice sounded harsh, like his father's.

"The innkeeper took pity on me, a mother searching for her son in a foreign place."

An image of Giovanni's purpled face in the hours after the hanging filled Iacopo's head, and a pain stabbed behind his right eye. "I must not be disturbed. You know I am conducting important business that my father entrusted to me."

"I must speak to you." She closed the door behind her. There were lines around her mouth and at the corners of her eyes. *She is old*, he thought, *but not too old to interfere.* "I know you seek the man who testified against your father," she said.

Her words made his heart drop in his chest, but he willed his voice not to tremble.

"It is no concern of yours."

"Iacopo, I fear for your safety in this city that took your father's life. Come back with me, and let us find a way to heal the wound of your father's loss without more violence." He could not allow this conversation to go further, this awful pleading.

Once Immacolata might have reached out to touch her son, but now her hands remained at her sides. "If you will not speak to me, then at least find a confessor to hear your sins. I shall pray for your deliverance from whatever gnaws your soul."

Deliverance from whatever gnaws my soul. Can I even hope for that? He imagined the words flowing from him and the absolution a priest could provide.

"I shall consider what you have said," Iacopo said with finality. "But leave me now, for my father's business demands attention."

Immacolata looked into her son's face, searching as if something might be found there. Then, without another word, she left, pulling the door shut behind her.

After she had gone, a memory came to Iacopo unbidden from his boyhood, as real as if he were still crouching unseen against his mother's bedroom wall. He saw his mother's arms raised in defense, saw her cringe and plead for mercy as his father's blows rained down relentless upon her head and limbs and back. Iacopo had longed to help her but instead crept away, afraid to become the subject of that awful wrath. *Do I wish to be that father's son?* Whether he wished to or not was of no consequence for it seemed he had no choice.

*　*　*

We questioned Baldi until the sun rose, but he didn't know much, or didn't reveal it. Baldi didn't know where Iacopo (he called him "the Medici boy") was staying—he'd been at Semenzato's before, but wasn't any longer. Baldi was to await a letter with their next meeting place after the deed was done. I grimly imagined what Baldi's success would have meant. Yes, he'd orchestrated the letter denouncing Gabriele, and the scaffolding accident. There was nothing else we could get from him. With a smirk he reminded us of our promise, and we ushered him out the front door. Now we knew what Iacopo had planned, but not where to find him.

Ysabella went upstairs to bed and Bianca put Gabriella in her cradle; after the night's uproar the child had fallen asleep in our bed, one arm thrown over her head and her long red child's gown wrapped about her legs.

Gabriele and I sat at the kitchen table. It felt like a year had passed since our wedding—had it really been just the day before?

"Our married life is not as peaceful as I'd imagined," Gabriele said. He smiled, that sweet smile I'd seen him give only me, and took my hands between his.

"Peace is not very likely when the two of us are involved," I answered, wryly. "Baldi probably won't make more trouble, but his boss is at large somewhere."

"We could search the local inns," Gabriele said. I nodded, but now I was remembering what I'd learned in my trip back and forth between two centuries. "I think that attack on you is just a tiny piece of a larger plan." Gabriele raised one eyebrow quizzically. "No offense meant; your life isn't tiny of course."

"A single man's life is an infinitesimally small flicker of a candle in the bright light of the divine presence," Gabriele replied seriously.

I smiled at my medieval husband. "True, but that's not what I meant. I should have told you all this before, but it's been kind of busy around here." I'd only been able to talk to him twice since I'd returned to this century, and once had been our wedding night. But now there was time to talk, and I did. It reminded me of our night on the ship: the flood of words, the relief of putting my thoughts together and pouring them into the ear of a sympathetic, thoughtful listener. Gabriele listened, his head at that falcon's angle, all attention.

When I got to the Signoretti-Medici connection, Gabriele suddenly sat up straight, with a sharp intake of breath. "Now I see it," he said, his voice taut. He took his hands from mine and sat back.

"See what?"

"What I ought to have seen before. What I must have seen, many months ago, that made me put the faces of the two men together in my sketches . . . but I did not realize the import of what I'd seen, until now." A chill came over me, listening to Gabriele describe the drawings that I'd found in my flooded modern Siena kitchen. He continued, not realizing the effect that his words were having on me. "Sometimes the truth is invisible, because it is so far from what can be imagined. The night of Cristoforo's murder, I stayed late to finish a section of Ser Signoretti's chapel fresco. As I left, I observed two men leaving Signoretti's house, later than any honest guests ought to be walking the streets. And, as you well know, that night I witnessed the crime that has set the forces of evil in motion against not only me but against both of us, and our family." Gabriele stopped to take a breath. "But now, now that you have told me what you know, I believe it was the Florentines I saw leaving Ser Signoretti's palazzo that night, the same two men who, moments later, threatened and killed Cristoforo Buonaventura."

"So Giovanni and Iacopo were visiting Signoretti that night?"

Gabriele nodded gravely. "I believe so. But I cannot imagine how we might be certain."

I stood up out of my chair, my heart pounding. "I can. We can go visit Signoretti ourselves. Right now."

"At least find a confessor to hear your sins. I shall pray for your deliverance from whatever gnaws your soul. . . ."

A confessor. Yes, he would seek out a priest, and with the relief that the act might bring, would steel himself for his next and final task. Iacopo donned his cape and hat and followed the winding streets that would lead him to the Duomo.

The looming cathedral always took him by surprise. The narrow street opened suddenly into the courtyard where Siena's duomo and ospedale faced off as if for a duel, two forces meeting in a surprisingly small space. The scale felt even more distorted to him than usual, buildings angling sharply against the uncomfortably bright sky. He climbed the long flight of white steps and into the cathedral's dim interior.

The confessional was in a small side chapel. He slipped into the narrow wooden seat and bowed his head at the metal grille.

"Bless me father for I have sinned . . ." He heard the creak of a wooden seat on the other side of the screen as the priest shifted to receive his confession.

"Speak my son, for God's ear is open to your prayers." The intimacy of those words startled him. There was no other ear but God's now, to hear what he had to say. And in the rush of sudden freedom—the anonymity and promise of absolution—Iacopo began to speak, slowly at first, and then more and more quickly, telling the story from its terrible beginning. He told of his father's last requests, the hanging, the despair. Then of Baldi's hire, the scaffolding, the orchestrated ambush, the doctored evidence and new trial, the attempt on Accorsi's life on his wedding night. He spoke in a headlong rush, the weight lifting from his soul as he gave his sins to God. But when he told the story of meeting with the Becchini, the confraternity's dark purpose and success, he heard a sharp intake of breath from the invisible priest. He paused, feeling a flush come into his face. Had he told too much? But it was just a breath, nothing more. Iacopo realized he had been pressing his head against the grille, and when he reached a hand up to his forehead, he felt the imprint of the metal grate upon it.

"Pray with me now," the priest said, "and with me implore God for absolution." Iacopo matched his words to the disembodied voice. "As a penance you shall pray as we did today for these departed souls every day that remains of your life. Now go and sin no more." Iacopo lifted his head for the priest's last words. "*Te absolvo*," the priest intoned at last, and the sound filled Iacopo's ears, the first balm since his father's death. He rose stiffly and walked out of the confessional, back toward the cathedral's great doors, and into the winter sun.

Bartolomeo sat immobile in the confessional, filled with the horror of what he had heard. *God give me strength, for your succor will comfort us all, those who serve you in truth.* But his prayer provided scant comfort. The stranger's confession burned in his ear. *Three attempts at murder, one false witness.* Alone that would have been too much, but then came the worst: the dispatch of an army of Plague-ridden criminals to sweep through Siena, ensuring her doom. No penance could ever atone for such a sin. *The sanctity of the confessional is absolute. . . .* Father Lupini had said innumerable times. *But for this?* No other sinners came to confess that day, but Bartolomeo remained in the little booth behind its heavy curtain until the bells rang for Vespers, paralyzed by the sins he had heard in God's holy name.

* * *

Immacolata did not go back to Firenze. *You may be your father's heir, Iacopo, but you are not my master, not in this.* Iacopo had looked like a puppet animated by his father's invisible hand. He had been twisted by the forces that pushed his father into acts of violence, and then to his grave. Immacolata feared those forces now drove Iacopo toward the same fates: murder, and death. *God, please hear this mother's prayer, and keep my son from damnation.* But she would go beyond this maternal plea for divine intervention—she must oppose her son's plan on this mortal earth.

*   *   *

When we got to the Signoretti palazzo, the huge wooden doors at the top of the stairs loomed over us, an ominous symbol of the threshold we intended to cross. I looked at Gabriele. "Are we crazy?"

"Bravery must be fueled by a bit of madness, else we should all stay huddled in our beds rather than face adversity."

We headed up the stairs to knock. The manservant who opened the door knew us both—me from my visit with Cane, and Gabriele from his time spent painting Signoretti's chapel—which helped us past the first hurdle. He led us into an audience room where we waited, standing, for Signoretti to descend. It took an uncomfortably long time; by the time I heard Signoretti's heavy, measured tread on the stairs, I was sweating.

"To what do I owe the pleasure of this unexpected visit?" I got a closer look at Signoretti than I had during the trial, and now I saw the signs of age in his face. Only a year and a half had passed, but his face was more deeply lined, his thick hair grayer. The Mortalità left its mark on those lucky enough to survive.

"We are sorry to disturb you at this hour, but Ser Accorsi and I have a matter of grave importance to discuss."

Signoretti's eyes flickered from my face to Gabriele's, then back again. "I was not aware that you two were so well acquainted."

"I am fortunate to call this good lady my wife," Gabriele said.

Signoretti raised one eyebrow. "Indeed you are. Now, let us

put pleasantries aside, for I am certain that it is not to announce your betrothal that you have sought me out. Will you sit?"

Behind his enormous desk, Signoretti looked as if he were in a fortress, while Gabriele and I huddled unprotected on stools outside the fortified walls. Gabriele spoke first.

"Let me begin by saying that I do not begrudge your honest testimony at my trial, Ser Signoretti. I am a free man now, with the law on my side. We may put the matter of the trial behind us." *Bold move*, I thought, but it seemed to have dealt with the huge gorilla in the room effectively.

Signoretti nodded once. "I am happy to see justice served. Is this the reason for your visit? If so, good day, and enjoy your well-deserved freedom."

Not yet Signoretti; we've got more for you. "Thank you for your wishes on my husband's behalf; I am glad to see no animosity remains between us. But there is another reason we've come. We are looking for a Florentine gentleman, a Ser Iacopo de' Medici. Perhaps your wide-ranging business interests put you in a position to know his whereabouts?"

There was a long, awful silence. As we sat there, I realized how ridiculous it was, that Gabriele and I, powerless and totally unimportant, might expect this nobleman to worry about anything we had to say. In fact, we were probably risking our lives—he could easily wipe us both out for making trouble. I saw him reach for the bell on his desk to call his servant; now we were either going to be dismissed, or worse. I searched my mind for a backup strategy, ideally one that would get each of us out of his palazzo in one piece. My brilliant idea came just in time.

"I'm sure you know Suor Umiltà?" Signoretti's hand withdrew from the bell and returned to his lap.

"Indeed, I am well acquainted with the good sister," he said carefully.

"She is also looking for Iacopo de' Medici. In fact . . . she sent us here to ask for your help. And she has your best interests in mind . . . yours as well as ours."

It looked like the lie was working, because Signoretti's bell hand stayed down. "Suor Umiltà is involved in the matter?"

"Quite involved." I crossed my arms over my chest and waited for my words to sink in.

After another agonizingly long silence, Signoretti spoke, his voice low. "And if I should have dealings with this Iacopo de' Medici, why might you seek him out at such an unusual hour? Surely a routine business matter could wait."

I looked at Gabriele, and he gave a small acquiescent nod. "Ser de' Medici sent a killer to our house last night, whose deadly aim was, fortunately, foiled. From the would-be killer's confession, we learned of his master's intent. I mean in no way to implicate you in this crime, but I hoped that you might have information that could lead us to him. Our lives, we believe, depend upon it."

"And may I ask what had led you to hope for such information from me? Other than my 'wide-ranging business interests,' of course." He was being careful, I saw, not to give us any information, while acquiring as much as he could.

"Perhaps you have had business with this man without realizing his criminal intent," Gabriele began, "but as I was leaving your chapel late, on the fateful night about which you testified, I saw two men leaving your palazzo. Only moments later, those two men, it appears, were stopped by Cristoforo Buonaventura, an act which hastened his departure from this world." Gabriele was treading carefully through a minefield here—somehow not directly accusing Signoretti of perjury, harboring a criminal, maybe even conspiring with one. "In the event, perhaps, that you were deciding whether to continue to do business with the young Medici, in the aftermath of his father's death, I hope this information will help your decision. And if, in return, you might be able to inform us of his whereabouts, we would be in your debt."

My heartbeat sounded like a drum in my ears. "It seems," Signoretti said after another long, tense silence, "that if I should be in a position to encounter Iacopo de' Medici in the future, it might be wise to avoid further entanglement. Do I take your meaning well?"

"Wise, indeed," Gabriele said.

"Your information is well received. But, I am afraid, I have no knowledge of the man's whereabouts. I wish you God's help with your search." With that, Signoretti bowed to signal the end of our meeting, and called his servant to usher us out.

"He didn't exactly confess," I said to Gabriele. I had a flashback, as I stood outside the Signoretti palazzo, of my unpleasant brushes with the modern Signoretti, this man's descendant. Now I saw why the future Signoretti would want to suppress, and even steal, the documents Ben had been working on. Beyond being a competing scholar hungry for his own academic credit, the modern Signoretti would not likely enjoy seeing his noble family implicated in a conspiracy with Florence to overthrow Siena's government. Even a seven-hundred-year-old conspiracy.

"He did not have to confess," Gabriele answered, bringing me back to the medieval present. "But perhaps we have foiled one aspect of the Medici plan through our efforts."

I hoped it was true. "But we still don't know where Iacopo is."

With the relief that confession had brought, Iacopo steeled himself for his next effort—a visit to the Signoretti palazzo to establish the certainty of that alliance. He had not seen his father's co-conspirator since the failed trial. Ser Signoretti received Iacopo in the small chamber rather than the large one made for his most esteemed guests: not a good sign. The meeting did not go as Iacopo had hoped.

"Ser Signoretti," Iacopo began, "I am here to forward my good father's cause, and reassure you of my continued dedication."

"Messer de' Medici," Ser Signoretti replied, but with a raised eyebrow that implied the "Messer" was not deserved. "The trial was a disaster. Were you not aware of the witness, the Ospedale scribe with her documents?"

"Ser Signoretti, the scribe was certainly a surprise but—"

"There should be no surprises. Particularly not when I take the stand in court."

"Yes, Messer, of course. But the Brotherhood of San Giovanni remains committed to the alliance, as do others of the confraternity. Our plans for Siena, and your role in particular, should not be altered by the outcome of the trial."

"I have had enough of your plans, Iacopo. You may be Giovanni de' Medici's son, but I am afraid that legacy is no longer sufficient."

"But Ser, I—"

"You are dismissed." Before Iacopo could consider any response, a manservant appeared from the shadows against the *sala*'s wall and took his arm firmly. Iacopo found himself on the marble lintel of the palazzo, the great double doors closed behind him.

* * *

Gabriele and I had no luck finding Iacopo at the inns—and we tried them all. Some innkeepers might have been lying, and many were tight-lipped, protecting their patrons. But my empathic efforts did not ferret out any particular crucial lie.

"I can't imagine that none of these places has a small dark Florentine staying in it," I said indignantly—we had gotten a minimally helpful description from Baldi to fuel our search.

"It seems we shall not find out from asking," Gabriele said.

"We can't just sit around waiting for him to hire someone else to kill you."

But neither of us had a better idea. We headed home as the bells were ringing for Vespers.

We all slept together in Gabriele's and my room with a heavy trunk pushed against the loggia doors from the inside. I fell asleep to the sound of my new family breathing around me.

The next morning as I prepared to go to the Ospedale, there was a knock on the front door. Bianca was seated at the kitchen's trestle table, showing little Gabriella how to pick stones from a bowl of dried lentils. Ysabella turned from the stove with a frown.

Gabriele appeared at the bottom of the stairs, his hair still ruffled from sleep. "I am not expecting visitors—might you be?" I shook my head. Whoever was at the door knocked again, and Gabriele's face changed, alert and wary. He looked through the front door's grilled window. "Whom do you seek?"

"Is this the Accorsi household? I have a message for Ser Gabriele Accorsi, from Ser Luciano Datini di Padova."

"I do not know this Datini," Gabriele said, his hand on the door. I noticed he did not move to open it.

"He is a well-established merchant in Padova who seeks a commission from a Sienese artist. You came highly recommended by the rector, Ser." After a moment's hesitation, Gabriele unlatched the door and swung it open. The messenger stood on the doorstep with the letter in his hand, and Gabriele reached out to take it.

"Does Messer Datini require an immediate response?"

"He is eager for an answer."

Gabriele hesitated before inviting the messenger in. He broke the letter's seal. "Messer Datini seeks to commission a panel painting for his collection. He says he watched me paint the Ospedale fresco, in the last days before its completion, and knows the quality of my work."

"Of course he sought you out," Ysabella said, her tension softening into a smile.

"Perhaps because so many of our finest masters have died," Gabriele responded modestly. "I am certainly in need of work; I have had none since Messina and we have many mouths to feed."

He looked back at the messenger, who was still standing in the doorway.

"When does Messer Datini wish to meet?"

"He hopes you will be able to meet today at Nones. This trip to Siena is brief."

Gabriele read through the letter carefully again. "You can tell Messer Datini I will meet him at the appointed time and place." Gabriele let the messenger out.

"I think I met Datini before I left for Pisa," I said. "He was admiring your fresco outside the Ospedale." It was nice to have good news, but I didn't like the timing. "You're going to trust him?"

"Would you have me ignore the commission? Long-standing interest in my work seems adequate proof of his intent." I frowned; in a normal situation it would have made sense, but this was not a normal situation. "Beatrice—my art is my livelihood, and my life. If I ignore commissions, I will soon be out of work."

"I could support us for a little while." I wasn't sure whether I'd just introduced an idea that could result in our first public marital argument.

"Of course you could," Gabriele said without a trace of anger, "but for now we have more immediate worries." He pointed at Gabriella, who had pulled a chair over to the hearth and was trying to stir Ysabella's pot of soup. Bianca rescued her, and the soup, with a gasp. With that domestic crisis settled, I decided to head to the Ospedale, where I could talk to Umiltà about finding Iacopo de' Medici. Gabriele followed me out, stopping me with a hand on my arm.

"Beatrice—be careful in your travels today."

"You too. Maybe you could ask Tommaso to go with you?"

Gabriele smiled. "He would be most amused to know that I was afraid to meet alone with a potential patron." I took that as a polite rejection of my advice. Gabriele kissed my cheek softly, then released my arm. I turned and made my way to the Ospedale.

After accepting Umiltà's good wishes on my marriage, which she delivered with a probing look that made me blush, I gave her an abridged version of the story—that Baldi had broken into the house, and had confessed to being sent by Giovanni de' Medici's son.

"Revenge," Umiltà said, her expression darkening. "I shall call upon the communal police to find Baldi and throw him in prison."

When I explained to her how we'd promised Baldi freedom in return for information, I was afraid Umiltà might actually explode with suppressed fury. I managed to convince her to leave Baldi alone, but she insisted on sending a team of Ospedale guards to search the city for Iacopo. "And since you are here," Umiltà added, as if she'd been in the middle of a sentence, "you can write out a letter of direction to the guards, describing the man they seek and authorizing his detainment under the Ospedale's writ."

The warrant required several versions before it met Umiltà's approval, but eventually the guards fanned out on their errand with my warrant in hand and I headed out into the Piazza del Duomo. I hadn't been back inside the cathedral since my return to the fourteenth century. Looking at its striped facade made me nervous, though now I knew a visit wasn't likely to fling me through time against my will. *The person is the portal, not the place.* As the words popped into my head I remembered the little priest with the head injury. Had Father Bartolomeo survived the Plague? I walked up the marble steps and inside.

A group of priests had gathered in the oratory to chant the hour, and I was relieved to recognize Bartolomeo among them. I sat in a pew until the chanting stopped, and Bartolomeo came down the nave in my direction.

"Father." He turned toward me with a look of apprehension. "It's Beatrice Trovato, the Ospedale scribe. I'm glad to see you're alive and well." Since Bartolomeo was extremely unlikely to have heard about my recent wedding, I didn't have to deal with the decision of whether to call myself Accorsi yet. I wasn't sure of the medieval position on newlywed wives keeping their names, but I guessed it wasn't favorable.

His deer-in-the-headlights look faded only slightly. "God be with you, Monna Trovato," he said. Bartolomeo was thinner than when I'd last seen him, and his eyes seemed larger than before. His close-cut hair looked downy, like the fuzz on a baby chick.

"And with you also," I said reflexively. Bartolomeo was the most porous person I'd ever met; the emotion streamed out around him like a shimmering psychic halo. Today I felt a current of uneasiness in his presence. He didn't look well. His skin was ashen, and he had dark circles under his eyes. He swayed on his feet, and I guided him to a pew. The other priests had disappeared.

"Is there something I can help you with?" I sat down next to him.

"None can help but God."

"I have some knowledge as a healer," I said. "Maybe I can move God's intent along?"

"The silence of the confessional is absolute," he said, I thought irrelevantly. "Absolute," he said again, and then, suddenly, I was inside his head. I heard a voice—a thin, wavering voice that grew louder and more insistent as it went on. It was like listening to a recording of an old radio program, blurry and full of static. The words wormed their message through Bartolomeo's head and into mine.

. . . I made a man fall to his death, but, though the bolts on the scaffold gave way, the man was unhurt. Forgive me Father for I have sinned. I brought an innocent man to trial, but he was acquitted. Forgive me Father for I have sinned. I sent an armed man to kill another, and I hoped for its success. Forgive me Father for I have sinned . . .

Bartolomeo was moaning, a counterpoint to the words inside his head.

Bent on Siena's destruction, I hired the Becchini to do my bidding . . . The last confession was magnified a thousandfold by

Bartolomeo's own terror, the penitent's voice distorted to a demonic howl.

Then I was back, my heart hammering as if I'd run a flight of stairs. "Father, tell me what you've seen."

"Absolute, absolute," Bartolomeo said, putting his head in his hands.

"This is not a secret anyone should keep."

"I saw nothing," he said, miserably.

"Then what did you *hear*, if you *saw* nothing?"

Bartolomeo began to rock back and forth on the bench. "The sanctity of the confessional is absolute. Bless me Father for I have sinned . . . *te absolvo . . . te absolvo . . .*"

"Bartolomeo, if you are a witness to a crime, you are *required* to speak." Bartolomeo looked up from his hands, tears streaming down his face.

He did not need to tell me everything he knew, because I saw it then, with awful vivid clarity, blooming in his mind. I'd found Ben's anti-Siena conspirator, and I knew now exactly what he had done, and how.

I left Bartolomeo in the hands of a solicitous older priest and walked home in a daze. Ysabella embraced me at the door. "You look like you've seen a ghost, Beatrice. Has something happened?" Something had certainly happened, but it was hard to believe, and harder to explain—this story from a priest who'd heard the anonymous confession of a mass murderer.

"Too many hours staring at a contract," I said. She looked at me sideways but did not press me further. Bianca was upstairs with Gabriella, who was teething and grumpy; Gabriele was out at his afternoon meeting. *I cannot live my life in fear, Beatrice,* Gabriele would have said. But it was hard not to.

I'd barely hung up my robe when there was a knock on the

door; Ysabella and I both jumped at the sound. A woman stood outside whom I'd never seen before.

"I am Immacolata de' Medici," she said in a low voice. "Is this the Accorsi household?"

Her name was like a thunderbolt.

Ysabella stepped forward, never liking to be on the periphery of anything. "To what do we owe this unexpected visit, Signora?"

"It regards my son," Immacolata said. My vision grayed, and for a moment I saw a receding figure in a rowboat, moving without rowing. Then I was looking into Immacolata's face again. "His name is Iacopo de' Medici." *So she is his mother.*

"Signora," I said, "will you sit down?"

Immacolata remained standing. "My son was searching for a Messer Accorsi. I was told the painter lived here, with his wife."

"I'm his wife. But Messer Accorsi is not here."

"Do you expect him this evening? I would prefer to stay until he returns."

I might be the wife, but Ysabella was still the mistress of the house. "Please sit," Ysabella said, guiding our visitor to a chair and fetching a cup of wine. When Immacolata brought the cup to her lips, her hand trembled, and she spilled several drops into her lap. The dark liquid pearled on the wool of her cloak.

"I thank you." She emptied the cup but did not put it down. Ysabella leaned forward and gently took it from her hands.

"May I ask why your son was looking for my husband?" It was the first time I'd said *my husband*. I wished it had been under happier circumstances.

"I fear my son plans Messer Accorsi's death," Immacolata said, "even as we speak. And I wish to prevent him from succeeding." The only sound in the room was the cup falling out of Ysabella's hand to shatter on the stone floor.

PART XV

FEAR OF HEIGHTS

Iacopo paced in the inn's small bedroom, rehearsing the words he'd planned. *Ser, I have heard much of your artistic prowess, and would be delighted to have one of your works in my collection. Too frivolous. Honored? Too deferential. I would welcome one of your works in my collection. Better.* The discarded versions of the letter now lay crumpled in the grate where a low fire burned. He reached the wall and turned back again. The hidden knife moved against his thigh. Never mind that Iacopo had never killed a man—flesh must give way to steel.

Iacopo could not stay here with his intended victim—there would be too many witnesses. He would suggest somewhere secluded, a point from which an excellent view of Siena might be had, a view that could find its way into a painting. He would convince Accorsi to follow him, so that they might discuss the vantage point from which the commission might be painted.

Iacopo wished he had some confidant now, someone to shore up his strength for what was coming. But there was no one left. Just as that thought came into his head, Iacopo heard a familiar voice, as real as if the speaker stood beside him.

-Iacopo.

    Father?

-Do you not know my voice?

    The man I hired to carry out our mission informed upon me.

-He was ill-chosen.

    The Brotherhood has discarded me, though I served them well.

-They would have followed a leader strong enough to move them to action.

Even in Iacopo's imagination, the words still stung.

    What have I left, Father?

-You will avenge my death, and bring Accorsi to justice. That will have to serve.

Iacopo stopped in front of the fire, watching the flames writhe like molten snakes.

    And if I do not?

This last question went unanswered. Iacopo wondered whether his father's spirit truly spoke from beyond the grave, or whether the voice was the product of Iacopo's own tortured soul. Then there was no time to ponder, for the visitor had arrived at last.

Gabriele had still not come back from his meeting. Ysabella stayed to wait for him and I left with Immacolata, my unexpected guide. She led me to the tavern where Iacopo was lodging. It was, as I suspected, a place we'd visited on our hunt the day before.

I tried the handle of his room, and the door, unexpectedly, swung open. It was an ordinary room—a small bed, a scratched desk and rickety chair, a low fire burning in the hearth. But no one was there. A discarded letter lay on the desk, crumpled and spotted with ink. As I read it my hand began to shake.

> *Ser Accorsi:*
>
> *I have heard much of your artistic prowess, and would be delighted to have one of your works in my collection. . . . It is said the Torre del Mangia has a view from which Siena can be seen in all her great beauty, a view worthy of painting. There, high above the city, we will also find a private place to talk undisturbed.*

I had not feared the worst, but I should have.

I tore out of the inn, running as hard as I could. Immacolata, surprisingly fast, followed me. I burst out into the milling crowds of the Campo, and scanned the sea of people for Gabriele. A troupe of theatrical performers suddenly blocked my view, bright in yellow and red; I pushed through them and kept running. As I pounded down the slope of the Piazza del Campo the wind picked up, the sky darkened, and there was a sudden flash of lightning, followed by an ominous rumble of thunder. I reached the doorway of the Torre and stepped inside just as the rain hit.

There are heights and then there are heights—some so extreme that they unnerve all but the most extreme thrill seeker. The last time I'd been in the Torre I'd been a tourist, and I remembered the narrow stone spiral staircase and the dizzying view. But this time there were no electric lights or security rails. It was a menacing tower with a dangerous ascent, at the top of which Gabriele might be about to die, or perhaps already lay dead. Immacolata was a few steps behind me, breathing in short gasps. I kept climbing, my legs and lungs burning, looking only at the few feet of stone ahead of me.

I reached the level of the Torre's great bell, with the harrowing open view I remembered. The wind was blowing hard, making a high whining sound. But there was one more set of steps, the steepest and most frightening of all, leading to the very top.

Iacopo had been surprised by Accorsi: his height, the unnatural color of his hair, his low quiet voice, which made Iacopo's own seem overly high by contrast. The painter did not appear to suspect danger, nor could he hear the violent pounding of Iacopo's heart. Iacopo strained to keep up with Gabriele's long strides as they walked.

The first few flights of the Torre were bearable, closed in and dark. But as the view appeared through the window slits, Iacopo's head spun and he had to press one hand against the wall. By the time they reached the bell, Iacopo was drenched with sweat from exertion and fear. Accorsi walked ahead, showing no sign of fatigue. *But of course—he has been climbing scaffolding most of his life; an artisan, not a nobleman.* Iacopo's reasoning gave him little comfort.

Accorsi moved to the tower's edge, putting one hand on the waist-high wall and looking out across the city. "I have always longed to paint this angel's view of our beautiful city, kept safe within her encircling walls."

Now, it must be now. While he is lost in his precious view. Just there, beneath his ribs—one hard thrust of the dagger. Iacopo willed his feet to climb the last two steps. The dizzying spread of the Campo fanned out below them, red-bricked and impossibly far down. A flash illuminated the sky, and the thunder that rolled behind it made Iacopo jump and stumble, until he was just behind the painter. *Now, it must be now.*

As I stepped out from the dark stairwell onto the Torre's top, I saw the Duomo stark against the looming clouds, outlined by the storm's electric light. Around the cathedral spread the red roofs of Siena's buildings, then, beyond the curve of the city walls, the *contado*'s brown hills rolled on until they met the sky. Framed by that view were Iacopo and Gabriele, both still standing. I was not too late. Iacopo stood with his back to me, dark hair whipping in the wind. Even from behind, I recognized the man I'd seen watching Gabriele paint months before. I remembered the strange, out-of-focus gaze, the silently moving mouth. A patron of the arts, he'd called himself, when in fact he was a killer. Iacopo's long cloak reached nearly to the ground, dwarfing him. But his clothing was not what caught my eye—it was the knife in his hand, that triangle of bare iron aimed at Gabriele's back. Gabriele leaned against the parapet, looking out at the breathtaking view, oblivious to the danger behind him. There was no way I could get from the stairway in time to stop the knife's descent. But something else did.

Immacolata burst out of the stairwell and screamed her son's name. Once in my modern life I saw a toddler step off a curb into a busy intersection. His mother, too far away to use her body to save his life, let out a bloodcurdling yell that not only stopped her son, but also brought traffic to a grinding halt, and along with it a thirty-foot radius of adults responding to that primal parental imperative. Immacolata's voice stopped the dagger in midflight.

Iacopo half turned toward his mother's voice but kept his grip on the knife, pointing at his target. Gabriele turned too, and saw what he had failed to before in his absorption with the view.

"Sheath your dagger, Iacopo," Immacolata said.

"This is the informant who caused my father's death." Iacopo had the incongruously high voice of a child.

"I know what *he* has done," Immacolata said, "but what have *you* done?"

"I have done my father's bidding." Iacopo advanced a step, moving the blade to point at Gabriele's throat. He held the knife awkwardly, as if he'd never held one before.

My mouth was so dry it was hard to speak. "I know what you have done, Iacopo."

"She knows nothing!" Iacopo's voice edged toward panic.

"I know that you used the Mortalità as a weapon against Siena, Iacopo de'Medici."

Immacolata's face shifted. How must it be to be a mother of a son who has murdered thousands? "Is this true?"

"Two informants have confirmed it." I thought of my sources: Bartolomeo and Ben.

"Iacopo, do you deny this charge?"

"You would trust this painter's wife over your own son?"

"I would, if she told the truth and you did not. You have lied to me for months. Do not lie to me again now."

Iacopo flinched. "I did as I was told," he said, but now his voice wavered. Still, he did not drop the knife.

"Then it is true?"

"I hired the Becchini to come to Siena, bringing contagion in their wake. I brought the *commune* to her knees, as the Brotherhood bid me do, and as my father would have done, had he lived. And it was well done—it was well done!" Iacopo's voice rose, shrill and desperate.

As the Brotherhood bid me do. Even if Iacopo were stopped, there were others out there, still plotting. Was this the conspiracy Ben had discovered? The fall of Siena's Nine was only six years away, the beginning of the weakening of the great regime, and Siena's independence would end under Florentine rule more than a hundred years from now. Would this Brotherhood, whoever they were, have a hand in it? What if the meeting with Signoretti had been part of the plan? What if the Plague's devastation was only the beginning?

While my mind was racing, Gabriele spoke quietly to Iacopo, as if he were trying to calm a frightened horse. "If it was my death you sought, you should have left my fellow citizens alone."

"I saved your death for last, Accorsi."

Immacolata's words were edged with steel. "Iacopo, you have used a weapon no man should wield. And if you kill this honest man who stands before you, this man who did his duty to his *commune*, I shall not pray to save your soul."

"My own mother would forsake me?"

"I will deny I ever had a son."

"My father's blood runs in my veins. His blood and his cause." Because I had failed to find the record of Iacopo's birth, I did not need supernatural empathy to know what Immacolata was about to say.

"You do not share his blood, and need not share his cause. You are a foundling whom I called my own. And now I see the evil in the child I chose." Immacolata's words created a stillness after them. The wind whistled through the breaks in the Torre's top, a high, mournful keening. Then Iacopo's shoulders straightened, as if a weight had lifted from his narrow back.

Giovanni de' Medici is not my father. At first the words brought Iacopo sweet relief. *My father did not beat his wife until her shoulders bloomed with bruises. My father did not rain blows down on my head while I cried for help that never came. My father did not kill a man of Siena's night watch and hang from the gallows for his crime.*

"If he is not my father, then I am free of him, and free to do as I wish." Iacopo's heart lifted as the words left his mouth.

Immacolata had not moved from her spot at the top of the stairs. "You are free to spare the life of this innocent man. But any sins you have already committed, and any sins you commit from this day forth, will rest upon your head, and upon your soul for eternity."

In the wake of his mother's words, Iacopo's relief faded as fast as it had come. For if he could not blame his birthright, he had only his own miserable self to blame. His words in Angelo's ear had carried the Mortalità's curse to Siena's most noble citizens, and his own shaking hand now held a knife to Accorsi's neck. All that Iacopo had once thought to be true crumbled beneath him—his parentage, and his purpose.

"He despised me, because he knew I was not his. Do you despise me too?"

"I am your mother, and I love my son as much as any woman who bears a child from her womb. What I reject in you is not your blood, but your evil acts. Listen to me now, and drop the knife. Let no more sin stain your soul."

Iacopo lowered his hand slowly, letting the knife slide out of his grip. The three watched him: Accorsi, wary and still, the black-haired woman who had discovered his secret, and his own mother, familiar and strange all at once. Iacopo felt as if he were receding irrevocably away from the shore on which they stood. They belonged to the world of the living, a world he could not rejoin.

Iacopo climbed the wall separating him from the dizzying drop to the Campo.

"Iacopo, come down." Now his mother's voice held fear. *Perhaps she does love me. But her love is not enough.*

"I will let the painter live, Mamma"—even now Iacopo could not keep from calling her by that lovely name—"but I shall not come down. There is nothing that holds me to this earth now, neither your fear nor your love. I am beyond both."

Iacopo edged sideways along the wall until he was out of Gabriele's reach. Seconds stretched as the four of us stood, one above and three below. It could have been a painting: Iacopo's shape loomed dark against the backdrop of moving clouds, and Immacolata's hands emerged white from the sleeves of her cloak like a pair of doves. I had the feeling that Iacopo was part of the wall, the sky, the wind that blew his cloak out around him like an angel's wings. Then into the silence, the tower's bell began to ring for Vespers: the evening prayer.

"God forgive me," Iacopo said, "and keep my mother safe." Then he stepped off the wall, and into the view around us.

Immacolata's howl split the air as Iacopo's body hurtled toward the distant shell-shaped Campo below. For a fraction of a second Iacopo looked, splayed out with his arms and legs outstretched, as if he might fly.

PART XVI

HOME

S omehow I was standing with my hands pressed against the cold wet stone of the parapet. From the Torre's height, I watched Immacolata run across the crowded Campo, her cloak a blur of dark green. The crowds parted before her as she fell onto Iacopo's prostrate body, covering him like a blanket while the rain beat down upon them both.

Gabriele and I stood next to each other, silently looking down. We watched city officials in their black and white take Iacopo's body away. We kept watching until the crowds dispersed, and then until the wind died and the heavy rain faded to a quiet mist.

In the stillness after the storm, I began to hear sounds around us—a flock of sparrows chittering in the Torre's overhanging roof, the drip of water from a beam to the stone floor, Gabriele's breathing next to me. I could feel the warmth emanating from him, and I smelled his cloak's wet wool. The sun was low over Siena's surrounding hills when Gabriele turned from the view to face me, and took my hand in his.

"*Andiamo a casa?*" Gabriele said—*Shall we go home?*

Home. The weight of all that *home* meant—what it used to mean and what it had come to mean for me—rested on those three sweet Italian words.

"*Sì,*" I answered. *Yes.*

And we walked home together in the fading light.

PART XVII

EPILOGUE

The night after Beatrice confirmed her flight to Siena, Ben dreamed that he took her to the Museo. In the dream they were walking hand in hand from one empty room to the next. Beatrice kept consulting a creased museum brochure; the outlines of the gallery map wavered in the dim light. They walked for hours, the odd surreal fabric of the dream stretching and distorting the passage of time. At last they reached Ben's favorite gallery, where the unfinished Accorsi Messina altarpiece hung alone against the back wall, filling the space with its power.

Hey Little B, here's a painting I've always wanted to show you— Ben's waking thoughts infiltrated the realm of sleep—*even half done, doesn't it blow your mind?* But in the dream he felt Beatrice moving away from him, the contact between their two hands lost.

He stood in the doorway of this last gallery, unable to cross the threshold. Beatrice walked to the altarpiece and stopped, looking at the painting as if it were a window rather than a work of art. He could tell from the set of Beatrice's shoulders and the angle of her head that she was thinking hard, her black hair falling down behind her like a dark waterfall. Beatrice's hand disappeared into the flat canvas, then her other hand, then her body and head, moving into the painting as if it were a still lake. The long strands of Beatrice's hair were the last to vanish, and the painting closed over them without a ripple.

Ben woke alone in his Siena bedroom, where maps of the city covered the walls and piled books formed unsteady towers by the bed. But as the dream faded, the image of Beatrice stayed behind in his mind. She'd be here soon, his little sister neurosurgeon who wasn't so little anymore. "Maybe you'll end up getting into history after all, Little B," Ben said aloud, smiling in the dark, "just like me. That wouldn't be so bad, would it?" And this time, he drifted off into a sweet, dreamless sleep.

*　　*　　*

It was Sebastiano's second birthday. Donata knew she must leave work soon to buy ingredients for the ricotta cake Felice and Gianni loved. Her youngest child was not quite old enough to choose a dessert for himself, but would eat it willingly, as he did most things. Donata lingered in the reading room of the university library on that bright March afternoon, fingering the binding of the book she'd requested from the archives. The leather cover was worn and stamped with a faded pattern of leaves and vines in gold. Donata rested the manuscript on the velvet-lined stand. A painting of Siena's Campo illuminated the flyleaf. Donata knew that perspective well—it was a view of the piazza seen from the Torre's height, its nine sections fanning out from the Palazzo Pubblico, the Duomo rising gravely over the city it protected.

Donata bent to look at the next page, and as she read a feeling came over her, as if someone were standing at her shoulder, close enough to touch.

To my beloved Siena
The city that opened her gates and heart to me across the
  centuries
And in my Brother's memory
Written by my hand in this year of our Lord 1349
  Beatrice Alessandra Trovato

Donata sat staring at the inscription. Outside, the trees had not yet begun to leaf, and the light streamed in through the tall leaded glass windows. She sat without moving until the bells began to ring the hour of Nones, then put away the book and went home to make a birthday cake.

Siena University News; Issue 213; March

Three scholars, working consecutively, have uncovered surprising new information about Siena's medieval past. However, this work appears to have taken a toll on those scholars who undertook it. Beniamino Emilio Trovato, the well-known Sienese historian who began the project, died suddenly of a heart ailment before he could complete his work. The second scholar to become involved, his American-born sister, Beatrice Alessandra Trovato, mysteriously disappeared before she could finish the project. The trail of their efforts to uncover the secret of a six-hundred-and-fifty-year-old conspiracy has been picked up by Professoressa Donata Guerrini, a notable scholar of art history at the Università di Siena. Prof. Guerrini has publicly declared the work to be Beniamino Trovato's discovery, and insisted that it be published in his name, angering some competing scholars who would speak against the veracity of his sources and methods of scholarship. Most disturbingly, the evidence appears to implicate members of the well-known Signoretti family of Siena as co-conspirators of the Medicis in a plot to overthrow Siena's Nine more than six centuries ago. Since Prof. Guerrini began work on the project, her office has been broken into twice, fortunately without loss of any crucial documentation or injury to her person. The reason for the break-ins is suspected to be related to the alleged Signoretti controversy, though it remains unproven at this time. In an interview, Prof. Guerrini has revealed startling facts regarding the Medici involvement in Siena's terrible losses during the Plague, and implications for the violent fall of Siena's Nine seven years later.

With the assistance of local archivist Emilio Fabbri, Prof. Guerrini has identified the writings of a previously unknown Sienese medieval chronicler. Interestingly, the author shares her family name with Dr. Trovato and her brother. Dr. Guerrini, when interviewed about this remarkable coincidence, had no comment. In a harmonious marriage of text and art, the chronicle is illustrated by the fourteenth-century painter Gabriele Beltrano Accorsi, a pupil of Simone Martini. Accorsi's work was not previously known to include manuscript illustration, and the numerous illuminations will provide academics dedicated to post-Plague Sienese art with a wealth of new material. The chronicle itself gives insight into the appearance of the original Fonte Gaia and suggests that Accorsi himself was the painter of the long-debated fifth fresco on the Ospedale facade. Finally and most dramatically, the research into this trecento chronicler's work has uncovered evidence to illuminate Siena's particularly devastating losses to the Plague, and its failure to recover after the Black Death's retreat. These Trovato historians, both past and present, have together added a new and startling chapter to Siena's great history.

†††

AUTHOR'S NOTE

This book is a particular sort of historical fiction—an invented narrative embedded in a real place and time. Historical fiction demands accuracy, and that requires research—research to answer not only large questions about major historical events and conflicts—such as the centuries-old bitter rivalry between Siena and Florence—but also smaller questions about daily life. Does a medieval Italian child drink milk? What language was spoken in what would eventually become Tuscany in the 1340s, and would it sound like Italian? Was intellectual life and literacy possible or likely for women in fourteenth-century Italy? And how were criminals denounced and tried?

But research, though it provided the necessary scaffolding for this story, wasn't enough. Because this isn't history, it is fiction. And fiction, by definition, goes between and beyond the facts. That is the privilege, and the heady pleasure, of the novelist.

Where do the facts end and where does this fiction begin? Medieval Siena did fall from its economic, cultural, and political prominence after—and partially as a result of—the great Plague. And it fared worse during and after the Plague than other Tuscan cities that were its contemporaries and rivals. A number of Medici ancestors were tried for capital crimes in the fourteenth century, but sources vary as to whether one was executed for his crimes, and when that might have occurred. There was a failed plot backed by Florence's Walter of Brienne to unseat the Sienese regime, and powerful Florentine families appear to have been involved—but the specifics of the Medici family in this plot are my own fabrication, and there was no well-known Signoretti family in Siena in the fourteenth century. There was a Giovanni de' Medici born a few years after the one in this book; I did not intend to portray him, but his existence planted the seed of an idea. Immacolata and Iacopo are invented, too. There is also no mysterious conspiratorial text written by a plotter against Siena in "real" history. And, as far as I know, there is no painter named Gabriele Beltrano Accorsi who trained with the very real Simone Martini. There is, however, uncertainty about the creator of the Ospedale of Siena's fifth fresco, which has proved to be a useful foundation for invention. Uncertainty is inherently interesting, and it has allowed me to create people and events. You won't find them in primary sources. At least, I don't think you will.

ACKNOWLEDGMENTS

It was a delight to write this book, but readers made the words take flight. I owe enormous gratitude to the dedicated people who gave comments and encouragement: Hannah Stein, Alex Bassuk, Heidi Hoover, Christine Leahy, Paul Josephs, Loren Levinson, Michael Rose, Jason Wexler, Julia Stein, Helaina Stein, Adam Grupper, and Carol Higgins-Lawrence. Some emailed me at 2 a.m. pleading for the next installment, some spent vacations buried in my book, some copy-edited on a buggy Google doc across time zones, and some, solo parenting heroically, put their children in front of a screen for hours so they could keep reading.

I am indebted to two scholars—Jane Tylus at New York University and Neslihan Şenocak at Columbia University—whose generosity and expertise helped me bring the fourteenth century to life. Rita Charon, head of the Narrative Medicine Program at Columbia, in the hallways of the medical center and over wine and oysters, illuminated the delicate balance of the physician/novelist's existence. Heartfelt thanks to my eleventh-grade English teacher and poet, Harry Bauld, who, decades after he'd last taught me, helped my book find a home.

I had the good fortune to work with three skillful editors—Judy Sternlight, Julie Mosow, and Tara Parsons—who made the challenges of editing exhilarating and genuinely fun. I am deeply grateful to my publisher, Susan Moldow, president of the Scribner group, who championed my book, and to my assiduous and insightful copy editor, Shelley Perron. I am indebted to Richard Mayeux, Chair, Department of Neurology, Columbia University, who provided an academic second home and unflagging support of my career as a physician, scientist, and author. I also owe special thanks to the MTA of New York City for providing and maintaining the subway trains where I wrote most of this book.

The manuscript would still be languishing on my laptop without my wonderful agent, Marly Rusoff. Her belief in my story, intellectual companionship, and unflagging emotional support are more than I could ever hope for. Michael Radulescu, unflappable master of foreign sales, provided constant good humor and enthusiasm while guiding me through incomprehensible international paperwork.

Finally, thanks to my mother, Bonnie Josephs, who was my first editor, a devoted reader, and much more than that; to my father, Herb Winawer, who died while I was writing this book but who knew it would be published someday; and to my children, Ariana, Chiara, and Leo, who listened to me tell the story, gave me courage and good ideas, and followed me to the top of Siena's Torre del Mangia during a terrifying thunderstorm. And I could not have done it without Susanna Stein, who told me the book was good in my gravest moments of doubt, read and commented and criticized and complimented, played medieval music and cooked medieval dinners, and did everything I couldn't do because I was (and still am) writing.

ABOUT THE AUTHOR

Melodie Winawer is a physician-scientist and associate professor of neurology at Columbia University. A graduate of Yale University, the University of Pennsylvania, and Columbia University, with degrees in biological psychology, medicine, and epidemiology, she has published numerous nonfiction articles and book chapters. She is fluent in Spanish and French, literate in Latin, and has a passable knowledge of Italian. Dr. Winawer currently lives with her spouse and their three young children in Brooklyn, New York. *The Scribe of Siena* is her first novel.

THE
SCRIBE
OF
SIENA

MELODIE WINAWER

INTRODUCTION

After Beatrice Trovato's brother, a scholar of medieval history based in Siena, Italy, dies unexpectedly, she travels to Siena to take care of his estate. As Beatrice delves deeper into her bother's affairs, she discovers files from his unfinished research—all of which seem to point to a 700-year-old conspiracy to annihilate the city of Siena.

After uncovering the journal and paintings of Gabriele Accorsi, the fourteenth-century artist at the heart of the plot, Beatrice finds a startling image of her own face in his work and is suddenly transported to Siena in the year 1347. She awakens in a city on the eve of an unimaginable disaster—the Plague's imminent arrival. Yet when Beatrice meets Accorsi, something unexpected happens: she falls in love—not only with Gabriele but also with medieval life. As the Plague and the ruthless hands behind its trajectory threaten Beatrice's survival and the very existence of Siena, Beatrice must decide in which century she belongs.

FOR DISCUSSION

1.   Discuss the significance of the title. Does it give you any insight into Beatrice's priorities throughout the novel? How do you think she would choose to identify herself?

2.   On her first morning in 1347 Siena, Beatrice goes to the Santissima Annunziata where she hears a prayer she remembers from Catholic school. She says, "It was nice to hear the familiar words; that familiarity and sense of belonging across centuries was one benefit of religion." What other benefits, if any, does religion offer the people of medieval Siena?

3.   Albizzi warns Iacopo that his knowledge places him in danger with the confraternity. What makes Albizzi issue this warning? What does Iacopo know that places him in danger? Do you think that the members of the confraternity have used Iacopo for their own means? If so, how and why? Why was Iacopo so willing to go along with the confraternity's scheme?

4.   Giovanni de' Medici's absences "provided a certain relief" for his wife, Immocolata. Why does Immacolata feel this way? Describe Giovanni. Did you think he had any good in him as a husband or father? Explain your answer.

5.   When Beatrice first sees Gabriele, she says that seeing him "as real as my own solid self, unnerved me." Why is seeing

Gabriele unnerving for Beatrice? What were your first impressions of Gabriele? Was he as you had pictured him?

6. Beatrice says "oddly enough, I felt more at home in the *scriptorium* of the Ospedale della Scala than I had almost anywhere in the past month, even in my own time." Why do you think Beatrice is able to find refuge in the *scriptorium*? Describe Beatrice's duties as a scribe. What benefits does working as a scribe afford her?

7. Discuss the epistolary elements of *The Scribe of Siena*. Were you able to gain any additional insight into the characters through their letters? If so, what were they? How did the letters help further the plot?

8. Describe Beatrice's relationship with Gabriele. Did you think that they were well suited for each other? In what ways? Gabriele asks Beatrice, "What is a husband for, if not to comfort you?" What roles did a spouse serve in medieval Italy? Were there benefits to being married? What were they?

9. In a letter, Ben jokes with Beatrice that "I try to get into people's heads too, but my subjects are already dead." Are there any ways that the work of a surgeon is similar to that of a historian? Describe them. Does Beatrice's background as a neurosurgeon help her as she investigates the high levels of the Plague in Siena? Does her medical background help in any other ways in medieval Siena? What are they?

10. Were you surprised by Gabriele's reaction when Beatrice shares the truth about her origins with him? Why or why not? In her gratitude, Beatrice tells him "the last thing I'd imagined in return was sympathy." Why does

Gabriele correct her, telling her that he's responding to her disclosure with "empathy"? How have Gabriele's actions demonstrated that he is able to empathize with Beatrice? What effect has keeping her origins hidden had on Beatrice?

11. Umiltà tells Beatrice, "The Pestilence has brought its share of regretful behavior in its wake, but I would not have imagined it from you." Why does Umiltà believe that Beatrice has been callous toward Gabriele? Do you agree? Why or why not?

12. When Beatrice is not able to open her mind to the perspective of another, she "supposed it was safer to be free of it, if safety was my goal." What is Beatrice's goal? Why might she miss her extreme sense of empathy? Are there any benefits to having it? How does it help Beatrice both as a surgeon and in medieval Italy?

13. Beatrice says, "I was beginning to realize that it was never quite safe to make assumptions about Clara." Do you agree? What were your initial impressions of Clara? Did your opinion of her change? In what ways and why? Beatrice posits that Clara has been able to survive so long as an orphan because she has learned "to make her rescuers feel at ease." How is Clara able to make her rescuers feel comfortable? Clara has also been able to survive by making herself indispensible. How has she been able to accomplish this feat?

14. Compare and contrast Beatrice's life in present day Italy and New York with her life in medieval Siena. What are the advantages to staying in each time period for her? What would you choose and why? Were you surprised that Beatrice made the choice she did?

ENHANCE YOUR
BOOK CLUB

1.   Beatrice recounts how she and her brother would visit the Cloisters on Sundays and how "the unicorn tapestries were always my favorite. This is probably true of all kids who visit the Cloisters." Visit the Cloisters virtually and learn more about the Unicorn tapestries: http://metmuseum.org/exhibitions/listings/2013/search-for-the-unicorn. Discuss them with your book club. Why do you think that Beatrice liked the tapestries so much?

2.   Beatrice says, "I'm cautious about who I get recommendations from, but Nathaniel knows how to pick a book, at least for me." Discuss how you get book recommendations with your book club. Go through your last few book club selections, taking the time to talk about whether or not you would recommend them to others.

3.   When Donata's family gives Beatrice a Civetta scarf, she is overcome with gratitude. Why is the scarf such a meaningful gift to Beatrice? Do you own any objects that have particular significance to you? Tell your book club about them.

4. The Bubonic Plague took a particularly heavy toll on the population of Siena. To learn more about the Bubonic Plague and the effects it had on medieval society, visit: www.historytoday.com/ole-j-benedictow/black-death -greatest-catastrophe-ever.

A CONVERSATION WITH MELODIE WINAWER

Congratulations on publishing your first novel! What's been the most rewarding part of the experience of publishing *The Scribe of Siena* so far? Was there anything that surprised you about publishing fiction?

The most remarkable thing about the publishing process is that the story I'd been telling—first in my head, then on the page—got into someone else's head. Many other people's heads! Being read makes my words take flight. The exhilaration of having someone gasp at a plot revelation, or fall in love with a character who was born in my imagination, or stay up all night reading words that kept me up all night writing—that makes all the hard work worthwhile. Writing is an unimaginable delight, but being read . . . being read is beyond belief.

You've written more than fifty nonfiction articles and book chapters throughout your medical career. How was the experience of writing fiction different? What made you decide to write a novel?

There are some definite similarities in the process and some drastic differences. The similarities: I'm a research scientist (and a doctor). The way I do scientific research goes something like this: I come up with a question I don't know the answer to. I try to look up the answer. If I don't find an answer, I look harder, and in more sources. If I still don't know the answer, I ask colleagues with expertise. If no one knows the answer, or even better, if there is disagreement or even controversy about the answer, that's when I know I've found my next research project. That happened with *The Scribe of Siena*; the minute I started thinking and reading about Siena as a foundation for a story, I started running up against the question of why Siena fared so badly during the Plague. And I didn't find an answer—I found conflicting answers. That became the historical question at the center of my story. Now, in scientific research, my job is to explore the uncertain systematically, and be absolutely true to fact or to experimental results. But in fiction . . . uncertainty is a foundation for invention. That means I get to make things up. And that is intensely pleasurable—the absolute antidote to my satisfying but highly structured scientific work, in which I never get to make things up.

What made me decide to write a novel? I was in a funny time in my life. We'd just sold our house, and bought a new house, but it needed renovations so we—my spouse and I and our three kids—moved into my mom's apartment. We lived with her for two months. Almost all of our belongings went into storage, and I moved into my childhood bedroom. During those two months my spouse, an ex-professional violinist, was working on a Stravinsky trio four hours a night, and I was left to my own devices. I was between books—not reading anything, and missing the feeling of being in an absorbing story, at the same time as being in a limbo of life stages, too, between homes. I'd always written—since childhood—short stories and essays, and I'd even made notes for a novel when I was fifteen before I realized I was too young to write it. During those few strange months where I was longing to be absorbed in a story, in a deep, compelling imaginary world, it came to me that I wanted to MAKE my own story, not READ one. So that's what I did.

As a debut novelist, do you have any advice for aspiring writers? Is there anything that you wish you had done differently in hindsight?

First: Write for the joy of it, not to please some imagined audience or market. Don't worry if people say "no one is buying historical fiction [insert your genre here]," or "no first novelist should write a book over 400 pages," for example. Both those things were said to me, and I ignored them. Write your story because you love it or must write it. There's no point otherwise.

Second: Don't give up. The only thing that will ensure your failure is if you stop trying.

What I wish I had done differently . . . at first I said—I'll never write a book blind like this again, without a clear plan and detailed outline right at the beginning. But I'm not sure I really would have done it differently. It was exhilarating, the free fall into fiction, into a story that evolved as I wrote it. And to some extent, I don't think it is possible, at least not for me, to really plan fully before writing. Most of what actually happens in my stories happens on the page as I start to write, and even when I plan, the outcome eludes me until that magic moment and surprising things happen as the words start to appear in front of me. That's part of the mystery and pleasure of writing.

Can you tell us about your writing process? *The Scribe of Siena* **is intricately plotted, moving seamlessly between two time periods. Did you know how Beatrice's story would end when you began writing?**

The quick answer is . . . no. And yes. I knew some things, but many things were obscure to me. It's like driving in the dark, in a snowstorm. You know where you are heading, and you can see a few feet in front of you. But the road appears as you go, and sometimes you take a wrong turn and end up somewhere you didn't expect, or maybe it wasn't a wrong turn but you can't tell until you go miles down that road. Some scenes I wrote very early on, and they stayed (like the scene where Gabriele and Beatrice hold hands for the first time). Sometimes a character would show up and I would have no idea why—like Bartolomeo. It was years before I fully knew why he was there and what role he would play in Beatrice's life. Some scenes that I wrote early on never got into the book at all. Some came, left, then came back. They all give the story depth, whether they are there or not—invisible layers that make it richer even if they are not read.

In present day New York, Beatrice works as a neuro-surgeon. In addition to being a writer, you are an associate professor of neurology. Are you similar to Beatrice in any other ways? If so, what are they?

This question gets at one central autobiographical issue—not just about being a doctor and a writer at the same time but also about the possibility of being a doctor first, THEN leaving the doctor's life and becoming a writer. Beatrice leaves her medical life and moves toward writing. People are always asking me whether I'm going to "quit my job and write," which doesn't really make sense to me, since medicine and science are fundamental to who I am and influence how I write fiction. I have the privilege of being allowed into the most intimate and powerful moments of my patients' lives, and I also work at the edge of scientific understanding on a daily basis. This is deeply rewarding. But writing fiction exerts a powerful pull on me, and the pull is not always in the same direction as the rest of my work. It's a challenge! So there was a deep satisfaction in allowing Beatrice to leave the medical world, to choose *writing* a history instead of *taking* it. Ben articulates that for her, and it's one of the key lines in the book for me.

Other ways I'm like Beatrice? Oh, millions of ways! But here's a funny thing: Someone quite close to me once told me that Beatrice was funnier than I am. How is that even possible? How unfair? She IS me! How can she be funny if I'm not funny? I MADE her, for heaven's sake! That is one of the odd things about fiction. I'm not Giovanni either, but he must be in there somewhere. . . .

As Beatrice settles into her life in medieval Siena she grows to find pleasure in "something intangible, a surprisingly pleasurable medieval-ness." From your writing, it's clear that you also value the "pleasurable medieval-ness" Beatrice describes. What attracted you to this particular historical period?

I've been entranced with medieval life since I was a child. I read eight different retellings of the Arthurian legend, and even played King Arthur in my girl scout camp drama production. I remember getting a set of calligraphy pens and bottles of ink and practicing forming the medieval letters (like Beatrice)—I fantasized for a while about a life sitting in a quiet room illuminating manuscripts. Once, when I was very young, I told my parents I wanted to be a nun. I remember that not going over very well since I was growing up in a secular Jewish household. The impulse to the contemplative life wasn't religion though, it was something else. When I was little I couldn't articulate what it was I loved so much, but now I've managed to get a firmer understanding of what I found so compelling about the idea of living a medieval life.

Modern life is fast. It prides itself on speed and efficiency. Fast food, fast delivery, fast transmission of information. This is all useful, but it is not pleasurable. When I was writing *The Scribe of Siena* I studied historically accurate medieval Italian recipes and held several dinners based on traditional dishes and menus— *poratta*, *lasana fermentatam*, *limonia* of chicken, pumpkin tart . . . these are even more delicious than they sound. I spent three days preparing for the first meal I ever served: making almond milk from scratch, squeezing bunches of grapes with my hands to make pink garlic sauce, steeping wine with galangal, cinnamon, ginger, and honey for the hypocras. Three days of cooking and a six-hour, luxurious, slow dinner for seventeen people, with music and flickering candles and the feeling that the evening need never end. Three days to prepare a dinner—and I was using an oven and electric equipment! I loved the slowness, the physical immersion in the process of cooking for people I loved. This encapsulated much of what I see as a major contrast between the medieval past and our fast-moving, convenient present. Sometimes I feel that there is hardly any time to taste what you are eating, let alone enjoy it, or the people you are sharing a meal with.

The Scribe of Siena has been compared to Outlander and The Time Traveler's Wife. Were those works inspirational to you? Were there other books that inspired you? Can you tell us about them?

Inspirational is an understatement! It is absolutely mind-boggling to be compared to Diana Gabaldon and Audrey Niffenegger, both of whom I think of as luminaries of fiction, particularly in the absorbing, believable, and emotionally gripping portrayal of love across centuries, transcending the traditional shape of time. I stayed up all night reading both *Outlander* and *The Time Traveler's Wife*, and I would be honored if *The Scribe of Siena* affects readers even a fraction as much as those books affected me.

One of the most inspiring things about *Outlander* wasn't the story itself, it was Gabaldon's trajectory—the way she started writing, the way she continues to write, the way her life has evolved into that of a celebrated novelist. She was a scientific writer who knew she wanted to write a novel. She wrote without asking anyone how, because she had a story she wanted to tell. She had a bunch of kids, no time, and another job. She didn't get an MFA, join a writer's group, write essays about point of view or narrative structure. She had no extra time but she used the time she had. When I read why she chose historical fiction it was so like what I had said that I laughed out loud. I knew how to do research already so that's what I did. I can do it too, I thought—with my scientific career, my medical life, my three kids. And I did. I wrote on the subway during my ridiculously long commute. I wrote after the kids were asleep, in the passenger seat of our minivan on the way home from a trip upstate. I wrote whenever I could, hungry for every moment I had. And when I couldn't write, the story hummed in my head.

Do you have any favorite moments in *The Scribe of Siena*? What are they?

I absolutely loved writing the wedding night scene—I really enjoyed the combination of the tension of Gabriele and Beatrice's challenging conversation, the clash between their two worlds, and their desire for one another.

I also loved writing chapter 9—Beatrice's return to modern life, that underlines her longing for the medieval life she left behind. That was probably my favorite to write. It was hard too, though, figuring out the balance of the mystery and the emotion, and how to make her decision make sense.

I have a special connection to the scene in the elevator, when Beatrice dreams about Gabriele, and reflects on how he becomes part of the objects around him, how much he would like that. This comes from a real experience of my childhood. My grandmother died when I was fifteen, and I missed her all the time. We'd been very close, talked a lot, traveled together, went to museums—she was an amateur late-life historian who loved art and must have instilled a lot of that joy in me. After she died I had recurrent dreams that would take place in the elevator of the apartment building where I lived, and we would meet there. I'd update her about my life, and I knew instinctively in those dreams that elevators were a place between the world of the living and the non-living, where we could connect and still share our thoughts. . . . It was strangely reassuring at the time. I would say, if one of my children asked me now whether that was magic, that the mind creates wonderful ways of solving problems of emotional loss that are magical . . . it was certainly that for me.

Finally, there's a piece of dialogue that is easily missed but is one of my favorites because, although it is ostensibly about Gabriele's process of painting, it actually describes my experience of writing:

"Do you know what you're going to paint before you start?"

"I spend many days preparing studies before I approach the unpainted wall, and outline my intended image in red-brown *sinopia*, well before I begin to paint. But I can only plan so much. The full execution eludes me until the moment I lay pigment on wet plaster, feeling the brush move in my hand as if a force other than my own propels it. That is the moment I live for, and that I cannot explain . . ."

What would you like your readers who are interested in medieval Italy to take away from *The Scribe of Siena*?
I like historical fiction because I want to bring the past to life. I don't just want to write about history, to record what happened. I want to give readers (and myself!) a way to sink into history—to be time travelers, like Beatrice. I want my book to help people go to medieval Siena, not just read about medieval Siena. I want my readers to feel transported, to believe that it is possible to move from one time and place to another, and even for just a moment, to believe that these invented people are real, the way I did while writing it, and in some ways still do. I want to provide a bridge into a living, breathing past—a past that might even coexist simultaneously with the present.

Are you working on anything now? Can you tell us about it?

Yes, yes! Always—if not on paper then in my head. At the moment I'm working on a novel set in late Byzantine Greece. It focuses on the now abandoned city of Mystras, in the Southern Peloponnese, which is mostly in ruins but still standing. You can walk through its streets, into the churches and crumbling houses, the great fortress on top of the hill at the foot of the Taygetos mountain range—and of course I have walked through it—it's even more magical than it sounds. It has a mysterious, tumultuous history, with moments of great triumph, as the center of the late Byzantine empire after the fall of Constantinople, and also great despair. I keep coming back to this question of the shape of time, and how the past and the present intersect—that plays a role in the story I'm writing now too.